Kiss Me Soldier Boy

American Wars with the Rainwater Sons

Julius Rainwater

iUniverse, Inc.
Bloomington

Kiss Me Soldier Boy
American Wars with the Rainwater Sons

iUniverse books may be ordered through booksellers or by contacting:

iUniverse
1663 Liberty Drive
Bloomington, IN 47403
www.iuniverse.com
1-800-Authors (1-800-288-4677)

ISBN: 978-1-4502-7320-6 (sc)
ISBN: 978-1-4502-7321-3 (ebk)

Printed in the United States of America

iUniverse rev. date: 1/25/2011

Dedicated in memory of the author's grandson, David William Rainwater, who loved to try on my old World War II uniform and to listen to my war stories as a young boy. History is David's First love. Sadly, he was killed in an automobile accident at age 18.

Acknowledgements

Thanks for the many people whose contributions in my life have made the writing of this possible; special thanks go to my family for their support and encouragement. My wife, son, daughter, and grandsons have by their examples made me a better person and created the desire in me to write about our family involvements throughout history in past American Wars. Acknowledgement goes to the web and its many resources, making the writing easier. In addition, much appreciation goes to Erin Leongomez for providing a thorough genealogy of our family back to the George Washington era.

Introduction

In today's instant news coverage through television, satellites, Internet, Web sites, cell phones, etc. we see immediately what is happening almost as it happens, as the media presents the events. Listening to commentaries about the war in Iraq and Afghanistan, the author began to visualize in his mind's eye and ear about past wars in our American history and how these played out in the public's opinion in their time.

The author remembers questions asked by his grandson about the Rainwater war experiences. *American Wars With the Rainwater Sons* reflects on the stories from memory as told by the author to his grandson. This story depicts people and their thoughts and opinions of the wars in their time.

Soldiers falling in love, the marriages, and family struggles are all intermingled with the stream of American wars in America's history.

Julius Rainwater chose his family lineage of the Rainwaters as the characters in the stories that unfold. While some events and people in the stories are real and true, many are fictitious.

Chapter 1

Going Back to Pre-revolutionary Times

The Irish Beginnings

The smells of leather color Michael Rainey's memories, as he grew up in Ireland **as** the son of a leather fabricator. On a bright sunny day in April 1501, Michael discusses with his son, Jordan, the news of Columbus who has just returned to Spain. The news has spread throughout the European countries. One of Columbus' crewmembers has spotted the New World on twelfth of October in 1492, just nine years ago.

Michael says to his son, "Christopher Columbus, born only fifty years ago in Italy in fourteen fifty one, and grew up in Portugal to be an excellent seaman."

Jordan asks, "Why did he make this voyage in the name of Spain?" "That is an interesting question son; the fifteenth century has become a time when many merchants and enterprises seek expanding geographical territories for their companies. I have heard Columbus tried to persuade King John II of Portugal to back his plan to start a company called 'the Enterprise of the Indies;' but he could not convince the King."

"Well how did he get the money from Spain?"

1

"He moved to Spain where he connives Queen Isabella into financing the voyage. I have heard she had a secret love affair with Columbus. And it's interesting to know she has financed three voyages in all and will pay for his upcoming voyage next year."

Jordan ponders in his mind; *I would love to go to the New World one day.* Little does he know that his great grandchildren might be there in a little over one hundred years?

I enjoy telling stories to my grand children; probably more than any other of the fun activities we share together. My grandson, David Rainwater, at his young age of nine, has a keen interest in the history of the Rainwater family, and especially in past wars. David is very bright and inquisitive for his age. The story that unfolds is one of the stories I have told David to satisfy his interest in the Rainwaters as they served in wars from the time of George Washington to the present time. The Rainwater sons served both militarily and politically in these war times. One will experience the adventures and the very interesting questions from David. I see David raising his hand to ask a question now.

"Granddaddy, were you in a war?"

"Yes, I served in the Second World War in the South Pacific from 1943 to 1946."

"How old were you?"

"I was 18 when I entered, and I was 21 when discharged."

"How about your father, did he fight in a war?"

"David, you have a million questions."

"Granddaddy, I am interested in the wars in which our ancestors were involved. It might give me some stories to tell to my children when I grow up."

"Bless you child! When I was a little boy like you, I was interested just as you are. My father died when I was too young to ask him about those things; but I did ask my grandfather, when I was about your age."

"Did your grandfather ask his grandfather about the wars of old times?"

"You ask a great question. Yes he did and I can tell you about times even before the founding of America."

"Granddaddy, tell me about those times, please, please."

"Oh! All right, but we'll start with how our ancestors came to America."

"Thanks Granddaddy!"

"Okay, here is the story passed down from our grandfathers and grandmothers, all the way back from Ireland Scotland."

"Granddaddy, did Jordan get his wish to go to the New World?"

"David, let me finish the story and you'll find out. Just be patient son."

"I will Granddaddy; but tell me more about the love affair Queen Isabella had with Columbus."

"David you know as much as I do about that."

"Okay, tell me the rest of the story."

I continue telling David about the Rainwater beginnings.

Jordan Rainey marries Francis, a lovely Irish girl who is not only an excellent homemaker, but helps her husband in the family leather business from time to time.

Jordan's father and mother soon pass away, leaving the business for Jordan and Francis to run. The business continues to thrive, providing a good income for the young couple.

Jordan and Francis soon have children of their own. There are three: Dorothy and then the twin boys, Roger and Kenneth.

As the years pass, Jordan's dream of going to the New World fades; he never has the opportunity to go to this mysterious place. However, Roger and Kenneth believe that perhaps their father's dream can become theirs since many prominent people are talking about the possibilities for expanding into the New World.

Roger reads about how most of the European countries are establishing colonies in the new world except the Germans. He thinks about his father's dream, hoping he will explore this new world one day.

Meanwhile, Roger and Kenneth Rainey and their dad, Jordan, become quite wealthy in their growing leather business. Horsewhips, saddles, carriage seats, and carriage coverings are in great demand as the horse and buggy provides the primary means of travel.

In her 50s, Jordan's wife endures a long illness. When she passes away, his heart was broken. As he grieves and offers comfort to his children, he tells them, "Death is so final, but we, the living, must go on."

Little does Jordan know about events in the '*going on*' that will bring to the family?

At age thirty-five, Kenneth, the hotheaded Irishman of the twins, yells out one day to a Catholic neighbor, "I do not like the remarks you made about me and my brother; I challenge you to a dual, you idiot."

"I accept your challenge." Is the neighbors answer.

Sadly, Kenneth dies in the dual, in 1566 leaving his young widow and his son Kenneth, Jr. It is a sad day for this Irish family;

but they maintain a stiff upper lip. The family is strong, as most Irish families are.

Roger and his aging father, Jordan, maintain the leather business, grieving over the death of the twin brother. *Why do men have to fight each other?* Roger ponders in his mind. He has hardly gotten over Kenneth's death, when his father passes away.

After his father's death, he falls madly in love with his brother's wife, Jane. Jane is left to provide for her son, Kenneth, Jr.

After Roger and Jane date each other, the two find their love is mutual. One evening under a full moon shining brightly, Roger bends down on one knee to propose to Jane.

Jane's quick answer to this romantic proposal is "Yes, oh yes, Roger!"

After the wedding, Jane's young son, Kenneth, Jr., becomes active in the leather business with his uncle, now his stepfather. Kenneth Jr. grows from boy to a man very quickly. Kenneth, Jr., having heard the stories of his grandfather, wonders if he will be able to go to the New World.

At the age of twenty-four, Kenneth, Jr. feels his childhood friend is the girl of his dreams and is eager to propose marriage to her. At just the opportune time he asks, "Florien will you become my soul mate in marriage?"

Florien quickly answers, "No!"

"Shocked and saddened by Florien's quick negative answer he asks, "But Florine we have known each other since we were children. Don't you love me?"

"Well I think I do; but my mother knew your real father. She feels you might be a hotheaded Irishman as he was. She says I should not marry you."

Therefore, Florien and Kenneth, Jr. go their separate ways, although in their hearts they both still love each other very much.

Several months later, the two are at a mutual friend's birthday party. Florien sees Kenneth Jr. out of the corner of her eye as a warm feeling sweeps through her body. She thinks *my man is not hotheaded. He is kind and I do not care what Mama says; I do love him.*

About the same time Kenneth Jr. watches Florine and wonders, *does she still not want to marry me. I will let her make the first move. I wish she would since I am deeply in love with her.*

To his delight, Florien shyly approaches Kenneth and asks him to take a walk in their host's garden. There she confesses that she realizes what a terrible mistake she made in refusing his offer of marriage. She has spent many sleepless nights in regret over this decision.

Kenneth realizes how difficult it must be for Florien to be so bold in expressing her feelings in this way and quickly takes charge of the conversation. "Florien", he says as he bends down on one knee, "if you will still have me, I'd like to ask for your hand in marriage once again."

Despite the objections, she knows her father will make, she says, "Yes, with out a shadow of a doubt, I know I want to be your wife. Would you be willing to elope to avoid a confrontation with my father?"

"Oh, yes, Florien. You have made me a very happy man!"

Florine and Ken slip off the next day to the justice-of-peace in the next village and become husband and wife. Florien's parents are devastated and refuse to have anything to do with the young couple. Kenneth's stepfather and mother are disappointed but give the two their blessings. Ken stays busy in the family leather business. He wonders if the dream of his Grandfather to travel to the new world will be his.

Nine months later, in 1585, a baby boy is born to Ken and Florien. Roger is pleased to have a grandson. They name him John.

John soon becomes a teenager with a restlessness that his father Kenneth, Jr. wonders if John will take over the family leather business one day. John shows little interest in the business.

As a restless soul, young John later thinks about fulfilling the family dream to travel to the new world. He decides to leave his father's leather business and go do some traveling, wanting to see more of the world than just Ireland. So he moves to London. He enjoys London very much. Six months after he arrives, he receives word his father has sold the leather business and has retired. John loves his family in Ireland but he wants more in this world as he wonders, *will I ever live the family dream about going to the New World.*

> **My grandson, David, speaks up again saying, "Did John get to go and fulfill the dream?"**
> **"David, how can I finish this story if you keep interrupting me."**
> **"I'm just anxious to know what happens."**
> **"That is all right David; if you don't ask questions you won't learn. I'll go ahead with the story and you'll find out if he fulfilled the dream."**
> **Pleased that David is so interested, I continue.**

As luck would have it, John receives word about a prominent English business, The London Company, which has plans to expand into the New World. He talks to the owners and fortunately, they ask him to join this group planning to settle in this New World that few know about. It thrills John, knowing he will be fulfilling the dream of his Great-Grandfather Jordan Rainey.

The First Settlement in America

After a long voyage from England, The London Company docks in the new land. They establish the first settlement, in what is now Jamestown, Virginia. The year is 1607. The companies' purpose is financial success and expansion. To a lesser extent, some of the people desire to convert the Native American Indians to Christianity. The first few months are very hard as the people have a rough time growing food, building houses, setting up the business, and protecting themselves against the more hostile Native Americans. However, they soon find the fertile lands will produce tobacco, which will provide a great cash crop for the company. The Native Americans have taught the English settlers how to grow tobacco and to use it by smoking it.

**David interrupts again,
"Granddaddy, did the people know tobacco is not good for their health?"
"No, they didn't know what we know now, son."
"Well why did they smoke it?"
"Smoking tobacco was something most men did, but they just didn't know how harmful it is, David"
"Thanks Granddaddy. What's next?"
"Now let me tell you about the other side of our family beginnings."**

The Scottish Beginnings

There is a man who lives in Scotland who will change John Rainey's family future. The man is from a family active in the government for centuries. This man, James Waters, an adventuresome person, is a friend of Lord Baltimore. Lord Baltimore knowing that James is looking for adventure, tells him about a group in England that is secretly planning to go to America. Baltimore, a close friend to the King of England does not want the Royal Family to know about this secret group, so he asks James to keep it a secret.

James travels from Scotland to England where he sought out the group's leader, William Bradford and asks him, "Sir, do you mind if I join your group? You do know that I am a Presbyterian?"

William replied, "Son you'll fit in nicely. Welcome to our group."

This group of Separatist—mostly Catholics—in England flees to Holland in the year 1608 where they decide to find refuge in America where they can build homes for themselves. After several weeks of preparation, the group leaves on the ship Mayflower.

During the voyage over the Atlantic, James Waters suggest to William Bradford an idea expressed in this question, "Since we have so much time during this voyage, why don't we use some of the time to form an agreement which will be the bases for our newly established government. Such an agreement must let the will of the majority rule?"

"Say, that's an excellent idea." Bradford replies.

They do just that and name it the Mayflower Compact. This becomes the precedence for a future written constitution.

The Second Settlement in America

The Mayflower lands in the new land in 1620, where these pilgrims form a colony and name it Plymouth. William Bradford and James Waters are elected governor and lieutenant governor respectively with elections to be held annually. Over the years, the people elected Bradford governor seven times while electing Waters lieutenant governor only twice.

Eight years later and after many more settlers reach the area from the Old world, a commercial group forms the Massachusetts Bay Company. Many Puritans are employed and have their home in and around Boston.

The first marriage to take place in this new colony is between James Waters and a lovely Indian squaw named Jobba Runningwater from the nearby tribe of Nipmuck Indians. William Bradford serves as best man at the wedding. Since a white man

9

is marrying a Native American Indian, this wedding surprises many of the Puritans.

In less than a year, the two give birth to their first child, a baby boy they name John. Many people still look critically on James' Indian marriage. When criticized in public one day, James responded, "We came to America to be free did we not?"

However, this prejudice prevents James from being elected to a public office again, even though most of the people still respected his peacemaking leadership abilities.

A feud between the New England Colonies and three tribes of Indians, Wampanoag, Narragansett, and Nipmuck escalates to war. The war became known as King Phillips War, named for the main Indian chieftain.

James ponders, *why does this war have to be?* He knows the answer; it is because of the tribe's great displeasure at the intrusion of the white man on their lives. It is a bloody first war in the colonies and James's son John, half American Indian & half Scottish, fights along side the English. His mother, a Nipmuck Indian stays neutral during this one-year war. Soon after John's father James's death, his widow Jobba returns to live with her Indian tribe and John loses contact with his mother.

With the loss of his father and the ending of the Indian War, John decides to move south to the Virginia Colony. He receives word that his mother is content living with the Nipmuck. So, prompted by news that his father's friend Lord Baltimore is now in the Southern area of the new world, he plans to move to the Virginia settlement.

> **Little David interrupted again, this time by raising his hand.**
> **"What is the question this time David?"**
> **"May I go to the bathroom?"**
> **"Sure David, are you getting tired of listening to the story?"**
> **"Oh no! I just need to pee."**

"Go do it."

As I waited, I wondered if David was getting tired of my story. It seemed to take him a long time. In a little while, he came back buckling his trousers as he walked anxiously and jumped on the sofa beside me

"Do you want me to continue?"

"I sure do Granddaddy! It is interesting to me, but when will you let me know what happens to the Rainey's."

"Just listen and you'll learn about that."

As I continue, I begin telling David about the early Colonial days in America.

The Colonial Days

Lord Baltimore helps to establish Maryland as the fourth English colony in 1628 after receiving the charter from the King several years before. As a Roman Catholic, he is fed up with persecutions by Protestant Englanders and Maryland becomes a refuge for Roman Catholics. Even though Lord Baltimore's friends, the Waters family of Scotland are Presbyterian, the two families believe in religious tolerance. Both families respect the other's faith.

Lord Baltimore receives news that young John Waters has moved to the Virginia Colony, and looks forward to seeing the son of his friend soon, especially since the Maryland Colony is so near to Virginia.

The Rainey Family in Virginia

The Rainey family prospers in their business at the Virginia settlement, just as the Waters family has in New England. John Rainey marries a girl that caught his eye while making the long voyage aboard the ship over the Atlantic Ocean. Mary O'Leary, a girl of Irish descent, is attractive as most blue-eyed red haired Irish women are. The two newlyweds live in Williamsburg, carrying on the Rainey family tradition at the leather business store. It prospers as the demands for leather goods grow rapidly in the colonies.

John says, "My father and Grandfather would be proud of us Mary. Everyone in this new land needs our goods for their horses, oxen, buggies and carriages."

"I'm proud of you John! The trade that your father and grandfather handed down to you puts food on the table."

"Thank you Mary, you are the one who cooks the food that we put on the table."

The two hug each other and kiss with passion that shows the love they share.

That night at dinner, John has news he shares with Mary, "King James has given us royal colony status here in Virginia"

"That is good news John!"

"Our colony will be the first self-government instance in America."

"Does that mean we have to pay more in taxes?"

"I hope not. The King is taking too much already."

Rainey's leather business continues to prosper as the demand for leather products doubles each year. While John is at the store in town, Mary tends to a small garden near the house. The Raineys own a small farm out in the country. Farm hands are hired to farm t he land for major food crops.

John works hard and so does Mary. Her garden provides easy access to fresh vegetables spring, summer and early fall. Several mules, horses, cows, pigs and chickens, provide transportation, as well as meat for food year round. Fresh vegetables canned by Mary during the summer provide the taste of summer vegetables during the cold winters.

This day finds Mary aware she needs to reveal her secret of several weeks to her husband. She decides that today when John comes home from the store, "I'll tell him."

That evening she sees John's carriage trotting down the long sandy road to their farm. After the normal hug and kiss she says, "Guess what?"

"What dear?" John has a puzzled look on his face as he faces Mary.

"Are you ready for a little one?"

"What do you mean 'little one'?"

"Oh John! We are going to have a baby!"

"How do you know?"

"Well, women just know those things."

"Tell me how you know sweetheart."

"I talked to Mrs. Williams, she has eight children and she knows what to do."

"You are right, she does, but when is the baby due?

"Next Spring isn't that the perfect time to have a baby!"

John jumps up and down as he hugs Mary. "I can hardly wait for spring!"

In the years to follow, the Raineys have ten children in all, five girls and five boys.

"Honey, we must count our blessings. God has given us ten precious children." Mary looks at john with a smile on her beautiful face as she thanks God.

"Yes we should Mary. We could not keep the crops farmed without our boys."

"Do not forget about the girls. They help me in the garden and around the house they cook, wash clothes, and do ironing and all those things you men do not like to do"

"I will not forget about the girls. The five girls are our jewels."

"You know I love our boys very much."

"Yes you do and I love the older ones that help me in the leather business.

"Granddaddy, did people have slaves back then?" David asks as he interrupts once again.

"Some did, but they claimed that these people were working out their passage cost that brought them to America.

Dutch traders during this time in history bring in several ships loaded with Africans periodically. These Negroes are *indentured servants* and serve out their time to pay for their passage across the Atlantic. Some poor Europeans also pay for their voyage to the new world by serving as servants for a period for wealthy colonist.

"As the story continues you will learn more about slavery and what people thought about it."

"Okay Granddaddy, thanks."

Irene, the Rainey family's youngest daughter, an especially beautiful child, is quite bright and continually pesters her mother with numerous questions. Mary does not mind these questions; she knows its Irene's desire to learn more about the world.

One day Irene questions her mother, "Do you think I'll ever marry?"

"Of course you will, Irene Rainey, don't you worry! You are just a little girl, be patient."

Mary's thoughts reflect to when she asked her mother the same question and to the romance between herself and John aboard the ship over the ocean.

Lord Baltimore

In 1636, Lord Baltimore of Maryland receives a letter from John Waters. John respects the Lord's opinions, because of his royalty, but mainly for the long relationship with his family. Since John's father James passed away, he has sought guidance from Lord Baltimore on several occasions. In this letter, the subject is John's possible marriage to an Irish girl in Virginia. Many people seek guidance from Baltimore, especially since he is a favorite of King Charles I of England. Baltimore reads the letter from John Waters:

Dear Lord Baltimore,

I have a favor to ask you. I am in need of some more advice from you. This time it is about a matter that is very personal for me. I have fallen in love with a girl here in Virginia and I need your wisdom about what to do before I ask for her hand. In addition, this will give us the opportunity to visit for the first time since you came to the colonies. Can you come? Please let me know soon.

Sincerely,
Your friend, John Waters

This is an inopportune time for Lord Baltimore. He has a governmental crisis and cannot leave the colony. He does write John as follows:

Dear John,

I am so sorry about the delay in getting back to you. As you know, we have our hands full with all the colonies with the Indians, French, and other scrimmages that have kept me busy. I am so glad to hear about your possible marriage. I will come to James Town in six weeks. Unless I hear from you otherwise, I will be knocking on your door in the afternoon of April 13. I look with pleasure the chance to talk to you. It should be beneficial to both of us.

Kindest regards, Lord Baltimore

John has been anxiously awaiting this message from the Lord. He now can breathe a little better while anticipating the meeting with Baltimore. It seems like an eternity for April 13 to come around. John does not want Irene to know his intentions until after he meets Baltimore. Each time he dates Irene he thinks, *why not just propose now.*

Irene smiles at John on one of their many dates and asks, "Do you think we should stop dating?"

"Uh Uh! Of course not! Why do you ask such a silly question?"

"Well we have been dating for sometime now and we both know that we love each other; but where do we go from here?"

"I do love you Irene and love just being with you. I want to think about our future before we make any major decisions. Give me some time, but I want to date you during this time."

"John, I think you have given me the answer to my original question. I do want to continue dating."

John and Irene hold hands and skip down the path leading to a beautiful lake. There they sit on a bench looking out over the lake hugging each other.

Two weeks later John wakes up realizing that April 13 has finally come.

As promised, Lord Baltimore ties his horse to John's front hitching post. He knocks on John's door. John opens the door, smiling because he is happy to see Lord Baltimore standing there.

The first words come from Baltimore as he says, "John you look so much like your father when he was your age."

"Thank you sir, you are a looking great yourself! I am so happy to meet you in person."

John invites Baltimore in for tea. The two make small talk for a while, and then Lord Baltimore asks, "So you have fallen in love, eh? Tell me about it."

"You bet I have and with a wonderful beautiful woman that I love very much. When you meet her, you will know why I want so much to marry her."

"Good for you John. I'm sure that the time in your life is right for marriage."

"I can hardly wait! I want you to be my best man at the wedding, sir."

"Wait John, have you asked her to marry you already? You can not plan the wedding until she says yes to your proposal"

"Not yet, that's why I want the advice you have given me. I know in my heart that she will say yes."

"I am looking forward to meeting this girl of your dreams."

The two continue to talk and enjoy their tea, discussing all that is happening in the colonies. The conversation leads into a discussion about the various Indian wars.

John asks, "Were you involved in the King Philips War?"

"Thank goodness, no! That was primarily involved the New England colonies. You should know you once lived there; in fact, one of the tribe of Indians was the one your mother is from, as I remember.

"Yes, you remember correctly."

"You know what it is about, it is about who will control this continent, France or Great Britain."

"Yes I understand Lord; it has to be us British. I guess you know about the English trying to capture and burn the Spanish-held fort at St. Augustine."

"Yes, but do you know they were unable to take the main fortress. The English ran away from that one."

"No I did not know that. I have not received the latest news. It is just too slow getting news these days here in our town."

As John ponders the discussion about wars, Baltimore changes the subject by asking, "Before you ask Irene to marry you, you must ask her father first."

"I have not thought about asking him first. Thank you for reminding me sir."

"Who is the father?"

"Mr. Rainey."

"I know about him. He is prosperous leather goods fabricator here in the colony, isn't he?"

"That's him. He has ten children and they are all good folk."

"Well, John, if she says yes to your proposal I will be honored to be your best man at the wedding. When do we get to meet this girl that is the dream love of your life?"

"Would tonight be a possibility?" John says, barely holding his excitement.

Before nightfall, Lord Baltimore and John ride out to the Rainey farm in John's shiny new buggy. Knowing the Raineys and their leather business, John equipped his buggy with all the finest leather trim, seating, garnishes, and other delightful accessories. As they pull up to the hitching post in the front yard, John Rainey walks out to greet the two.

The Rainey home is beautiful with its four tall white columns on the front porch that extend upward to support a lovely veranda at the front of the second floor. A pair of beautiful winding stairs lead to the basement area where the kitchen is located. This style of architecture is unique to the Southern Colonies and unlike any of the houses in the fatherland of Briton.

"Mr. Rainey, please meet Lord Baltimore." John Waters says politely, as he introduces the two men.

"Pleased to me you sir, I have heard so much about you and your efforts in the Indian and French wars that have so troubled the colonies to the North." John Rainey says, as he extends out his right hand to the Lord.

Baltimore seems to appreciate the beautiful home as he shakes Rainey's hand and says, "I love those modern white columns in the front of your front porch. The portico above is so modern, too."

Mr. Rainey says, "Thank you sir, it is the newest designs here in Virginia. The British may copy this style, we hear."

The three men walk into the house to find it well lighted with several candles in each room. Mrs. Rainey welcomes the men into her house. Mary Rainey, a very beautiful and gracious woman, looks much younger than her age. The ten children she has birthed and the years have not taken away from her beauty. John Rainey however shows his age a little.

After proper introductions, Lord Baltimore asks, "Where are the children?"

Mary speaks up first, "They are all married except the three youngest, Jack and his wife live in a town house in Williamsburg. The other married children decided to move to the Carolina Colony, south of here where they live in Charles Towne. Robert and Irene are out back and our youngest, Charles, is playing with a friend down the road."

"Mrs. Rainey, may I go fetch Irene and introduce her to Lord Baltimore?" John asks anxiously.

"Sure, and bring in Robert also" says Mary.

Everyone knows that John is deeply in love with Irene, as it is obvious by his actions, but they wonder: when he will pop the question.

While John is getting Irene and Robert, Mary gives Lord Baltimore a tour of the house. Baltimore turns to Mary and says, "What a wonderful house design you have here, I love it."

In the back door walking hand in hand come John Waters and Irene Rainey followed by little Robert.

Now that all are home and seated, John stands and says, "I have a question to ask Irene and also her dad. Irene, will you marry me? Mr. Rainey may I have your daughter as my wife?"

Everyone is surprised. Not at his questions, but because of the way he does it in front of everyone.

Mr. Rainey smiles and says, "John I will be happy to have you as a son-in-law. All I ask is that you just take good care of my Irene."

"Yes sir, you know I will."

"John, you already know that I love you and yes, yes I will marry you!"

Although, this is an unusual public manor for a young man to ask his lover to marry, it pleases everyone.

After dinning later in the evening, Mr. Rainey asks Lord Baltimore. "Give us a report of some of the wars that have taken place in the colonies to the north."

"Daddy, why do we have to talk about wars at a happy time like this? Irene pleaded.

"Irene, wars do affect our lives. That is why I have an interest in what is happening."

"Yes Daddy, you are right."

The Lord speaks, "I'll be brief. The French agitated the situation in the North by allying with the Indian tribes and everyone knows that France is just trying to gain more territorial control of the continent.

"We may still have to confront a problem with Spain down south below the Carolina Colony."

The conversation returns to the subject of John and Irene and their impending wedding when the youngest Rainey son, Charles blurts out, "Hey, since Rainey is marrying Waters, why don't you change your name to Rainwater?"

Lord Baltimore comments, "I've thought about that, too, and think it's a great idea."

Little Robert says, "Lots of our friends have been talking about this very thing; you two changing your name to Rainwater. What do you think John?"

"It is great idea and all right with me if it is all right with Irene. What do you think Irene?"

"You know I have thought about the Rainey Waters combination a lot my self. Let's do it!"

The Rainwater Name Begins

Before the marriage, the couple legally changes their last name to Rainwater. The name, Mr. and Mrs. John Rainwater, appears on the marriage license, dated June 21, 1629. Since Irene's new husband, John, is active in the governmental processes, he makes it happen smoothly. Mr. John Waters is now Mr. John W. Rainwater and Miss Irene Rainey is now Mrs. Irene R. Rainwater.

David interrupts asking, "I have heard that Rainwater is an Indian name. Is it true?

"Yes, I know of some Indians named Rainwater, especially in Oklahoma."

"In your story you tell about James Waters marrying an Indian squaw. Does that make us part Indian?

"Very observant David! Yes, we do have a little Indian blood, but we are mostly Scotch-Irish."

"That's cool!"

"Do you want to continue?"

"Yes, yes, please tell me more Granddaddy."

"Would you like to hear about the war with the Cherokee Indians?"

"Okay, that will be cool!"

"In the South, the Cherokee Indian tribes become suspicious of the English and declare open war. Cherokee raids on frontier settlements capture several English-American posts. The governor of South Carolina raises an army of over one-thousand men to march

to the most southern area of the colony to seek
a peace treaty with the Cherokee. After several
attempts fail and several years of fighting,
the Cherokee sign a peace treaty with South
Carolina, ceding most of their eastern lands.
This Cherokee War seemingly ends; however,
mistrust on both sides continues."

"Granddaddy, my school teacher says that
the white man took the lands from the Indians
all over America."

"Your teacher is correct; however, let me
continue telling about the early rainwater
family."

"I'm ready!"

The Rainwater Children

John and Irene are exited when their first child is born in the
spring of 1630. The proud parents disagreed on the name for
their baby boy. Irene wanted to name him Robert after her little
brother. John wanted to name him Homer.

John suggests, "Let's name him Homer Robert Rainwater."

"I agree sweetheart."

With this compromise, they embrace each other while
promising to agree on future babies name in advance of the birth.
Over the next twenty years, John and Irene have the joy of naming
five more healthy babies.

John and Irene's oldest child, Homer, is a *'chip of the old block'*
as he shares the same interest in governmental affairs. John serves
in the Virginia Colony Assembly and is a close friend and advisor
to the Governor. At age 21, Homer wins a seat in the General
Assembly, joining his father as a member.

John is a proud father as Homer takes his seat in the assembly.
John remarks, "Like Father like son."

"It just runs in our blood, father, my grandfather and great-grandfather was active in government, too."

"Yes son, you have the same attitude and willingness to serve our people. I know our King in the fatherland appreciates our services.

Homer Rainwater

Young Homer marries Dorothy O'Callahan, a young woman who shares his interest in the political arena. Homer wonders about her aspirations when, soon after the honeymoon, she posed the question. "Why can't women vote?"

"Dorothy, a woman's place is in the home to care for the children and her husband's needs. Men have always looked after the governmental affairs and worked to provide for the women."

"I still think I should be able to vote."

"Dorothy, men do the voting; but I will get your opinion before I cast my vote."

"Yes dear and I'll look up to you as the head of our family because I love you so much."

"I love you Dorothy and will respect your opinions."

Mary thinks, *this is the custom and I will not cause a ruckus because even the Bible teaches that the husband is the head of the wife.*

Homer and Dorothy are blessed with three children in the first ten years of their marriage, all girls.

Homer asks Dorothy, "When will the Lord bless us with a son?"

"Aren't daughters good enough for you since they can't enter politics?"

"You don't have to say that Dorothy. You know I love these darling daughters. I suppose you will want them to serve in the Kings Army one day."

"Of course women should not be soldiers in war; but, let's not argue, Homer, let's keep trying to have a boy, okay:"

Homer hugs his wife as he thinks, *she is a wonderful women and I do respect her very much. However, with the Indian wars going on I certainly would not want my daughters involved.*

During these times, each village has grown up around a palisade built as a defense against Indian attack. The small village is composed of stores, mills, a tavern, a church, and assorted homes. Williamsburg, named after William III, King of England, has many plantations surrounding the village. Homer and his father, busy in the assembly, are responsible for selecting young men to serve in the militia to protect the people in the village and on the plantations. Homer assumes the responsibility as an honor for which he served and has the respect of the citizens.

At the age of 42, Homer receives a wonderful birthday gift: a baby son. They name their son, Floyd.

"Thank you Dorothy! Now I have a male to help me stand up to you women."

"Oh, you silly man! You have always stood up very well and you know it."

Floyd grew to be a young boy who idolized his father. His Grandfather John and Grandmother Irene try to spoil him along the way. In spite of all the attention, Floyd receives as a boy; he becomes a sharp young man with excellent work ethics.

"Mother will you be alright with me if I join the militia?" Floyd asks Irene.

"Son, I know your father would be proud if you volunteer for the militia. I will, too.

Homer is very proud of Floyd as he commissions Floyd as an officer in the militia. Dorothy along with her three teenage daughters attends the ceremonies.

Future Rainwater Generations

Several years later, after Floyd completes his service to his colony in the militia, he marries Katherine Murphy, his next-door neighbor's daughter. As sweethearts, since the two were twelve years-old, they continue the Rainwater generations by giving birth to a son. Named John, he will carry on the John Rainwater tradition of his great-great-grandfather, John Waters Rainwater.

When John grows into a young man, he marries a beautiful Irish girl. Her name is Ann Randolf and she still has the Irish brogue of her mother. The young couple plans to move to South Carolina where there is more land available at practically no cost since the South Carolina Colony subsidizes new landowners.

Katherine asks, "John, why are you and Ann leaving Williamsburg? Floyd and I will miss you and future grandchildren. I think I'm gong to cry."

"Mother, we can visit each other and that way you will not have to miss us all the time. Ann and I wish to help establish Spartanburg in the lower Carolinas just as your generations helped establish Williamsburg. "

"Please take care of Ann and do not let the Indians get you."

"South Carolina has a peace treaty with t he local Cherokee Indian tribes. I know that we will be safe, Mother. We love you and promise to visit.

"All right John, take plenty of food supplies for your journey south."

South Carolina – "Here we come"

It is the year 1716, when John and Ann move to South Carolina, believing it a safe place to raise children, now with the two Carolinas. The land is rich and best of all safe.

"John it is time to start a family." Ann tells John.

"Why is now a good time?"

"Because I am pregnant, that is why!"

"Oh! That is great sweetheart, I am so happy."

John and Ann name their first born a junior, so the John Rainwater tradition continues.

Over the next few years, Ann and John Sr. have another son, George, and a daughter, Katherine. The three children, John Jr., George and Katherine grow up in Spartanburg. John Sr. continues in politics and becomes the mayor of this town, a small town west of Charles Towne, approximately in the center of the colony.

John Jr., as a young teen-ager, is as diplomatic as his father is.

Elizabeth Ramsey has her eyes set on John Jr. On the way home from school one afternoon she asks him, "Hey John, how about carrying my books for me?"

"I sure will Elizabeth, here put yours on top of mine."

"John, when are you going to ask me for a date?"

"What would you say if I ask you?"

"What would you do if my answer is yes?"

"I would run for the hills!"

"Don't tease me John!"

"All right, how about going to the barn dance with me this Saturday night?"

"Yes! Yes! Will you bring your father's horse and buggy to pick me up?"

"Sure, I think he will let me use it."

"Come by early and I'll cook supper for you."

"Girl, you are trying to win over my heart."

"Boy, we'll see about that!"

My grandson, David, speaks again saying, "Will John Junior and Elizabeth fall in love?"

"David, how can I finish this story if you keep interrupting me."

"I'm just anxious to know what happens."

"That's all right David; if you don't ask questions you won't learn. To answer your question, yes John Jr. and Elizabeth do fall in love,"

"What happens to John Junior's brother and sister?"

"That is a good question David. George and Katherine move to the Georgia Colony."

"Why is it called it Georgia?"

"It is named after King George II, who charted it in 1732."

"That is the year George Washington was born!"

"David, how, in the world, do you know that?"

"My history teacher told us."

"You are a real history buff!"

"I guess so, but what does buff mean?"

"It means you have a lot of knowledge about history. I do not belief buff has that definition in the dictionary, but I use it anyway.

"Granddaddy, when you tell me this story, I learn a lot about history."

"Thank you David. Now let me tell you what happens to John, Jr. and Elizabeth."

"Okay!"

Ann and John Sr. love their three grown children, but wish the two boys and their daughter were still young children.

Ann says, "John, I wish George and Katherine still lived here. I miss them so much."

"Yes, I feel the same way; but, as you know, both of them love the adventure of starting a family one day in the new Georgia Colony."

"We still have John Jr. here with us. He loves politics just as much as you do, John."

"John Jr. will make a great addition to the King's colonies because he is so diplomatic,"

"Honey, do you think he and Elizabeth are in love."

"Ann, your guess is as good as mine. They are seeing a lot of each other lately."

"Maybe one day we'll have some grandchildren."

"I am looking forward to that time, sweetheart."

When John Sr. retires, he and Ann look forward to having Grandchildren.

Thirteen Colonies

By 1732, thirteen colonies have now been established: Massachusetts, Rhode Island, Connecticut, New Hampshire, New York, New Jersey, Pennsylvania, Delaware, Maryland, Virginia, North Carolina, South Carolina and Georgia. King Charles Jr. gave eight men a charter to settle in the area south of Virginia. They name the area Carolina in 1663. Charles Towne is the main port. In 1729, the colony splits into two colonies, North and South Carolina. James Oglethorpe establishes Georgia in 1732 after receiving a charter from King George ll. This colony provides a place where imprisoned debtors may form a new life. Georgia provides a barrier between the Spanish in Florida and the other twelve colonies to the north. This offers some safety.

Chapter 2

The American Revolution

"Hey John Jr., when are you going to talk to me about our future?"

'Elizabeth, I have been busy tending to the colonies' future. I guess I have been waiting for you to ask me to marry you!"

"You know that the man is supposed to propose to the woman. Does your last statement mean you are asking me to marry you?"

"Yes! I love you so much. Will you marry me?'

As Elizabeth throws her arms around John's shoulders she says, "You have just made me the happiest girl in South Carolina!"

John Jr. and Elizabeth have a church wedding in Spartanburg. Elizabeth begins a school teaching career at the local schoolhouse. John Jr. continues his political ventures with other leaders in the colonies.

John Rainwater Jr., knowing that much unrest and dissatisfaction exists between many people in the colonies have concerns that it might lead to war. He also believes that the King of Great Britain is not treating the colonies properly. He and his wife Elizabeth, having tea in the morning, are discussing this very subject.

John comments, "We are treated like a step-child. The Brits are taking our money through taxes, but we cannot vote on these matters. What do you think Elizabeth?"

"I agree with you but hopefully the leaders in each colony will rise up and lead us to a peaceful solution; whatever it may be. I feel that someone will emerge as a leader in the colonies"

"Your statement 'Whatever it may be.' leads me to wonder what will happen. I hear great things about young George Washington. Perhaps he can be that leader of which you speak. You know that I will keep my ear to the ground and help out where needed."

"Yes John, you are always there when needed. Perhaps it is time for Rainwater to emerge as that leader." The year is 1735.

David comes running in from his school bus shouting, "Granddaddy, I'm home. You promised to tell me the rest of the story."

"Why don't you wash up and get some cookies and milk first. Then I'll tell you some more."

"Good idea. I'll get some now."

When David has finished, I begin to tell him about things I remember about the times leading up to the American Revolution.

George Washington

In his late teenage years, George Washington is an accomplished hard working surveyor, having responsibility for the layouts of several towns in the Virginia Colony. In addition, his knowledge in the rules of civility along with mathematics and the classics make young George stand out in his community. . After the deaths of his parents, who were of English descent, he eventually inherits their Mount Vernon estate.

George becomes active in the nearby Military District, gaining public notice of his abilities and ambitions. At the young age of 22, Gov. Robert Dinwiddie dispatches him to warn the French about their encroachment on territories claimed by the British. Even though nothing much came of the warning, George Washington is recognized as a man of abilities.

The Governor promotes him to Lieutenant Colonel because of his quick mind. George Washington's personality, a combination of brashness and innate abilities, makes him a potential great leader.

Once George Washington is satisfied that Virginia's border is safe from the French, he elects to leave the military to make repairs on the farm at Mount Vernon. After a while, he becomes bored and enters politics serving in the Virginia House Assembly.

In 1759, George marries Martha Dandridge Custis, a wealthy and attractive young widow with two children. George and Martha experience a happy marriage.

Many colony leaders, including George and John Jr., are dissatisfied with the treatment they receive from the British. This leads to the formation of the Continental Congress. As a delegate to the First and Second Continental Congress in 1774 and 1775, Washington is the first choice as their commander-in-chief of the continental forces.

The Revolutionary War Begins

Washington organizes a 14,000-man army, spending months training the undisciplined men and at the same time gathering gunpowder and other supplies for his army.

He has foresight enough to know that he would need diplomatic help by someone skilled in the political arena, so he writes this letter to John Rainwater, Jr. in Spartanburg.

Dear Mr. Rainwater,

Your political skills are well known. I fear that war with England is inevitable. I invite you to meet with me to discuss the political position of our relations with all the colonies. Please reply.

With sincerity,

George Washington
Commander In Chief

John knows that Washington is a man of unquestioned integrity and possibly the greatest leader in the colonies, so he is happy to be of service. He bids his young wife in Spartanburg goodbye and travels several days by horse back to New York where a battle with the British is ensuing.

George Washington greets John saying, "I know I can depend on you. With your help, we need to rally the leaders of all the colonies behind our effort to defeat the British. John, you must work through the Continental Congress in this endeavor."

"Yes sir, I'll get right on the job."

"Thanks John, I'll notify the Continental Congress in Philadelphia about your appointment as my assistant for political affairs."

With that assignment, John mounts his horse and heads south to Philadelphia to begin his task. To his surprise as he arrives in Philadelphia, many have fled the town, fearing an attack by the British. John takes note that the civilian morale is at an all time low and soldiers have been deserting like crazy. *It does not sound good*, he thinks.

In his first address to the Congress, "Gentlemen, the time is now when all colonies must pull together. We need the support of the military and the people in all thirteen colonies. War is at hand now!"

The congressional representatives all agree with his comments.

April 14, 1775 is a day to remember; John has news from the Massachusetts Colony.

The report:

> *The Massachusetts Governor has secretly been given orders by the British to suppress 'open rebellion' among colonists by using all necessary force. Four days later seven hundred British soldiers come to Concord to destroy the colonists' weapons depot and that night, Paul Revere and William Dawes ride*

from Boston to warn the colonists. Revere reached
Lexington about midnight and warns Sam Adams
and John Hancock who are hiding out there.

After receiving this report, John announces to the Congress, "Gentlemen this news tells us that the war with the Brits has started for sure. Let us pray for our colonist militiamen wherever they are."

News of the events at Boston, Lexington and Concord spreads like wildfire throughout the Colonies. Colonial volunteers from all over New England assemble and head for Boston, where they establish camps around the city and begin a yearlong siege of British-held Boston. The first real major fight between British and colony troops occurs at Boston in the Battle of Bunker Hill on June 17, 1775.

Washington retreats from the British in New York because the British out number his forces. However, the clever strategy devised by Washington revived moral as Rainwater reports what happened at the Delaware River.

John reports, "Washington has made a surprise crossing of the Delaware River on Christmas night and captures the British fort at Trenton, New Jersey.

"He goes on to Princeton, New Jersey and routs the British troops there this January 3, 1776."

"Hear hear!" is the sound from the congress as the delegates applaud the report Rainwater has given.

Washington loses some battles and wins some. One of his greatest wins is at Valley Forge, where it is a difficult fight in the bitter coldness of winter.

Washington and his troops are cheered when hearing this latest news from Rainwater.

John's report:

France has sent word to me that France has
recognized the Independent America. King Louis

> *XVI of France commits one million dollars in arms and munitions. Spain then also promises support. The French also promise navy and army help for George Washington.*

Washington and his troop's morale improve greatly. Washington sends congratulations to Rainwater for his efforts in recruiting France and Spain's help in the colonial war for independence. Rainwater is instrumental in rallying the 13 colonies to get behind the efforts to achieve independence from Britain.

John Rainwater receives word from George Washington to return to South Carolina since the War with the Brits has elevated in the south. His primary duties are to rally the Southern colonies in their war efforts. This also gives John a most welcomed opportunity to see his wife, Elizabeth.

John quietly slips in the back door, anxious to surprise Elizabeth. She is busy drawing water from the back porch well as John tiptoes and hugs her around from her back.

"Who is it?" Elizabeth says as she turns her head around and sees John's face. "This is such a surprise John"

"It's so good to be home. I love you! I love you! I love you!"

"I love you, too John. I have missed you so much. Please tell me you are here for good."

"Sweetheart, I will be here taking care of the war situations in our colony."

"Will you be joining the militia?"

"No, Washington wants me to rally the troops and the people in the south."

They embrace as what seems an eternity.

In John's South, Washington is not present; however, as commander-in-chief, he assigns other generals to that area. In South Carolina, colonial forces at Fort Moultrie successfully defend Charles Towne against a British naval attack and inflict heavy damage on the Brits fleet in June of 1776. It is such a great victory for the colonist.

In the middle of June, after John receives word of this victory he says to Elizabeth, "Good news! Our troops have won a battle against the British at Fort Moultrie."

"That is good news! I heard the horse outside and wondered who it was."

"It was the messenger from Charles Town. I need to go to Fort Moultrie."

"Why do you have to go?"

"The troops need to hear congratulations from Washington's representative, me."

"I know you need to go. Please congratulate the wife's of the soldiers, too."

"Good idea Elizabeth, I will do that."

"When are you leaving John?"

"This afternoon and I'll be back in two days."

John and Elizabeth kiss each other goodbye, after John has saddled and packed s his horse.

John and his horse gallop from Spartanburg to Fort Moultrie to congratulate the militiamen and their families in person.

When John returns to Spartanburg, he receives orders to return to Philadelphia as a quasi-delegate to the Continental Congress.

Elizabeth and John bid each other goodbye once again.

On John's journey to Philadelphia, he receives a message in Baltimore About a massive British war fleet that has arrived in New York Harbor consisting of 30 battleships with hundreds of cannons and thousands of soldiers and sailors. Over two-hundred supply ships are in the fleet to supply the massive number of military personnel. As a show of force, two British frigates sail up the Hudson River blasting their guns.

"Granddaddy, when does the revolution end and the 'Declaration of Independence

'begin? David asks as I realize he is trying to jump ahead in my story.

"Son, I'm getting to this part of the story."

"Who signed the 'Declaration of Independence'?

"David you ask great questions. As you know, it was signed on July 4, 1776. I do not remember from my history books in school who all signed it. I do remember a few of those early forefathers."

"What is a forefather?"

"The men who helped to begin our great country are called forefathers. Sometimes we call George Washington the father of our country; do you know that David?'

"Yes I do Granddaddy; I learned that in the third grade."

'Getting back to your original question about who the signors were, I know that Thomas Jefferson, Benjamin Franklin, John Adams, Roger Livingston and Roger Sherman were a few of the men who signed that important document. My Great-Great-Great-Grandfather acted as the scribe for this document."

"Really Granddaddy?"

"Really David. Now let me tell you what led up to the 'Declaration of Independence'

"Okay Granddaddy."

Peace Delegates are appointed by the British to the Americans and under the direction of Admiral Howe meet with Gen. Washington in New York. Sadly, only vague offers of clemency for the American rebels are given. Washington politely declines, and then leaves the meeting.

The Continental Congress meets on June 17 and at John's request, his good friend, Richard Henry Lee, a Virginia delegate to the Continental Congress, presents a formal resolution calling for America to declare its independence from Britain. Congress decides to postpone its decision on this until July.

On June 18, Congress appoints a committee to draft a declaration of independence with committee members: Thomas Jefferson, Benjamin Franklin, John Adams, Roger Livingston and Roger Sherman. Jefferson is chosen by the committee to prepare the first draft of the declaration.

Just 10 days later, June 28, Jefferson's Declaration of Independence draft is ready and is presented to the Congress, with changes made by Adams and Franklin at the suggestion of John Rainwater.

On July 2, twelve of the thirteen colonial delegations (New York abstains) vote in support of the resolution for independence. On July 4, John Rainwater reads the completed document, once again to the Congress. The Congress formally endorses the Declaration, with copies to be sent to all of the colonies. The actual signing of the document occurs on August 2, as most of the 55 members of Congress place their names on the parchment document.

At a failed Peace Conference held in September on Staten Island, the British demands the colonists revoke the Declaration of Independence.

Washington's army continues to defend New York City against British attacks. In the battle, fire engulfs New York City and destroys over 300 buildings during September. On September 22, Nathan Hale is caught spying on British troops on Long Island, and is executed without a trial.

His last words, "I only regret that I have but one life to lose for my country."

Rainwater is summoned by Washington, "John. Try to influence Congress to seek peace treaties with other European governments."

"Yes sir, I'll get right on it."

John meets with congress and announces, "Washington request that we seek peace treaties with other European countries. Men, I urge you all to act on this immediately."

Congress agrees and conducts a quick but thorough discussion, which leads to the appointment of a committee to seek a treaty with the French. The committee appoints Thomas Jefferson to negotiate treaties with France and other European governments. Jefferson seeks from France, not only a peace treaty, but financial and military aid.

Rainwater reports to Washington, "Sir, as we speak, Thomas Jefferson is going to Paris to engage the French to offer additional help in our war for independence from the British."

"Good job John, we sure could use their help as many soldiers are dying on both sides, as those damn British are intent on controlling the continent no mater what it cost in lives."

"George, we know you will win. Keep up your positive attitude and do not get discouraged,"

"Thank you John, I pay you to keep the spirits up for the colonies; and here you are cheering me up!"

"George, as you know, we have some victories and some defeats, but in the long run we will kick the butts off the British."

"Yes we will John! Go tell the congress about Benedict Arnold's troops defeating the British at Ridgefield, Connecticut the other day." (April 27, 1777)

"The Continental Congress needs to hear good news like that."

When Congress receives the news of Washington's successes against the British, it gives them a sense of great optimism.

"Granddaddy, what flag are the colonies flying?"
"You know David, you ask great questions!"

"I know Granddaddy; I just want to know
if you know."

"Son, are you trying to trick me?"

"No, I just want to hear it from you. I will
learn more that way because you are more
interesting than my school teachers."

"Thanks; the flag in the beginning of
America has a design consisting of 13 stars
and 13 white and red stripes. It is submitted by
Betsy Ross, a local seamstress and is mandated
by Congress."

"I knew that!"

"Let me continue with the story and you
will learn some new stuff about John, Junior
and Thomas Jefferson."

"Okay."

In the summer of 1777, John speaks with Thomas Jefferson, "I am afraid the civilian population is turning against this war; and most everyday I hear complaints about why a war with so many of our young men being killed. What do you suggest I do, sir?"

"Don't get discouraged. You have been the one who has kept up our moral during the past three years. No one likes to see our boys killed; but their deaths will not be in vain. As you know, we have lived under a virtual dictator King who takes our taxes without representation leaving us in debt as our citizens try to make ends meet. Just look at the Declaration of Independence, which you scribed, to see the terrible things to which we have suffered. We are in this war to win, not to retreat. John, you must keep up your spirits and let the people know that we need to stay the course and do not forget, the Congress, which represents the people, is behind this war."

"Thank you, sir. I agree with you whole-heartedly. We will win and become a great free country because of the heroes that have made the ultimate sacrifice."

"That's the spirit, son."

New England and the Dutch Colonies

It seems as though New England and the Dutch colonies New York, New Jersey and Pennsylvania are getting their worst beating from the British during this year 1777. In June, a large British force invades from Canada, sailing down Lake Champlain toward Albany, planning to link up with Howe who will come north from New York City, thus cutting off New England from the rest of the colonies. In July, British troops stun the Americans with the capture of Fort Ticonderoga on Lake Champlain. Its military supplies are greatly needed by Washington's forces; making the loss a tremendous blow to American morale

During all of this, there is a breath of fresh air: Late in July, Marquis de Lafayette a 19-year-old French aristocrat arrives in Philadelphia and volunteers to serve without pay. Congress appoints him as a major general in the Continental Army. Lafayette will become one of Gen. Washington's most trusted aides.

Rainwater reports to congress, "In August, the Battle of Bennington, militiamen from Vermont, aided by Massachusetts troops, wipes out a detachment of German Hessians who have been sent to seize horses.

"In October, the Battle of Saratoga results in the first major American victory of the Revolutionary War as our generals Gates and Benedict Arnold defeat the British, inflicting many casualties with American losses at a minimum.

"In the middle of October we have a great day as the entire British army in the area surrenders to the Americans. As a result the British march to Boston, board ships and go back to England after swearing not to serve again in the war against America."

There is a complete uproar of joy in the hall, but still the war is not over. Yet the congress votes to go in recess.

A report from Paris cheers Rainwater and the Congress members, now in recess—the report:

> *News of the American victories and especially the
> victory at Saratoga has traveled to Europe and has
> boosted support for the American cause. In Paris, the
> victory is celebrated as if it has been a French victory.
> The French Royal Court gives our ambassador an
> audience as the France reaffirmed the independence
> of America.*

Washington suggests to Rainwater, "Now might be a great time for Congress to reconvene and begin to prepare a new constitution."

John uses his influence and the Congress decides, first, to adopt the Articles of Confederation as the government of the new United States of America. Under the Articles, Congress is the sole authority of the new national government.

John reminds the members, "These Articles must be ratified by the individual states before it will become law."

During November, Rainwater begins his long trip to each of the thirteen states to promote and seek ratification of the articles.

Early in January of the New Year, John goes to Philadelphia to talk to Benjamin Franklin, who has just returned from Europe.

"Ben, what is happening in France?"

"Great news John, next month our representatives in France will meet to finalize a treaty of agreement."

On February 6, 1778, the American and French representatives sign not one but two treaties in Paris: a Treaty of Amity and Commerce and a Treaty of Alliance. France now officially recognizes the United States and will soon become the major supplier of military supplies to Washington's army. Both countries pledge to fight until America wins its independence.

Rainwater and Washington are encouraged and can see the end of the tunnel at last.

A message from Washington to Rainwater, Franklin, and Jefferson: "I have enlisted additional troops and will provide training to prepare for what will surely be winning battles." John passes this information on to Congress.

Rainwater remarks to some friends at dinner, "The American struggle for independence has enlarged to the extent that I am afraid it will soon become a world war."

This prediction is right, for soon after, British vessels fire on French ships, the two nations declare war and surprisingly Spain enters as an ally of France.

Britain has its hands full; In addition to the war in America, the fighting in the Mediterranean, Africa, India, the West Indies, and on the high sea is spreading their resources thin. All this is happening while at the same time facing possible invasion of England by the French.

Rainwater asks Washington, "With the Brits thinly spread out situation, should we ask congress to organize a Peace Commission to allow them a way out of our war?"

"No! We need to have Britain in a massive retreat from our land after being totally defeated. This will give us the upper hand in any peace negotiations."

"You are right as usual, George."

Washington and Rainwater are unaware of the British Parliament's creation of a Peace Commission in to negotiate with the Americans.

The commission travels to Philadelphia where its offers granting the entire American demands, except independence. The members of Congress reject this offer saying privately to each other, "Do the Brits think we are idiots?"

At the end of June '78, the Battle of Monmouth occurs in New Jersey as Washington's troops and British troops fight to a standoff. The Brits try to move on into New York but Washington out maneuvers them and sets up headquarters at West Point, New York.

Rainwater, with instructions from Washington, passes the news on to the public about France declaring war on Britain in July '78. Although this is goof news, the fighting continues.

In early 1779, the British began a major southern campaign with the capture of Savannah, Georgia, followed a month later with the capture of Augusta. British troops burn Portsmouth and Norfolk, Virginia. The year 1779 is turning out to be one of the worst years in the Revolution. With the Loyalists, the Indians and the British using terrorist tactics, the Colonists are having a very rough time.

John, worried about his wife in South Carolina, has a premonition that something has happened so he leaves Philadelphia to travel home.

After a tiring trip, John arrives in Spartanburg to find Elizabeth in tears.

John puts his arms around her trying to comfort her as he asks, "What is the matter Honey?"

Elizabeth begins to cry even more and through her red-rimmed eyes, she looks to John and says, "I've missed you so much. The war has me scared to death. John, what is going to happen?"

John understands her concern, but is inwardly relieved that she is not ill, as he feared.

Being the encourager he is, John says, "Everything will be fine as soon as those damned British get the hell beat out of them and run back to England. I am here with you now for a while, so you are protected."

She hugs and kisses John and threw her arms around his neck. John melts in her arms and they go into the bedroom where they make love! They are so ecstatic to be reunited after such a long time.

"Granddaddy, why do they have to make love?" David asks.

Knowing that it is an innocent question from a nine year old, I answer carefully,

"David, they are already in love so 'make love' means that they just continue loving each other as husband and wives should. Does that answer your question?" *I hoped so.*

"I understand Granddaddy."

Thank goodness, **as I continue, trying to remember where I was.**

The next morning news arrives that John Adams has been appointed by congress to negotiate peace with England.

Hearing this Elizabeth says to John, "That is good isn't it?"

"Yes it is. John Adams is one of our great leaders.

"When we win this war and become an independent America, Adams will be an excellent choice to be our President."

"But I think maybe George Washington will be a great choice; don't you think so?"

"Oh he probably wants to stay in the military and not get into politics. But you are right he would be a great President."

John remains in Spartanburg on into the spring of 1780 keeping up with the war efforts through couriers from George Washington and his friends in Congress. One such report reads:

> *The British attack Charleston (formerly Charles Towne) as warships sail past the cannons of Fort Moultrie and enter Charleston harbor.*
>
> *Washington sent reinforcements; but, as of May 6, the British occupy Fort Moultrie.*

John reads this report to Elizabeth.

She cries out, "Why, oh why, do we need this war?"

"It is because we want our freedom!"

"But, John, so many young men are being killed."

"It is not a lost cause. We will win and the generations to come will call those soldiers heroes. I know it seems so much harder since it is in our own state."

She placed her hand on his cheek saying, "Dear, I know you are right; but I still don't feel good about what's happening."

"I don't either, but sweetheart, we must remain patient and loyal."

Elizabeth and John enjoy several weeks of quality togetherness before John must return to Philadelphia.

"I need to return to Philadelphia because the need for renewal in spirits and the uplifting of morale in the American people is especially important at this time."

"I understand John, but please do not stay away so long."

"I will be back soon, Honey." John kisses his wife and heads to the stable to mount himself and his baggage on his horse.

His return to Philadelphia in May of 1780 is very timely because things are not going well with our troops. Washington faces a serious threat of mutiny at a camp in Morristown, New Jersey. Two Continental regiments demand immediate payment of several months back pay. Troops from Pennsylvania put down the rebellion; resulting in the hanging of two leaders of the protest.

Benedict Arnold

In August, Washington appoints Benedict Arnold commander of West Point. Unbeknownst to the Americans, Arnold has been secretly collaborating with the British since May of 1779, by supplying information on Washington's tactics.

One month later, a British major in civilian clothing is captured near Tarrytown, New York. He is carrying plans indicating Benedict Arnold is intending to become a traitor and surrender West Point. Two days later, Arnold hears of the spy's capture by the colonial army and flees West Point to the British ship *Vulture* on the Hudson. Later the Brits name Arnold a Brigadier General in the British Army to fight the Americans.

"Granddaddy, I learned in my fourth grade history book that Benedict Arnold was a traitor."

"Yes he was, and that is punishable by death as a treasonable offense."

"Why didn't they hang him for treason?"

"As you know from the story, he escaped to the British side. Washington just missed catching him before he was able to flee to one of the British ships."

"Why did he do it?"

"I guess he did it for money."

"I wish he was captured."

"I do too. He eventually moved to London where the King praised him for his actions."

"Granddaddy, you can tell me some more of the story."

The British, now low on supplies, are forced to steal from any Americans they encounter, thus enraging the population. The British abandon their plan to invade North Carolina after Americans capture their reinforcements in South Carolina; however, in the cold winter in January of 1781 there is mutiny among the Colonial soldiers in Pennsylvania and New Jersey. The crisis is eventually resolved through negotiations, but over half of the mutineers abandon the army.

Down in the dumps himself, John Rainwater, Jr. penned his wife as follows:

Dear Elizabeth,

I hope things are going well with you today. I love you so much and I miss you. I would be with you now but Congress and George Washington need me here. They think that I have been helpful in creating hope in the people and uplifting their hearts at this time of great struggle with the British. Washington has some problems with the troops recently especially in New Jersey where two cases of mutiny occurred this month. The cold winter conditions and the battle with the British and Loyalist perhaps are hard to take for some of the soldiers. So far, I have not heard of these type disturbances occurring in the South, have you?

I see that there is a group of Loyalists in the South just as there are in the North. I do not think that the British with their Loyalists will win. We have fought hard for our freedom and independence and I have a feeling that the war is nearing an end soon and we will win that for which we have fought. The past wars with the French and Indians did not hurt our relations with France, especially since the regime in France changed. Thank goodness for their help.

With Love,
John.

——————————————

With a glimmer of hope, victory does seem near, as the British are defeated in more and more scrimmages. John, now encouraged, sends this report:

——————————————

We win a victory at Cowpens, South Carolina, as our General Daniel Morgan defeats the British troops, this January 1781. The British suffer heavy losses in the Battle of Guilford Courthouse in North Carolina and their campaign to conquer Virginia is thwarted as our troops have formed a combined French and American force in Virginia to oppose them.

——————————————

Word comes to John that Thomas Jefferson narrowly escapes capture by the British at Charlottesville, Virginia. John rushes to the side of Jefferson to find that he is safe.

Rainwater desires for Congress to appoint a Peace commission, so he addresses Congress again exhorting them about the prospects for peace.

He speaks, "I am here representing the voice of our citizens; as do each of you. I urge you appoint a Peace Commission so that we can bring an end to this war with the British without sacrificing our independence."

In June of 1781, two weeks after John's address, Congress appoints a Peace Commission comprised of Benjamin Franklin, Thomas Jefferson, John Jay and Henry Laurens. The commission supplements John Adams as the sole negotiator with the British.

However, the war continues, as signs of the troublesome times reveals itself locally, when the slaves at Williamsburg, Virginia, rebel and burn several buildings. Rainwater comes to the aid of the slaves; calms down the rebellion to let the slaves know they will be a part of the new free America. He knows that all people are created equal and Negro Slaves should be treated as equal humans in society. Many of his Southern friends do not hold to Rainwater's beliefs. Some states in the north are considering abolishing slavery; the State of Massachusetts has written a new constitution, years earlier that stated *all people are created equal* abolishing slavery. John remembers, however, that George Washington has slaves on his farm at Mount Vernon.

As the war progresses, the British are unsuccessful in their land attempts; establish a base of operation aboard their fleet of war ships off shore in the Atlantic.

**"Granddaddy, the Revolutionary War sure
did take a long time, didn't it?"
"Yes it did, David."
"Did the people think it was worth it?"**

"From what I've told you so far, what do you think?"

"I believe they did. I know I'm glad they gave us an independent free country."

"I'm sure that most of the citizens during that time felt the same."

"Well, what's next Granddaddy?"

"Listen and you'll find out."

As I continue, I will tell David how the French came to our rescue.

The French Connection

While the British are considering their next move, General Washington has received a letter from a French Admiral indicating his entire 29-ship French fleet with thousands of soldiers is heading for the Chesapeake Bay. With this bit of good news, Washington abruptly changes plans to coordinate with the French.

By the end of August, the French fleet arrives and deposits troops, linking with the American troops, cutting s off the British troops from any retreat by land.

Near the end of September, Washington has a combined Allied army far out numbering the British. The Allied lines slowly advance and encircle the Brits as British supplies run dangerously low.

As the British Army is about to be taken, the British send out a flag signaling a truce. General Washington and his officers then work out terms of surrender. Two days later, on October 19, 1781, the British band plays while the British army marches out in formation and surrenders at Yorktown. Hopes for a British victory in the war against America are dashed.

Peace!

Rainwater now knows that peace and independence is near, although fighting in the North is not completely ceased. Random skirmishes exist, as some British units have not received news of the surrender.

On New Year's Day in 1782, Loyalists begin leaving America in droves, heading north to Nova Scotia and New Brunswick; the majority of Americans, including Rainwater, are glad to see the Loyalists leave. During January, the British withdraw totally from the Carolinas as the war in America is over. Rainwater sends the good news to congress and on to the public throughout the colonies. John and Elizabeth Rainwater are especially happy when the British leave Charleston.

"April 11, 1783 will certainly go down in history." Rainwater remarks to Congress as it officially declares an end to the Revolutionary War. Washington reports that about100,000 Loyalists have now fled America.

Rainwater, when hearing this, says, "If you didn't want to fight for our freedom, then you should go to Canada because we do not need traitors."

Congress applauds John after hearing his comments as *Hear-Hear* roars through the hall.

David raises his hand to let me know he is about to ask a question.

"I always thought the *Declaration of Independence* was when the war would be won. Now I know from your story that July 4, 1776 was really the beginning of the Revolutionary War."

"Son, you are correct; that document was just the beginning of our fight for independence from the British. It was almost seven years later before the end."

"Why is it called the Revolutionary War?"

"It is called that because the people in the colonies revolted against the government of

Great Briton. They were tired of sending tax money to the British government without being able to vote by the people in the colonies."

"Thanks Granddaddy, you know how to explain things really good."

"Well thank you David."

"What happened after the war?"

"I am going to tell you about how America set up its government."

"You know Granddaddy; we have a lot to be thankful for all our forefathers died for us."

"We sure do David! America has the best system in the World. Thank you for saying that. Are you ready to continue?"

'What happened after the Revolutionary War?"

"The leaders of the colonies join together for the purpose of establishing a government for the new independent country."

"What did they do?"

"Let me tell you; are you ready?"

"Yes! Yes!"

George Washington delivers his farewell address to his army on November of 1783. The next day, the remaining troops accept discharges. General Washington temporarily moves to Manhattan.

Congress decides to meet in Annapolis, Maryland on November 26. Just before Christmas, George Washington 'the hero of young America' makes a triumphant journey from Manhattan to Annapolis. The victorious commander-in-chief of the American Revolutionary Army appears before Congress and voluntary resigns his commission, shocking members of Congress and especially shocking John Rainwater.

John Rainwater, believing his job is finished, now that Washington has resigned his commission, prepares to head south to his first love, Elizabeth.

"David, should you do your homework?"
"My mother thinks so. I guess I should. When will you finish telling me some more about this story?"
"How about after you finish your homework?"
"I can't wait."
David scurries off to do what he hates the most. This gives me a chance to gets some Z's.

Chapter 3

The New Independent America

The few minutes of rest go by too quickly as David jumps into my lap and I lurch suddenly and open my eyes from the drowsy state. The few minutes actually are an hour-and-half. After regaining my composure, I say, "David, are you sure you want to hear more?"

"Yes, Granddaddy, I am still wondering what happens after the war."

"Well, let's see what happens. My great-great-grandfather will be in this part of the story."

"What's his name?"

"James Rainwater is his name and guess what?"

"What!"

"He was born before George Washington died."

"Granddaddy you have a long list of Rainwaters in your family tree."

**"Yes I do, but let's get on with the story so
you can meet some of these people."
"I'm ready."**

The story continues.

John gathers his belongings and horse gear and heads south. He discovers that the oxcart trails made during the war from the Northern states to the Carolinas make a much safer journey for him and his horse. He reflects back on the teams of oxen, which pulled huge cannon artillery and other warfare supplies by both the Colonist and the British to fight the war and feed the troops.

Oh, I am so glad the war is over. He thinks as his horse trots southward on a sunny day in November of 1783.

"Well, what a surprise!" Elizabeth shouts as John walks in the door.

The happily married couple enjoy this time of peace in the new country and dream of the future. They discuss Elizabeth's school teaching position.

John asks, "Are the children in your school learning anything?"

"Yes John, however, some learn more than others."

"Why is that so?"

"You know, some listen and some are just daydreaming."

"I guess it's your job to get them all to listen so that they learn."

"John, you do know I try to achieve that as my goal."

"Good girl, I'm proud of you my dear!"

"Thanks John! Say, are you ready to settle down into the local political world here at home?"

"I am, however, as a new country, much has to be done to organize the states into a great functioning nation. Maybe I'll be needed at our new Capitol city."

"You know I'm ready for you to stay at home with me, but I understand."

"One of these days we need to start a family. That's when I'll be here all the time."

"Then, let's start a family right now!"

"That sounds wonderful." John murmurs through a happy smile as he anxiously hugs Elizabeth and engages her in a long smothering kiss, leading her to their bedroom.

John and Elizabeth enjoy their time together for several weeks before John receives word from Thomas Jefferson; he wants John to come to Philadelphia. John knows that something important is in the air.

"Elizabeth I have just received word from Thomas that I am needed in Philadelphia."

"Oh John! You are not going to have to leave so soon are you?"

"I'm afraid so sweetheart. It's my duty to serve my country at this pivotal point in its beginning."

"I wish I could go with you. I would if I did not have the children in school to teach."

John bids Elizabeth goodbye, packs up his gear and makes the trip to see his good friend and mentor, Thomas Jefferson.

John detects questions on Thomas' face when he first greets him in Philadelphia.

The first thing out of Thomas' mouth is, "John, what should we do with the sprawling western territories and what are your thoughts about the slavery situation?

"That's two questions; on the second question I think you know my ideas about slavery."

"I know that you would like to ban it in all states; but, what are the farmers, throughout the nation who depend on the slaves to work the crops do, especially in the South, where you live?"

"Thomas, I haven't changed my mind."

"What about the western territories?"

"I have some ideas, but need to give more thought to these first."

"John, when is it convenient for us to meet and discuss your ideas?

"Next Thursday morning? That will give me time to bring myself up-to-date with some of the other men and to benefit from their perspectives."

"Good idea, my son. However, can we meet at my home in Virginia?"

"That's even better for me."

Thomas bids John goodbye and John heads south.

Mount Vernon

As John approaches Mount Vernon, he notices that the place is in dire need of repair. After the war when Washington returned to Mount Vernon, his goal, to bring it back to the pre-war shape.

George, working in the front yard, notices a man coming down the road on horseback. As the man came closer, he recognizes the man as his friend and advisor, John Rainwater.

"John, what in the world brings you here?" What's going on?"

"I am sure glad to see you George; Oh, I'm coming to pick your brain."

"You mean what's left of it; the war took its toll on my brain John."

The two friends make small talk about old times while standing in the front yard.

After a bit, John says, "May I water and feed my horse?"

"Sure thing, and then come in out of the cold and have some hot tea with me."

After John leads his horse to the water trough and feed trough, he goes into the house and greets Martha as he expresses his great pleasure for the opportunity to serve her husband during the war years.

Just before leaving the parlor, Martha says, "I am so glad to have George home for a change. Now he can get some much needed work done here at Mount Vernon."

The conversation then returns to a discussion between George and John as they sip tea one of the house slaves brings in from the kitchen.

"George, I was surprised at your resignation from the army. What are you going to do with yourself now? We need to get you back into the government someway."

"You know that I served in the Virginia House of Burgess several years ago. Maybe I should consider politics again; but, right now I need to get the home place back into shape."

George and John discuss many subjects well into the night. George invites John to spend the night in the guest room.

The next morning Washington shows John the home improvements he has already made in the short time since he left the army. He not only is in the process of restoring his home, but he has added a mill, an icehouse, a greenhouse and several acres of new land to the estate.

John thinking, *Due to Washington's popularity, many visitors will come to visit him at Mount Vernon.*

John thanks George and Martha for their generosity and then heads further south in Virginia to meet with Thomas Jefferson on Thursday.

I see David getting a little restless and ask, "David, are you getting tired?"

"No! I was wondering if Mount Vernon is still in Virginia."

"Yes, it is and it's a national treasure. Your grandmother and I visited it several years ago when we were in Washington D.C."

"Can I go to see it Granddaddy?"

"Do you mean '*May* I go to see it?'"

"That's what I mean. May I?"

**"We'll see about that. Maybe we can plan
a trip sometime."**

**"Granddaddy, tell me some more about
what happens in the story."**

**I was getting a little tired myself, but I
wanted to please my grandson, so I tell him,
"Okay here we go."**

On Thursday, John meets with Jefferson as promised. The two
spend the day and evening exchanging ideas about the upcoming
congressional committee agenda. John's ideas presented in detail
seem to please Thomas as he thanks John for his help.

Jefferson, who is to lead the committee the next day says,
"All right, from what you have suggested, I will propose to the
committee that we divide up the sprawling west into separate
states, each to be considered equal to each of the thirteen states
now in America.

"That's good, but what about the slavery issue?"

"Banning slavery would be a hardship on many farmers;
however, I believe that we should propose that slavery be banned
in all of the United States after 1800. This will give people time
to prepare for it."

The next day the committee meets at Jefferson's home and
to the disappointment of both Thomas and John, the proposal is
narrowly defeated, six for it and seven against it.

Before John leaves, he asks, "Thomas please write so I can
keep abreast of what's happening in our new government."

John returns to his wife in South Carolina.

**"David, David" screams my grandchild's
mother.**

**He squirms out of my lap and answers,
"Yes Mama."**

"It's time to go to bed and I mean now!"

"Do I have to Mama?

"Yes and I really mean right now."

I whisper in to his ear, "You better go, son."

"Oh, okay" The child makes a slur out the corner of his mouth as he slowly walks away.

I am tired and ready to go to bed too, so I was happy his mother came in to get him.

The next day, Friday, David hurries in from school yelling for me. I answer, "What?"

"Let's get back to the war stories."

"Don't you need to study your homework?" I ask.

"You know I don't have to study on Friday."

"Oh, that's right. Come on over here and we'll hear some more about the story."

David makes himself comfortable by my side as I continue the story.

John Rainwater is one of Thomas Jefferson's special friends. The feeling is mutual; but since John has not spoken with Thomas in a long, time, he wonders *what is going on with Thomas?* That very day he receives this letter from his friend:

_____

Dear John,

I hope this letter finds you healthy and prosperous – both in your profession and in your marriage to your dear wife, Elizabeth. I have not heard from you since February of eighty-four. Let me bring you up to date on what is going on. Congress has relocated to New York City temporarily. This will be the capital of the United States for now. This happened in January around the eleventh.

You probably know about the many post-war problems our country faces. There is an economic depression including a shortage of currency, high taxes, nagging creditors, farm foreclosures and *bankruptcies. In August of 1786, Congress adopted a monetary system based on the Spanish dollar, with a gold piece valued at $10, silver pieces at $1, one-tenth of $1 also in silver and copper pennies. Many farmers in several states have shown anger at the high salaries for their state officials. There is a demand for paper money as a means of credit and on October 16, 1786, Congress established the official United States mint.*

Please let me hear from you John.

Sincerely, Thomas

––

Happy to hear from his friend Thomas, John writes:

––––––––––––––––––––––––

Dear Thomas,

Thank you for your letter and updates on recent events. Please excuse me for neglecting writing to you in the past years. We have been in Georgia visiting my brother and sister, George and Katherine. George now has two children and Katherine has six. Since we have no children, we are free to make it a long and lengthy journey. Elizabeth does have to engage a substitute teacher for her school class while we were away.

Thomas, there will be a constitutional convention this May in Philadelphia. Many are looking for a stronger central government. I know your ideas about protecting the rights of the individual states; I certainly agree with you; but I believe that a strong central government is a way to strengthen the individual states rights. I know James Madison will have many good ideas, which will be of value at the convention.

I will be in Philadelphia in May. Since you will still be in France, I will pass on your ideas to the others. Take care of yourself.

With kindest regards, John

––

In May of 1787, the constitutional convention begins in the state house in Philadelphia. Several veterans of the Revolutionary War and some signers of the Declaration of Independence are among the delegates.

John's friend, the brilliant 36-year-old James Madison and the inventor, 81-year-old Ben Franklin are included in the delegation.

The delegates vote to keep the proceedings secret. George Washington is nominated as president of the constitutional convention.

Rainwater will be available if needed. George does seek Rainwater's advice and although John could not be at the secret convention, he promised to guard the secrecy of this important meeting.

George asks John, "What do you think about simply revising the Articles of Confederation which are already in place?"

"No! No! We need to create an entirely new form of national government separated into three branches - the legislative, executive and judicial - thus dispersing power with checks and balances, and competing factions, as a measure of protection against tyranny by a controlling majority.

"That type of tri–governmental division will provide a stronger central government and at the same time protect the rights of each state."

"I like that John, it's a brilliant plan! I'll propose it to the delegates."

He does just that as the delegates vote unanimously to consider such a proposal. Simultaneously at a meeting in July, the Congress enacts the Northwest Ordinance, which establishes formal procedures for transforming territories into states. It provides for the eventual establishment of three to five states in the area north of the Ohio River, to be considered equal in size to the original 13. The Ordinance also includes a *Bill of Rights* that guarantees freedom of religion, the right to trial by jury, public education and a ban on slavery in the Northwest.

As the constitutional convention holds long discussions, Connecticut's delegate takes the floor.

"Fellow delegates I propose a compromise, we should allow for representation in the House of Representatives based on each state's population and an equal representation for all of the states in the Senate. Under this plan, the numerous Negro slaves in the South should be counted at three-fifths of their total number."

The delegates approve his proposal and form a rough draft of the constitution.

Discussions continue for weeks, debating the length of terms for the president and legislators, the power of Congress to regulate commerce, and a proposed 20-year ban on any Congressional action concerning slavery. If John Rainwater knew about the decision on slavery action he would object, but he was not at the secret meetings.

In general, John Rainwater likes what he reads, when the proposed new Constitution is made public for the first time; although, it draws a storm of controversy as most people want only a revision of the Articles of Confederation, not a new central government similar to the British against whom they have just waged a bloody revolutionary war.

The Congress, in session nine days later, votes to send the Constitution to the state legislatures for ratification, needing the approval of two-thirds of the states, nine in all. By June of 1788, nine states ratify the Constitution.

John Rainwater, an anti-Federalist, is happy with the new constitution because it includes amendments, which guarantee civil liberties for the citizens of America. He loves the fact that it is a more decentralized system of government.

The congressional leaders ask Rainwater to visit George Mason in Virginia to see if he can persuade their state to ratify the new constitution. He visits the Virginia leaders and after talking with Mason, he finds them receptive to a compromise.

"George what can I do to help move along Virginia's ratification process?" Rainwater asks.

"John several of our members are calling for a bill of rights and a lower house set up on a more democratic basis."

"As we speak, James Madison is working on a bill of rights. I think you will have your answer to the dilemma holding back your state's ratification approval."

Sure enough, Madison's bill of tights proposal meets with approval in congress and Virginia becomes the tenth state to ratify the new constitution.

> **Out of the corner of my eye, I see David raising his hand as he asks, "What's a constitution?"**
>
> **"You know David, you ask good questions."** **I am *tap dancing in my mind* as I try to come up with an answer that he will understand.**
>
> **Finally, I say, "A constitution is a document stating the basic principles and laws of a nation, state, or social group that determine the powers and duties of the governmental leaders and guarantees certain rights to the people in it. Do you understand?"**
>
> **"I think so; but, can it ever be changed?"**
>
> **"Yes, it can be amended with approval of two-thirds of the states. You know something David; I think you could make a great politician when you grow up."**
>
> **"Do you think so granddaddy?"**
>
> **"I sure do and you will be a great one."**
>
> **"When will this new constitution come into effect?"**
>
> **"Listen and I will tell you."**

The state of New York is still a hold out in the ratification of the new constitution. Rainwater is to visit that state to convince them of the importance of their state's ratification. He addresses their leaders.

"Gentlemen, as the temporary seat of our U.S. government, it is important that we have your approval of the new constitution. As you know, the constitution is in affect since the majority of the states have ratified it. I have some information that will change some no votes to yes votes."

"What is this information Mr. Rainwater?" the leaders roar back.

"We have a congressional committee to plan for an orderly transfer of power from the old government to the new government under t he new constitution. Just a few of the agenda items include procedures for electing representatives from the states and procedures for choosing the electors of the first president."

After John explained other items on the agenda, New York voted for ratification with a vote of 34 for and 29 against.

John Rainwater, known for his past public diplomacy is chosen as an advisor to the public for the congressional power transfer committee.

The national economy begins to recover to pre-war levels of prosperity as the public begins to feel good about their government, thanks, in part, to the public relations efforts of Rainwater and others.

John writes his friend Thomas Jefferson:

———————————————

Dear Thomas,

We miss you here in the newly formed United States! As you know, the Constitution of the United States of America is now in effect. Plans to implement it are being made even though North Carolina has not yet officially endorsed it. I have friends there that say it is just a matter of a few days. I passed on to the Congress your ideas. We need you over here. When will you return?

Sincerely,
Your friend John

"Granddaddy, why was New York chosen as the temporary capitol?" David interrupts.

I reply, "It was the largest city and the center of business in the states at that time. I guess that's the reason."

"When did it move to Washington?"

"That's a good question, so I'll tell you how that came about, when I continue telling the story."

"Go ahead now Granddaddy. Please."

"Okay I'll tell you now. New York, being the largest city and the center of commerce in the colonies at that time, makes it the logical choice. May I proceed with the story now David?"

"Yes sir, I'm ready."

First President

Charles Thomson, secretary of Congress, arrives at Mount Vernon on April 14 to inform George Washington of his election to the Presidency of the United States. Two days later, Washington leaves for New York City. John Adams arrives first in New York and is sworn in as Vice President, then takes his seat as presiding officer of the Senate. Washington arrives in New York City after an eight-day triumphal journey. Seven days later, on the balcony of New York's Federal Hall, George Washington, at age 57, is sworn in as the first President of the United States. He then enters the Senate chamber to deliver his inaugural address.

The first inaugural ball occurs on May 7 in honor of President Washington. John Rainwater and Elizabeth attend as special guest of the President.

**Out of the bright mind of David I hear,
"Granddaddy, will there be anymore wars?"**

"Why do you ask, David?"

**'Well your story is a war story, that's
why."**

**"David, I wish there were no more wars,
but you know from your fourth grade history
that there are many wars. In our countries'
early years, there is a war with France called
the Franco-American War."**

"But I thought France was our ally."

**"Yes you are correct. Keep listening and
I'll tell you about this war and some other
wars, too."**

In the summer of 1789, France begins its own internal
Revolution. Both French and American diplomats have knowledge
of a small naval battle brewing in the Atlantic Ocean over France
and American commercial ships. The U.S. Navy captures more
than 80 French ships although neither country officially declares
war. It is all about France interfering with American trade. The
British delights in the anti-French uproar in America and moves
to assist the United States against a common foe, revolutionary
France. Although the Franco-American negotiations initially
deadlock, France finally agrees to cancel the Treaty of Alliance
of 1778 if the United States drops financial claims resulting from
recent seizures of American merchant shipping. The resulting
agreement terminates the only formal treaty of alliance of the
United States. This war known as the Franco-American Naval War
is never officially declared and America does not need to accept
the British offer of help. The undeclared war ends peacefully.

About the same time, George Washington invites John
Rainwater to meet halfway at Mount Vernon. George travels
from New York and John from Spartanburg. The two discuss

ways to unite all of the people of America in mind and spirit. John suggests a national day of thanksgiving.

"That's a great idea, I'll do it."

He then declared Thursday November 26, 1789 as a Day of Thanksgiving established by proclamation and approved by Congressional resolution.

Washington City

In 1790, Maryland proposes giving a 10-mile-by-10-mile diamond shaped land area along the Potomac River for the establishment of a federal town to be the new seat of the U.S. government. Many of the states feel that the seat of the new U.S. government should be located near a central point between the northern most states and thee southern most states. Maryland's proposal certainly fits the states desires.

Maryland's offer for this site is considered and agreed upon at a dinner by James Madison, John Rainwater and Alexander Hamilton and hosted by Thomas Jefferson. Rainwater suggests that the exact location should be left up to the Congress and the President. Everyone agrees.

On July 10, 1790, the House of Representatives votes to accept Maryland's offer and locate the national capital on this site along the Potomac, asking the President to choose the exact location within this area for the location of the governmental buildings. President Washington likes this site on the Potomac River because of its natural scenery.

The city is officially named *Washington* on September 9, 1791. Out of modesty, George Washington never referred to it as such, preferring to call it *the Federal City*. Despite his approval of the site, he chose to live in nearby at Mount Vernon.

The federal district is named the *District of Columbia* since 'Columbia' is a poetic name for the United States at the time. The city's plan first laid out in 1791 by Pierre Charles L'Enfant, a French-born architect, engineer and city planner who first arrived in the American colonies as a military engineer. The cornerstone of the White House, the first newly constructed building of the new capital, is laid on October 13, 1792.

John Rainwater, dividing his time between Washington D.C. and his home in South Carolina, has been home for the past five years enjoying local and state politics and the living with his dear wife. The year is 1794 and Spartanburg, South Carolina has grown in the past several years to a size that now requires a second schoolhouse. Elizabeth has the task of choosing a site for the new school since she is the main teacher at the present school. She seeks help from her husband, John, in this task.

"Elizabeth, your school is crowded with pupils because of the new settlements west of here. Wouldn't it be best to locate the new school near these new settlements to the west?" John offers this suggestion to his wife.

Elizabeth answers, "I believe you are right, but let's ride around the area before we make a decision."

"Hey, that's a good idea."

He hitches up the buggy and off they go; after touring the areas in the east and west sides of town, they both feel that John's original suggestion is right. Elizabeth will make the recommendation to the local school board.

John and Elizabeth, both, know that education is very important for the children of the day.

John comes close to Elizabeth, looks straight into her face and says, "I feel sad for the children of the slaves who are not being educated.

Elizabeth, with teardrops in her eyes, places her arms around John and says, "I share your sadness John. Since we have no children of our own yet, let's invite some of the Negro children from our neighbor's farm to come here for instruction in English, mathematics, and history."

"That is a great suggestion Elizabeth! Since we have no slaves, we can help those next door. Let's do it!"

"What do you mean let's do it? I'm the teacher John!"

"Yes you are Honey, and a great one, too. But I'll help you when I can."

Elizabeth jumps up and down with a big smile on her face and says, "John this is going to be so much fun!"

John and Elizabeth enjoys seeing the bright young Negro children learn so quickly. They are relieved that their owners are supportive of this, especially since teaching Negroes to read is against the law at this time. The children retained most of their Creole dialect, nonetheless.

Time passes on, Elizabeth asks, "Guess what John?"

"What?"

"You are going to become a father!"

"Are we going to adopt a child?"

"No silly, I'm pregnant!"

"You have made me one happy daddy to be! When is our baby due?"

"Some time early next January, according to the doctor."

John is so excited that he sends word to his friends in Washington that he would be home in Spartanburg for a long while. As time goes slowly by, Elizabeth begins to show her pregnancy more and more.

James Rainwater

Born January 1, 1795, James Rainwater, who bares the name of John's great-great-great-grandfather James Waters, becomes their first-born and the parents are delighted!

"John isn't this just one of God's miracles?"

"It sure is."

The Rainwater family is fortunate to have such a good mid-wife to perform the birth of their son, the wife of a neighbor's slave hand. Everything went smoothly, although, John has to boil six washtubs of water during the birthing process.

Elizabeth's assistant teacher is handling the teaching at the little red schoolhouse during this important time in the Rainwater's life.

John thinks back to his childhood days with his dad, John Rainwater, Sr. and his grandfather, James Waters as he hopes he can be a good influence on little James the same as they were on him.

James reaches his second birthday as Mom and Dad have a second baby. Named Veasey, he is loved just as much as their first one.

George Washington refuses to run for a third term and, after a masterful farewell address in which he warns the United States against permanent alliances abroad, he returns home to Mount Vernon. His vice-president, Federalist John Adams, succeeds him.

About this time, David asks, "Why didn't Washington run again?

"I really do not know. Maybe he was getting old and tired."

"I was just wondering."

"That's good. Let me continue."

In mid-December, Washington contracts quinsy or an acute laryngitis

"What's quinsy?" David asks.

"It's an abscess in the tissue around a tonsil usually resulting from bacterial infection and often accompanied by pain and fever."

"Did the doctors know how to cure it back then?"

"I don't think the doctors knew as much as we know now, and I'm not sure if they did have a cure for quinsy."

**"What happened to George Washington?
"Let me continue with the story."**

The doctors are unable to cure the president. He declines rapidly and dies at his estate on December 14, 1799.

When John Rainwater receives the news of Washington's death, he and Elizabeth rush to Mount Vernon to express their deep condolences to Martha.

After being comforted by the Rainwaters and other friends, Martha remarks, "George's last will and testament specifically states: his express desire that his corpse may be interred in a private manner, without parade, or funeral oration."

Nevertheless, his friends and family could not avoid the overwhelming desire to commemorate George Washington as a national figure.

John asks, "Martha, what can Elizabeth and I do to help you?"

"Just being here is help enough because his Masonic brothers have taken care of everything."

Upon arriving at the humble red brick tomb sunk in a hillside below the mansion house, the Reverend Thomas Davis, rector of Christ Church, Alexandria, reads the Episcopal Order of Burial.

After the funeral, the mourners return to the mansion to pay their respects to the widow and then they go out into the cold December night.

John and Elizabeth spend the night with Martha. They mostly sat by a roaring fire in front of the parlor fireplace, chatting to ease each other's sadness. The only disturbance is the servants tiptoeing in to bring a light supper and fresh hot tea.

As I think about Washington's funeral, my grandson seems to be rustling about beside me.

"What's the matter David?
"I feel sorry for Martha Washington."

**"You are such a tender hearted boy, aren't
you?"**
"I guess so, Granddaddy."
**David is especially thoughtful when it
came to other people's feelings. This is just one
of his many good character qualities.**
"Do you want to continue son?"
"Sure!"

Home again in Spartanburg, John remarks to Elizabeth,
"John Adams has a relatively uneventful tenure as President."

Elizabeth is quick to say, "I don't know about that, as you
know he is negotiating with the French about the commercial sea
'undeclared' wars. Those skirmishes are keeping him busy. Just
because he hasn't called on you for help, don't get upset"

"Oh, I have been busy myself so it has been great that he
hasn't called on me. I remember what he once said to his wife,
Abigail, when he was Vice President"

"Yes. I do too! President Adams, a man of such vigor, intellect,
and vanity that being Vice President was so frustrating that he
complained to his wife Abigail, *'My country has in its wisdom
contrived for me the most insignificant office that ever the invention
of man contrived or his imagination conceived.'*" Elizabeth finishes
the story that her husband has started.

Martha Washington dies at Mount Vernon and the burial
takes place on May 22, 1802 with John and Elizabeth present.
Both are there to pay their respects to a much-admired person.

After the funeral, Elizabeth says to John, "She was such a
beautiful and gracious woman. We will miss her.

"It seems like only yesterday when you and I were in New
York attending their first inauguration grand ball."

John nods his head and says, "Yes, time does fly by doesn't
it?"

He does not expect an answer as he thinks about the great
times over the years with George and Martha Washington.

Elizabeth, seeing him in deep thought, asks, "Say wasn't that the time we stayed at the Duke of York hotel?"

"Yes it was and that was a fine hotel and one that I really enjoyed. Say, why don't we catch the Stage Coach and go up there tonight?"

"John, don't be silly; we have two children waiting for us in Spartanburg!"

"I was only dreaming. We do have to get back before the servants go crazy."

Later Back Home

"Who is going to bake the cake?" John wonders as he plans for his son's birthday.

James is eight years old that January 17. It does not seem possible eight years have passed since James' birth, that cold day in '95.

Elizabeth, sitting across the room, is preparing to answer him, although he is not really asking her. She knows he is mumbling out his question, while deep in thought.

She says, "Honey, I will."

"You will do what?"

"I'll bake the cake for James' birthday."

It has been a good eight years for the couple. God has blessed this family with two fine boys. Veasey, the younger brother, will be six soon.

Elizabeth enjoys teaching in the little red schoolhouse on the eastern side of town. James is in the second grade with his mother as his teacher and though he loves her dearly, really wishes for another teacher. It is hard for an active eight-year-old boy to be taught by his mother! Veasey will be in the first grade next school year. John keeps busy in local politics and in their church, the First Baptist Church of Spartanburg.

Elizabeth notices the keen mind James possesses. John tells her that James' intellect comes from himself.

Even though he is only joking she says, "Don't be so conceited."

The birthday party goes well according to plans and all have fun!

John receives a letter from his brother in Georgia and after reading the letter, he shouts to his wife in the next room, "Honey, George is moving his family back to England to be close to some of our kinfolk."

"Really? I am surprised. How about your sister, Katherine and her family, are they going back to England, too?"

"No, she and her family still live there in Georgia."

"Why don't we go visit George before they move?"

"We can't now. You do know that Thomas Jefferson wants me to visit him in Washington, do you not?'

"I have forgotten about that. What does he want to see you about?"

"I really do not know; his message just tells me that I am needed there. It must be important so I am expected to be there next week"

John, on his horse, is galloping toward Washington thinking about what a great President Jefferson is, despite the controversy surrounding his election.

As John approaches the city, the more he wonders why Jefferson asked him to come. John ponders in his mind—is *another war in the making? Goodness, I hope not. Oh, it cannot be that; if it is I would already know about it.*

He recalls Jefferson sent a naval squadron to fight the Barbary pirates, who were harassing American commerce in the Mediterranean. Further, although the Constitution made no provision for the acquisition of new land, Jefferson suppressed his qualms over constitutionality when he has the opportunity to acquire the Louisiana Territory from Napoleon and now here he is in his second term.

John arrives on Thursday afternoon tired and exhausted. He checks by the White House to be sure Thomas is home. He is. John asks the marine sergeant on duty if he could see the president. The sergeant asks him if he has an appointment.

John says, "I sure do and I believe he is anxious to see me."

The sergeant opens the door and tags John to check with Jefferson's secretary.

The secretary says, "Hello Mr. Rainwater, the president is expecting you. Would you like to wash up, sir?"

"Thanks, I sure do."

Shortly, Thomas comes out of his office just as John is walking down the hall from the water closet. They greet each other like the old friends they are.

Thomas says, "You know, John, we've been through a lot over the years, haven't we?"

"That's right sir and I've enjoyed working with you through the years. I surely missed you when you were in England and France."

Comfortably seated in his office, the President speaks first, "Let us get to the reason I sent for you. I need your diplomatic perspective about the Napoleonic wars. You know that I have been trying to keep the nation from involvement in that chaos.

"England and France have interfered with the neutral rights of American merchantmen. The embargo upon American shipping I have tried has not worked and has been very unpopular.

"What do you suggest John?"

"Stay neutral. If we get into a war about it, we know from experiences that the populace will be against it. If we stay neutral, some will be against that also. The lesser of two evils is to stay neutral. That is my opinion."

'Then I am on the right track, do you think?"

"Yes you are Thomas."

The two walk into the men's poolroom. They relax, drinking bourbon with water and smoking cigars. After a few shots of bourbon, the two discuss the two separate political parties, the Federalists and the Democratic-Republicans.

John says, "I'm glad you have championed the rights of states and have opposed a strong centralized government. You and I agree on those two paths for our country. You are a good Republican."

> **"Granddaddy what's a Republican?" The question blurted out of David's inquisitive mind.**
>
> **"David, you amaze me with your questions.**
>
> **"There have always been political parties that represent the people. The Republican Party is also called the Democratic - Republican Party at that time. The Republican Party believed in states rights with a moderate central government. There were those who believed in a large controlling central government. Those who believe this are in the Federalists Party. Is this clear to you?"**
>
> **"I think so."**
>
> **"May I continue?"**
>
> **"Please do. Tell me some more."**

Some years later, Jefferson retires to his home in Monticello to ponder such projects as his grand designs for the University of Virginia.

Elizabeth is delighted when she and John receive their invitation to the presidential inauguration of James Madison. Madison's buxom wife Dolly compensated for her husband's deficiencies in charm with her warmth and gaiety. She is the toast of Washington. Elizabeth noticed that her own husband gets excited when Dolly walks into a room.

John has favorable memories of Madison; he consulted with James and Thomas when they were delegates to the Constitutional convention in Philadelphia. Jefferson mentioned to me how

Madison took a frequent and emphatic part in the debates. Many now claim Madison as the *Father of the Constitution*; but John remembers the statement James made several years before when he said, "The document was not the off-spring of a single brain, but the work of many heads and many hands."

Dolly Madison's entertainment made this ball an event to surpass all presidential balls since Martha and George held theirs in New York twenty years before. John and Elizabeth dance until almost midnight interrupted only when James and John slip out to talk politics.

Madison respects the public diplomacy skills possessed by John so he seeks his opinion as he asks, "What advice do you have for me in the new regime?"

"James, you should be careful of the 'War Hawks' especially Henry Clay and John Calhoun. Those two will press you for a more militant policy."

"I may have no choice if the British continue to attack American seaman illegally capturing our cargoes. I understand that the British have agreed to stop this practice, but I do not trust them. I certainly do not trust that Napoleon.

"I understand what you are saying; however, you must do what is in the best interest of America."

As David squirms next to me, I wonder if he is loosing interest in my story so I turn to him and say, "Are you awake, David?"

He sits straight up and looks at me as he says, "I'm awake, but I'm wondering how a President knows what's best for America. What do you think Granddaddy?

Puzzled at such an adult type question, I answer in the best way I know, "The President has many advisors that help him to make intelligent decisions and then he decides based on this knowledge what is best for America.

Sometimes history tells us that the Presidential decisions are best for America even when many do not agree with him at the time."

"Thanks, I like your answers Granddaddy."

Pleased with his comments I continue the story.

On their way to South Carolina after the inauguration, John and Elizabeth travel to Monticello to visit Thomas Jefferson. They find Thomas in good health and enjoying retirement. John and Elizabeth learn while visiting their friend that he is planning to donate land for the building of the University of Virginia.

It is such a nice visit with Thomas, they wish they could stay longer, but must get back to the children.

Traveling south from Monticello on their way home, their thoughts turn to wondering about their children's week.

In Spartanburg their son, James, unbeknownst to his parents, has a spat with a bully at school. It happens when the bully, Tom Martin, asks James, "What does your father do for a living anyway?"

"He is in politics." He proudly continued, "And moreover, my dad has been an advisor to all the presidents since George Washington."

"You're a damn liar!" Tom remarks.

At that ugly remark, James threatens to hit Tom, but he decides it best not to start a fight.

Instead, he tells Tom, "Don't ever use words like that because God doesn't respect you for it and I don't either."

Tom walks away not exactly understanding or knowing what to say to James.

When mother and father came home, James does not tell them about the incident.

War of 1812

After the British impressments of American seamen with the seizure of cargoes, Madison, is pressured to ask Congress to declare war. On June of 1812, Congress votes to declare war on Britain. The young nation is not prepared to fight and its forces take a severe trouncing in the early stages.

One particularly devastating event: the British enter Washington and set fire to the White House and the Capitol. However, a few notable naval and military victories, climaxed by Gen. Andrew Jackson's triumph at New Orleans, convince Americans that the War of 1812 is gloriously successful.

The Battle of New Orleans is the biggest U.S. military victory of the war. Though the war resolves very little between the two nations, the United States comes away with a new feeling of national pride and unity. An upsurge of nationalism follows.

The nation unites behind Madison, as news reaches America in early 1815 of the signing of the peace treaty with Britain. The end to the war is now official.

James Rainwater

James Rainwater has grown into a fine young man; attending the University of South Carolina where he hopes to follow the example of his father and grandfather. However, politics do not seem to interest James at this point in his life. More and more he feels a calling to preach the Gospel. When he tells his mother and father of his calling to preach, they give him their blessings.

James completes his degree in divinity at the University and, fortunately, the local Baptist church invites young James to preach on several occasions, putting some money in his pockets, which he needs very badly, even though still living at home with mom and dad.

Despite James's chosen profession as a minister, he still keeps up with what is going on in the nation, as did his father. He has concerns when an Indian uprising in the South brings a war with

Creek Indians. Creeks, living mainly in Alabama and Georgia are alarmed by encroachments on their lands, become convinced by Tecumseh, the Shawnee chief, to unite with many other tribes against the settlers. The Creek war ends as General Andrew Jackson defeats the Creeks at the decisive battle of Horseshoe Bend in Alabama. James thinks to himself, *I hate wars.*

James, like all young men, becomes interested in the girls, and one girl in particular has caught his eye. He has dated Polly Ann Mason for a while, since she attends the small Baptist Mission church where he preaches. James' heart begins to beat rapidly every time Polly Ann comes close to him. The two are so romantically involved and are together as often as possible.

One evening, sitting under a spreading oak tree sipping lemonade, James looks at Polly with longing in his eyes and says, "Polly would you like to be a preacher's wife?"

"Which preacher?"

"You know! The one you are looking at right now."

Polly reaches over kisses him on the lips and says, "I thought you would never ask! Of course I will!"

The two are married in the fall of 1817.

John and Elizabeth adore Polly; giving them a nice home-warming party to begin the two on their journey as newly weds.

James continues preaching at the mission church where he and Polly met. It is James' custom to give his listeners a chance to respond to his message by walking down the aisle to the front of the church to express their responsiveness. One Sunday morning during this invitation time a man, about the same age as James, walks down the aisle to accept Jesus as his Lord. James is surprised to see Tom Martin coming down the aisle. His first convert is the boy with whom he confronted several years before. This convert is not his last.

Katherine's Visit

John's sister, Katherine, travels from Georgia to visit the family in the summer of 1818. It has been a long time since they have been together and this is such a great visit. She enjoys James' new wife Polly, as she is such a joy.

Katherine casually mentions to Polly and James that a little church in Georgia is looking for a pastor. James' eyes pop open as he hears his aunt.

Polly looks at James and says, "Do you want to move to Georgia?"

"I might."

Katherine says, "My family would love to have you in Georgia. It is a beautiful place and with many sinners, too. James you could have a field day there."

Rev. James Rainwater and his wife Polly move to Carroll County, Georgia in the fall of 1818. His brother Veasey, a business student, still lives in Spartanburg with mom and dad. James and Polly settle down in Georgia and start a family of their own. The original church meets only on the first Sunday of each month giving James and his two slaves plenty of time to farm.

Eventually three other churches establish in the surrounding counties. James is offered the Pastor's job at one newly established church. He agrees on the condition that they meet on the second Sunday of each month. They agree and eventually James ministers to four churches, meeting on the four Sundays of each month. He travels by horseback to the churches, alternating Sundays and resting on the fifth Sunday once every three months.

July 4th is normally a day of celebration at the Rainwater home in Spartanburg. John, now in retirement, relishes memories of past Independence Days since the first, July 4, 1776. He was young and full of energy back then. This particular July 4 of 1826 is a particular sad day for John and Elizabeth. They lose two good friends on the very same day. Thomas Jefferson and John Adams both die within hours of each other on July 4, 1826. John and Elizabeth travel to Virginia to attend both funerals.

John's son Veasey moves to Georgia to be near his brother and Aunt. By now, James and Polly have three children and welcome Veasey to Georgia near them.

John, consumed by many thoughts, remarks to Elizabeth; "The United States has been free of wars since the War of 1812 and the Creek War." John wishes for this time of peace to linger.

In retirement, he has spent less time in Washington. While he knows President Monroe, John has not been called on for advice. However, he hears rumblings about Texas wanting their independence from Mexico. He wonders, *'do they want my opinion.'*

Changing the subject, John blurts out to Elizabeth, "Say let's go visit James and Veasey and all the grandchildren in Georgia."

"That's a great idea. We can take the stage coach to Terminus (Later Atlanta) and have James pick us up for the journey to Carroll County."

Crickety cracety crickety cracety goes the sound of the stagecoach wheels on the dirt road as John and Elizabeth roll toward Terminus. They feel safe as the coach goes through Cherokee and Creek Indian territories since the two coachmen up above both carry rifles for protection against attack. The crack of the coachmen's whip and the shiny leather seats trimmed in mahogany frames bring back memories to John of his maternal grandparents' leather business in Virginia.

Sitting across from John and his wife are two men in their thirties talking about states rights and the strong central government in Washington. John, having many years of experience in these type discussions, knows better not to engage in conversation with the two young men. He thinks to himself; *young people do not listen to old men anymore as they did when I was young.*

Instead, he engages in conversation with Elizabeth, "I can't believe James has three children now. Remind me of their ages"

"Yes that's right. The oldest is Zebulon Miles; he is four years old and Joseph is two years old and the baby, Clariah, is two months old."

Waiting under a shade tree at the Terminus coach station, with their bags beside them, they wonder when James will arrive to pick them up. In her letter, Elizabeth gave them the time of arrival. An hour passes before the buggy arrives. It is Veasey coming to pick them up.

Veasey informs them, "James is busy with his slaves picking cotton; so he asked me to pick you up."

John knows that his son is a farmer during the week and a preacher on Sundays and he aware of the two slaves his son bought at the slave house in Macon. John still feels that having slaves is wrong; but most people in the Southern part of America have slaves. Many of the northern states have already abolished slavery.

After a three-hour drive, the three arrive in Carroll County at the farm home of Polly and James. Polly, running out the front door greets them as she dries her hands with her apron around her waist. James is still in the field with his slaves picking cotton.

Polly asks John and Elizabeth to come in and get comfortable. She has a nice cool pitcher of lemonade, which is cool from the well out back. After putting their bags away, they sit in the rockers on the front porch drinking lemonade. Polly is holding Clariah while John entertains Miles and Joseph. Veasey, who owns a small general store in town, has to leave.

Elizabeth says, "Thank you Veasey. We do appreciate the ride from Terminus. We wish you success in your store."

James is happy to see his dad and mom, but he is surprised to see how much they have aged since their last visit. They have a great time during the week with the family. One of the special treats of the week is the watermelon that James placed in the spring near the edge of the woods to cool. As James serves everyone, they all exclaim how delightful the cold melon is.

In a private conversation with his son, John says, "Son, why do you have slaves? You know my feelings about that. You were never raised to have slaves at our house in Spartanburg."

James looks puzzled as to what he should say, "Well Daddy, it's like this. We are family to our two slaves and they love us. They have their own home here on the farm and they have married and are raising their own families.

"They are God-fearing people and anyway, where would they go and what would they do if I set them free?"

"Mark my word, one day slavery will be abolished in this country. Did you know that in George Washington's last will and testament he freed his slaves upon his death?"

The conversation turns to other subjects as son and father enjoy each other's company. Elizabeth enjoys the grandchildren as grandmothers do.

After three days, it is time for John and Elizabeth to leave. They would love to stay longer, but they need to get back to the comfort of their home in Spartanburg.

John Quincy Adams

Back home, John continues his interest in the events and other happenings in Washington, yet he is not as active as in his younger days. He pays especial attention to the presidency of John Quincy Adams, the son of his dear friend John Adams. He is the first President who is the son of a President and in many respects parallels the career as well as the temperament and viewpoints of his illustrious father.

As a child, Adams watched the Battle of Bunker Hill from the top of Penn's Hill above the family farm.

Rainwater admires this Adams just as much as he admires his father.

President Andrew Jackson

In the fall of 1835, President Andrew Jackson, seeking advice on the situation brewing in Texas, visits John. The Texas war of Independence has begun.

The President says to John, "I know of your reputation and I need your thoughts about what is going on over there."

"You know I haven't been active for several years; but, I do know that the American settlers in Texas are fed up with the Mexican rule and their lack of independence for themselves.

"The Mexican President has sent in army troops to quell the unrest. Most of the Texas volunteer guard troops were killed at the Battle of the Alamo.

"I have a cousin in that area who keeps me informed. Jessie Rainwater, my cousin, said that if the United States would send in an army of troops that we could not only help them win; but could eventually get Texas to join us as a state.

"So, Mr. President that is what I suggest to you, sir."

The President thanks John and takes his advice.

Republic of Texas

The war ends at the Battle of San Jacinto where General Sam Houston leads the Texas Army to victory over a portion of the Mexican Army. The conclusion of the war results in the creation of the Republic of Texas. Mexico does not recognize The Republic of Texas and in its brief existence, it teeters between collapse and an invasion from Mexico.

John's Last Days

James Rainwater and his brother Veasey receive word that their father is deeply ill in November of 1836. They leave immediately to be with their mother at his bedside. When they arrive in Spartanburg, they find their daddy somewhat improved but still very seriously ill.

He is able to speak to them saying, "Did you know that James Madison passed away in June? I am sorry that I could not go to his funeral. You know he was the one who made the Louisiana Purchase.

"George Clinton, whom I didn't like much, served as Vice President under both Thomas Jefferson and James Madison."

John has always been the public servant. He becomes very still and quietly smiles just before he passes on.

James weeps, kneels and prays.

At the First Baptist Church, four days later, there is standing room only at the funeral of John Rainwater. His family and many cousins along with several dignitaries from Washington attend, including President Andrew Jackson.

Elizabeth requested that her son James deliver the eulogy. James praises his father as a public servant, especially as a parent, and as the husband of his mother. He can hardly hold back the tears that swell up in his eyes.

Among the crowd after the funeral, an old acquaintance from James' school days comes up to speak to James. James is surprised to see Tom Martin as he walks up to offer his condolences.

Tom says, "That was great what you said about your father since he was a great man and so are you James. You turned my life around for the better. Did you know that?"

"No, But I'm glad you are doing well; thanks for your comments."

President Andrew Jackson walks over to James and says, "Your Dad was an unsung hero and this country owes him much credit for all the *'behind the scene'* things he has accomplished."

"Thank you very much Mr. President for your kind words."

It is a long sad trip back to Carroll County, Georgia for James and his family. His mother decides to continue living in South Carolina. After her retirement, she decides to start a small secret school for the children of the Negro slaves.

James had said to his mother, "Don't let the authorities know about what you are doing."

She had replied, "I won't, but it will be a good deed and keep me occupied. I am only involving the children from owners who are sympathetic to our cause."

Polly gives birth to several children over the next several years. In addition to Zebulon Miles, Joseph, and Clariah there came Cristina, Frances, Benjamin, and three other babies that died shortly after birth. The children enjoy holidays to visit Grandma in Spartanburg.

Their father, the Reverend, continues to preach; but now he has only one church. He is full time pastor at the Ramah Baptist Church in Palmetto, Georgia. His children enjoy going to Sunday school with their mother and daddy. Little Benjamin the youngest child has to be held by Polly. He is only two.

The oldest son Zebulon Miles, now 20, joins the U.S. Army and is to be assigned to a base in Virginia for basic training. In Virginia, he visits with some of his distant cousins. One of them introduces him to a local girl who catches his eye. A romance begins between the two. They spend many evenings together sitting by a nearby lake looking up at the moon and watching the ripples in the water as they do what comes naturally for a young man and woman in love.

One night he and his girl friend, Lilla Ann Thompson, are caught lying together on a haystack in a barn. They are embarrassed trying to explain the situation to the owner of the farm. However, this incident does not hinder their love affair.

When Miles receives notice that he is to be transferred to Louisiana, he asks Lilla Ann, "Will you marry me?"

"I do, but not until you are out of the army; please, I hope you understand."

Miles is disappointed, but knowing he will have to go away, understands.

In Louisiana, Miles corresponds with Lilla Ann frequently, as often as the army permits him to do so.

Zebulon Miles Rainwater
(His Military Career)

Miles, who has just received a promotion to Captain of his 39th Infantry Company, receives orders from his General to place the company on alert since the Republic of Texas is in deep trouble. Miles will not be surprised if the USA gets involved in a Mexican War. All military personnel are confined to base with no outside correspondence is permitted.

Miles recalls that President Tyler spoke of the annexation of Texas as his 'ticket' for a second term; however, James Polk won primarily for his promises to bring Oregon and California under American control. In the waning days of President Tyler's term, he sent messengers to the Republic of Texas for the purpose of annexation, with congressional approval. This action upsets the Mexican government since they believe any annexation is an act of war.

The massing of Mexican troops on the southern bank of the Rio Grande, coupled with the refusal of the Mexican government to achieve peace, leads the President to order General Zachary Taylor to move to the borders.

David asks, "Wasn't Texas like a lone star state?"

"Well, it was actually a separate country called the *Republic of Texas*. Some of its people did call it the lone star state; however, neither the United States nor Mexico controlled it. But Mexico still wanted it as part of Mexico."

"You explained it good, Granddaddy, I understand I think."

"Let me tell you what happened and you'll understand it even better."

"I can't wait Granddaddy, please hurry. Okay!"

It pleases me to see David's eagerness to learn. So I continue.

All of the 39th Infantry Company, with Miles Rainwater in charge takes part in the military campaign with Mexico. Miles knows that war is as terrible as he feared when he hears about the Mexicans crossing the Rio Grande and ambushing 63 Americans from a sister company. Sixteen Americans are killed. General Zachery Taylor orders the 39th company to attack. With Taylor in command, Miles and the other Captains are able to drive the Mexicans back to the south bank of the Rio Grande.

Six days later Miles and his troops cross the Rio Grande and occupy the Mexican frontier town of Matamoras. Miles is pleased when he receives a message from Taylor that the Americans have been able to capture the capitals of three of the Mexican provinces. The General commends Rainwater for his bravery and that of his men during the battles.

California and New Mexico

As the war spreads west to the pacific, a squadron in the Pacific receives orders to seize California. Simultaneously, General Stephen Watts Kearny follows orders to invade New Mexico.

The occupation of California is practically undisputed by Mexico, as it held little resistance to the American invasion. Most of the people are thrilled to see the American flag raised in the territory.

Kearney sends a request to Taylor, "General Taylor, we need assistance from your 39th Infantry Company to help in the invasion of New Mexico."

Taylor asks Miles, "Captain Rainwater, since your company has chased the Mexicans from Texas, Please go to General Kearney's position in New Mexico."

"Yes sir. I'll move our troops over to meet up with Kearny's troops right away."

The Mexicans put up a good fight in New Mexico; however, Miles and his men fight admirably, defeating the Mexicans.

With the war going so well for the U.S, President Tyler sends this message to the Mexican embassy in Washington.

November 2, 1847
The United States is willing to sit down at the table with your president to reach a peace treaty agreement between our country and the great country of Mexico. You may choose the time and place. This offer will not be extended after one month has passed from this date.
Signed, United States President Tyler

The Mexicans refuse and General Taylor and General Kearny advance deeply into Mexico.

The Mexican Government has second thoughts and begins to worry that Mexico could become a United States territory. So, Mexican commissioners are sent to make advances for peace. Remembering the past Rainwater reputation for diplomacy, Miles is invited by the Generals and the President to attend a meeting between U.S. Army Generals and the Mexican commissioners. The Generals convey the conditions for an agreement from the President.

Peace Conditions

To achieve peace, Mexico will be required to cede California and New Mexico to the United States and to recognize the Rio Grande as the southern and western boundary of Texas. In return, the United States will pay Mexico $15,000,000 cash and assume some $3,250,000 more in claims of American citizens on the Mexican government.

In the discussions with the Mexicans, Miles Rainwater, with permission from his General, speaks saying, "This is a very generous offer. If you do not accept it, we have the power to annex Mexico as our state!"

The Mexicans agree and the Peace Treaty signing takes place on February 2, 1848 with Miles Rainwater serving as one of the witnesses. Miles has some of the genes from his grandfather, although he is not quite the diplomat John Rainwater, Jr. was.

In Virginia

After the Mexican War, Miles and his 39th Infantry Company return to their home base in Virginia. As soon as possible, Miles visits his sweetheart Lilla Ann. Sitting on a park bench the two lovers embrace each other making up for lost time.

Lilla Ann says, "It's so good to see you Captain. By the way, congratulations on your promotion."

Miles snuggles closer to Lilla Ann and says, "Thanks, great to see you honey."

"Miles have you heard from your Father recently?"

"No, I haven't heard from Daddy because there is no way of corresponding while in Mexico. You know because that is why I could not contact you."

"Well I have some sad news and some good news. While you were gone, I wrote to your father to see if he receives letters from you; however, he gave me some news about your family. Which do you want first, the sad news or the good news?"

"Give me the sad news first."

"Your grandmother, Elizabeth Rainwater, passed away two years ago. She died peacefully in her sleep."

"Oh I'll miss her! My grandmother was such a grand lady and she loved life to the fullest, always doing good things for others. I am so sorry to hear that she passed away. Now, what is the good news?"

"You have a new baby sister at home. Her name is Catherine."

"That is good news!"

"Now, what about us?"

"I've got some good news too! I am going to be discharged this week from the Army; now answer this question; will you marry me?"

"Yes Yes! I thought you would never ask."

Zebulon Miles Rainwater and Lilla Ann Thompson

"Zebulon Miles Rainwater and Lilla Ann Thompson, I now pronounce you, man and wife." Announces Reverend James Rainwater, as he officiated at his son's wedding. He continues by saying, "You may now kiss the bride."

The newlyweds kiss as everyone applauds and the couple runs up the aisle and out the door.

Lilla Ann lost both of her parents several years ago, when they were captured and killed by the Creek Indians. She knows that Miles wants to live near his Daddy, so she had asked Miles if they could marry in Georgia, at her future father-in-law's church.

Miles brother, Joseph served as best man and Miles sister, Clariah served as the Matron of Honor.

"Is Miles your Great Grandfather, Granddaddy? "

"Yes he is David."

"Well, then Rev. James is your Great-Great Grandfather, right?"

"Yes son." I answer, knowing David has my lineage correct.

One of Miles's fellow officers in the Mexican war, General Zachary Taylor, taking time from his busy campaign running for President of the United States this fall, is a guest at the wedding,

Just under a year later, Miles and Lilla Ann are proud parents to their first child. They name him after Miles grandfather, John.

In the years to follow, Miles helps his preacher father run the farm. He and Lilla Ann are fortunate enough to have several more children. Their young son John now has two new sisters, Catherine, named after Miles youngest sister, and Sarah.

Miles youngest brother, Benjamin, now 12, is always getting into trouble, even with Miles helping and showing him how to do things the right way. Never the less, Benjamin would steal from his neighbors and do things that grieve and anger his Daddy. A frustrated James asks Miles to continue trying to straighten him out.

The Rainwater military involvement continues as Joseph, the second son of James, joins the National Guard. He and his wife live off base in the growing town of Atlanta. The city, formerly named Terminus after the new railroad crossings in the city during the 1830's, is later renamed Marthasville. In 1847, the city now incorporated, chose the name Atlanta, a feminized version of *Atlantic*.

Although farming is the main livelihood of most men, many are also joining the National Guard in the 1850's.

Miles' family continues to grow with two more children, Blewn born in 1853 and Ephraim born in 1855.

The year 1857 starts as a great year. Miles and Lila's youngest daughter, Martha, born the year before is growing into quite a cute toddler.

One day James has asks, "Miles I am planning for the future and would like to appoint you as the executor of my will. You can do that can't you?"

"Daddy I'll do it but you are going to be around a long time you know."

"I know but I am ready whenever the good Lord is ready for me."

Miles' younger brother, Benjamin becomes very angry and jealous when he hears that Miles has been appointed t executor of his father's will. He thinks he should be the executor, even as his father tries to reassure him that his brother is older and more experienced in legal matters.

James says, "Son, do not forget that Miles is a captain in the Army."

"I can't forget because you are always throwing it up to me."

"A statement like that is why I do not think you should handle my will."

The year is nearing the end and on December 8, everyone seems to be getting into the Christmas spirit, but unbeknownst to the family, Benjamin has stolen a pistol from Miles' gun collection. Later in the day, Benjamin, in a rage, rushes to the home of Miles and shoots him in the head. He leaves his bleeding brother and flees into the nearby woods.

Soon thereafter, Lilla Ann walks into the house and upon seeing her husband lying dead on the floor starts screaming as she runs next door to her father-in-law's house crying, "Miles has been shot, come quickly."

James and Polly run quickly to find that Miles is dead. They send word for the sheriff to come and when he arrives, a search of the area is made and late that night they find Benjamin hiding in the woods behind a large tree with the gun still in his hand.

The sheriff takes Benjamin to his father and since this is a family feud, the custom is to let the family decide the fate and the punishment. The sheriff leaves Benjamin in the custody of his father.

That very night, James saddles up a horse packs Benjamin's belongings in a saddlebag, and forces his youngest son to mount the horse. He says to Benjamin, "You are banished. Travel west and don't stop until you reach Texas."

As Benjamin heads west, his father yells, "Do not ever come back to Georgia. You are now considered dead to this family, just like your brother, Miles"

"Your Great Grandfather was shot dead?
"David looked at me with puzzlement in his
eyes as he asks or states his question.
"Yes he was David."
"Well, that's bad, bad, bad!" He replied.

It is a terrifying and sad day for all. A horse drawn hearse of the Palmetto Funeral Home picks up the body. Polly invites Lilla Ann and the children to spend the night at her house.

The Army receiving word that the family desires to have a military funeral and burial notify President James Buchanan, who immediately sends word to the military base at Fort McPherson to organize and cooperate with the Rainwater family on this solemn occasion.

Lilla Ann asks her father-in law to officiate. He thinks about asking someone else, but then he remembers he conducted the funeral of his father and surely, he will by God's grace, do this for his son.

Three days later the funeral takes place at the Ramah Baptist Church. Several officers from the military base speak on behalf of Captain Zebulon Miles Rainwater. His body is taken to rest in the church graveyard where the family plots are located. An American flag drapes the casket and the soldier folds it in a precision fashion and politely hands it to Lilla Ann. All heads hang in reverence, as the three-gun salute seems to echo throughout the Georgia blue skies. Afterwards the soldiers march off in a tight column, leaving the family beside the casket above the grave. It is a cold and sad December day in Georgia as friends begin to mosey away from the grave toward their carriages and wagons.

"**Granddaddy, did your great-grandfather ever know his father?**"

"**No, he was only two years old at the time.**"

"**What happened to Lilla Ann?**"

"**Let me tell you.**"

Lilla Ann, widowed by her husband, starts teaching at the local school to support her six children while her oldest child, John, now eleven, is helping work the fields with his Granddaddy.

Catherine, the 10-year old, helps her mother with ironing and house keeping and caring for the baby, Martha. The other three children, Sarah 8, Blewn 4, and Ephraim 2 are a handful, but the young aunts and uncles next door are very helpful when Lilla Ann needs them.

Polly Ann Rainwater

Two years later, James' wife Polly Ann dies peacefully in her sleep. She would have been 60 on her next birthday. She is laid to rest in a grave beside her son Miles in the Ramah Baptist Church cemetery lot. Her husband, Rev. James, asks a fellow pastor friend to officiate at the funeral.

Later James has a black wrought iron grave marker made. It bore these words in this shape:

POLLY WIFE OF

REV. JAMES RAINWATER

BORN   MCH 14 1799

DIED   JAN   8   1859

ASLEEP IN JESUS

Many reflect back twenty years before when Polly Ann gave support to the Cherokee Indian Nation in North Georgia. It was her belief that the Cherokees should be free to govern themselves and not forced to move west of the Mississippi river. Nevertheless, President Andrew Jackson put a policy in place to relocate all Eastern Indians; Congress passed the *Indian Removal Act* to force those remaining to move west. Polly saddened by the brutal treatment of some 100,000 American Indians as they moved west. Many Indians die in this forced walk. It became known as the *Trail of Tears*. She never forgave the U.S. and Georgia governments for this act. While many politicians disagreed with Polly Ann as they justified the action by referring to the peace treaties signed by the Indians and the generous gift of $5,000,000 allocated by the United States to help the Indians in their move. People in Georgia will always remember the kindness of Polly Ann Rainwater.

Joseph Rainwater

Joseph Rainwater, the oldest living son of James Rainwater, lives in Atlanta near the National Guard headquarters at Fort McPherson with his wife Catherine. He is now 36 years of age and the father of three children: Tom, Yvonne, and William. His military career has been a great thing for him and his family. His new promotion to First Lieutenant in 1860 means more money in his pocket for his family.

Joseph has an opportunity to involve the military in the new technology called telegraph. It has been 16 years since the message, '*What hath God wrought?*' was sent by Samuel Morse from the old Supreme Court chamber in the United States Capitol to his partner in Baltimore on May 24, 1844 through wires from Washington to Baltimore.

"What's a telegraph? Do we still use it?"
David asks.

> "Son, the telegraph was a new discovery by Mr. Morse to send messages over wires for long distances. The system used dots and dashes to represent letters of the alphabet. For example, *dot-dash* is the Morse code for the letter *A*."
>
> "But is it used now?"
>
> "No it hasn't been used for sometime. Western Union, the former telegraph message company, now provides a service to send money over long distance. With e-mail through the Internet, fax messaging and cell phone text messaging, the telegraph became obsolete. Do you understand?
>
> "I think so Granddaddy.
>
> Tell me some more about the telegraph, please."
>
> "Sure, here we go!"

Samuel Morse and his associates obtain private funds to extend their line to Philadelphia and New York. Small telegraph companies meanwhile begin functioning in the East, South, and Midwest. Dispatching trains by telegraph started in 1851, the same year Western Union began business.

Now, Joseph Rainwater has an important assignment to integrate the new technology into military communications. There are rumors that the South's military forces might be called on soon to defend states rights and fast communications will be a helpful tool. Joseph devises a means of stringing wire from one point to another and using a small hand–operated generator, an operator can send the dots and dashes as a full message over the wire.

The Captain of Josephs Company congratulates Joseph when he sees it demonstrated across a field 800 yards wide.

The rumors Joseph hears have become a reality as his unit is put on alert to prepare for a battle.

Joseph says to his wife, "I'm not sure what is happening, but we hear that South Carolina is planning to secede from the United States!"

"That is awful. What are we going to do?"

"My Captain informs me this morning that we must stay on alert and be ready for whatever happens."

You are still paid by the U.S. Army, aren't you?"

"Yes, for now."

The couple is puzzled as to how this will affect their lives.

Chapter 4

The American Civil War

It is just before Christmas 1860 when Joseph Rainwater hears of South Carolina's decision to secede from the Union of the United States of America.

Joseph says to his father, "If my grandfather John were still alive, I don't believe this would have happened."

"I am sure that Lincoln's bid for the presidency triggered South Carolina's declaration of secession from the Union. President Buchanan should have taken action to prevent it, but being a lame duck president, he has not done much of anything.

"And yes, my father probably could have influenced the present governmental leaders of South Carolina in a diplomatic way to avoid such a drastic action.

"You may remember that your grandfather did not believe in slavery. He felt very strongly about the abolition of slavery in all states."

"Dad, do you think that this is all about slavery?"

"Some people think so, but Lincoln has promised not to change the slavery laws that exist in the Southern states."

"If it is not about slavery, what is it about?"

"It's all about states rights! After all the states were here before the Union was constituted."

"Do you think that other states will join South Carolina in seceding?"

"I hope not, but it looks as if more will join South Carolina's lead."

By February 1861, six additional Southern states make similar declarations of secession and on February 7, the seven states adopt a provisional constitution for the Confederate States of America and establish their temporary capital at Montgomery, Alabama. The remaining eight slave states reject pleas to join the Confederacy.

> **"Granddaddy, what does secede mean?"**
> **I "When a member of an organization withdraws from that organization, that is called secede."**
> **"Do you mean that these Southern states are withdrawing from the United States?"**
> **"That's what it means**
> **"Why did they want to do that?"**
> **"Listen to the story and you'll learn from history the reason."**
> **So the story continues.**

Jefferson Davis
(Confederate States of America)

Jefferson Davis, born June 3, 1808, an American political leader is elected President of the Confederate States of America.

After his election, Catherine asks Joseph, "Why did you vote for Davis?"

"I heard him speak once and believe that he is a man of experience and one to be trusted."

"What is his experience?"

"Davis believes that political corruption has destroyed the old Union and that the Confederacy must have ethical integrity to survive. Davis has never been touched by corruption, to my knowledge. He is a West Point graduate, and he served in the Mexican-American war as a colonel. I remember Miles speaking highly of him in that war and you do know he served as U.S. Secretary of War under Franklin Pierce. With these credentials, don't you think he's the right man?"

"I hope so! Sometimes I wish we women could vote."

"That'll be the day" Joseph responds and then thinks—*that was unkindly of me.*

Noticing David seems to have another question, I ask, "Do you have a question son?"

Why could women not vote?"

"Traditionally men were considered the head of the family and were entitled to vote. I suppose the women could influence their husbands but it was the man's privilege to legally vote. This was just the way it was in the 19th century and before."

"But women can vote now, can't they?"

"Yes they can, this privilege was granted to women early in the 20th century. Before that time, men felt that women should stay at home and birth their children. They considered politics as a man thing,""

I am thinking- *it is amazing how much my nine year-old grandson is learning.*

A Peace Conference meeting in Washington fails to resolve the crisis. Confederate forces seize all but three Federal forts within Southern boundaries. President Buchanan makes no military response aside from a failed attempt to resupply Fort Sumter via the ship *Star of the West* and no serious military preparations are being made. However, governors in Massachusetts, New York, and Pennsylvania quietly start buying weapons and training militia units.

President Abraham Lincoln

Abraham Lincoln, sworn in as President on March 4, 1861 delivers his inaugural address saying, "Our Constitution promotes a perfect union and it is a binding contract. Any secession is legally void. We do not intend to invade the Southern states. We will not end slavery where it exists.

"We will use force to maintain possession of all federal property. I ask for the restoration of the bonds of union of the American states."

Fort Sumter at Charleston, South Carolina, is one of the three remaining Union-held forts in the Confederacy, and Lincoln is determined to hold it.

Confederate President Jefferson Davis orders troops to bombard the fort with artillery. Northerners react quickly to this attack, and rally behind Lincoln, who calls for all of the states to send troops to maintain the fort and to preserve the Union.

Tennessee, Arkansas, North Carolina, and Virginia have repeatedly rejected Confederate overtures. Now these states refuse to send troops to join the federal forces against their neighbors. They declare their secession, and join the Confederacy. As a reward to Virginia, the Confederates move the capital to Richmond.

Joseph Rainwater becomes an important member of the Confederate Army. Although he silently does not believe in the war, his military training requires him to be loyal to his superiors and to defend his land. Promoted to Lt. Colonel, he takes charge of all communication within the Confederate army. He finds that laying lines through the battlefields is no easy task for his men. He commandeers the telegraph lines belonging to the railroad lines to provide communication between Richmond and points south. Through these means of communication, he is able to notify military commanders of events taking place more rapidly than in the old pony express days.

One such message:

An informant has passed word to us that Winfield Scott, the commanding general of the U.S. Army, has devised a plan to win the war. His plan is to form a Union blockade of the main ports to strangle the rebel economy, then to capture the Mississippi River and split the South.

Even with this fore knowledge, the rebels are unable to stop the blockade. They try, but do not have the technology to compete with the U.S. Navy. The blockade succeeds in shutting down *King Cotton* shipments to Britain and other European countries.

The South suffers a shortage of everything, including food. This shortage only adds to the devastating effects of foraging by Yankee soldiers and seizure of crops by Confederate armies. This results in hyperinflation and even bread riots.

In July of 1861, Reverend James hopes to hear some good news from Joseph as he receives this letter:

Dear Daddy,

Things are very difficult for us in Virginia, but I do feel that we might have a chance to win. It is so frightening to be fighting fellow Americans, some of whom may be our kinfolks. Please pray that the war will end soon.

This past week our Confederate troops were able to push the Union troops back from Virginia and into Washington with General Thomas Jackson in charge. We nicknamed him 'Stonewall Jackson' because to the Union troops he was like a stonewall, impregnable to their advances

Daddy, I hear that the U.S. Congress is alarmed at the loss, and in an attempt to prevent more slave states from leaving the Union, they plan a resolution, which states that the war is being fought to preserve the Union and not to end slavery. Perhaps that position will save some lives in the future.

It looks like Atlanta is safe for now and I know you hope this war does not get into Georgia. Hope things are going well with you all down there.

Love, Joseph

––––––––––––––––––––––––––––

The Atlanta Dailey News printed this article on September 3, 1862,

WAR NEWS

The war really began in earnest after the strong urging of President Lincoln to begin offensive operations. McClellan attacked Virginia in the spring by way of the peninsula between the York River and James River, southeast of Richmond. Although McClellan's army reached the gates of Richmond, Confederate General Joseph E, Johnston halted his advance, and then General Robert E. Lee defeated him and forced his retreat. McClellan was stripped of many of his troops to reinforce General John Pope's Union Army of Virginia. Pope was beaten spectacularly by Lee in the Northern Virginia Campaign and the Second Battle of Bull Run in August.

The Confederacy made its first invasion of the North, when Lee led a very large number of troops across the Potomac River into Maryland on September 5. Lincoln decides to restore Pope's

troops back to McClellan, where the Union
troops and Lee's troops fought near Sharpsburg,
Maryland, on September 17, 1862, resulting in
the bloodiest single day in United States military
history. Lee's army, checked at last, returned to
Virginia before McClellan could destroy it.

This first part of this news cheered James and his fellow
Georgians in Atlanta, although all are saddened because young
soldiers, by the thousands, are being killed on both the Union
and the Confederate sides. Interestingly, this news is actually
considered a Union victory because it halted Lee's invasion of the
North and provided an opportunity for Lincoln to announce his
Emancipation Proclamation.

> **David asks, "What's Emancipation
> Proclamation?"**
> **"Those are big words and they mean, in
> this case, that Lincoln is making a statement
> that all slaves are to be set free."**
> **"I understand. Did your granddaddy have
> slaves?"**
> **"No, but his granddaddy did have two
> slaves."**
> **With that, I continue.**

Joseph reads the *Emancipation Proclamation* transcript, given
to him by a friend in Richmond, on the train heading for Atlanta.
Two years have gone by seemingly rapid since he has been on
leave. Joseph imagines seeing Catherine after two years; he is
anxious to get home to her.

In his thoughts about his grandfather he thinks, *my
grandfather would be pleased to know that a president will free the
slaves.* Joseph knows that this proclamation might enrage many of

the slave owners in the Confederate states, but he knows that his grandfather would have said, "Lincoln is doing what is right."

My own father has two slaves; Joseph thinks about as he wonders how this would affect him. James Rainwater has always treated Thomas and Zack, his slaves, with respect and assured them of a good life by providing a home, work, food, and all the other necessities of life. To many Southern plantation owners the slaves are considered members of the family, yet in reality they are still property owned by their masters.

Having telegraphed Catherine, Joseph knows that she will be at the train depot in Atlanta to pick him up. As the train begins to slow down approaching the depot arrival platform, he can see Catherine out the window. She looks as beautiful as ever to Joseph as he watches her smile. He is so excited.

The train abruptly comes to a stop and he anxiously stands up and walks toward the door. Stepping off the train and into the arms of his wife brings a warm feeling all over his body. They kiss and embrace each other for what seems an eternity—yet only a few seconds.

Quite a few soldiers are at the station awaiting the train to take them back to the battlefields in Virginia. As Joseph passes each one, they salute him, as is the military custom. He returns the salute politely. Hand in hand, he and Catherine walk over to the row of baggage where the porters placed them.

Traveling to their home, near the Fort McPherson, Joseph asks Catherine, "What do you think about Lincoln's *Emancipation Proclamation?*"

"What is that? I haven't heard anything about it."

Joseph suddenly realizes that this document has not been circulated throughout the South.

"Well I'll tell you. It is a presidential proclamation that sets the slaves free, taking effect January 1 of next year. In it the Confederate states are mentioned as being in rebellion against the United States of America."

"Joseph, do you think that the proclamation will help to end this terrible war?"

"It's my opinion that it will intensify it and not bring it to a close. As you know, this fight is not just about slavery, but about economics and states rights. It is really a *War Between the States*, more so than a war between people. The cotton plantation owners would lose most of their profits if they have to pay wages to the cotton pickers. In answer to your question, the war may be continuing for several hard years yet to come."

"That is not very hopeful; will you be serving that long?"

He has a sad frown on his face as he says, "Yes, I'm afraid so, but between you and me, my heart is not in it."

Finally, at home, they make up for lost time in their love lives. It is so good to be together again.

"Joseph, when do you want to go see your Daddy?"

"Let's go tomorrow, if that is okay wit h you Catherine."

"I will love to go tomorrow."

The next day, they ride down to Palmetto to visit Joseph's father and their brothers and sisters, leaving early right after breakfast.

They arrive just in time for dinner at noon. James is happy to see Joseph and since Miles was killed, he depends on Joseph more and more, especially since his other children are all girls. Of course, he will never see Benjamin, now somewhere in Texas.

After dinner, James and his son have a nice discussion about what is going on in the war. Joseph tells his dad about the Lincoln proclamation.

James says, "You know I treat Thomas and Zack like members of the family. They have, in the kitchen, the same dinner that we just ate."

"Yes I know, but Dad they have to eat in the kitchen while we ate in the dinning room."

"What's wrong with that Joseph; that's how it has always been?"

"Dad, I know you are a good man and I know that you love Thomas and Zack and I'm sure they love you, too."

Joseph does not want to confront his dad.

That night after supper, James begins to think about the conversation with Joseph that day after dinner. He decides to go down to see Thomas and Zack to find out how they feel.

As he arrived at Thomas' house he says, "Thomas, I need to talk to you and Zack; would you go get Zack"

"Yasu, I'll gets him."

In a few minutes in walks Zack with Thomas and Zack says, "Mausu James, whats can we duz fer ya?"

James began to think how he should broach the subject, knowing that these men are smart, but without much education, he finally says, "Have you heard about how some slaves can be set free?"

Thomas speaks up, "Yausu, we done hear dat talk, but don't yuse worry Mausu James."

Then Zack speaks. "Yausu, I done heared dat talk, too."

James ponders what to say next and then he says, "Zack would you want to be freed so you can go up North?"

"Nawsu Mausu James, Yuse been good to us and deys nobody would treat us like yuse."

"How about you Thomas?" James asks.

"I's kinda like Zack, I's loves it here likes it is."

"Well okay, but if you do change your mind I'll set you free. Do you understand?"

The two slaves answer in unison, "Yausu Mausu James!"

Then, James asks, "What would you do if Yankee soldiers came to our farm?"

Thomas says, "I'd be scared, and come getcha Mausu James."

Zack speaks, "We'd hide our misses and our chilens sos dey wouldn't gets hurt."

"You and your families will always be family to me; don't worry, we will take care of you."

109

Both slaves smile and say, "Dats good su!"

**David asks, "Why did the slaves talk like
that?"**

**"Most all of the negro slaves came from
Africa. They spoke the *Creole Language*. It is
a broken language used by the slaves as they
learned to communicate with their English
speaking masters."**

"Why did people have slaves?"

**"That is a complicated situation to explain,
David. Perhaps as I continue with the story,
you will discover the answer to your question.
"**

"Okay, Granddaddy."

The Rainwater slave relationship may not be the exception;
however, many large plantation owners do not treat their numerous
slaves with such love. Sadly, many slaves are mistreated or are sold
away from mothers, fathers or even spouses. Most Southerner
plantation owners look on slavery as a normal way of life and
do not even consider the real fact that slavery is morally wrong.
Even God-fearing men, like James Rainwater accepts this evil
institution.

These thoughts keep flashing through Joseph's mind, as he
looks at Catherine he says, "why is it going to take a civil war to
end slavery?"

She answers, "Let's pray that this war is over soon."

Too quickly, Joseph must return to Richmond to his service
duties with the Confederate armed forces. His nephew, John J.,
the oldest son of his deceased bother Miles, has also joined the
service as required by law for all eighteen-year-old boys. John J
has just turned eighteen.

The war continues and the news from the front lines in
Virginia troubles Lincoln. He transfers General McClellan back

to headquarters and assigns Maj. General Burnside to confront Lee. Lee defeats Burnside at the Battle of Fredericksburg where over twelve thousand Union soldiers are killed or wounded. Lincoln replaces Burnside with Maj. General Joseph 'Fighting Joe' Hooker, who, also proves unable to defeat Lee's army. Despite outnumbering the Confederates by more than two to one, Lincoln is humiliated in the Battle of Chancellorsville in May 1863. Lincoln then gives Maj. Gen. George Meade a shot at Lee.

Union forces under the command of General Meade stunningly defeat Lee at the Battle of Gettysburg in July of 1863, which turns out to be the bloodiest battle in United States history.

> **David's eyes seemed confused as he says, "It looks like Lee is going to get defeated, Granddaddy."**
>
> **"Yes it does, but let me tell you what happens in this war and you'll learn more of the details." I continue to tell David the war story.**

While the Confederate force has seen great success in the Eastern Theater, they crucially fail in the West. Driven from Missouri early in the war, the invasion of Kentucky enraged the citizens there who previously declared neutrality in the war, turning that state against the Confederacy.

The Union Navy captures New Orleans without a major fight, allowing the Union forces to begin moving up the Mississippi River. Only the fortress city of Vicksburg, Mississippi prevents unchallenged Union control of the entire river. Gen. Ulysses S. Grant is the Union's key strategist and tactician in the war. He commands the West Theater and has many key victories, including his win at the Battle of Vicksburg.

"I know about Lincoln's 'Gettysburg Address'; do you know about that Granddaddy

"Yes, but you probably know about that famous address from your most recent fifth grade American History studies.

"I remember from my own history studies that it begins with the sentence *'Four score and seven years ago our fathers brought forth on this continent, a new nation, conceived in Liberty, and dedicated to the proposition that all men are created equal.'*

"Lincoln goes there to dedicate a battlefield in Pennsylvanian where many men have been killed fighting in a civil war to eliminate slavery and to preserve the union of the states. What do you know about it David?"

"I guess about the same thing you do Granddaddy."

"Shall we continue the story about the Rainwaters in the war?"

"Yes sir, Granddaddy."

Joseph Rainwater

Joseph learns through a telegraph message from a friend in Washington about Lincoln's announcement to Congress and to the Northern public that General Grant will be commander of all Union armies with Maj. Gen. William Tecumseh Sherman as his second in command. Joseph thinks *this is the beginning of the end of this terrible war.* He keeps his thoughts to himself. Many in his Rainwater family feel the same and wish Jefferson Davis would not be so stubborn.

Joseph's beliefs turn out to be true as General Grant's strategy is to strike at the heart of the Confederacy from multiple directions. Many in the South now have their worst fears this 1864 autumn.

Joseph receives orders to move down to Atlanta to provide for backup communications for the troops in the Georgia area. Many fear that since Lee's forces are being pushed further south there will be trouble if the Union forces approach Atlanta, in the near future. This concerns Joseph but he is happy to be with his wife and near his father in the Atlanta area.

Joseph has a long trip by train from Richmond to Atlanta and as he steps down the train car steps, his wife and three children are there to greet their father soldier. They can hardly hear each other due to the train noises as they hug each other. Walking through the terminal, they pass dozens of men in uniform scurrying back and forth catch trains. Joseph returns their salutes as they pass.

Joseph has a few days off before his company expects his return to the military base. He uses the time to be reacquainted with his family. His children are growing up before his eyes; Tom is 16, Yvonne 14, and William 10. All three are old enough to ask many questions about the war, especially Tom as he asks, "Daddy why are the Yankee's trying to kill us?"

Joseph says, "Son, it's not that they are trying to kill us; it's that the Confederate States want to rule themselves and the Union wants to keep the Union together including all the states. You might call this as a '*War Between the States*' instead of a '*Civil War*'."

"But Daddy, people are being killed and some of them are civilians. Isn't that a civil war?" Tom asks.

"In that sense it is a civil war, but hopefully it will end soon."

Catherine sitting quietly in the chair in the corner of the room has been listening to her husband trying to explain a war that is not easily understood.

She stands up and announces, "Let's go to Palmetto and visit Granddaddy, okay?"

"Yes! Yes!" Comes shouting out from the three children.

"Let's go!" says Joseph, who is anxious to see his father.

They can hardly wait as the one-horse-buggy rolls through the dirt roads to Palmetto, south of Atlanta. The children noisily express their excitement over having Daddy home and making a visit to see Granddaddy. The carriage pulls into the red sandy yard of Rev. James, just before the farmers go back to the fields. James seeing the carriage, runs out to greet the family as he calls out to Zack and Thomas, "You fellows take care of things in the fields; I'm going to spend this afternoon with my son's family."

"Yausuh Mausuh James." The two slaves say as they return to the fields.

James, now 69-years old, yet still a strong man, looks forward to sitting down with his grandchildren and the son whom he has not seen in many months. They sit on the front porch talking about how things are going in the war. The two grandsons, Tom and William, go out into the sandy yard and start playing marbles, as James yells out, "Don't play for keeps!"

"We won't Granddaddy. Tom yells back.

James, a very conservative Baptist minister, feels that playing marbles for keeps is a form of gambling and against what the Bible teaches.

John J. Rainwater

Everyone has a fun afternoon and the grandchildren are able to see their cousin, John J., who has just been transferred to Atlanta from Tennessee, where he has served in the Confederate infantry for only a short six months. He was originally sent to Tennessee to fight with General John Bell Hood in the battles against Sherman and the strong Union forces. He is home now with his mother next door.

Tom asks John J., "do you think I will have to go into the army?'

"Some 16-year-olds have volunteered, but my suggestions to you is that you don't volunteer

"Okay, I won't."

James asks his grandson, John J., "When are you reporting back for duty?"

"Day after tomorrow, Granddaddy."

Joseph speaks to his nephew, "Say John J., tell us about what you experienced in Tennessee."

"It was pure hell! Our company was under the command of General John Bell Hood, who is a great commander, but the Union troops continuously pushed us southward down the railroad line from Chattanooga. Our company was transferred to General Joseph Johnston's command near the Tennessee and Georgia border."

"What happened after that transfer?" Joseph inquires.

"That's when they shipped us down to Atlanta, and I'm glad to be back down here!"

Joseph understands what is happening more than does young John J. and he speaks up, "Since Atlanta is the most industrialized city in the South and has the busiest railroad center, the Union forces plan to capture it to stop the flow of supplies to our troops throughout the South. John J., now we know why we are in Atlanta. Something big is about to happen."

James says, "It doesn't sound good to me; I think we need to pray about the situation."

He then bows his head, as do the others, and prays that God will intervene and stop this terrible war.

After the prayer, Joseph speaking to Catherine says, "Honey, we need to be heading back to Atlanta with our children."

"Yes we should."

They bid farewell to James and John J. and travel back to Atlanta in their black one-horse-carriage. On the way home, Yvonne, ask her Dad, "Is Granddaddy going to be hurt if the Union troops come to Atlanta?"

"Probably not, Yvonne, you see over where he lives it's mostly a farming area and I believe the Union forces will want to attack our industry and our railroad hub in the Atlanta area other than out in the countryside." Joseph reassures his daughter.

Tom says, "Daddy, does that mean we are in danger where we live in Atlanta?

"Tom, I'm afraid so. Your mother and I have discussed this possibility. We will send you all to live with Granddaddy if we see a real danger. But I'll be with the army trying to defend our family and our land as much as possible."

Catherine joins in by saying, "Both your dad and I will protect all of you, whatever it takes. One thing I think about is that the soldiers in the Union are also from families or have their own children and will not seek out and kill innocent mothers and children. At least I don't think that they will, so please don't worry too much about this."

Little William, looking at his Mother says, "But, didn't Cousin John J. say that the Yankee soldiers are mean?"

"Well, he means they are tough, but that's not mean. Your dad is a soldier and he has to be tough, but he is not mean. Do you see the difference?"

"I guess so Mama."

The Union's Progress

President Lincoln summons Grant to Washington to discuss the progress of the war.

He asks, "Ulysses, It still doesn't look great in Virginia against Lee. Where do we stand?"

"Mr. President, as you know, we now control all of the Border States: Maryland, Delaware, Missouri, Kentucky and the new state of West Virginia. We have taken all of Tennessee, all of territory west of the Mississippi River, and most of Alabama and Mississippi. We control the Mississippi and Tennessee Rivers and all the seaports. We are about to start the battle for Atlanta. However, Lee is still giving us a hard time in Virginia; but we should have him routed out in a few weeks."

"How long will it take to have the entire Confederacy surrender?"

"It's hard to pinpoint the exact length of time, but I think, by the summer of 1865, we should be at that point. But, sir, do not hold me to an exact date because warfare is unpredictable, as you know."

"Thank you General, you have accomplished much so far, just keep up the good work. What is your strategy in Georgia?"

"Georgia has some of the best railroads in the South with a great hub in Atlanta. We are going to take those railroads to cut off the supplies to the Confederate troops and burn the agricultural crops as we go. If we can't kill 'em, we'll starve 'em. We are planning to do that in Virginia too."

Lincoln is pleased with what he hears, although he hated to hear the phrase, *if we can't kill 'em we'll starve 'em*. Now, Lincoln is very anxious to end the war and to get the Union back together as it was before the war.

The South's War Progress

General Lee, a brilliant military strategist and a man of unquestionable personal integrity, is serving as general of the Confederacy only to protect his home state of Virginia and then only after Virginia left the Union. Joseph Rainwater has great respect for this man and shares in many of the general's beliefs.

Lee does not hold back the truth when President Davis asks for a report of the South's progress in the war. He reports a grim picture to his Commander-In-Chief as he points out the lack of a sufficient number of men to win the war. Lee reports that his troops are being pushed back on all fronts and we don't have time on our side to increase our troop count before we are defeated.

As a good soldier, Lee is not ready, at this point in time, to through in the towel. He is strengthening resources in the Atlanta Theater since it is such an important rail junction to supply the troops. In addition, Lee has plans to defend the Confederate Capitol in Virginia.

> **"Granddaddy, I understand that Robert E. Lee was a smart man. Is that right?"**
> **"In my opinion, yes he was."**
> **"Well why didn't he win the war?"**
> **"That's a good question David, but listen to the story and you'll learn why."**
> **"Was General Lee on the wrong side?"**
> **Surprised at David's perception of the situation, I say, "Maybe, but let me finish and you'll see what happens."**

Lee's popularity grows because of his aggressiveness in attacking the Union forces; even the people in the Union states admire him. One woman, sitting on her front porch in Pennsylvania as Lee and his troops passes by, says, "I wish he was on our side."

However, in the autumn of 1864, Lee and his troops are wearing down because of the greater manpower the Union possesses. The Confederate army also experiences great losses from within, from both casualties and desertion. Lee knows he is being pushed southward from all geographical directions, but he keeps fighting in his usual tenacious style, annoying the Union Generals.

General Robert E. Lee

Lee offers to resign in August of 1863, but Davis refuses to accept it. Lee is a disciplined soldier with a keen engineering background and knows how to outsmart the enemy on the battlefield; but he can do very little to stop such a powerful enemy. In his mind, he knows that a defeated Confederacy would be the best for all people in these American states, both in the North and in the

South; but he never let these beliefs affect his efforts to accomplish the task assigned to him by the Confederate President.

The Yankees Are Coming

The Union forces in Georgia are advancing south from Chattanooga toward Marietta, Georgia in June of 1864. Confederate General Joseph Eggleston Johnston retreats from General Sherman and his stronger Union forces. Along the railroad, heading southward to Atlanta, Sherman's troops confiscate chickens and any other foods that feed the men. One woman tries to run them away from her house with a broom. She runs after the soldiers saying, "You Yankees get out of my yard."

Sergeant George McKenzie, as he dodged her swinging broom, says, "Hey lady we won't hurt you! We just need to get food for our men and then we will go."

"You can't have our chickens because then we won't have any thing to eat. So ya'll just get outahere!"

Sgt. McKenzie has one of the privates hold her while they round up all the chickens. After that, they burn the fields in her farm as Sherman has instructed. Sherman's ruthless plan to 'starve 'em' is working. They know that an army travels on its stomach. For as long as man has warred, the toughest tactical feat is feeding men who fight battles. Many times important tactical and strategic decisions are based on the ability to provide food.

The Kennesaw Mountain Battle Field

The Union forces advance to the area around Kennesaw Mountain near Marietta, Georgia, with Sherman on one side of the mountain and Johnston on the other side, Sherman decides to launch a full-scale frontal assault against Johnston's entrenched Rebels. John J. Rainwater is smack in the middle of this battle. He is at the top of the mountain as he writes in his diary these words: *The valley is full of men coming towards us for as far as the eye can see."*

John J. wonders how his uncle Joseph is making out in Atlanta. Little does he know that Joseph is busy with General Hood making plans for the eventual invasion of Atlanta by Sherman. Joseph already knows what is happening at Kennesaw as he communicates with the troops via telegraph along the Western and Atlanta Railroad line, which skirts the north end of Kennesaw Mountain.

Johnston's headquarters is located in a plantation home on the south side of the mountain. During the battle, artillery shells begin to land near the house and Johnston must evacuate the home. With his troops, numbering nearly 100,000 men, entrenched along the top of the mountain and in the valley near the railroad line, which he needs to protect, General Johnston decides to wait and let Sherman attack first.

A simple plan devised by Sherman gives his field commanders great leeway in their choices of an attack plan. Generals Schofield and Hooker, at the southern end of the line, shoot cannon fire to keep Johnston in place. Hooker launches the primary attack somewhere along a front nearly two and half mile long south of Pigeon Hill. To the north, McPherson launches a secondary attack.

With his men in position and the Union Army on the move in front of them, Johnston can't reinforce the actual areas of attack and Sherman wants to split two holes in the Rebel line and drive to the Western and Atlantic Railroad in downtown Marietta.

Young John J. sits at the top of the mountain knowing that a huge battle is ready to commence. He is scared but holds his rifle ready to fire when the need arises Hundreds of Rebel soldiers now sit in waiting just like John J. He wonders if they are as terrified as he is as he tries to think of pleasant thoughts to take his mind off the impending battle. His thoughts turn to his Grandfather James Rainwater in Palmetto, hoping that all is well with him.

The Union line has formed far enough back on the hill that a *'dead area'* beneath the Confederates might offer the attackers brief relief from the hail of lead they would surely face.

Sergeant George McKenzie of Ohio is frightened as he thinks about what is about to happen, when orders to attack are given. He thinks about the chickens he has taken from that farmwoman in North Georgia, just a few days before. He wonders if the Rebel soldiers are as afraid as he is. Of course, he does not let on to his fellow soldiers that he is scared.

The morning of June 27, the ranking Union officers give orders for the artillerymen to begin bombarding the Rebel line. For fifteen minutes across parts of the eight-mile front, Union cannoneers lob shells at Confederate positions. The barrage is designed to *'soften up'* Rebel defenses; however, it may do more harm than good since it forewarns of the impending attack.

The Union attack plans almost immediately go awry. One division does not start until an hour after schedule and the assault runs into several unexpected physical barriers. At 8:15, the cannon bombardment halts and is quickly replaced by the staccato bursts of gunfire as the men move forward. Nearly 5,500 infantry pour into a small area to battle the entrenched Rebels.

Noyes Creek, which runs north south just west of Mountain Road, provides the first physical barrier for the infantry. Behind the creek sits the 63rd Georgia Regiment, along with other groups on the skirmish line and instead of withdrawing when others moved back, the recently transferred 63rd stays on the line. Regiments of Federals, six in all, pour out of the forest and over the line held by the Georgians.

With orders to reinforce the skirmish line, reserves come forward as support. Brief hand-to-hand fighting routs the Georgia Regiment, who head for the Rebel line followed closely by boys in blue. Punishing Confederate crossfire halts the Union forces and the commander orders retreat within ten minutes.

John J. Rainwater is relieved for the moment as is George McKenzie, his enemy on the other side. John J. enters these words into his diary: *This morning has been terrible as I dodged cannon fire and bullets flying by. Many of my fellow soldiers have been wounded or killed. If I get out of this, I'll never fight in a war again.*

George McKenzie does not keep a diary; however, he has similar thoughts, wishing he were back in Ohio with family. He thinks to himself, *war is terrible.*

As the Union men regroup and again attack, the heavy woods, large rocks and a stone palisade at the top of Pigeon Hill, doom the assault. Even further, north the men overrun the skirmish line but fail to take the main line in the heavily wooded gap.

Johnston assigns two of his best commanders to defend the area as Union commanders plan to rush the Confederates en masse, with hopes of breaking through and routing the boys in gray. The Union Army launches a charge at nine o'clock with 8,000 men committed to the assault across a two-mile front, many waiting for a breakthrough to exploit.

Leading the charge for Sherman is George McKenzie, the Ohioan most noted for sharing a law office back home with his commanding officer, William Tecumseh Sherman. Simultaneous charges are being made from the southern side, as well as the northern side.

Prepared for the attack by the unusual artillery barrage, the Rebel line watches the green valley become a sea of blue as the Union assault sweeps across the creek below them. Advancing men try to punch holes in the line but word from the battle is not good. Men are falling left and right and as the Rebel line rakes the Union boys with cannon fire and rifle rounds. John J. fires many rounds and is hardly aware of his surroundings as he fights, thinking only about surviving.

Wave after wave of Union soldiers advance towards the Rebel line, withering gunfire kills hundreds of boys, mostly from Illinois and Ohio. Incredibly, McKenzie and some of his men make it to the Rebel line, only to be shot, stabbed, or captured by the Rebels

Just to the north of the hill, some woods catch on fire during the attack. Wounded Union soldiers, left during the hasty retreat, scream as they burn to death in the blaze. A Rebel colonel from Arkansas steps on top of the entrenchments with a white flag and calls to the opposing force, "Come and get your men, for they are burning to death!"

Rifleless Union men approach and begin to remove the bodies, aided by men in gray. The two forces that have been killing each other less than fifteen minutes earlier and now are working together to save the lives of fallen men. The next day the Union commander presents the Confederate Colonel with a matching pair of ivory-handled Colt .45 pistols.

The battle is over. Unable to pierce the Confederate line, the remains of the Union attackers withdraw to safer territory. In an hour and a half, the Union has lost more than 1,000 men, the Confederates one-third that total.

McKenzie is carried to the field hospital, badly wounded, dies shortly after his promotion to Colonel.

John J. rainwater is transferred back to Atlanta where fighting will soon require more of the Confederate Infantry. Johnston withdraws on the evening of July 2 to a position in defense of Atlanta.

John J. has no time to visit family, as he must stay with his Confederate troop group; however, he does contact his uncle Joseph through military communication channels. Having an uncle who commands all communications makes it easy for him to do this.

Joseph gave news about the family. Joseph has sent his wife and three children to live with his Dad in Palmetto to be out of harm's way.

All John J.'s brothers and sisters are doing fine. He especially is fund of his brother Ephraim Dawson Rainwater, who is now nine years old. He is happy that Ephraim and Blewn are too young to serve in the war. John J. sent this message via telegram to Joseph: *'Please tell me what the plans are for the Battle of Atlanta.'*

As part of the Confederate upper command in Atlanta, Joseph cannot pass on restricted information to his nephew because the Union forces may have means of intercepting such information.

Retreating from Sherman's advancing armies, Gen. Johnston has withdrawn across Peachtree Creek, just north of Atlanta. Johnston has drawn up plans for an attack on part of Sherman's army as it crosses the creek.

On July 17, Johnston receives a message from Confederate President Davis relieving him from his command. The political leadership of the Confederacy is unhappy with Johnston's lack of aggressiveness against the larger Union army and so they replace him with Hood. In contrast to Johnston's conservative tactics and conservation of manpower, Hood has a reputation for aggressive tactics and personal bravery on the battlefield.

Hood takes command and launches an attempt at a counter-offensive. Joseph hearing this is afraid that the President has made a big mistake. *The Confederacy will probably lose more lives and lose the war in the end* Joseph thinks to himself.

Sherman has placed Maj. General Henry Thomas as the commander in charge of this phase of the battle to take Atlanta facing Hood at Peachtree Creek

On July 19, Hood learns that Sherman has split the Union army; Thomas's Army is to advance directly towards Atlanta, while John Schofield's Army moves several miles east, apparently an early premonition of Sherman's general strategy of cutting Confederate supply lines by destroying railroads to the east.

Thomas will have to cross Peachtree Creek at several locations and will be vulnerable both while crossing and immediately after, before they can construct a temporary fortification. In addition, the Confederate East Atlanta corps will enjoy a rare three-to-one numerical advantage over the Union corps in that area. Hood thus hopes to drive Thomas west, further and further away from Schofield and Sherman will be forced to divert his forces away from Atlanta.

This advantage evaporates when the Confederates arrive late to their starting positions, to find the bulk of Thomas's command already on the south side of the Creek, and on prepared high ground, giving the Union an advantage over the Confederate forces. Casualties are extremely high on the Confederate side and low on the Union side.

Joseph's personal predictions have sadly become a fact. He discusses his fears with his superior, Maj. General William J. Hardee, who agrees with Joseph.

Hardee says, "President Davis' move in changing the command to Hood and the losses at Peachtree Creek are probably the *'straw that broke the camel's back'*. It doesn't look good at all for Lee in Virginia at this time either."

Joseph leaves Hardee's office very troubled.

Sherman issues orders to burn every building in Atlanta and round up all the supplies needed for a long trip to the sea at Savannah. In the battle that pursues, many civilians hide out to avoid being caught in the crossfire of the battle.

The Burning of Atlanta

Sherman shells the civilian population of Atlanta and sends his troops on raids west and south of the city to cut off all supply lines from Macon, Georgia. On August 31 at Jonesborough, Georgia, Sherman's army captures the railroad track from Macon. Confederate trains and its crew are confiscates and many farms and homes in the area are burned and destroyed.

In Jonesborough, a woman runs from a Union soldier as he makes improper advances toward her. Her slave, standing nearby, comes to her rescue just in time, as they are able to defend themselves from the soldier's advances. The woman and her slave are able to hide upstairs in a closet as the soldier ram sacks the house and then leaves with food from the kitchen.

"We are lucky." The woman says to her faithful slave.

The slave is shaking all over her body but answers, "Yasum, we show was."

The fall of Atlanta, extensively covered by Northern newspapers significantly boosts Northern morale. Lincoln feels this news will help him in the fall campaign when he will be running for reelection for his second Presidential term.

Just the year before, the polls showed that most Northerners wanted to stop the war and pull the troops home to save lives, but now most polls show that most people are behind Lincoln and want to win the war and not give up.

His Democratic opponent, former Union General George B. McClellan, is running on a peace platform calling for a truce with the Confederates. Lincoln, a Republican, maintains that the war must continue by staying the course to rid the country of Rebels and to bring the Union back together.

Grandfather James' House

It is a cold dreary day as the Reverend James stands in the front yard of his home watching the smoke fumes rising into the sky above Atlanta, more than thirty miles to the North. Accompanied by his three grandchildren along with Zack and Thomas, having just finished dinner, they take their afternoon break. Wondering how his son Joseph and nephew John J. are fairing in the battle in Atlanta, he doesn't know it is all over except for the remaining fires flickering throughout the city.

Luckily, the Yankees have not been to Palmetto and he hopes they will not. He says to his two slaves, "Well boys, so far the Yankees haven't bothered us."

"Yausuh, and dats good ain't it Mausuh James." Zack remarks, as they started to the fields to gather the remaining corn before winter sets in.

Joseph's son Tom asks, "Granddaddy, when can we see our daddy?"

"Tom, I really don't know. Soon, I hope."

"Is he all right?"

"Yes I'm sure he is because we haven't heard any different news."

That reassurance seems to satisfy little Tom and his sister Yvonne and the younger brother William, as they huddle together, wondering what war means.

Atlanta

Wandering through the simmering fires and smoked filled air, Joseph is walking down Peachtree Street, not going anywhere in particular, but in deep despair with his thoughts lingering about the terrible time everyone experienced during the past few weeks. As a chicken flutters out of a bush in front of him, he thinks, *that is one Sherman did not get.*

A two-horse drawn fire engine with four men hanging on and its bell clanging as it rushes down Peachtree Street toward a burning building distracts Joseph from his grim thoughts. Suddenly, as the red fire wagon passes, he sees a familiar face leaning against a gas lamppost on the corner. The closer he comes to the young soldier; he realizes it is someone he knows. It is his nephew John J. He runs up to John J and says, "Man, it's good to see you!"

"Uncle Joseph, it's a surprise to see you too. What's going on with you?"

"Oh, I'm just wandering around trying to get my mind off this war. What about you?"

"Me, too. I can still hear the bombshells exploding and the rifle bullets whistling by my head. I wish this war would end."

"Son, I think we are nearing the end now. John J, tell me are you scheduled for any special duty?"

"I don't know for sure, but it has been rumored that my outfit may be heading toward Savannah. What about you?"

"We are busy trying to maintain the telegraph lines between here and Savannah. I guess you know that we have lost all communications from Macon, and that's where most of our supplies are stored."

"No, I did not know about Macon. If we lost the telegraph lines, did we lose the railroad tracks to Macon?"

"Yes, I'm sorry to say Sherman and his troops captured the railroad leading out of Jonesborough to Macon."

John J., knowing his uncle is part of the Confederate command asks, "When do you think we'll be going home?"

"Your guess is as good as mine, John J."

"Have you heard from Aunt Catherine?"

"The last I heard, she and the children are doing all right at Daddy's house." Joseph says, as he realizes he is due at a meeting with his superiors soon, continues, "I need to get back to my tent, but I hope to see you again soon and good luck to you."

"Goodbye Uncle Joseph, It is good to see you. May God bless you."

As the uncle and the nephew depart in opposite directions, neither knows what to expect in the coming days.

David seemed to be crying as he asks, "What's going to happen to John J. and Joseph?"

"It's a sad story—this war, but you'll have to let me tell you what happens in the story as I continue."

"Granddaddy did Lincoln know about the terrible things happening in Atlanta?"

"David, Lincoln did know and so did Jefferson Davis. However, that is part of the price of war and men never seem to remember this when wars are started. Let me continue and you'll learn more, okay."

"Granddaddy you are cool in knowing how to explain things."

I smiled as I continue the story.

Lincoln Reelected

In Washington, the Republicans celebrate the reelection of Lincoln.

General Grant says, "Mr. President this will stop the Democrat's pressure to cut the war short." Grant knows that the Civil War will end only if the Confederacy's strategic, economic, and psychological capacity for warfare is decisively broken.

Sherman knowing Grant's desire to end the war decisively applies the principles of scorched earth, ordering his troops to burn crops, kill livestock, consume supplies, and destroy civilian infrastructure along their path.

Atlanta to Savannah

Sherman leaves the captured city of Atlanta, Georgia, on November 15, 1864 knowing that Grant's armies in Virginia continue to be in a stalemate against Lee's army as fighting continues in Petersburg, Virginia.

Sherman addresses his officer staff, "The task before us is to march to Savannah and then move up and attack Lee's rear to allow Grant to break through the rebel lines. Keeping Southern reinforcements away from Virginia is also primary in our campaign.

"We will be out of touch with our North Headquarters throughout this campaign so I have prepared explicit orders regarding the conduct of the campaign. Sherman issues these field orders to all of his commanders before leaving Atlanta.

1. The army will forage liberally on the countryside during our march.
2. You are to destroy mills, houses, cotton gins, etc.
3. As for horses, mules, wagons, etc., belonging to the inhabitants, the cavalry and artillery may appropriate freely and without limit, discriminating,

> *however, between the rich, who are usually hostile,*
> *and the poor or industrious, usually neutral or*
> *friendly.*
>
> *4. Negroes who are able-bodied and can be of*
> *service to may be taken along.*

With a force of about 60,000 men remaining, Sherman divides this army into a left and right wing with the cavalry supporting both wings. The Confederate opposition from Gen. Hardees's remaining army is quite meager with only about 25,000 men. Of these, about half remain at Lovejoy's Station, south of Atlanta and the Georgia militia has about 3,000 soldiers, some of them boys and elderly men.

At 7 a.m. the following morning, Sherman writes in his journal describing the scene as he leaves Atlanta. Marching in convoy style, he turns his ears as he hears his Army band striking up the anthem *'John Brown's Soul Goes Marching On'*. Later the troops begin a chorus of *'Glory, Glory, Hallelujah'*.

Sherman says to his two Corps commanders, "I want your two wings to confuse and deceive the Rebels about your destinations."

The Confederates could not tell from the initial movements whether Sherman will march on Macon, Augusta, or Savannah. The right wing, marches south along the railroad to Lovejoy's Station, which causes the defenders there to conduct a fighting retreat to Macon.

The Union cavalry captures two Confederate guns at Lovejoy's Station, and then two more and fifty prisoners at Bear Creek Station. The infantry marches through Jonesborough to Gordon, southwest of the state capital, Milledgeville.

Sherman accompanies the left wing as it moves to the east in the direction of Augusta. They destroy the bridge across the Oconee River and then turn south.

The Georgia state legislature flees the capital. Hardee arrives from his headquarters at Savannah and realizes that his city, not Macon, is Sherman's target. He orders the Confederate cavalry to harass the Union rear and flanks while the militiamen hurry eastward to protect the seaport city.

On November 23, Sherman's staff holds a mock legislative session in the state capitol, jokingly voting Georgia back into the Union and playing cards.

Several small scrimmages ensue along the way as Confederate troops make several flank attacks against Union troops in seemingly unplanned fashion. The Union units rejoin the army at Louisville and on December 4, the Union cavalry routs the Rebels at the Battle of Waynesborough.

Sherman's armies reach the outskirts of Savannah on December 10 only to find Hardee entrenched with 10,000 men in good positions, and his soldiers have flooded the surrounding rice fields, leaving only narrow causeways available to approach the city.

Sherman, blocked from linking up with the U.S. Navy as he has planned, dispatches cavalry to Fort McAllister, guarding the Ogeechee River, in hopes of unblocking his route and obtaining supplies awaiting him on the Navy ships.

Now that Sherman has connected to the Union's Navy fleet, he is able to obtain the supplies and siege artillery he requires to take Savannah. On December 17, he sends this message to Confederate Hardee in the city.

I have already received guns that can cast heavy and destructive shot as far as the heart of your city. I have for some days held and controlled every avenue by which the people and garrison of Savannah can be supplied. I am therefore justified in demanding the surrender of the city of Savannah

> *Should you entertain the proposition, I am prepared to grant liberal terms to the inhabitants and garrison; but should I be forced to resort to assault, or the slower and surer process of starvation, I will.*

Hardee decides not to surrender but to escape; so, on December 20, he leads his men across the Savannah River on a pontoon bridge hastily constructed of rice flats.

Sherman's men occupy the city the next day.

On December 22, Sherman telegraphs to President Lincoln,

> *I beg to present you as a Christmas gift the City of Savannah, with one hundred and fifty guns and plenty of ammunition about twenty-five thousand bales of cotton.*

From Savannah, Sherman plans his destructive march north through the Carolinas to complete the devastation across the south and combine his armies with Grant's against Lee.

A Cold December Day

On a cold December day, struggling Southern soldiers, fresh from the Savannah defeat, are returning to their homes in Georgia, South Carolina, Alabama and Tennessee. Joining, they find transportation wherever possible, hoping to get home for Christmas. Along the way, several Atlanta area veterans of the war pool their resources and obtain a wagon and horse to make the long journey to Atlanta. The leader of the group is Joseph Rainwater, stranded in Swainsboro, just north of Savannah.

Joseph is on the look out for his nephew John J. along the way. When the group reaches Sandersville, he learns from the civilians that one of the Confederate soldiers killed there was his nephew, John J. This makes an already difficult journey even more so.

Joseph finally arrives in Palmetto on December 24, the bearer of sad news about John J. He first tells his dad, James, then John J's mother, Lilla Ann. He then gathers his wife and children to tell them of John J.'s death.

Lilla Ann brakes down crying and says between sobs, "Why is Jefferson Davis prolonging this war? There must be other young soldiers like my son, still fighting in Virginia and some will surely die, too."

Joseph, knowing she isn't expecting him to answer says, "It is bad, but let us take care of you and the children at Christmas tomorrow."

For the sake of the children, the adults in the Rainwater family put on a brave front on Christmas morning. However, the grief they are all feeling casts a dark shadow over what is normally a joyful event.

Lincoln's Second Term

Abraham Lincoln begins his second term as President in January 1865. In his inaugural address, he talks mostly about war events of the past years.

Lincoln's last words impress General Grant more than anything else in his speech does.

What Lincoln said is, "With malice toward none; .... and to do all which may achieve and cherish a just, and a lasting peace, among ourselves, and with all nations."

In February, the Union cavalry attempts to intercept Confederate supply trains in western Virginia. Another Union Corp positions itself to prevent interference for the Union's cavalry operations. Two other divisions shift west to cover the right flank. Late in the day, the Confederate division attempts to turn the Union's right flank but is repulsed. During the night, two divisions further reinforce the Union units.

As the siege continues, Grant attempts to break or encircle the Confederate forces in multiple attacks moving from east to west, and both armys' lines are stretched out until they surrounded the city.

By March, the siege has taken an enormous toll on both armies, so Lee decides to pull out of Petersburg, Virginia. He amasses nearly half of his army in an attempt to break through Grant's Petersburg defenses and threaten his supply depot. The Union overpowers the Confederate garrisons who suffer under killing crossfire.

The loss is a devastating blow for Lee's army, resulting in the fall of Petersburg. Lee considers telegraphing President Davis about surrender, but decides against it.

After this victory, Grant chases Lee out toward the southwest where Lee hopes to join up with Confederate forces in North Carolina. Lee is taking maximum advantage of the two Southern forces in a determined stand against the converging armies of Grant and Sherman. However, Grant moves too fast for the plan to materialize. The Union infantry continues to dog the Confederates at every turn.

On 6 April, almost one-fourth of Lee's trapped army is captured. Lee receives news of the disaster and leads his remaining men in a north-by-west arc across the Appomattox River toward Lynchburg. In the meantime, Grant, with four times as many men, blocks Lee's only line of advance.

> **Looking into David's eyes, I noticed he has a tear in his eye, so I ask, "Son, what's the matter?"**
>
> **"It looks like Lee is going to lose the battle and that makes me sad."**
>
> **"In every war someone loses and someone wins. Most times the good people win and**

the bad people lose. In this situation it is my opinion that the United States wins and that's all of us, right?"

"Right, if you say so, but tell me some more please."

On the morning of April 9, Confederate probes test the Union lines and find them to be impregnable. Lee's options are now gone as General Johnson's North Carolina army has already surrendered to Sherman.

That afternoon, *Palm Sunday*, Lee meets Grant in the front parlor of Wilmer McLean's home to discuss peace terms.

The actual surrender of the Confederate Army occurs three days later, an overcast Wednesday in Appomattox Station, Virginia. As Southern troops march past silent lines of blue uniformed soldiers, one Union general says, "An awed stillness, and breath-holding, as if it is the passing of the dead."

Months later, Robert E. Lee energetically campaigns for inter-sectional reconciliation as he publicly announces, "So far from engaging in a war to perpetuate slavery, I am rejoiced that slavery is abolished. I believe it will be greatly for the interest of the South."

Lee rises above the fray.

Abraham Lincoln

On Good Friday, April 14 one of Lincolns most trusted Generals comes stumping into the President's office and demands, "Mr. President, what are you going to do with our enemy?"

"Let's make friends with them and then they will not be our enemies."

Hearing the President's statement and observing the pleasant smile on Lincoln's face the general walks out unsure if they can accept the Confederates they battled as friends. Lincoln however is at peace and looking forward to attending a performance at Ford's Theatre with his wife that evening.

He and his wife, Mary goes to the theatre, seating them in the special booth reserved for the President. Mary turns to tell Abe how much she is enjoying the play, when the sound **"POW"** drowns out all other sounds in the theatre. Her husband slumps over in his seat, as she notices that everyone in the theatre is looking up at them, including the actors on the stage. She cries out. "Lincoln is shot."

His bodyguards and two men standing by quickly make a makeshift stretcher and carry the President down to a waiting horse-drawn ambulance, where he is taken to a house across the street where a doctor treats him. The other bodyguards capture the shooter.

The next day, on Saturday, April 15, 1865, President Abraham Lincoln dies. John Wilkes Booth, an actor, who somehow thought he is helping the South, is charged with his assassination. The opposite is the result, for with Lincoln's death, the possibility of peace with magnanimity dies.

> **David jumps up to say, "We studied about Lincoln's assassination in our history class."**
>
> **"This story is sort of like a history study, don't you think?"**
>
> **"But you make it come to life better than the boring history books."**
>
> **With that complement, I smile and continued the story.**

Jefferson Davis

The defeat and surrender of the armies of Lee and Johnston all but dissolve the defeated Confederacy. The abrogation of the ordinances of secession initiated by the Southern States puts an end to the rebellion. A shame faced and weary President

Jefferson Davis is made a captive by the United States military and imprisoned in chains. He is charged with crimes for which he demands a trial in vain. After two years of imprisonment, he is released on bond.

After his release, the former Confederate President enjoys an enthusiastic reception at Richmond, Virginia. He then avoids ostentatious display, appearing before the public, only in rare addresses. He counsels the South to recover its wasted resources and maintain its principles. Secession he frankly admits to be no more a possibility, but he remains to the last in unyielding opposition of power centralized in the Federal government.

Andrew Johnson

Andrew Johnson, who has been a U.S. Senator from Tennessee at the time of the secession of the southern states, is the only Southern Senator not to quit his post upon secession. Johnson won the Vice President slot on the Lincoln ticket in 1864. Johnson became president upon Lincoln's assassination.

As president, he takes charge of the first phase of a Presidential Reconstruction Program, which lasts until the Republicans gain control of Congress in the 1866 elections. His conciliatory policies towards the South, his hurry to reincorporate the former Confederates into the union, and his vetoes of civil rights bills embroil him in a bitter dispute with the Republicans. The radicals in the House of Representatives impeach him in 1868, and he is acquitted by a single vote in the Senate.

"Granddaddy, what does impeach mean."
Little David asks.
"It means they wanted to fire Johnson as President."
"Can the Senate do that?"

**"Yes, but by a two-thirds vote and Davis
was not impeached because the Senate needed
one more vote for the two-thirds required."**

After War Reconstruction

As post-war reconstruction begins, James Rainwater feels a need
for the family to get together in Palmetto for a reunion. James, the
oldest in the Rainwater clan, is the patriarch of the family.

James asks his oldest living son, Joseph, to contact the various
family members, "Joseph, since you are the great communications
man, will you send out invitations to our kinfolk for a family
reunion? Let's meet at the Ramah Baptist Church on Sunday
September 5, 1866. Every family should bring a covered dish to
share with the others. Will you do this?"

"Sure, Daddy. That gives me about four weeks to get it done.
I'm looking forward to seeing my cousins and aunts and uncles;
and hearing what's going on with our kinfolk."

"Thank you, son, that'll take a lot of pressure off of me. You
know I'll be 81 next month and you're just in your young forties,
so I need your help."

"No problem Daddy. By the way, it looks like Thomas and
Zack are happy working for you as freed men."

"That's right, I'm so proud of those two boys. When I set
them free, they both wanted to stay and work for me. I really
appreciated their attitudes and now I pay them salaries and let
them manage their own families. We even have suggested they
enroll their children in the new colored school over in Fairburn.
Lilla Ann has been teaching the adult Negroes at her home to read
and write. She also teaches them arithmetic."

"Hey, that's great! My brother Miles would be proud of her,
if he were still alive."

"It's hard to believe that it has been nine years since Miles was
killed. Poor Lilla Ann has much heartache, loosing her husband

and then her son. I sure miss not having John J. around." James reminisces.

"I guess I better get back to Atlanta before Catherine sends the sheriff after me."

"How is the reconstruction progressing up there?"

"There is still a lot of construction everywhere, with new buildings sprouting up all over the place and the streetcars are running smoothly again. However, they have to import quite a few additional mules to pull the cars. The railroad terminals are open again; but some of the railroads still have rails that need repairing or replacing. Those Yankee carpetbaggers are trying to get rich off our people. It is just not right. I guess that is about it Daddy. See 'ya later. I'll get those invitations out for you."

"Goodbye son thanks, Joseph; don't let the carpetbaggers get to you. Oh! Please tell Catherine hello for me and tell the grandchildren to come see me soon."

Joseph travels toward home to Atlanta, all the way remembering his days in the U.S. Army and the bad days in the C.S. Army. His thoughts go out to Jefferson Davis. *Such a waste of lives and property, just because of Davis' stubborn desire for independence from Washington's rule,* were among other thoughts that blaze through his mind as his horse trots faithfully toward home. The nearer he gets to home, the more he thinks of Catherine. The great smell of turnips, greens, black-eyed peas, cornbread and buttermilk are imagined as he wonders what she is cooking for supper. It is interesting how much he enjoys this meal, once considered food 'fit only for slaves' before the war. However, with the struggling economy and lack of livestock, most southerners are happy to have this simply vegetable & cornbread meal.

Joseph walks in the front door greeted by his three children yelling, "How's Grandpa?"

"He's fine and he told me to say hello to ya'll."

"When are we going to see him?"

"Soon, he's having a family reunion over at Ramah Baptist Church and yall will be able to see all of your aunts, uncles, and cousins. Hey, where's Mama?"

"She's in the kitchen." The children holler out.

Joseph walks into the kitchen and wraps his arms around his wife.

She says, "Hey Honey how is your Father?"

"He's doing fine. You know he never seems to get tired. He wants to have a reunion and has asked me to send out the invitations to our kinfolk."

"When's it going to be?" Catherine asks.

"In four weeks, so I better get busy and send out the invitations. It's going to be at the Church."

"That's nice. I'll help you."

"Thanks Honey, what's for supper?"

"Something you like. Fried chicken, turnips, greens, fried green tomatoes, and watermelon. How's that sound to you?"

"Excellent!"

After supper, while the children are out playing with friends, Joseph and Catherine start working on the kinfolk list. Catherine asks, "Who all do we need to notify?"

Joseph, thinking aloud says, "Well, there's my sisters: Clariah, Christina, Frances, and Catherine and all their families, but no need to try to contact Benjamin, he's in Texas and Daddy wouldn't want me to invite him. Of course, there is Lilla Ann and all her children.

"My uncle Veasey and his family are down in Florida, I'll send him a telegram.

"I wish my grandfather and grandmother were alive so I could invite them. Many of their kinfolk are in England, so we will not send invitations to them. Does that about cover it?"

"I think so."

The children come running in from playing, get ready for bed, and are tucked in. Joseph blows all the kerosene lamps out, and being tired they lay down to go to sleep.

The Rainwater Reunion

Sunday morning, September 5, 1866 begins as a bright sun shiny day for a family reunion. Before the church services, James asked three of his deacons to bring six tables out into the churchyard before the family crowd arrive. They place the tables up in a long line about 48 feet long and drape white tablecloths on them. James figures that will hold all the covered dishes that everyone will bring. He bought two 60-pound blocks of ice from the icehouse that opened especially for him on Sunday. Sixty pounds should be enough to keep the iced tea cold.

About 11:00 a.m., the church is full of the preacher's kinfolks and his regular members. James makes the sermon short that day, preaching on family love, which he is led by the Holy Spirit and thinks is appropriate for the occasion.

Several women stay out in the yard laying out the covered dishes as people bring them to the tables. They place all the meat dishes at the beginning of the table and all the vegetable dishes next, with deserts last and there is enough food to feed an army. Even with limited funds, all the Rainwaters think the trip and the cost of food is well worth it. A short table is used to hold the washtubs of ice, which they crack up with ice picks. The iced tea is nearby on this same table. These women gather long branches of small tree limbs to be used to swish away the flies.

All of a sudden, the church doors open and outflows the congregation. The non-family members climb into their carriages and go their separate ways, while the Rainwater family members gather in the churchyard greeting each other and awaiting the time to start eating. James comes out and announces to the gathering, "I am so happy to see all of you. This has been my dream to get all of the family together, ever since the war ended. Thank you for coming and thank you women for preparing such a feast. After I say the blessing, you may start at the left end of the table where the plates and silverware are located.

"Let us pray,

"Dear Lord, we thank you for bringing us together today. We are thankful for those who cooked the food. May it strengthen our bodies as we partake of it. Guide us and let us enjoy being together this afternoon. I pray in the name of our Lord, Jesus Christ. Amen."

A line forms as the families hustle to get their food and after everyone has served himself or herself, it becomes very quite as everyone enjoys eating.

There is enough food for everyone. Because of the lingering poverty created by the war, a few fried chickens provide the only meat, but the women more than make up for the loss with lots of delicious dressing. The Rainwaters know how to cook. Plenty food for seconds lay in the bowls and platters on the serving tables. There is fried okra, squash, black-eyed peas, macaroni and cheese, green pole beans, collard greens, turnips and greens, rutabaga, cabbage and a melody of other good vegetables.

Little Ephraim Dawson Rainwater likes the desserts best of all. Ephraim is now eleven years old and quite a handful for his mother Lilla Ann. He was only two years old when his father was killed. Ephraim goes for the banana pudding first, and then comes back for blackberry pie. He spills some of the blackberry juice on his white Sunday shirt.

Lilla Ann asks, "Ephraim, what have you done?"

"I didn't mean to Mama!" he cries.

"Come here child. Let's see if some water will clean it off."

Ephraim walks over obediently and lets his mother try to wash it off. She cleans it some and smears it some.

"Well, that'll have to do. Tomorrow is wash day and it will come out then."

Little Ephraim runs to the edge of the church yard to play with some of the other children.

The adults pull up their chairs, borrowed from the church, into a large circle as James begins to speak, "I think it would be nice if each family gives a report of what's going on in their family. I'll start first.

"I'm happy to report that my brother Veasey, his wife and children are here from Pensacola, Florida. They have traveled the furthest, I believe. He's thinking about getting into some sort of beverage sales. I wish him well. His son Veasey, Jr. has grown into quite a young man.

"You can see all of my children, except Miles and Benjamin, are here. Miles' oldest son John J was killed in the war at Sandersville. Lilla Ann, Miles' wife, is here with her children and my oldest living son, Joseph, and his wife, Catherine, and their children are here. You all probably know that Joseph was heavily involved in the war. He is still serving, but now he is back in the army of the United States, thank goodness.

"Hey, I'm going to shut up and let each family give their report."

About three o'clock in the afternoon everyone has reported on their individual families. Each family prepares to go home. Despite the hardships that have resulted from such a long and bloody war, the whole family has much for which to be thankful. As they are packing up the left over food a terrible rain and thunderstorm begins. The tied down horses are bellowing, but cannot run away. James encourages his family not to travel in this weather and invites them inside the church to wait out the storm.

Inside, James lit the lamps so people could see, as the dark clouds outside are not allowing much light through the stained glass windows of the church sanctuary. James asks everyone to make themselves comfortable in the church pews.

Veasey says, "Brother you ain't gonna preach to us again are you?"

"No Veasey, I'm not.

Looking at Joseph, James says, "Joseph, since you as an officer in the Army and know what's going on in Washington, would you give us a report."

Joseph stands and comes to the front of the group and begins to speak, "As you know, many soldiers were killed or wounded in

143

this past war, both Yankees and Southerners, and we now estimate the number to be about a million. Out of our overall population of a little over 31 million, that many is horrendous, and most of these deaths and casualties occurred here in the South.

"The physical damages from the war are tremendous. Just look at the blown up bridges, the twisted railroad tracks, burned out buildings and other physical properties destroyed and we know it is going to take a lot of money to reconstruct this Southland. Most of the damages occurred here in Georgia. Since our Confederate money is worthless now, everyone is wondering how the reconstruction cost will be paid. This is our greatest concern. That is the big picture of what the politicians in Washington are talking about these days. I do not have to tell you how it affects each individual southern family.

"Our Constitution did not imagine that states would ever secede from the Union, so there's no precedence for handling the situation. Lincoln proposed a reconstruction plan as early as 1864, but nothing was done about it and now he is dead. Johnson cannot accomplish much because he is opposed by the Republican majority in Congress. As you know, Johnson switched to the Democratic Party after the war started. So what are we to do? That is the big question.

"Another problem we have to overcome is how we treat the freed slaves. I know that my father, sitting here, has done the right thing, but some Southern states like Mississippi and South Carolina are trying to pass local laws that makes all Negros second-class citizens. The Yankees don't like that and I don't either, frankly speaking. As you know Congress is proposing the 14th Amendment to the Constitution to addresses this situation."

David raises his hand to ask, "What's the 14th Amendment?"

"The Fourteenth Amendment to the United States Constitution is one of the post-Civil War amendments, intended to secure rights

for former slaves. It assures that Negros will have equal protection under the laws, the same as for all citizens. Proposed, I think, in 1866 and ratified two years later making it the law. It is now regarded as one of the most important components of the Constitution."

David says, 'Thanks Granddaddy, you know a lot don't you?"

I encourage David as I say, "If you study hard in school, you too will learn about stuff."

Joseph continues his report, "Getting back to the reconstruction solution, it looks as though we, as the defeated, will have to depend on the victors of the War. I know that we remember this as the *War of Northern Aggression*, but now we must put that aside if we wish to see any progress. We also must remember that our country actually withstood a civil war and is now reunited is nothing short of miraculous.

"Here's what's going to happen. I have this on good authority from my commanding officer. The U.S. army will oversee the rebuilding of the South. Some may not like it, but the military presence will get the job done by keeping the states in line. My unit will be involved in this nation re-building effort.

"That's what I know about what's going on in Washington. Oh yes, don't forget to vote this fall for our Congressional leaders."

Everyone sits in silence as Joseph ends his report. Some agree with him and some do not. Most of the Rainwaters are Democrats and many harbor great resentment against the Union. Joseph is extremely rare as a Southern Republican.

Most Congressional issues passed by the majority Republican Congress, Andrew Johnson vetoed many and is becoming more and more ineffective as President.

Ulysses Grant

Ulysses Grant becomes the 18th President of the United States of America on March 4, 1869. Grant pushes the 15th Amendment to the Constitution through Congress, which is passed in his first year as President. This Amendment is a follow up to the 14th and it assures that all male citizens have the right to vote regardless of race, color, or past servitude.

The reconstruction of the South continues with many Southern farmers planting cash crops of tobacco and cotton, borrowing money to do so. The lenders demanded a lien on the farmers' profits from these cash crops, but this does allow them to buy seed, pay for laborers, and feed their families while they wait for the harvesting of their crops.

James Rainwater is one of the few who can provide adequately for his family mainly because of the small income from his church. His two Negro hands, Zack and Thomas, are also unique because, of James' generosity toward them. James has deeded property to each of them, so that now they have their own small farms. Zack and Thomas have learned much from the teaching they received from Lilla Ann. James is very proud of the progress they have made. Their children enrolled in the colored school in Fairburn are fortunate. Most Negros are not as fortunate as these two. Many whites still look on the Negro as a second-class citizen. This is true for some in the North, too, sadly enough.

Reverend James Hospitalized

James is admitted to the hospital in Atlanta on June 22, 1874 with pneumonia. Lilla Ann and Zack, his former slave, insisted he go because of his difficulty breathing. The two took him to the Grady hospital in Atlanta. As soon as they could, they notified Joseph, who came quickly to the bedside of his daddy. James is having trouble breathing and the doctors are doing everything they can to relieve him of his suffering, by using packs of ice on his chest and having an orderly fan him to move the air into his face. In his suffering, he reassures Joseph and other family members that he is all right. They have their concerns that he might not make it, although he does seem to be gaining some strength. That night, Joseph and Lilla Ann will remain with him through the night, while the others return to their homes.

The nurse on duty checks him every two hours and says to Joseph, "I think he's breathing a little easier and if he continues to improve he may be all right."

Joseph said, "Thank you, nurse that makes me feel better."

James sleeps through the night and eats a little breakfast the next morning. That morning, most of his children and some of his grandchildren are at the hospital in the hall just outside the room.

After breakfast, James whispers in a low voice, "Joseph, you have been here all night, why don't you go home and get some rest?"

"I'm okay; I did sleep a little last night."

Clariah speaks up and says to Joseph, "Let me stay here and you go get some food and rest."

"All right, but I'll be back soon."

On the afternoon of the 23rd, James seems to have more trouble breathing, so the doctors decide to use a new technique where an oxygen tent is placed around the person and raw oxygen is released into the tent. Everyone is asked not to smoke in the room. The doctors explain to Clariah that this is new for Grady Hospital and worth trying. All hope that it works.

After a while, James asks his daughter, "Where is Joseph?"

"He's out in the hall."

By that time, Joseph returns from the few hours break James says, "Ask him to come in; I need to talk to him."

Clariah steps out into the hall and relays the message to Joseph who immediately goes into the room leaving Clariah in the hall with the other sisters.

James asks Joseph to come closer, speaking in a very low tone. Joseph walks up to the head of the bed and leans over to his dad and through the tent asks, "What can I get you daddy."

In a very feeble voice James says, "Joseph, I feel like the Lord is calling me home to Heaven. Before I go please be sure my will is followed. Please have a grave marker for me, made similar to the one we did for your mother. Will you do this for me?"

"Daddy, you are not going to die! But, your wishes will be carried out whenever you do pass on to Heaven."

"Thank you, Joseph; I have always known I can depend on you. Let me go to sleep now for my head fills a little woozy."

Joseph tiptoes out of the room and gives his sisters the news about their daddy. Several of the women began to cry with their heads held in their cupped hands, while the others stare up into space. Joseph walks down the hall to find the doctor.

When he locates the doctor, he asks, "How long will my father live?"

"That's hard to say. His lungs seem to have fluid in them, so it could be within the next few days."

"Is their anything that can be done now?"

"Joseph, we have given him some medication that will make him sleep and are giving him oxygen. That is about all that we can do. He may fill woozy in his head, but that's normal."

"Thank you, doctor."

Joseph returns to his sisters to let them know about the doctor's prognosis.

His sister, Christina, says, "I'll notify the family that he is in very serious condition and not expected to live."

Joseph says to his sisters, "Thanks, Christina, I'll send Uncle Veasey a telegram and get a message to our kinfolk in England."

The next day, 24 June 1871 about 10:00 o'clock in the morning, the family surrounds his bed, looking on, as their father glances at each of his children's face, smiles and then lays his head to the side, when all motion in his body becomes perfectly still. They begin to weep knowing that he has gone to be with his Heavenly Father.

In a just a few minutes, the doctor and nurse confirm what they already knew. They all walk down the hall to a little room where they could begin the grieving process. In a few minutes, the hospital Chaplain enters the room and says, "I know how you feel; I lost my father and it's hard to say goodbye. May I notify someone for you?"

Nobody answers because they are all still in shock. Finally Joseph says, "I'll call Hemperley's funeral home in College Park, Georgia and let them make the arrangements."

The chaplain says, "Let me do that for you, but y'all will need to meet with him tomorrow morning to complete the details."

"Thank you Sir."

The news spreads through out the community. When the family returns to James' home, the friends and neighbors have a table full of delicious food waiting for the family. Zack and Thomas let them into the house and helped place the food on the table. That night the house is full of people coming to express their sympathy.

The next morning, James' children meet at the Hemperley's Funeral Home to make the final arrangements for their father. The body will lie in state at the Ramah Baptist Church, for viewing, on 29 June 1871. The funeral is to take place the next day at 11:00 a.m. at James' church. The Reverend George Perkins, a very close friend of James, agrees to deliver the eulogy. Perkins is the minister at Bethlehem Baptist Church in Fairburn, Georgia. Several grandsons will serve as pallbearers along with the Deacons of the church as honorary pallbearers.

On the day of the funeral, the churchyard and adjacent roads fill with horses, buggies, carriages and wagons, as people from all over attend the funeral. There is standing room only in the church as Rev. Perkins gives a fine eulogy in honor of a great man of God.

Many Baptist leaders of Georgia attend to pay their respects to this important and Godly man.

Zack Murry and Thomas Washington, the faithful ex-slaves, sit in the balcony of the church along with their wives and children, out of respect for the *Master* they love.

Six weeks after the funeral, Joseph, fulfills his father's request by placing the black wrought iron grave marker on the grave next to his mother's grave. It matches it perfectly as depicted here:

REV. JAMES RAINWATER

BORN   JANY 13 1795

DIED   JUNE 24 1871

OUR LOSS WAS HIS GAIN

Ephraim Dawson Rainwater

Joseph has a favorite nephew, although he never mentions this to Lilla Ann's other children. His favorite, Ephraim Dawson, the son of Miles, turns 18-years old next March 14, 1873. Joseph invites him to his Fort McPherson office in Atlanta on his upcoming birthday as a gift.

Joseph speaks privately to Ephraim, "Say, Ephraim, would you like to visit my base on your birthday?"

"I'd love it, Uncle Joseph."

Ephraim has no memories of his father since he was only 2-years old when Miles was killed. His Uncle Joseph takes the place of that void in his life. Ephraim has heard many stories about his father's military career and admired his uncle's service in the US Army and in the CS Army. Although his older brother, John J., was killed in the Civil War, he secretly wants to join the army, now that he will be turning 18-years old. Uncle Joseph's invitation excites him as he can hardly wait for his birthday.

Ephraim's older brothers and sisters are married and raising their families on their farms, but life on the farm is not something he wants for his future.

Ephraim says to his mother, "Guess what? Uncle Joseph has invited me to visit his military base on my birthday!"

"That's interesting, he asked me to visit with your Aunt Catherine while you are visiting the base with him."

"What about Martha?"

"Yes your little sister is invited, too."

Lilla Ann wants to keep the surprise birthday party they have planned for Ephraim a secret. It is to be at her brother-in-law's home in Atlanta.

On his birthday, Ephraim and his uncle arrive at the army base in Atlanta as promised. Fort McPherson, the U.S. Army post located near East Point, on the southwest edge of Atlanta, is the home of the Third U.S. Army, and U.S. Army Reserve Command for Major General James Birdseye McPherson. This base was used as a Confederate post during the Civil War and now is used by federal troops to occupy Atlanta for the reconstruction process.

Ephraim's eyes can barely take in the sights, as Joseph takes him on a tour of the base. He is especially interested in the artillery on display as they tour the Ordnance Department. From there, they walk over to the Communications building, where Joseph has spent most of his military career.

"Ephraim, this telegraph station has the latest technical instruments that allow us to communicate via Western Union wires across our nation to every military base. Can you imagine how difficult it would be if we have to rely on the pony express to communicate across our nation?"

"No sir." Ephraim says as he thinks about the fact that telegraph communications has been around all his young life.

"I don't like to brag, but I have major responsibilities for the military implementation of this great invention of Morse."

"Uncle Joseph, I see the telegraph operators are using keys to send the information. Are they using the Morse Code?" Ephraim asks.

"Yes son, that's the way we can translate English letters into electrical dots and dashes and then back into English letters on the receiving end."

"I see, isn't it great to be living in such a modern technical time?"

"It sure is. Even more technical advances in the communication field are now in the works."

"What can be an improvement over the telegraph?"

"It's not ready yet, but the army is working with Mr. Elisha Gray and Mr. Alexander Graham Bell on a new technology. These two gentlemen are now working on the same designs, and both asked for my input on what interest the military would have if they are able to obtain a patent for their ideas."

"What is this new design?"

"You won't believe this, but it will allow us to transmit the human voice over wires instead of electrical pulses like the telegraph. It's not available, but I believe that we will actually see this in the next few years."

"Man that will be something if it can be accomplished."

The uncle and the nephew travel by horse over the entire large base, finally arriving at the mess hall for lunch. Normally only military personnel eat at the mess hall, but Joseph's authority permitted Ephraim the privilege of eating there. They enjoy fried catfish with hot biscuits and plenty of vegetables for lunch.

Ephraim's Surprise

To Ephraim's surprise, when they arrive that afternoon, at Joseph's house, the house is full of kinfolk and friends. All have a fun time as they celebrated Ephraim's 18th birthday. His younger sister Martha and several cousins are all there. His best friend Jake from school is also there.

His mother has baked and decorated the birthday cake, his favorite chocolate. He blew all 18 candles out in one strong breath of air. His wish as he blew out the candles is that the army will let him join soon. After a good time at the party, Ephraim, his mother and sister, head for Fairburn, where they all live.

The next week, Ephraim visits the army recruiting office in Atlanta to fill out an application to join the army. Three days later, he receives notification that he is accepted. He runs to his Mother and says, "Mama, Mama, I've been accepted by the army!"

"I'm proud of you son and I know you'll make a fine soldier, like your father and your uncle and your poor older brother John J."

"I hope so. I wish I had known my father. I know you and others are very proud of his distinguished service. It's ironic that Uncle Joseph has served in both the U.S. Army and the C.S. army. Gosh, I hope I can be assigned to the Communications Department or the Signal Corpse as it is now called. Uncle Joseph gave me a great tour on my birthday and it made me want that part of the service."

"Ephraim, what ever they assign to you, I know you'll do well. Your father would be so proud if he were here." Lilla Ann says, hoping her son will be safe.

You Are in the Army Now

'Welcome to the U.S. Army Signal Center' is the sign Ephraim notices as he gets off the train at Fort Gordon, Georgia, just a few miles southwest of the city of Augusta. This is where he is to begin his basic training for the U.S. Army Signal Corps. He is happy to be assigned to the unit of his choice. Perhaps his uncle has a role in making it happen. He reports to the main office and signs in as a new recruit.

When he signs in the Sergeant says, "Private Rainwater, are you any kin to Lt. Colonel Joseph Rainwater?"

"Yes sir, he's my uncle."

153

"We sure think a lot of him; he's responsible for the latest technology used by the Corps. Do you know that?"

"Yes sir, he tells me about those developments and how the telegraph gives instant contact to bases all over the country."

"He's responsible for our total communications program."

As he hands Ephraim his orders he continues, "Here are your papers, private. First, you must report to the Quartermaster office to pick up your uniform and your other clothes, shoes and equipment you'll need. After that, report to barrack C9 for instructions from your Sergeant."

"Thank you, sir."

Ephraim is so excited about what is happening. After filling his duffle bag, Ephraim reports to barrack C9 where he meets the Sergeant.

The Sergeant speaks first, "I'm Sgt. Jack Cook and you must be Ephraim. Welcome to our barracks."

"Good to meet you Sergeant."

"Private, you'll need to read the schedule on the bulletin board at the end of the barrack for information about your schedule. What ever you do, follow it explicitly; do you understand?"

"Yes sir, I understand, Sergeant."

Ephraim walks to his assigned bunk, lays down his duffle bag, and then walks to the end of the barrack to read the bulletin board notices.

He begins to wonder if he has done the right thing. It is tough getting up at 5:30 a.m., eating breakfast at six, and then begin training in the field at 7:00 a.m. It gets a bit more bearable as he makes friends with the 29 other recruits, who are in the same boat. Sometimes he wonders what crawling on your belly under barbed wire has to do with army communications. Little does he know that the drill sergeants are making a man out of the boy and preparing him for the war conditions, he may face in the future.

A year later, Ephraim finishes his basic training and promotes to private first class. The real training in communications will now begin. He learns all about semaphore, a system of visual signaling by two flags held one in each hand. This method of sending messages is used extensively by the navy, but sometimes by the army under certain conditions. The hardest thing to learn is the Morse code. He knows his uncle will be proud of him now, since he can communicate in dots and dashes with electrical pulses through wires. Along with the technical training, he periodically receives refresher training by his drill sergeant in the fighting aspect of being a soldier. At the end of the year, he promotes to Corporal and receives a furlough of two weeks, for which he is deeply appreciative.

"Mama, I'm home!' He surprises his mother.

"Why didn't you let us know you were coming, Ephraim?"

"I wanted it to be a surprise."

"Well, it is and it's such a good one to see you. My you have grown into a man since you joined the army."

"They sure know how to make a man out of a boy. We have 30 in our unit to start with, but only 17 are able to keep up and remain in the unit."

"Mary Ann Hammond has been asking about you."

Ephraim always liked Mary Ann and says, "You know, I haven't seen her in a long time. Is she still as pretty as ever?"

"Why don't you go see her while you're home? How long will you be home, anyway?

"Two weeks, but I'm not ready to get with the girls, yet."

"Why?"

"Oh Mama, I'm not ready to get tied down to a girlfriend, because my military career is most important to me now."

"Okay, I understand what you are saying, son."

Going to Church

On a bright Sunday morning, Ephraim, his mother and younger sister hitch up the family buggy and head to nearby Bethlehem Baptist Church. All three are dressed in their Sunday best as usual.

On the way, little sister, Martha, asks, "Ephraim, are you going to sit with Mary Ann today?"

"Not that I plan to, why do you ask?"

"She asked me the other day if you would be in to church this Sunday."

Ephraim does not say another word the rest of the way to the church.

When they arrive, he sees Mary Ann out the corner of his eyes. Ephraim thinks how beautiful she looks. He then turns his head and looks straight at her as she looks at him with a smile and twinkle in her eye that he just cannot resist. They seem magnetically attracted to each other, but Ephraim thinks to himself, *I am not ready for this.*

Never mind what he has promised himself, he walks over to this pleasant and beautiful woman to say, "Mary Ann, it's good to see you, girl. What have you been up to?"

"Oh, since finishing school, I've been helping mother with the younger children and wondering how you've been doing in the army."

"I'm learning a bunch in the army; but I'll be going back this week."

"Let's sit together at the church service so we can talk while the preacher preaches, okay?"

"Mary Ann, you haven't changed much; you're still as funny as always."

"Does that mean we're sitting together, army guy?"

"Sure, let's do it!"

As the week goes by, Ephraim and Mary Ann spend everyday together.

On the first day together, Mary Ann says, "Kiss me soldier boy."

Ephraim is bashful but cannot resist as he kisses this beautiful woman.

So much for not being ready for the girls, Ephraim thinks, as he knows that Mary Ann is different from any girl he has ever known.

On Thursday, he tells his mother, "Mary Ann is taking me to the train station in Atlanta this afternoon."

"That's wonderful, but I thought you weren't ready for the girls."

"Mama, I know things about her that I never knew in School. I think I love her."

"Oh, don't move so fast. She is a special girl with a great sense of humor and a beaming personality; but, did you tell her that you love her?"

"It's too early to tell her that, don't you think?"

"Don't ask me; you have to decide that."

"Here she comes now!"

Mary Ann rides up in her two-horse buggy, trotting slowly. She is all smiles as usual greeting Lilla Ann and Ephraim, "Hi, Mrs. Rainwater, I see you have fed Ephraim well this week and good afternoon to you Corporal Rainwater."

"Mary Ann thanks for taking Ephraim to the train station."

"Well, I don't want to see him walk those 45 miles by himself."

Ephraim places his duffel bag in the back of the buggy, kisses his mother goodbye, and climbs into the buggy seat along side of Mary Ann.

She hands him the reins and says, "You drive young man."

On the way to Atlanta, she snuggles up close to Ephraim, causing him to feel tingly all over as he places his arm around her neck and she tilts her head to his shoulder. The two lovers enjoy the four-hour ride to the Terminal Station in Atlanta. As they arrive, the train for Augusta is almost ready for boarding. Ephraim lifts his duffel bag out of the buggy as Mary Ann prances down to stand in front of him.

Ephraim is a little bit bashful, so Mary Ann says, "Aren't you going to kiss me goodbye?"

With that invitation, he hugs her and gives her a big smack on the lips and she kisses him back several times.

She says, "Please write me often, Ephraim."

"I will. I'm going to miss you Mary Ann."

Mary Ann stands at the end of the boarding area, waving to Ephraim, as the train steams its way down the tracks and finally out of sight.

Mary Ann drives the horses as fast as possible to return home from Atlanta. She wonders *how the man that she knows she is in love with has swept her off her feet.* On the other hand, *has she swept the soldier off his feet herself,* she wonders.

When she arrives home, she says to her mother, "Mama, I think I'm in love!"

"Did you tell Ephraim?"

"Not yet, but I think he knows and I know he loves me."

"Did he tell you that he loves you?"

"Not exactly, it's just the way we both feel."

"Mary Ann, I'm happy for you and I know you'll make the right decisions in the relationship."

Mary Ann sleeps soundly that night as she dreams about what is happening in her life.

David laughingly says, "Isn't that a little mushy Granddaddy?"

"Well, that's the way it is when two people are in love."

"I don't like girls!"

"You should say 'you don't like girls, yet.'"

"Whatever!"

Return to Fort Gordon

Ephraim reports in to Fort Gordon and can't get Mary Ann out of his mind, but he sleeps all night dreaming sweet thoughts about his girl friend.

"Sir, Corporal Rainwater reporting for duty." Ephraim salutes and addresses his company commander the morning after his return from furlough.

The commander, Captain Davis, returns the salute and says, "At ease Corporal: have a seat. I have a new assignment for you Ephraim. You've been assigned to assist your uncle in the preparation of a status report on communications in the military and the latest technological advances now in use and those planned for the future."

"Sir, that's exciting. When do we start?"

"Rainwater, not too fast, you haven't let me finish. The report is for the President."

"You don't mean President Grant do you?"

"Yes I do mean the Ulysses Grant, President of these United States. You're new station is Fort McPherson with your Uncle Joseph, starting tomorrow."

Ephraim is thinking more of Mary Ann than writing a report as he excitedly says to his Captain, "Great news! I'm ready!"

He sends a telegram to Mary Ann about his transfer to the Atlanta base.

She jumps with joy as she reads the 'gram the Western Union boy hands to her in Fairburn.

Fort McPherson

Ephraim greets his uncle and says, "Uncle Joseph, I didn't think I'd ever have this opportunity."

"Well son, we'll have the time of our life doing this project for our President."

"When do we start, Sir?"

"How about now?"

"I'm ready."

Joseph and his nephew begin a closed conference to outline and make their research plans for the report Grant has requested. Joseph lays out to Ephraim what has occurred in the last 50 years in the military communication methods.

Joseph says, "Back in the 40's we relied on the pony express for fast delivery of information. U.S. mail relied on this and then came the railroads which provided faster delivery over long distances."

"When did telegraphing begin as our modern method of communications?"

"I'm sure you learned about that at Ft. Gordon, Ephraim."

"We did study about Morse's invention and his code, but I can't remember the exact time it came into being."

"As you know, I have made a career in the communications field, so let me give you a little history.

"The first telegraphs came in the form of optical telegraphs, including the use of smoke signals and beacons, which have existed since ancient times. A semaphore network invented by Claude Chappe operated in France from 1792 through 1846. It helped Napoleon enough that it was widely imitated in Europe and the U.S.

"Semaphores were able to convey information more precisely than smoke signals and beacons and consumed no fuel. Messages could be sent at much greater speed than pony riders could and could serve through line of sight and relays to entire regions. However, like beacons and smoke signals, they were dependent on good weather to work. They required operators and towers every 20 miles or so, and could only accommodate about two words per minute. This was useful to governments, but too expensive for most commercial uses other than commodity price information.

"The electrical telegraph was independently developed and patented in the United States in 1837 by Samuel Morse. His assistant, Alfred Vail, developed the Morse code signaling alphabet with Morse. America's first telegram was sent by Morse on January

6, 1838 across two miles of wiring. The message read *A patient waiter is no loser.* On May 24, 1844, he sent the message: *What hath God wrought,* quoting Numbers 23:23, from Washington to Baltimore, using repeater technology. The Morse/Vail telegraph was deployed in the 1850's and 1860's.

"Do you know that the first transatlantic telegraph cable was successfully completed in July of 1866, allowing transatlantic telegraph communications with Britain for the first time?"

"Uncle Joseph, I didn't need all that history, but it is very interesting and it answers my question. I now know about Western Union taking over the telegraph system in our country. What's this I hear about transmitting voice over wires?"

"I have talked to Elisha Gray and Alexander Graham Bell, two gentlemen who are working on devices that, hopefully, transmit speech electrically over wires. Bell has the one that is most promising for military use. They both received patents within hours of each other. There was a legal battle over the invention and Bell won.

"Bell tells me he is trying to improve over the telegraph which has been around for over 30 years. Success with his idea came as a direct result of this attempt to improve the telegraph. His extensive knowledge of the nature of sound and his understanding of music enabled him to surmise the possibility of transmitting multiple messages over the same wire at the same time. Although the idea of a multiple telegraph has been in existence for some time, Bell offers his own musical or harmonic approach as a possible practical solution. His '*harmonic telegraph*' is based on the principle that several notes can be sent simultaneously along the same wire if the notes or signals differ in pitch.

"I think he has a great idea. I talked with his assistant, Thomas Watson, recently and he thinks Bell will have a working model to demonstrate to the military very soon, maybe this year."

"That's great news Uncle Joseph; we should most assuredly include this new '*harmonic telegraph*' in our report to the president."

"Yes we will; hey, shouldn't we close up and go home. It's already 4:30 in the afternoon and I have a few items on my desk that need reviewing."

"Yes sir, I have someone I'm anxious to see!"

"She must be that cute Mary Ann."

"Yes, but how did you know?"

"Your mother mentioned it to me, Ephraim."

"Oh, okay, see you tomorrow?"

"Sure, bright and early. Goodnight Ephraim."

Ephraim goes to his barrack to freshen up before riding his military horse down to Fairburn where he will see the love of his heart. He can hardly wait.

Out at the front gate of the base, Ephraim is pleasantly surprised to see Mary Ann sitting in her buggy with a big smile on her face.

He hugs her and asks, "Mary Ann what are you doing here?"

"I came to pick up a handsome soldier boy!"

"Did you find one?" He snaps back.

"You'll have to do, Corporal Rainwater."

"Girl, I'm so happy to see you!"

They kiss and then he leaves to tie his horse to the hitching post at the base stables. When he returns she says, "How about taking me out to dinner here in Atlanta. Some fine restaurants have opened since the war."

"Great! Let's go."

"You drive, Ephraim."

"Okay, where to?"

"The *Aunt Mammy* is an excellent restaurant. It's on Whitehall Street near Rich's Dry Goods store. Is that okay with you?"

"I'm on my way."

The two lovers enjoy the evening, catching up on what's going on with each other. Mary Ann is impressed that Ephraim has been asked to help his uncle in the military communications report to the President of the U.S.

"I've heard how the Rainwater family has been active in the military and involved in so many wars in the past."

"You know, you're right; I guess I'm carrying on the tradition; but, I've got a question for you."

"What is it?"

"Will you marry me?"

"What brings that on sweetheart?"

"I love you and want to be with you forever."

"I love you to, but I'll have to think about it. I might say yes when you leave the military service."

Ephraim does not especially like her answer and the ride by to Ft. McPherson is a quiet one.

When she drops Ephraim off at the post, he says. "You think about it and I'll do the same."

He places his arm around her shoulders and kisses her as she returns the kiss affectionately.

He watches her as she takes the reins and heads toward Fairburn. His thoughts turn to the possibility of a future life outside the military. He knows that farming has been his life before joining the army and can be again after he marries, but that's a big if. He sleeps through the night, awakening often thinking about Mary Ann.

Joseph Rainwater

The next morning after reveille and chow, he goes to meet his Uncle Joseph, but the General-in-Command interrupts him with bad news—his uncle died at home during the night. This shocking news breaks Ephraim's heart.

The General says, "I'm sorry to bring such news to you, but I just heard about it through a messenger from the doctor at the hospital where he was pronounced dead. Corporal, please feel free to take leave and go to his family; I know they need you. Let me know how we can help, please."

Ephraim salutes the general, rushes to his horse, and heads to Aunt Catherine's home nearby. Walking into her front door, they console each other's grief with a hug.

Catherine cries, "Oh! Ephraim, it has all happened so suddenly, just within the last few hours. When he did not awake this morning, the children helped me to take him to the base hospital where the doctor pronounced him dead."

She cannot finish as the tears flow freely from her face. The children, almost grown now, are sitting in a state of shock, not knowing what to say. Cousin Ephraim tries to comfort them as best he knows how.

Ephraim says, "I'll go notify my mother and our aunts, uncles and cousins. Before I go, is their anything I can do, Aunt Catherine?"

Through tears she says, "No Ephraim. We'll go to the funeral home this afternoon to make arrangements."

"Do you want me to go with you?"

"I think Tom and Yvonne and I can do it, but thanks."

The funeral arrangements are made and all kinfolk notified. This will be a military funeral with the service at Ramah Baptist Church. The body will be laid to rest near Joseph's mother and father, James and Polly Ann.

Mary Ann is a constant comfort to Ephraim throughout the days before and after the funeral. She knows how much he loves his uncle. In fact, Joseph has been more like a father to Ephraim, since his own father's death, years ago when he was just two-years old.

The funeral is sad. Several days of mourning go by slowly.

The next day, Mary Ann asks, "Ephraim, when will you report back for duty?"

"I'm going back tomorrow."

"Okay, soldier boy, before tomorrow comes let's have some fun together."

"What do you have in mind?"

"Would you like for me to make a picnic dinner and we'll take it to the Grant Park and spread it out? Then we can enjoy nature the rest of the day; does that sound good?"

"Sure, I need something to get things off my mind. That's what I love about you Mary Ann; you are always planning things that make me feel good."

"Thanks a bunch, Honey."

It is a delightful day at the park even though Ephraim's mind keeps thinking about the loss of his uncle and about the report that the two are supposed to make to the President. Mary Ann has a way of making Ephraim feel at ease no matter what the situation. *She will make a great wife* is flashing through his mind, but then he thinks, *what about my military career.* The two love bugs do not discuss marriage during this day at the park.

Captain Ephraim Dawson Rainwater

The next morning Joseph walks into the General's office, salutes and says, "Reporting for duty, sir."

"Good morning Captain."

"What do you mean, *'Captain'*, I'm a corporal."

"It is unusual to move from corporal to captain, but we received special permission to do so. You are now a captain in the U.S. Army."

"I can't believe it, thank you, sir."

Ephraim is thinking as he shakes the General's hand, wondering what Mary Ann will think, but he asks, "General, what about the report that Joseph and I have been working on?"

"Son, we feel that you have the knowledge necessary to complete it. Do you think you can do it?"

"Yes sir, I can certainly try."

"We want you to move into your uncle's office and you will have the resources of his secretary to help you."

"Thank you, sir."

They salute each other as Ephraim leaves the office.

In the next few months, Ephraim completes the report about the latest methods the military is using in its communication technology. He visits Alexander Bell to discover the latest developments for the new '*harmonic telegraph*' and he learns that Bell has developed, not just a multiple message telegraph based on different tone pitches, but has discovered a way to actually transmit speech through wires. What a discovery!

The day the secretary presents him with the completed document, he discusses it with the general.

The general is pleased as he congratulates Rainwater and says, "When are you going to Washington with the report?"

"Next Tuesday is the day the President has scheduled to meet with me."

"Good Captain, you should take a few extra days off while there to tour the city."

"Thank you sir, I'll do that."

During the next few days, Ephraim practices and polishes his report to make it as interesting and as informative as possible for the President. His secretary works closely with him in the perfection of the report. He is so appreciative of her help that he invites her to go to dinner with him. She accepts and they go to a nice little restaurant on Peachtree Street for the noonday meal. He admires his secretary for her intelligence and politeness, but she is no match for the love of his life, Mary Ann.

When Mary Ann hears about Ephraim's promotion to captain, she hopes it would not mean that he would remain in the military. She wonders: *he knows that marriage is possible only if he leaves the service, but does he remember.* Perhaps when the two meet for supper tonight, she will just ask him about his intentions.

At supper, he says, "Mary Ann, I'm going to Washington Monday; please come with me? We'll be there all week until Friday. We can have a great time together."

"If we were a married couple I'd go with you! I don't believe it would be proper for a single girl to take a trip to a strange town and stay at a strange hotel with a man that's not her husband. Do you?"

"Hey! Are you pressuring me to marry you right now?"

"No sir. You are the one that needs to say when the time is right."

Ephraim asks, "If I resign from the Army will you marry me?"

"You know the answer to that question!"

Ephraim, torn between his career and the one he loves, says, "Let me think about it while I'm in Washington. I'll give you an answer when I get back."

"That's fair enough—you know how much I love you." Mary Ann reassures him.

"Granddaddy, did Ephraim and Mary Ann ever marry?"
"You'll find out when I continue the story."
"Well, okay."

Presentation to the President

Ephraim takes the train to Washington on Monday morning so he could be there bright and early on Tuesday for his meeting with President Grant. Wishing Mary Ann could have come with him; he has breakfast alone in the dining car. From Grand Central Station, he grabs a horse-taxi to go to the White House for his 10:00 o'clock appointment.

Grant as Commander-In-Chief returns the Captain's salute as they greet each other.

The President says, "Captain Rainwater I want you to meet these gentlemen: Henry Wilson, Vice President; William Belknap, Secretary of War; Benjamin Bristow, Secretary of the Treasury; George Robeson, Secretary of the Navy; and Marshall Jewell, Postmaster General."

"Good to meet all of you gentlemen, but I didn't expect to see so many important officials. I'm impressed."

"Captain, I am sorry to hear about your uncle's untimely death. Joseph is a respected member of the military and especially in the field of communications technology. I understand that your superior officers feel confident of your ability to complete this report, so please tell us what you have." The President says as all sit down leaving Rainwater standing.

Ephraim gives a very thorough and informative report as the recording secretary takes her notes. Everyone listens intently. When he is finished and answers all the questions, he expresses his thanks to the President and the other officials for giving him this opportunity. As he sits down, he hears applause and praise from the room full of important people.

Grant looks at Ephraim and smiles, saying, "Very good! Very good! They say that the army travels on its stomach, but I say the army with the fastest communication technology succeeds. You have convinced me that we have the best and will continue to in the future because of individuals like you and your uncle. Your presentation was well planned and very informative. Ephraim, did you know that I served with your father in the Mexican War and have known his brother Joseph for many years. The Rainwater family played a big part in the protection of our freedom in America. Thank you and I know you will have a great career in our U.S. Army, so keep up the good job."

"Thank you, Mr. President." Ephraim salutes the President.

Ephraim leaves the White House, feeling very good about his accomplishments, but still not sure about his career. On the one hand he has great opportunity for a wonderful future in the army, but on the other hand he could have a wonderful married life with Mary Ann, if he so chooses to. *What am I to do?*

The next few days in Washington, seeing the sights, will give him time to think about his future. As he settles back in his hotel room, he wishes Mary Ann could be there. *She brings joy to my heart* he thinks as his mind ponders about the decision he must make.

The next day he travels around Washington in a military two-horse-buggy, and driver courtesy of the government. He thinks about George Washington, John Adams, Thomas Jefferson, James Madison, and other founders of America. He remembers stories by his Grandfather James, whose own father, John, Jr., participated in the early events in Washington. Ephraim is proud to be an American; however, he feels badly about the blight of the Civil War on an otherwise positive American history.

Friday, Ephraim's guide drops him off at the Train Station for his long train ride back to Atlanta.

Ephraim's Big Decision

Ephraim is about to make the decision of his life—a choice between two very desirable paths. As he travels by train from Washington to Atlanta, his past military life blazes across his mind's thoughts. *Why marry a woman who wants me to give up a promising career? I grew up as a farmer, so why not go back to it and marry the girl I love.*

The train pulls into the Terminal Station in Atlanta and Ephraim grabs his duffel bag, jumps off the train looking for who might be there to pick him up, even though he has not given anyone his time of arrival. The mule drawn streetcar runs from the train station to Ft. McPherson, so he takes it to return to base.

Back in his barrack, sleeping is difficult for Ephraim that Saturday night. When he awakes Sunday morning, he decides to take a military horse, go to Fairburn, and attend church at Bethlehem Baptist Church. There, he will see Mary Ann and perhaps discuss the decision he must make.

At the church, he looks everywhere but con not find Mary Ann, to his disappointment.

Jane Cochran, a friend of Mary Ann happens to walk by as Ephraim asks, "Where is Mary Ann?"

"Oh! You have not heard. Her aunt in Macon died and she is there with her mother and father today."

"Thanks Jane. Do you know when she'll be back?"

"I think she will be returning Wednesday."

"Thanks, how have you been, Jane?"

"I am just fine and you?"

"Things are going fine with me, too. Thanks for asking. I'll see you later Jane."

"Bye Ephraim."

That evening, Ephraim, tosses and turns before finally getting to sleep. At reveille, he jumps out of bed feeling fresh and now satisfied in his mind that he will make the right decision about his future today. After breakfast, he goes to the general's office to report about the Washington trip.

The general is impressed and tells Ephraim, "You made all of us look good Captain. Grant sent me a telegram congratulating you last week. You have a great career ahead of you son."

"Sir, I have something I need to discuss with you."

"What is it?"

"My first enlistment period ends next month, as you know, and I have made the decision to leave the military."

"That is a surprise to me, Ephraim, what brings this on?"

"I'm planning to marry the love of my life and I she has no desire for army life. I have given this much thought sir. I would rather give up the army than to give up my girl. I have also grown to understand that army life can be hard on a family."

"What are you planning to work at after your marriage?"

"Farming. That was my life before I joined the army and that's what I'll do, sir."

"Captain, we are going to miss you, but you have to do what you have to do."

"Thank you, sir; I'll get everything passed on to the other people in my unit at Ft. Gordon during this month."

"That is great and congratulations on your upcoming marriage."

"Mary Ann doesn't know yet. I'll tell her Wednesday, so please don't mention it to her if she contacts you."

"It's just between you and me."

Now that Ephraim has made up his mind and has taken the first step toward leaving the army, he feels great about the decision and is anxious to tell Mary Ann.

He must ask Mr. Hammond for permission first. Mary Ann's father is a prominent farmer in Campbell County and seems to like Ephraim and the entire Rainwater family. Seeking his permission will only be a formality showing respect to tradition.

Wednesday finally arrives and it is the big day Ephraim travels to Fairburn to see his sweetheart. He makes use of the military vehicle and horse, since he is still an army man, although for only a few more weeks. An aide hitches the buggy to the horse for him and he takes over the reins, steps into the buggy and heads south to Fairburn with a glow in his heart and a smile on his face.

Trotting into the front yard of the Hammonds, he sees Mary Ann running out to greet him. He steps down from the buggy and ties the reins to the hitching post just as Mary Ann gives him a fierce hug and he returns the hug as their lips press hard together. This kiss last a long time. It feels like electricity is flowing from one to the other and back and forth.

After Ephraim regains his composure, he says, "I'm sorry about your aunt's death."

"Thanks, she will be missed by many! Hey soldier boy I've sure missed you."

"Sweetheart, I missed you all of last week in Washington. Everyday, I wished you were there with me."

"Well here I am standing in front of you. What do you want to do?"

"Let's go sit on the two-seat swing and talk."

"Is talk all you want to do?"

Ephraim turns red in the face as the two walk toward the swing. He knows what he would like to do with Mary Ann, but he also knows that marriage comes first. They sit in the swing resuming their kissing ferociously. The two are deeply in love and it is hard to hold back their true feelings for each other.

After a spell of time, Mary Ann, looking straight into Ephraim's eyes and with a grin on her face, asks, "What do you want to talk about?"

"Let's get married!"

"You know the answer is yes as soon as you leave the army."

"Guess what?"

"What?"

"I've notified the General that I'm leaving at the end of my enlistment period next month."

"Oh! Oh! Ex-soldier boy, you just made me very happy!"

The two embrace each other with such gentleness, yet with complete closeness, as both feel as if they are melting into each other's arms.

Ephraim looking up, says, "I need to talk to your father to ask for your hand. Do you want to do that now?"

"Why not, he'll probably be glad to get rid of me. You know I'm kidding you! He's inside. Let's go in."

They walk hand-in-hand into the house and she asks Ephraim to take a seat in the parlor as she goes to fetch her father.

When father and daughter return, Mr. Hammond says, "Hello Ephraim, good to see you. How have you been?"

"Fine Mr. Hammond, I'm okay. Thanks for asking."

"Mary Ann tells me you have something to ask me."

"Ye, Ye, uh Yes sir, I do. Mary Ann and I wish to get married soon and I want your blessings before we make our plans."

"Are you sure? I think Mary Ann wants to wait until after you leave the army."

Mary Ann interrupts quickly saying, "Daddy, he's leaving the army next month."

"Okay, well Ephraim you have my blessings and permission."

"Thank you sir and I want you to know I'll take care of her with all my might."

"I believe you son. What are you planning to do when you leave the military?"

"I have some land that my grandfather left to me when he passed away. I'm going to do what I grew up doing. I will farm this land and provide a good living for Mary Ann and me."

"Sounds like a good plan, if you need any help please just ask me."

"Thanks, Mr. Hammond that is kind of you."

Ephraim and Mary Ann go for a ride in the military buggy before it gets too dark. This gives the couple time to talk more about the upcoming marriage.

Ephraim says, "Sweetheart, should we have a church wedding or just go to the Justice of Peace to get married?"

"Ephraim, I can't believe you asked that question. Of course we'll have a church wedding and it'll be at the Bethlehem Church—our church."

"I agree. Let's think about the wedding date. What do you suggest?"

"You finish up at Fort McPherson on the 15th of next month, so how about Saturday the 16th?"

"Okay, that sounds good to me and it should give us time to get ready for the wedding."

It is a very busy three and a half weeks. Ephraim is busy on June 15 at Fort McPherson, bidding his friends goodbye and collecting his belongings as he leaves the military service. The General and all the officers have a special ceremony to wish him good luck and to congratulate him for his marriage, which takes place the next day. Most of the officers plan to attend.

Saturday's wedding on is simple, yet a beautiful ceremony with Reverend George Perkins, their pastor, doing the honors at Bethlehem Baptist church. The newly weds run to the hidden buggy, where their suitcases are loaded.

Their guest yells, "Where are you going on your honeymoon?"

"You'll never know!" Mary Ann yells back to them.

Being of modest means, Ephraim and Mary Ann do not plan an expensive honeymoon. They travel to Atlanta's Georgian Hotel on Peachtree Street, just three hours away from Fairburn. They dine and wine alone at the hotel restaurant, enjoying every minute of their time as husband and wife. The night is a wonderful time for the newly weds. They are made for each other and they now know it for sure.

The next few days go by too fast as the happy newly weds return to Fairburn. Their temporary residence is at Mary Ann's mother and father's home, until their new house is built on the land Grandfather James left for Ephraim.

Ephraim begins farming immediately on his land, even as the house is being constructed. He and Mary Ann have designed a comfortable home with a fireplace in every room and a well on ground that will be beneath the back porch. The neighbors love the idea of having water so convenient to the kitchen. Most homes have wells in the back yard, where they draw the water and carry the bucket back into the house.

The outhouse is a nice three-holler, as opposed to the two-hollers most people use. The outhouse is far enough away from the house so that they will not be bothered by odors. Ephraim feels that everything needs to be very special for his dear wife. The building of a home together is fun for both of them, although it is taking almost a year to build.

Ephraim finally announces to his wife, "Honey, we can move into the house in two weeks."

"That will be just in time for our new baby!" Mary Ann says, surprising her husband.

"What do you mean new baby?"

"Haven't you noticed?" she asks as she pats her protruding stomach.

"Are you sure? How do you know?"

"Women just know these things. We learn from our mothers and they learn from their mothers. I've already contacted Mrs. Jordon, the mid-wife."

"Whoopee! We're going to have a baby!"

They move into the house; the baby is born; the farm is prospering and God is blessing the family.

Ephraim says to Mary Ann, "I don't know how things could be any better for us. No wars and none in sight as I see it."

"Yes, Honey, isn't it great. God has been so good to us." Mary Ann says as she cuddles little Robert.

Over the years, Mary Ann and Ephraim continue to be blessed with several children. They name the second boy James after Grandfather James; the third child is a boy too, Amos; and then comes Charles, born on January 10, 1883.

Mary Ann says, "I love all my boys, but I wish we could have a little girl."

"It must be in the water. I'll get you some water from my mother's well; she has several daughters." Ephraim says as he laughs.

"Oh! Ephraim you are funny."

Sure enough, Edna, a little girl is born in 1885. Little Edna is a joyous addition to the family, Ephraim enjoys the help from his boys: Robert, James, Amos, and little Charles. Farmers can use as many boys as possible to help farm the crops, but Mary Ann needs help in the house, so little Edna will grow and provide that help.

Ephraim is sitting in the parlor, looking sad, one evening after the kids have been tucked in bed for the night. Mary Ann brings over a kerosene lamp, holds it close to his face so she can see what is bothering her husband.

"What's the matter, honey? Why do you look so sad?"

"I am sitting here wondering what ever happened to my father's brother Benjamin. I was only a baby when my dad died at the hands of Benjamin, so I never knew him. I wonder if my grandfather ever forgave Benjamin for what happened."

"I can understand how you feel. If he is still in Texas, perhaps you can contact him to find out about some missing links in your family history."

"Say, Mary Ann, I like that idea! Uncle Joseph mentioned to me once that he has heard from someone in Wood County, Texas who told him Benjamin lives in that county. I think I'll write to the Wood County Registrar to see if we can get any information about Benjamin."

"Let me know if I can help."

The Wood County Registrar replies to Ephraim's request:

Wood County, Texas
Registrar's Office

Dear Mr. Rainwater,   June 23. 1886

> *Thank you for your inquiry. Benjamin F. Rainwater does live in our County. He is married to Julie Morgan and they have seven children. He is now 48 years old and is employed as a carpenter for a local homebuilder.*
>
> *His address: 13 Lone Star Street, Fort Worth, Texas*
>
> *If we can be of further help please write.*
>
>
>
> *Sincerely,*
> **George Johnson**
> *George Johnson*
> *Registrar*
>
>

Mary Ann, I have a letter from Texas. Here you read it, too." Ephraim calls to his wife.

"Well now that you know where he lives, what are you going to do?"

"I know, I'll send him a telegram and ask him if he would like to communicate with us."

"That is kind of you Ephraim. After all he did kill your father when you were two-years old and this might be a way to let him know you forgive him."

"Yeah, that's what I'm thinking."

The text of the telegram Benjamin receives is as follow:

Western Union

To: Benjamin F. Rainwater   June 24, 1886
13 Lone Star Street,   Fort Worth, Texas
*   I am your nephew Ephraim Dawson Rainwater,*
the son of Miles Rainwater. I am now 31-years old
and have five children. I wish to let you know that
I have forgiven you long ago. Would you like to
communicate with my mother and us?
*   Love, Ephraim*

The Western Union message boy, riding his bicycle, presents the telegram to Benjamin. When Benjamin reads it, he is shocked. He remembers the last words he heard from his father *Go to Texas and never come back to Georgia.*

Would Lilla Ann my mother forgive me? Would my brothers and sisters in Georgia forgive me? These are frustrating thoughts that keep swirling around in his head. His wife, Julie, and his children do not know about what happened in Georgia. Nobody in Texas knows that he murdered his brother some 29 years ago. Things are good for him now and he doesn't want to stir his old problems into his new life, so he decides to sleep on it.

The next morning Benjamin decides not to answer Ephraim's telegram. He feels it best not to get involved with any connections to his old life.

Ephraim and Mary Ann wonder why he has never made contact with them.

Ephraim says, "Maybe he's ashamed of what he did and doesn't want the people in Texas to know about it."

"You are probably right and I'll bet his wife and children know nothing about his past either."

"I guess we must just leave him alone. If I ever go to Texas, I'll look him up and have a private meeting with him to avoid any embarrassment on his part."

More Children

"Another boy for me, I see." Ephraim says after his wife gives birth to their sixth child in the spring of 1887.

"Yes, I'm good at making baby boys, aren't I?"

"Oh, you will have some more girls, I'll bet."

"What shall we name this new baby boy?"

"I've been thinking about George Felton. What do you think?"

"That does have a great ring to it and now you will have another farm hand."

They do name their sixth child George Felton Rainwater.

Ephraim is right; Mary Ann does have more girls. By 1896, they have four more children: two boys and two girls. The boys are Allen Cleveland and Homer and the girls, Ida May and Christine.

Edna has just turned eleven when Mary Ann says, "I think we should buy an organ since Edna seems to have a touch for music."

Ephraim looks at his wife, with puzzlement on his face, as he says, "Organs are expensive-we'll have to sell a lot of corn and watermelons to afford one of those."

"I'll pay for it." Mary Ann says with a grin on her face.

"Where are you going to get the money?"

"We've been married 20 years and I've been putting a little aside in my cookie jar all the time."

"How much do you have?"

"Two-hundred-and-fifty dollars."

"Wow, we're rich!"

"No we are not rich, but we are going to get Edna an organ."

"Honey, you are something! That's why I married you."

"I know it sweetie pie. I've got the organ picked out already."

Their love for each other does not diminish as the years have gone by. It grew.

The next Saturday morning they take Edna with them to the Fayetteville Piano store in the next county to pick out the organ. They make it clear to Edna that the organ will be for the family, but she will be the primary user. Edna started learning to play on the church organ from the church organist when she was five years old and is quite good already. The store has several organs from which to choose. One with an easy foot pump would be good for a little girl like Edna to pump. They find the one with all the features they desire after Mary Ann has looked for months.

Mary Ann asks, "How much is this one?"

The sales clerk thumbs through his product guidebook then says, "Two-hundred-and-thirty-nine dollars. It's normally $299.00, but is on sale today."

"Can you deliver it this afternoon?" Mary Ann asks.

"We can, but there is a $10.00 delivery charge."

"We'll take it if you will give us free delivery."

"Lady you are a hard bargainer, but all right we'll deliver it free."

As promised, a mule and wagon deliver the organ that afternoon along with two men to carry it in to the parlor. After installing it, Ephraim slips the two men a five dollar bill each without Mary Ann seeing his tip.

The whole family enjoys the organ during family time most evenings and on many Sunday afternoons. Even Mary Ann learns to play it. The growing family works all week, rests in the evenings and attends church Sunday mornings. Saturday is a day off for the farm hands and for the family to do their shopping. Mary Ann is so happy with her family, but she knows that one day the children will grow up and fly-the-coop. In the meantime, Mary Ann and Ephraim will enjoy the blessings God has given them.

Chapter 5

The Spanish-American War

Robert Lee Rainwater

Ephraim's oldest child, Robert Lee, walks up to his father to say, "Dad now is the time for me to join the army."

"Why is now the time?"

"I'm 18 now; that is why."

"Are you sure? Have you talked to your mother about this?"

"Yes I'm sure and no, I haven't talked to mother."

"It's okay with me if it's okay with your mother."

Robert Lee has listened to the stories, all his life, about how is mother wouldn't marry his dad until he resigns from the army. Never the less, he still is anxious to join the military and plans to talk his mother in to it.

He catches her at an opportune time and announces, "Mama, I'm going to join the military."

"Well son it looks like you are going to follow in your grandfather's and father's footsteps. Are you sure?"

"Yes Mama, I'm sure. Daddy has already given me his approval if it is okay with you."

"Since there are no wars going on, I'm sure you'll be safe, so all right. When are you going to join?"

"Right away, just as soon as possible."

"Just be careful son."

Robert Lee visits the Army recruiter right away. Induction into the service will be at Fort McPherson where he receives assignment to a unit for basic training. His induction date is on the following Monday morning at 8:00 o'clock. This gives him time to get his stuff together and time to spend with family a few more days.

Robert Lee has never slept away from home except at Grandma Hammonds and Grandma Rainwaters nearby, so this will be quite an adventure for the young man.

Fort Gordon

Monday morning, Robert Lee reports as scheduled to Fort McPherson, where his first stop is the quartermaster to pickup his clothing and other gear. He learns his assignment for basic training is to be at Fort Gordon near Augusta where his daddy and great uncle Joseph served. The train leaves for Ft. Gordon in the afternoon, so he doesn't have time to notify his mother and daddy where he is to be stationed.

Telephone lines recently installed in Atlanta connect Ft. McPherson with the Atlanta area, but lines have not been installed in the Fairburn area yet. He looks in the telephone directory, which already has 3,009 numbers listed, and finds the number for Tom Rainwater. Tom, his father's cousin can send a message to let his father know that he will be in Ft. Gordon that night.

"Hello Tom, this is Robert Lee."

"Robert Lee, who?"

"You know, Robert Lee Rainwater."

"Oh! I'm sorry Robert Lee; what can I do for you?"

"Tom I'm in the army at Fort McPherson getting ready to board the train for Fort Gordon in Augusta to begin basic training. Can you send a message to my father where I am stationed?"

"No problem, I'll take care of that for you. Have a nice trip and good luck in the army. You know my father was at Ft. Gordon years ago and so was your father."

"Yes, I know. Thanks for letting my folks know where I'll be. Take care and goodbye."

"Goodbye."

Mary Ann is delighted to learn Robert Lee is stationed at Fort Gordon; she has pleasant memories of the time Ephraim was stationed down there.

She says to Ephraim, "I wish they would hurry up and install telephone lines here so we could talk to him."

"I'm afraid it will be a long time before they do install them since Fairburn is such a small town."

"Do you have any interesting places near Ft. Gordon where Robert Lee might enjoy going?"

"Yes, I know a lot of places where young single soldiers can have fun."

"Oh! You do, do you, and I believed you did nothing but military stuff when you were there."

"You would be surprised sweetheart."

"I'm glad I got you honey."

"I am too." Ephraim says as he reaches over and kisses his wife.

The couple cherishes the memories of Ephraim's Army service and desires the same for Robert Lee.

Mary Ann, right in the middle of a kiss says, "Let's ask Edna to play the organ for us tonight."

"Hey, that's a good idea. I'll enjoy hearing her play again." Ephraim agrees since he is always happy when his wife and daughter make music with the organ.

Mary Ann hollers, "Edna, Edna, We need you!"

"Yes Mama, I'm on my way."

It is a fun evening as Edna plays some of their favorite tunes on the organ. Even two-year old Ida May enjoys it. Mary Ann is thinking *what a wonderful family with which God has blessed us.*

Then she thinks she needs to check on baby Christine. It is timely, as the baby needs a diaper change. She makes the change and pats the baby back to sleep, then returns to the parlor to be with her family. Ephraim is sitting in the corner chair with little Homer in his lap as both of them are about to fall asleep.

It is getting late so Mary Ann suggests, "Don't ya'll think it's time to go to bed?"

"No Mama!" exclaim several children in unison.

Ephraim opens his eyes from his drowsiness and says, "Come on now, it's time to go to bed. Let's go boys and girls, right now."

They all scurry toward bed knowing that when their daddy speaks, he is serious.

Mary Ann lay in bed thinking about her firstborn, Robert Lee. *Wonder if he's okay and if he misses us.*

She says to Ephraim, "Do you think Robert Lee will be all right in the army?"

She hears nothing but snoring coming from Ephraim's side of the bed so she turns over and soon falls asleep.

Signal Corps

Most seasoned men recognize Basic Training at Fort Gordon as the toughest base for new recruits in the whole army. Robert Lee discovers this during his first few weeks, as his Sergeant is constantly on his back, but it seems to be necessary in order to develop a disciplined hard working man out of civilian boys. Hard work is nothing new to this farm boy, so it does not wear him out as much as it does some of the city boys. After his six months of basic training, Robert Lee is assigned to the Signal Corps. He is following the example of his father and uncle.

Robert Lee, having completed basic training, receives a two-week furlough and plans to spend it with his family in Fairburn. The morning he arrives home, he is greeted with sad news.

His mother hugs him and says, "Son, your Grandmother Lilla Ann Rainwater passed away last night. She died peacefully in her sleep and all of her children, including your father, were at her bedside when she took her last breath. Your father and uncles and aunts are at the funeral home making arrangements for the funeral now."

"Oh! I'm so sorry to hear that. I loved her so much and I wish I could have seen her before she died."

The funeral takes place on Thursday at the Ramah Baptist Church. She is laid to rest next to her husband, Zebulon Miles Rainwater. Many friends and family members attend.

Mary Ann does her best to cheer up the family the rest of the week. She knows that Robert Lee is returning to his base in a week-and-a-half and she wants the family to enjoy his stay.

She asks, "Son, where will you go for your duty in the Signal Corps?"

"I'm to report to Fort McPherson on Monday and from there, I do not know yet, but rumors are that I may go overseas. That's just a rumor because I really don't know."

"Please write us when you know."

"I will, Mama."

Robert Lee enjoys being with his mother and father and siblings during his furlough time; but, he returns to the base on Monday morning as ordered. Captain Jessie Lowe, his company commander, greets him along with the entire group after completion of basic training.

The captain says, "Gentlemen, your training is just now beginning. I'm sure y'all think basic training was it, but now you will be trained in the operation of the communication equipment used by our U.S. Army. We are the Signal Corps and we are the operating arm for all communication lines everywhere our military is stationed, so get ready men."

The extensive training lasts one year, so Robert Lee is able to visit his family most every weekend. At the end of the year's training, the men receive their orders. Robert Lee is assigned to a regiment in San Antonio, Texas. He telegraphs his mother and father, giving them the information. *San Antonio is certainly an interesting place,* Robert Lee thinks as he eats Mexican food at one of the town's restaurants down by the river.

Lt. Colonel Theodore Roosevelt.

Robert Lee's assignment to Lt. Colonel Theodore Roosevelt's unit as the Signal Corps coordinator is a recognition of the Rainwater legend of Signal Corps service. This new assignment comes with a promotion to the rank of Sergeant. Robert Lee develops respect for Roosevelt.

It is early in 1898, when Robert Lee reads Roosevelt's notification to his troops about an insurrection going on in Cuba. The newspaper article about President McKinley's request to Spain to resolve insurrection peacefully, before it affects America, gives Robert Lee a better understanding of the reason their entire unit is on alert.

At the request of Roosevelt, Robert Lee reports to the Lt. Colonel's San Antonio headquarters office. Rainwater salutes and asks, "Sir, what can I do for you?"

Roosevelt says, "Sergeant Rainwater please tell me about *'wireless telegraphy'*. I hear scientists are working on a wireless technology. What do you know about it?"

"Yes Sir, there are developments being made this decade by Messrs. Edison, Marconi, and Bose. Signals have been sent short distances, 30 miles or so. I think Edison has sold his ideas to Marconi. The goal is to send signals across oceans and from ship to ship. I personally think it will be several years before a practical solution is available for our use. However, as you know we can now send messages via cable beneath both the Atlantic and Pacific Oceans and from Cuba to Miami. Most all of the large countries of the world now have telegraph offices. The islands in the Caribbean use the world telegraph system and so do most of the islands in the Pacific. I have a friend in Havana who works in the Cuban telegraph office. Many areas now have voice over telephone communications, too. The Signal Corps has kept up with modern technology in the communications field. "

"Thank you Sergeant, you have enlightened me somewhat, please keep me informed."

"Yes Sir, may I ask you a question?"

"Sure, go ahead."

"Sir, what is happening in Cuba?"

"You know when I was assistant secretary of the Navy, before taking charge here in San Antonio, I always encouraged intervention in Cuba and I placed the Navy on a war-time footing. I ordered Commodore George Dewey and the Pacific fleet to head for the Philippines with sealed orders to be opened just before they arrive. This is an opportunity to drive the Spaniards from the Western World. That's what I still believe and I am training my soldiers to get ready for action, when it comes."

"Thanks Sir, I'll be ready."

After they salute, Robert Lee leaves and heads to his barrack. As he sits on his bunk, he writes a letter to his Mother and Father. He explains, in his letter, how tough Roosevelt is in his severe training of the men, but at the same time, he likes Roosevelt very much as a leader.

Mary Ann receives his letter and sits on the front porch rocker to read it. Later she yells to Ephraim to tell him about Robert Lee and his meeting with Teddy Roosevelt.

She says. "You know they call Theodore, 'Teddy', Robert Lee writes."

"May I read his letter?"

"Sure, he seems to be doing fine, and you'll find he is now a Sergeant."

"Maybe he'll become a Captain like I was, one day."

"I sure miss him; I want to see him so much."

Ephraim and Mary Ann love all of their children equally, but they treasure their first-born, Robert Lee.

> **David asks, "Will there be a war in Cuba?"**
> **"You are trying to get ahead of me again. Just be patient and you will see."**
> **"Alright, I'll be patient."**

Things begin to heat up in Cuba, as the insurrection is not being resolved by Spain soon enough to satisfy the politicians in Washington. On February 15, 1898 the American battleship, USS *Maine* mysteriously explodes in Havana Harbor. The Americans report that it is caused by a submarine mine. The blame is placed on Spain, but the Spaniards claim it is an accidental explosion and not an attack by their Kingdom.

American journalists, William R. Hearst and Joseph Pulitzer, widely publicize this as a Spanish conspiracy and this news results in the American public becoming fueled with anger.

Edison's new motion picture camera and projector allow people to see newsreels at the local theaters of things that are happening in Cuba. This, too, fuels the public's anger as the American cry of the hour becomes:

> *Remember the Maine!*
> *To hell with Spain!*

In mid March, Republican Senator Redfield Proctor in a speech to Congress announces, "The situation in Cuba is serious enough that war is the answer to resolve it."

While McKinley and Speaker of the House, Brackett, oppose war, the pressure from business and religious communities and the public outcry causes them to take action. On April 11, McKinley asks Congress for authority to send American troops to Cuba to end the civil war there.

On April 19, Congress passes joint resolutions proclaiming Cuba *free and independent* and disclaiming any intentions in Cuba, demand Spanish withdrawal, and authorize the President to use as much military force as is necessary to help Cuban patriots gain freedom from Spain.

War in Cuba and Pacific

In response, Spain brakes off diplomatic relations with the United States and declares war April 23. Two days later, Congress declares that a state of war between the United States and Spain has existed since April 21.

Cuba is not the only challenge for the U.S. and as the war progresses, rather rapidly, Guam, the Philippines, Hawaii and Puerto Rico are opportunities for America.

The first battle of the Philippines is in the sea near where, on May 2, 1898, Commodore George Dewey, commanding the United States Pacific fleet, in a matter of hours, defeats the Spanish sea squadron without sustaining a casualty at the Battle of manila Bay.

The Marines come into land later and attack the Spanish, successfully defeating them, ending with the Battle of Manila on August 13. The Spanish surrender Manila, but only after the U.S. Army makes a deal to protect them from Filipino persecution. This gives the U.S. control of the Philippines.

The Filipinos, angered because they are not consulted about the surrender agreement with Spain, demand independence for themselves, however, the American Troops remain for six years before having full control. The Japanese are upset at America's expansion into the Pacific.

During this same time, Captain Henry Glass, en route to Manila on the cruiser *USS Charleston,* opens sealed orders notifying him to proceed to Hawaii and seize those Islands for the U.S. and on to Guam to capture it.

The Hawaiian Islands present no problem for our Navy. It falls into American hands without a major battle. The native Hawaiians are happy to see the sailors. Japan is alarmed at America's triumphs, as many of the immigrants in Hawaii are Japanese.

Upon arrival at Guam on June 20, Glass fires cannon at the island.

The Spanish officer, not knowing that the war is on, comes out to the ship to greet them and asks, "May we borrow some gun powder so we can return the American's salute."

Glass responds by taking the officer prisoner and then demands, "I order you to return to the island to discuss the terms of surrender."

The scared Spanish officer returns in his small boat to the island and the following day, 54 Spanish infantry surrender, as the island becomes a possession of the United States.

San Antonio

In San Antonio, Colonel Leonard Wood asks Roosevelt to address the troops. Although Colonel Wood is in charge, Roosevelt calls the shots, however he depends on Wood for his medical advice for his troops.

Roosevelt stands on a high platform as he speaks, "Listen up men, we will be packing and moving in three days to an undisclosed location. I feel that your training is complete and we are ready for what may come ahead. You all will look back at the tough training and thank me later, I know.

"Several other regiments have joined us for the action that is before us to make up three divisions of about 15,000 troops. We will be reporting to General William Shafter appointed overall commander by President McKinley.

"The *buffalo soldiers*, a Negro unit with much experience in fighting the Indians in North Western Territories since the civil war will aid our Cavalry Division.

"They now call us the *Rough Riders*. A reputation we gained by the rough cavalry training you all have experienced. We are horse-mounted troops, but I warn you that we may have to fight un-mounted at times.

"During the next few days we will load all the horses, artillery, and gear into railroad cars and begin our trip to the undisclosed location. Everyman will be counted on to do his part to make this move happen efficiently, so get a good night's sleep because you will need it."

The men return to their barracks wondering *where we are going*. Robert Lee having made friends with many of the cavalrymen knows he will ride with them to maintain communications in battle conditions.

In the barrack, the men begin talking about Roosevelt's speech.

Robert Lee says, "We must be going on land, since he said we will be loading everything into railroad cars."

Jason speaks, "Maybe the railroad cars will take us to a seaport."

Robert Lee says, "You are probably right, Jason, since Texas does not have a ship dock for loading ships, perhaps we will go some place where there is a dock."

"There are docks in Savannah, maybe we are going there."

Jerry turns around to say, "Tampa has docks. Could that be where we are going?"

They all agree they will have to wait until later to know, so they begin playing polka to pass the time. Soon they go to bed to get good nights sleep Roosevelt says they will need.

The next morning, Roosevelt comes to Robert Lee with a question, "Sergeant, you have mentioned that you have a friend who works in the telegraph office in Havana; isn't that correct?

"Yes Sir, that is correct."

"Do you think this person would be willing to help the U.S. as a spy?"

"I think so; many Cubans want us to free them from the Spanish tyrants. I'm sure he will help us."

"Before you contact him about this, let me clear it through the President. I'll get back to you if we get approval from Washington. In the meantime, please do not mention this conversation to anyone. Sergeant, please have your men pack up enough supplies to lay telegraph lines for wartime conditions."

"Yes sir." Rainwater says to his commander as they salute and go about getting ready for departure in a couple of days.

Robert Lee, as a member of the Signal Corps attached to Roosevelt's Calvary concludes this conversation has tipped him off as to where they will probably end up in battle, however he keeps this knowledge to himself.

The next few days are pure hell, as every one is scrambling to pack up and load the train cars. It is springtime and not too hot, which makes a difference. General William Shafter, a former Confederate General, is scrambling with his men to get everything going. Although he is a very fat man, he is a very skilled strategist, and sweats along side his men. Shafter is an officer and a gentleman who leans on Roosevelt and his *Rough Riders* for a successful campaign.

One Southern Officer asks Shafter, "Sir, do we have to ride in these trains with those *Niggers*?"

"Those buffalo soldiers may save your life officer and I respect them as men in my command and they will ride with other soldiers in our mission. If you don't want to ride with them, I'll be happy to accept your resignation. Do you understand?"

"Yes sir," replies the Officer.

"Well, go get your group prepared for this long trip and don't use the word *nigger* in this army." Shafter demands.

"Yes sir, I apologize for bothering you."

"Apology accepted."

The Army is ready to move out on the trains leaving San Antonio, as the rat race is now crowded into boxcars and troop cars. The horses are bellowing, but there is plenty of hay for them as the train slowly moves out.

Along the way, through Texas, Louisiana, and Mississippi many civilians wave at the troops from the streets and roads. The train stops in towns for meals to feed the troops at local restaurants that have been notified before hand to be prepared for the large group.

At one stop in Mississippi, there is a sign in one restaurant: *No Niggers Allowed.* None of the soldiers, white or black, ate at this restaurant.

Three days after leaving San Antonio, the troop trains and boxcars arrive at Tampa Bay, where Shafter sets up temporary headquarters at the Tampa Bay Hotel. The hotel is well equipped with the new electric lighting and has an excellent bar where Roosevelt, Wood and Shafter enjoy mint juleps in the evenings. Those evening times are not often, as they have the men working sixteen hours a day loading the supplies, horses, and equipment on to ships.

Roosevelt is not an officer to complain much, but he asks Shafter, "Where are we going to put all the troops?"

"Several of those supply ships have been converted to troop carriers."

"I saw them and there is only one latrine in each ship."

"Roosevelt, it'll have to do and I know that the decks will be wall to wall with soldiers trying to sleep at night."

"Okay, we will make the best of it."

Roosevelt calls in Robert Lee to say, "Sergeant, we have permission from McKinley to seek your friend in Havana as a spy in their telegraph office. Please contact him by telegraph to see what you can do. Please keep this a secret for now."

"Yes sir, I'll get right on it."

Robert Lee used the telegraph office in Tampa to contact Cortez, his friend in Havana. Secretly, he is able to engage him to the aid of the United States in the fight for independence of Cuba.

"Having inside information will be an advantage for us." Roosevelt tells Rainwater as he surprises him with a field promotion to Captain.

, "Thank you sir, I didn't expect this."

"You deserve it Captain."

"My dad will be proud of me."

"Yes I remember your dad and his service to the Signal Corpse."

The next few days, filled with action along the docks at Tampa as soldiers, horses, equipment and supplies are loaded on to the several supply ships and troop ships, ready for the first time Calvary units will be engaged in a land away from the states. The loading is one experience most hope to never have to go through again.

Finally, the ships, men, horses, and supplies, crowded all together, set sail for Cuba. On board, one needs to step over men, spread out all over the deck, to get from one side to the other side. One could hear the horses in an adjacent ship bellowing as the ship rolls back and forth with the waves. Smoke flowing from the stacks of each ship makes a huge grey cloud in the blue sky as they slowly sail away from shore. Tons of coal has been loaded during the past few days, enough to power the ships to Cuba and back.

Robert Lee, now an officer has quarters in the ship's upper tower near Roosevelt, Wood, Shafter and other officers. He has contacted his friend Cortez in Cuba just before leaving Tampa. He arranged for Cortez to aid the U.S. Navy crews in the cutting of cables from Cuba to the outside world with the exception of the main cable to Miami. This maneuver will hinder the Spanish efforts, while aiding the Americans in their attack.

Meanwhile, the first successful U. S. Navy foray against Guantanamo Bay occurs on June 6, with the arrival of the cruiser *USS Marblehead* and the St. *Louis.* As the two ships come into the bay at dawn, Spanish soldiers cluster about the blockhouse on land near a hill. The blockhouse and the village are speedily cleared by fire from the *Marblehead's* six pounder and one five-inch shell.

With the help of Rainwater's friend Cortez, the telegraph cables leading east to Haiti and west to Santiago are cut by the *St. Louis* crew. The main cable to Miami is left intact leaving Cuba out of touch from the outside world except for the U.S.

Cuban soldiers, angered at the Spanish, cooperate with the U.S. Navy and U.S. Marines to capture and set up a base at Guantanamo Bay. The Marines arrive on June 10 from Key West on their transport, the *Panther*. The Spanish have fled in such a hurry that they left clothing, money, jewelry and weapons behind.

Sadly, Marine Privates William Dumphy and James McColgan are the first U. S. casualties of the war. Both die at night as they guard the base. The enemy slips in, fires at them and then escapes inland.

On the other side of the island, Spanish Admiral Cervera holds up his naval forces in Santiago harbor where they will be protected from sea attack. The U.S. Navy decides to block the bay inlet by sinking its own ship *Merrimac*. Thus, the brilliant idea forms a bottleneck to the entire Spanish fleet.

Finally, on June 21 and June 24, General Shafter and his troops land east of Santiago to establish an American base of operations. A squadron of soldiers with weapons has orders to scout ahead as the ships are being unloaded. With out a dock, the loading is very difficult. Small boats carry the men into shore. The horses are pushed into the sea; hopefully to swim to safety on land, however some of the horses become confused and swim in circles. One horse is seen swimming two miles out at sea. Fortunately, enough horses swim to shore to help the Calvary in the attack.

Rainwater and his men bring rolls of cable to splice into the cable from Miami on the Santiago side of the island. Cortez is instrumental in the achievement of gaining telegraphic communications with America. Shafter is able to communicate directly with McKinley.

Embedded news reporters use these cables to keep the public back home updated.

It requires two days to unload the ammunition, guns, and other supplies. The hospital ship remains ready to take care of the injured.

Pro-independence Cuban rebels greatly aid the American forces. Their advice saves lives as the troops fight their way inland. It is July 1 when the battle reaches its peak. Roosevelt's *Rough Riders* and rebel Cuban forces begin the attack in dangerous frontal assaults at the Battle of San Juan Hill outside of Santiago. Many American soldiers die in this battle; many more who suffer injuries are transported by medics to the hospital ship for treatment of their wounds.

Although Robert Lee and his Signal Corps men bore rifles, they mostly keep the cable lines extended to the tent of the general, but often do use their weapons not only to protect them but also to protect nearby soldiers. One of the signalmen on each shift around the clock copies the messages from McKinley for the general and sends the messages to Washington as directed.

Robert Lee remarks to Roosevelt, "It's a good thing we recruited Cortez to spy for us. He has helped us secure telegraph lines all the way from the ocean to here and without his help I don't believe we would be making the progress that we have made."

"Cortez is our jewel and did you notice many Cubans are on our side in the fighting of the Spaniards?"

"Yes I have noticed."

"Teddy, I worry about you! You are always up front with the *Rough Riders* and *Buffalo Soldiers* where the real fighting takes place. Please be careful."

"I will Captain. You just take care of Shafter's communication needs and I'll keep the front moving toward the top of the hill and you watch out for those cute Senoritas."

"I've been too busy to notice them, Sir."

Roosevelt takes off toward the top of the hill to lead his men in battle. Shafter has his headquarter tent about 600 yards down the hill where he plans the tactics for each change in maneuvers and informs the President periodically with the help of Robert Lee's men.

The battle of San Juan Hill is a success because of the bravery of the fighting soldiers and the help of the new Gatlin guns and their rapid fire, which supports the troops.

Roosevelt says to Shafter, "We couldn't have come this far in such a short time without the Gatlin guns."

The navy bombards the remaining Spanish fleet in Cuban waters and defeats them successfully. More powerful weapon systems and the fact that Americans and Cubans outnumber the Spaniards help in the success.

Puerto Rico

Meanwhile, on July 25, American troops land at Guernica, Puerto Rico and take the island without much resistance. Their way is paved by the constant bombarding of San Juan and other towns from Navy vessels during the preceding month. McKinley and the American public are pleased with the successes they see in this Spanish-American War.

With both of the Spanish fleets incapacitated in Cuba and Puerto Rica, Spain seeks a peace treaty; this halts hostilities on August 12, 1898. The formal peace treaty is signed in Paris on December 10, 1898 and ratified by the U.S. Senate on February 6, 1899. It comes into force on April 11, 1899. Cubans participate only as observers.

The United States gains almost all of Spain's colonies, including the Philippines, Guam, and Puerto Rico. Cuba is granted independence; however, the United States imposes various restrictions on the new government, including prohibiting alliances with other countries. The United States will control the land on both sides of the southern part of Guantánamo Bay under a lease set up in the wake of this Spanish-American War.

Time to Go Home!

The troops in Cuba now worn out from battle require much needed rest, but McKinley orders Shafter and his troops to remain for another six months to keep the peace with the Cubans. After several months, the troops demand to go home and are becoming quite restless. Many are sick with tropical diseases caused by mosquitoes and the extreme heat keeps wearing them down.

Rainwater suggests to Roosevelt, "Let's all sign a protest and send it to the President demanding that we return home."

"That's a wonderful idea. I'm surprised that I didn't think of it. Let's do it!"

Robert Lee, although feeling sick himself, goes to all the officers and men, including General Shafter, to seek signatures for this petition. Everyone signs the petition and Rainwater telegraphs it to McKinley.

McKinley telegraphs back to Shafter as follows:

To: General William R. Shafter
From: The Office of the President, United States of America
Date: 3 October 1898
Subject: Troop Return Plan from Cuba
All Calvary and attached Signal Corps will remain in Cuba for three more weeks. Replacements on their way will arrive then and your men will return on the same ship convoy to the U.S. Army base at Montauk, Long Island, New York. All arriving troops must be placed in quarantine until the Medical Corps releases them for returning to active duty or for

> ***mustering out. The quarantine is necessary in
> view of the several tropical diseases to which
> your troops have been exposed.***
>
> ***General, you may prepare the troops for
> the departure.***
> ***Signed,***
> ***William McKinley, President***

As soon as the typist completes this incoming telegraph, Robert Lee rushes it to Shafter and Roosevelt.

The very same day, Roosevelt calls all the troops to a meeting in a large clearing on the island and announces, "Gentlemen, I know you will be glad to hear that we have permission to return home. The actual departure will be three weeks from now, when our replacement troops arrive. We will go to the U.S. Army base at Montauk, Long Island, New York. We must stay aboard ship in quarantine until the Medical Corps releases us. That is an order from our President. We must begin preparing for this departure immediately."

Outcries from the troops begin immediately, "Why do we have to go to New York?"

"Why are we to be quarantined?"

No one, including Roosevelt and the General, like the idea of being quarantined and having to go to New York, but as military men, they are trained to follow orders and not complain. This is especially true when orders come directly from the Commander-in-Chief, the President.

Robert Lee sends a telegram to his mother and father advising them of the travel plans. When Mary Ann and Ephraim read the telegram together, they are excited to hear their son is finally on his way home.

Mary Ann says, "I'm disappointed that he's not coming home sooner, but he is coming home and that's great!

"It is wise to place them in quarantine to avoid transporting disease into our country. I hope Robert Lee doesn't have any of that stuff. According to the newspaper reports, many of our soldiers died of tropical diseases while in Cuba. Thank the Lord our son is coming home alive."

Roosevelt's troops load the ships, leaving horses and other heavy equipment for their replacements. Food, clothing and medical supplies are replenished for the long voyage ahead. The ships are not as crowded as before when they came to Cuba for the invasion and the general attitude of the troops is much improved, mostly because they are going home.

On the return voyage, the non-commissioned soldiers play polka and blackjack on the deck to pass the time.

Rainwater, as an officer, enjoys the comfort of extra space and other entitlements. He and Roosevelt and the other officers enjoy a Scotch whiskey and soda, or bourbon and water, with there Cuban cigars in the evenings before and after supper.

Roosevelt knows how to work hard and how to play hard. He makes the voyage quite enjoyable for everyone; however, Rainwater begins to feel ill and spends time in the infirmary and on his cot. He has flu like symptoms but not enough to remain bedridden.

The convoy of troop carriers arrives offshore near Long Island on 6 November 1898. The Medical Corps personnel come aboard to check the possibilities for removing the quarantine order. This check lasted seven days and in the process, medics discover several cases of yellow fever and malaria. Since these diseases are caught by mosquito bites and are not contagious, the troops are released to disembark.

Robert Lee reports into the base at Montauk, Long Island along with the other troops. They tell him he has malaria, so the infirmary gives him a supply of quinine water to use as a tonic during his long train trip to Atlanta.

Robert Lee says to Roosevelt, "I guess you'll stay in the army and rise up to the rank of general."

"Not really, Rainwater, I'm thinking about entering politics."

"You will make a great politician. I saw you in action in San Antonia and Cuba and it looks like you are the one calling the shots for President McKinley."

"Thank you, but I have good men like you that make the job easy. By the way, what are your plans?"

"I plan to stay in the army after a long furlough in Georgia."

"Rainwater good luck and get rid of that malaria."

"Thank you, sir. I have plenty of quinine water, so maybe it'll be cleared up soon."

Robert Lee telephones his Great Aunt Caroline in Atlanta. She answers, "Hello."

"Aunt Caroline this is Robert Lee."

"Man, good to hear your voice, where are you?"

"I'm in New York getting ready to return home."

"It's so good to hear from you, son. What can I do for you?"

"Send word to Mama that I'll be home soon. I'll have to check in at fort McPherson first."

"Sure, I'll be glad to do that for you Robert Lee."

During the train ride home, Robert Lee seems to feel better, probably because of the tonic he is taking. He sleeps most of the way, especially from Philadelphia and on into the Carolinas. The next day the train pulls into Terminal Station in Atlanta.

When Robert Lee steps down from the train steps, he hears, "Robert Lee! Robert Lee! Here we are!" It is his mother's voice.

To his surprise, there comes his mother and father running toward him. They embrace as Robert Lee gives his mother a kiss.

She says, "Did you learn to kiss like that from the Cuban girls?"

Embarrassed, Robert Lee says, "No Mama, I'm just glad to see you."

"Oh! I'm just teasing you son. We are so glad to see you. We've missed you so much."

Ephraim speaks out, "We have missed you son. What are your plans now?"

"First, take me to the base because I have to report in there before I start my furlough. Then we can go home."

They pick up the duffel bags, load up the two-horse carriage and head to the Fort.

It only takes about forty-five minutes for Robert Lee to check in at his base and then they continue toward Fairburn and home.

On the way home, Robert Lee tells his mother, "Mama, I have malaria, but I'm taking quinine water for it and I already feel better."

"I am so sorry! That is not good. What do the doctors say?"

"After my furlough, I'm to report to the hospital at Fort McPherson for further examination and treatment if necessary."

"You must take it easy and get plenty of rest while you are off duty."

"Yes, Mama, I will."

"When we get home I want you to tell us all about what you did in Cuba." Ephraim says.

"Sure, I'll be happy to do that."

They pull into the home place in Fairburn at 5:30 in the afternoon. Charles and Amos are playing in the yard. The two boys, already seven and nine are assigned gardening duties in Mary Ann's garden.

Mary Ann hollers to the boys, "Hey! Charles and Amos, did you get those turnip greens picked?"

"We did," replies Amos, and then Charles echoes the same words.

Mary Ann turns to Robert Lee and says, "We have a surprise for you."

"What is it Mama?" He asks.

"You have a new baby sister."

"Oh really! What's her name?"

"Anne."

"When was she born?"

"Last June the third."

"Well she's not even six months old yet."

Little Charles walks up to Robert Lee and says, "Who are you?"

"Don't you remember me? I'm your older brother. I guess you were too young to remember when I joined the army."

"I guess so." Little Charles runs off to play.

Amos speaks up and says, "I remember you Robert Lee. We sure have missed you."

The rest of the brothers and sisters are inside the house with Edna, who is playing the organ to keep the other children quite. James is out in the field and due in any minute. A larger than normal supper is in preparation to celebrate the homecoming of Robert Lee.

After everyone finishes eating, the adults sit around the table querying Robert Lee about the Spanish-American War and his experiences in Cuba.

Edna takes the little ones into the parlor to entertain them and to keep them from disturbing those in the dining room.

James asks his brother, "How was the food in Cuba?"

"Terrible, especially during all the fighting, but we got along on our meager rations of canned beef which tasted awful. I did have some better food at a restaurant after the battle was over."

Amos asks, "What do you think the United States gained from this war?"

"It has enabled us to emerge as a power on the world stage, though our colonial domain is smaller than that of Britain or France; I think that is significant when we look at our country's young age.

"This war probably marked the end of the Spanish empire. And don't forget we now have Puerto Rica, the Philippines, Guam and the Hawaiian Islands plus Cuba as our friend, even though we still have troops there and in Guantanamo Bay, which provides a base for our Navy and Marines."

Mary Ann asks, "Were the girls cute?"

"Yeah, they were cute and hot."

"What do you mean hot?"

"You know what I mean Mama!"

"Did you fall in love with a hot Senorita?"

"No Mama; I didn't have time. We were too busy fighting the Spanish troops."

Ephraim asks, "Son, what are the symptoms of malaria?"

"It feels like the flu, but not all the time."

"I hope they can cure it at the hospital at Fort McPherson."

"Pray for me Daddy."

"We will Robert Lee."

"Thank you. We should pray for the many other troops who have malaria or yellow fever. Some of my friends have died."

"You'll be alright son." Ephraim reassures his son.

During the next two weeks, Robert Lee is able to rest, but he still feels weak. On Tuesday, the day before he is to report to the base, he feels extremely tired. He asks his daddy and mother to take him that day to Fort McPherson.

They take him to his commanding officer in the afternoon.

The officer says, "Robert Lee needs to be admitted to the base hospital immediately."

Mary Ann and Ephraim stay with him until the doctors have him resting easily.

They return each day to visit their sick son. Many of his cousins and aunts and uncles come by to visit. The room is full of beautiful flowers.

Robert Lee is medicated to the point that he is asleep most of the time, but arouses enough from time to time to speak with those visiting him.

His mother and father and his adult siblings are there several days later when the doctor says, "He will not recover. He is now in a coma and it does not look good."

Mary Ann, crying on Ephraim's shoulder says, "Oh! Doctor can't you do something to save him."

"I'm afraid we've done everything medically possible to save him."

"Maybe a miracle will happen. Let's pray!" Mary Ann says as she bows her head.

The family bows their heads as Ephraim prays to God to save their first-born son.

It isn't time for divine intervention as God takes the boy to Heaven later that evening.

The funeral and burial take place at Bethlehem Baptist Church three days later in the family plot.

The family, still in shock, a week later, receives word that Aunt Caroline Rainwater has passed away in her sleep in Atlanta. Four days later, she is buried at Ramah Baptist Church next to Joseph, her husband.

That afternoon as family and kinfolk gather around the fireplace at Ephraim's house, Mary Ann says, "It's sad that two deaths have occurred in a short span of time, but the good thing is we get to see each other. You know we do need to visit more before we all die. Y'all have another piece of cake, there's plenty."

Ephraim's oldest living son, James remarks, "Our family does have a lot of men in the military. There is Daddy and Uncle John J. and Grandpa Miles Rainwater; of course, none of us was around when he died; and there was Great Uncle Joseph. Is there any more who served Daddy?"

"Yes, many of my cousins and my Granddaddy's people have served our country. By the way, I was around when my Daddy was killed. I was two years old but don't remember anything. Your mother and I were little children during the civil war. My older brother was killed in that war and my Uncle Joseph died from a brain tumor while still serving. So we have been in lots of wars."

Mary Ann perks up, saying, "Yeah, I remember the civil war. One day a Confederate soldier passed by our farm and says to me, 'Get inside because the Yankees are coming and there will be many bullets zooming by.' I was so scared that I ran in the house and hid under the bed."

Little Charles asks, "Did the Yankees ever come?"

"Not here, but they sure did in Atlanta and Jonesborough. Your uncle John J. and my Uncle were deeply involved in the battle of Atlanta."

Little Charles ask his Daddy, "Why do we have to have wars?"

"Son, we have to protect our freedom. That's why."

"Well, why don't other people just leave us alone?

"That's a good question Charles; but this world has evil greedy people and we must be ready to defend ourselves. Does that make sense to you?"

"Not exactly, my Sunday School teacher says we should always love our neighbor. If everybody went by that rule we might not have to have wars."

"I agree with your teacher, but everybody in the world does not practice love."

"Why?"

"It is because they don't believe in Jesus. He's the one that taught us the rule to love one another."

"Oh! I see Daddy."

Family conversations and chatter continue as the adults try to overcome the sadness of family member deaths.

Everyone leaves in the evening wishing the world could practice love and not selfishness, greed and hate.

Life goes on in Fairburn, as the Rainwater family gets ready for Christmas. Ephraim goes out into the woods to find a nice little pine tree that will be a good-sized Christmas tree for their parlor.

With him is Charles holding the axe as Ephraim says, "Doesn't this look like a good tree for us?"

"It smells good; I like it daddy, let's get it."

"Okay, hand me the axe."

Chop, chop sounds the cutting as Ephraim chops down the tree. After he completes the task, he gives Charles the axe to carry and throws the tree over his right shoulder and the two head for home.

They walk into the house with the tree and Mary Ann looks at it and says, "What a nice tree Hon; you did better than last year. I love it! I'm getting excited about Christmas; how about you Charles?"

"I am too, Mama!"

The next day, there is a knock on the door. Ephraim goes to answer the knock. As he opens the door, he sees a Western Union boy standing at the door.

The boy announces, "I have a telegram for Ephraim Rainwater."

"That's me.

The boy reads this:

_____

To: Ephraim Dawson Rainwater
From: Theodore Roosevelt
Date: 20 December 1898

Dear Mr. Rainwater:

I am deeply grieved about the death of my friend Captain Robert Lee Rainwater. I just learned of this today and am so sorry I did not know about it earlier.

Please accept my deepest sympathy in the loss of your son. Please express this to Mrs. Rainwater and your children.

You parents should be proud of how Robert Lee served his country. He is a hero in my eye and his loss will be deeply felt in the Signal Corps.

Signed,
Theodore Roosevelt

Mary Ann walks in and ask, "What are you reading, Hon?"

"It is a telegraph from Theodore Roosevelt."

"Let me read it."

She begins to cry as she reads the telegram. She says between her sobs and through her tears, "That is such a nice note from Mr. Roosevelt. We should have notified him about the funeral. Robert Lee really liked him. I sure miss our son."

She leaves, goes into the bedroom and has a long crying session. Ephraim walks in, places his arm around her and gives her as much comfort as a husband can in a situation like this.

"Mama, Mama can I go play with my friends?" Comes out of little Charles.

Mary Ann, drying her tears with her apron, says, "Charles, if you have two legs you can, but I guess you really meant *may I*, isn't that right."

"Yes Mama, may I?"

"Sure, but be home before dark."

"I will Mama."

Mary Ann walks out on to the front porch where Ephraim is smoking his pipe. She snuggles up beside him and says, "I love the aroma of that smoke; what kind is it?

"It's Prince Albert."

"Is it in the can?"

"Yes!"

"Well, why don't you let the Prince out?'

"That's not funny."

"I know, but I'm just trying to feel better."

"I've got something that will make you feel better."

"What?"

"Come in the bedroom and I'll show you."

"But the children will see us!"

"Charles is out playing and the other children are out Christmas shopping and Edna is out with Annie."

"Okay, you sweet man, let's go."

Mary Ann and Ephraim being the ideal married couple make the most of every opportunity. They walk into the bedroom and make love.

Atlanta versus Farm Life

In Atlanta, electric lights and electric streetcars are now operational, but the power system has not, yet, come to Fairburn, nor has the telephone system. Out in the country, people still depend on kerosene lamps, wood burning fireplaces and stoves, outhouses for toilets, and wells for water. The farmer families in Fairburn do not mind. The Rainwater family enjoys this simple life.

After a good night's sleep early in the morning, Mary Ann awakes to light the kerosene lamps thinking, *I wonder what it would be like to flip a switch and the electric lights brighten the room*, but she doesn't dwell on that thought as she places firewood into the fireplace to warm up the house on this cold December morning.

Ephraim and his older sons are already out feeding the livestock. The pigs, cows, horses and chickens all have to be fed.

The other children, who are old enough, start fires in the other bedroom fireplaces in the house and empty the slop jars into the outhouse holes. The children complain about having to empty the slop jars, as they hold their noses.

Mary Ann kindles the iron kitchen stove with old newspaper and small dried twigs beneath the coal and starts it with wooden matches. In a little while, it will be hot enough to cook the biscuits and fry the ham and eggs. This is a typical morning breakfast at the Rainwaters.

Such is the life of all the farm families in the rural country. Those who have moved into Atlanta are citified; and enjoy many of the modern conveniences, such as electricity, inside plumbing, and central heat. Mary Ann thinks *those people are spoiled.*

David shows interest as he asks, "Ephraim is your Granddaddy, isn't that right?"

"Yes he is David."

When did they get electricity and telephones in Fairburn?"

"David, I believe it was in the 1940's, to the best of my memory."

"Thanks, I am just wondering when it happened."

Mary Ann, thinking about recent events during 1899, asks, "Ephraim, do you know anything about the Panama Canal project."

"Yes, the US Congress has created the Canal Commission to examine the possibilities of a Central American canal and to recommend a route. The United States and the new state of Panama have signed a treaty. The United States has guaranteed the independence for Panama and has secured a perpetual lease on a 10-mile strip for the canal. Panama is to be compensated by an initial payment of $10 million and an annuity of $250,000, beginning in 1913."

"That is interesting. It'll be quicker to ship to San Francisco."

"That's right, Honey. You know we've seen a lot of histories during the 1800's haven't we?"

"Lord yes! I'm looking forward to the 1900's."

Chapter 6

The Great World War

Mary Ann says, "Ephraim, do you know that next Monday is New Years Day!"

"Well we only have seven more days to live in the 19th century and then we begin the 20th century."

"Hey, let's have all the family over Sunday evening and celebrate the coming of the New Century together. We can get some fireworks and really have a blast. What do you say?"

Getting excited Ephraim says, "Let's do it! You plan the food and I'll get the fireworks and invite all of our family. We'll get in touch with our cousins and uncles and aunts, too."

> **My smart grandson asks, "Granddaddy didn't the 20th Century actually begin on January 1, 1901?**
>
> **"You are technically correct. How did you know that?**
>
> **"My teacher in school said that the year 1900 is the last year of the 19th Century and the 20th Century begins on January 1, 1901."**

"Back in 1900 most people celebrated January 1, 1900 as the first day of the 1900's as far as I know."

"I have heard that also."

"Let's go on with the story and see what happens."

"Okay, Granddaddy."

1900

What a beautiful night it is on Sunday evening December 31, 1899. The sky is dark with millions of stars shinning brightly through the blackness. The full moon gives enough light to see each other as all await the lighting of the fireworks. Ephraim's teenage sons, Charles and Felton are standing by ready to help their father with the fireworks at the stroke of midnight.

Everyone enjoys the fried chicken Mary Ann cooks for the stand-up to eat supper. Some of the elderly aunts and uncles are sitting in the few rocking chairs on the front porch. Ephraim places lamps on the porch, which make the event more romantic as all enjoy the last hours of the 1800's.

As the clock strikes midnight, Ephraim and his two young helpers begin the shooting of the fireworks. They place them far enough away from the family to provide save explosions.

Mary Ann hollows, "Don't let 'em burn you boys!"

The beautiful fireworks last for about thirty minutes, at which time all are ready to head for their homes to start the new Century.

Uncle Veasey Jr., who came from Florida, spends the night with Ephraim and Mary Ann.

Veasey says to Ephraim, "If my dad were still alive he would be 102-years old."

"My Granddaddy, your dad's brother, would have been 104-years old."

"I loved your Granddaddy, my Uncle James, the preacher."

"Veasey, how is your Coca Cola bottling business prospering?"

"I'm glad you asked. It is growing like wildfire; you should invest in the business and get rich!"

"I don't have the money to invest; but I hear Asa Candler is now advertising and pushing the product all over the country."

"Asa Candler has a great vision for the company. That's why I'm building bottling plants in all of North Florida."

After reminiscing for a while, Mary Ann notices Ephraim yawning and says, "I guess we need to go to bed, don't you think?"

"Yes it's getting late."

Veasey says, "It's not late; it's really early in 1900."

They all laugh and turn in for the night.

"Do you like to fish Granddaddy?"

"Sure, why do you ask?"

"Will you take me fishing?"

"That'll be fun!" I agree as I think *I can't refuse my precious grandson.*

"Can we go right now?"

"Yes, let's go."

We travel across town to my house, grab my fishing gear, dig up some worms and then head to the nearby lake.

Fishing is very relaxing for me and David seems to be enjoying it, too. After an hour, with no bites, we both are getting bored. At least I am.

All of a sudden, David has a bite. He is so excited that he is pulling in his first fish for the day.

"Look! Look! It's a big cat fish, Granddaddy."

"Good for you son."

We both begin fishing with greater intensity.

Another hour passes with no bites. I am not very patient and David must notice that I am impatient

"Granddaddy tell me some more of your war story."

We pack up our fishing gear and move over under a big spreading oak tree. I continue the story as David listens.

September 1904 is a special month in the life of Ephraim and Mary Ann. Their oldest living son, James Barnett Rainwater, is to be married on the 18th. Mary Ann is excited, yet sad as she is about to loose her son to another woman.

James now engaged to Lamora Hart has been in love for six months and is very anxious to marry. He feels fortunate to become the husband of such a beautiful and kind loving woman. However, he worries about his mother, who seems to be sad that her first child to marry will be leaving home to live with another woman.

James say, "Mama, think of it this way, you'll be gaining a daughter-in-law and I'm still your son."

"I know son, I guess I'm happy for you, but since Robert Lee died before he could marry I just hate loosing you. Do you understand, son?"

"You are not loosing me Mama. Lamora and I'll be living near home and will visit you frequently."

"Alright James, I'll look at it as gaining a daughter." She does shed a few silent tears.

The wedding on Sunday September 18 goes according to plans. Mary Ann accepts the fact that she now has a new daughter-in-law. The Hart family is a good family and Lamora is such a sweet and adorable girl. She is such a likable person and she knows that Lamora will be a good wife for her 26-year-old son.

She still has Amos and Charles at home as well as all the younger children. She wonders when Amos and Charles will marry. Amos now is 24 years old and Charles is 21.

Mary Ann tells Ephraim, "I guess we need to get used to loosing our boys to new wives."

"Do you remember when we married? Maybe our parents were glad to get rid of us"

"No they weren't. Your mother always liked me and I know my mother and daddy like you."

"I guess I'll be the one that gets upset when one of our daughters decides to marry. I'm not sure there is a boy good enough for our daughters."

Mary laughs as she says, "I know your time will come, but we'll be gaining a son-in-law, so don't worry. Edna is only 19 and hasn't found the right fellow yet, so your time is still way off."

Their times come sooner than they imagine. Amos marries the next year and Charles is dating a schoolteacher. Edna has her eyes on one of the Brock boys.

Mary Ann says to Ephraim, "I guess we will just have to get used to our children leaving home. You know I'm beginning to not mind so much because we are gaining great in-laws and that makes me happy."

When Charles nears 25, he announces to his mother and daddy that he and Bertie Belle Henderson are planning to marry on December 24. The year is 1908 and the wedding is still two months away. Bertie turns 23-years-old on October 10.

The Henderson family, a respected name in Hapeville Georgia, is a large family, much like Charles' own family. Bertie the oldest child is already working as a schoolteacher at the Flat Rock School.

Mary Ann asks Charles, "Son, you gotcha self a pretty lady with a smart brain. Do you think you can keep up with her?"

"Oh, Mama, just because she's smart doesn't mean I can't keep up with her. She's smart enough to pick me as her husband. I guess that's enough for me."

"Well Charles, I guess you got me that time."

December 24th comes around too quickly, but everything is all set for the wedding. It takes place at the Hapeville Methodist Church. It is a simple wedding without much fanfare. Only the close family and friends attend. There is no reception and Charles and Bertie Belle slip of to Atlanta in a T-Model Ford for the honeymoon.

Mary Ann is glad it isn't a big formal wedding since she is still has memories of the death of her first-born, Robert Lee. It was near Christmas time when he died of malaria just after the Spanish-American War. She thinks *I hope we don't have any more wars in my lifetime.*

"If President Theodore Roosevelt has anything to do with it we will not e in another war." Mary Ann says to her son Charles after he returns from his honeymoon.

"I hope you are right, but he only has one more year left in office."

"Whatdo you plan to do son? You haven't let me know where you and Bertie will be living."

"Mama, we have a place over at Flat Rock near College Park that we will be renting. I'm going to start a truck farming operation. Bertie will be teaching school nearby where we live."

"You are not going to forget about your Mama, I hope."

"Of course not Mama!" Charles loves his mother dearly and thinks *I will never forget her.*

The truck farm becomes very successful for Charles and Bertie. The city folk love to buy fresh produce from Charles' truck all year long and especially during the summer months. The income from the farm and from Bertie's teaching job provides a good income for the young married couple.

Charles and Bertie's Family Grows

Charles and Bertie's celebrate the birth of their first child on November 30, 1909. The first-born is a son. They name him Earl

Edward Rainwater. Bertie has to take leave from teaching for a while after the birth. Charles pays several Negro men who help with the farming.

Charles says, "Bertie we will have another farm hand when Earl is old enough."

"The way our truck-farming business is growing, you'll need him."

Two years later Charles and Bertie are blessed with another child. This time a girl, they name Agnes Mae. She is born on February 11, 1911. Bertie is still enjoying her teaching job at the Flat Rock School. Charles has two more trucks, three more mules and a need for two additional Negro farm hands.

Charles and Bertie continue to be blessed with children as a second daughter is born on January 30, 1913. They name her Evelyn Edna after Charlie's sister Edna. Bertie loves teaching school and watching the boys and girls learn at her school.

One of the fun things that Charles and Bertie love to do is to take their toddlers to Mary Ann and Ephraim's house in Fairburn. Usually in the summer, they spend a week at Grandma's house.

Bertie says, "Charles, I don't know who has the most fun at your mother's house, Earl or your mother."

"My mother has always been fun to be around. I guess she has fun with Earl and Agnes because of her fun loving spirit. She also loves to cuddle little baby Evelyn, have you noticed?"

"Yes, I noticed that. She has a way with babies."

Little Earl now 4-years old comes running into the parlor and says, "Mommy, I found the tea cakes!"

"Where did you find them?"

"Where Grandma hid them, behind the churn in the kitchen."

Mary Ann, listening to Earl, says, "Come here Earl, let me hold you while you eat the tea cake. I'll try to find a better hiding place next time."

"Why do you hide them Grandma?"

"Because tea cakes taste better if you think you are sneaking around to find them."

"Well I like 'em Grandma!" Earl turns toward Granddaddy to say, "Hey Granddaddy why did you marry Grandma?"

"Because she makes great tea cakes."

Everyone knows that Ephraim became enamored with Mary Ann because of her winning smile and quick wit.

Still sitting under the spreading Oak tree, looking out at the lake, David asks, "What's a tea cake?"

"You know those butter cookies that Mema cooks, well that is what a tea cake taste like."

"Hmmm, that's good. May I have some now?"

"Well go wash your hands in the lake water and I'll see if I can find some for you."

I packed a bunch in the tin lunch box, before we went fishing. I will open the box as David washes his hands.

When he returns, he spies the cookies, grabs a handful, and says, "Granddaddy, thanks for bringing these."

"My pleasure, just enjoy and thank Mema when we get home."

The story continues as David munches.

Bertie rings the dinner bell at the farmhouse. When her husband hears the bell ringing, he knows it's not dinnertime, so there must be a problem. He asks his farm hands to continue turning over the land for the next spring's crop as he hastily rushes to the house.

At the house, standing on the back porch, Bertie yells, "Charlie, the baby is coming, and I'm having labor pains already."

After three births already, Charles does not worry.

He calmly helps Bertie to the bedroom and says, "I'll fetch the midwife, you just lie down and rest."

He gets into his old T-Model Ford and rushes to the midwives' house down the road. She is on ready because she expects Bertie is about ready. She gets her stuff together and jumps into the car with Charlie.

They are back just in time. When they arrive at the farm, Bertie is having the labor pains very close together.

About an hour later the midwife brings out a cleaned up precious little baby boy. Charlie is so pleased that it is a boy since the last two were girls. Bertie is happy. They name the baby boy Charles Emory, after his dad and Bertie's brother, Emory. The birth date is January 10, 1915.

The Great World War

Charlie and Birdie sit around the kitchen table reading the Saturday morning newspaper and discussing the news about Europe.

Birdie says, "I don't know too much about Austria-Hungary, do you Charles?"

"I have never known much about geography, especially about Europe. Why do you ask?"

"In the paper today there is an article about the tensions in that country and Bosnia. There have been a lot of killings over there."

"That is over there. Why should we worry about that over here?"

"I'm not worried Honey. Since it is headline news, it may be serious."

"You know our government will not let us get involved with the feuds over there."

The tensions covered in the local Atlanta newspaper continue across the continent of Europe. The war really begins to escalate as Germany declares war on France and invades Belgium. This act violates Belgian neutrality, the status to which Germany, France, and Britain are all committed by treaty. Many consider it inconceivable that Great Britain will remain neutral as Germany declares war on France.

As David and I pack up our stuff at the lake and get into my car, David asks, "Did the Austria-Hungary country really start this war?"

"That was just one of many causes, David. There were a lot of cultural differences among the people in Europe and these differences caused problems then and still do today."

"I guess it is a complex situation, isn't it, Granddaddy? Why don't you call it World War 1 in your story?"

"It is complex David. When The Great World War started, no one dreamed of there being a second world war so my story describes the Great World War as it is known to the people in that era."

As I tell David this, I remember that David's mother said that he could spend the night with Gloria and me.

"David, your mother said you can spend the night with us tonight."

"Hot-digity-dog!"

Driving toward our home in Conyers, I continue to tell David what I know about the war and the Rainwaters.

Woodrow Wilson

As Charles Rainwater hopes for, President Wilson, in his first three years as president, steers a path of neutrality for the United States. Our ally, England, enforces a naval blockade of Germany in the hopes of cutting off supplies. Wilson and many in America feel neutrality is best for America. Germany responds to England's blockade by unleashing its U-Boats. U-Boats are submarines capable of staying submerged for long periods. They can sneak up upon their victims, often at night, and torpedo them. The Germans do not limit their attacks to military vessels. They consider any ship sailing in the war zone an enemy.

When the British cruise ship Lusitania sinks off the coast of England, killing over a thousand passengers including many Americans, America is furious at the brutality and demands a stop to this type of attack. After several other attacks, Germany agrees to end such attacks.

This agreement with Germany puts off the inevitable American entry into the war, although America shares a cultural bond with England and France.

Woodrow Wilson begins to actively campaign for Americans to support the allies. America increasingly sees Germany as the enemy. Germany is a dictatorship fighting against the great democracies of the world. America, as a democratic nation, feels the threat and is obligated to support them.

As America becomes increasingly less neutral, the British government intercepts a message from the German ambassador Zimmerman to the Mexican government. In this message, Zimmerman asks Mexico to attack the United States if America enters the war.

The British government turns this note over to the American government. It is eventually published in the newspapers, outraging Americans,

Wilson campaigns for a second term promising to protect freedom of the seas and now it seems he has little choice, so he asks Congress to declare war. There is much debate in Congress.

Wilson closes his speech to Congress by saying, "It is a fearful thing to lead this great peaceful people into war, but the right is more precious than peace and we shall fight for the things which we have always carried in our hearts."

On April 6, 1917, the Senate and House of Representatives vote overwhelmingly to declare war on Germany.

America has a small army; but it drafts millions of men and by summer of 1918 is sending 10,000 fresh soldiers to France every day. Germany has miscalculated the early arrival of so many U.S. troops. The German efforts to use U-boats to stop the arrivals from America fail. The British and French need American units to reinforce their troops already on the battle lines.

James (Jim) Rainwater

Jim bids his wife, mother, father and children goodbye as he leaves to board the train with other volunteers from Georgia for New York. He and forty other young men having completed their basic training at Fort McPherson are now on their way to France by way of train to New York and a troop ship across the Atlantic.

When Jim arrives in Europe, he and his fellow soldiers mix into an English infantry group deep in the farmlands of France. The Germans push back into a retreating formation and the worn out Brits welcome the Yank's help. Jim thinks *fighting in trenches is hell!* The food is terrible and baths are far and few in between. The fact that freedom for the western world is the goal keeps Jim and the other soldiers going. These boys are the heroes of their time.

As bullets zoom overhead, Jim remembers his young brother Robert Lee and his premature death he experienced as a soldier. *Now I'm fighting to keep the democracies of the world free* Jim thinks, giving him some comfort in spite of the bullets zooming overhead.

The troops are able to move forward the next day as the Germans retreat again. This means digging deep trenches again in this advanced position. The armored tanks help to chase the Germans closer and closer to the border between France and Germany.

Jim finds himself dazed and lying in a wheat field, not knowing how he got there or what is happening. It is twenty-seven hours before the medics reach him. They rush him, along with several other wounded soldiers, back to the field hospital.

Jim says, "Nurse, what is wrong with me?"

"Soldier you have been hit by the Germans with mustard gas, but you are one of the lucky ones."

"My skin is burning, why am I lucky?"

"If you inhaled any more of the gas, you might not be alive today. We are treating some of your fellow soldiers for inhalation of mustard gas and some have died. Your skin will heal and you'll be okay in a few weeks."

"I guess I understand; thanks for taking care of me."

Jim lay in a covering, much like a tent, made of propped-up sheets for weeks. It is a very painful experience and for these weeks, he receives great treatments with a special healing salve. After six weeks he feels like sitting up since the skin blisters on his skin are now small red spots and not as agonizing as before. *War is hell* he thinks.

The use of poison gas in this war is a major military innovation. The gases range from disabling chemicals, such as tear gas and the severe mustard gas, to lethal agents like phosgene. The killing capacity of gas is limited as compared to explosive artillery; however, the proportion of non-fatal casualties is high, and gas remains one of the soldiers' greatest fears. Both sides soon utilize effective countermeasures to gas attacks, such as gas masks.

As soon as Jim is able, he writes his wife a letter.

Lamora,

I'm sorry I haven't written to you lately but I am all right, so don't worry. I was in the hospital recovering from burns I received from mustard gas. The Germans are vicious in warfare, but I am back in my outfit now.

How are you and the children? I miss you all so much. I miss that good southern cooking that you are so good at in the kitchen. Tell my mother that I'm doing fine and will be home when this war is over.

Love you,

James

The year the United States enters into the war to join Britain, France and Russia in a war to end all wars, Bertie gives birth on May 30, 1917 to another son. The proud parents name him Oliver.

Bertie says to Charlie, "I hope Oliver never has to fight in a war."

"Maybe this war will be the one to end all wars."

"Charlie, did I hear right, that your mother has heard from Jim?"

"Yes, he's fighting in Germany with the French and Brits. He has been gassed but his recovery is alright."

"I know Lamora misses him and your mother does too."

"When I talked to Mama last, she said there were enough tears flowing to float a ship. We need to pray for my brother's safety."

"When you were in the Second World War did you have gas problems from the enemy?"

"We did not experience that problem. I think most nations agree not to use gas in warfare."

"Hmmm, but what if you did have gas shot at you?"

"We were prepared with gas masks, but never did use them."

"Granddaddy, I'm glad."

We drive into my driveway and as soon as I park, David jumps out yelling, "Mema, Mema I am here!"

He meets Gloria at the door and she gives him a big hug. David loves his grandmother very much.

"Granddaddy, I'm going to help Mema in the kitchen; you can tell me some more about the war story later."

David runs into the house with his grandmother.

This is fine with me, so I decide to get a little rest.

The rest is short lived, but enough; David is ready for more war story.

He asks, "Did they use airplanes during World War 1?"

"Airplanes were first used toward the end of that war. Let me go on with the story."

"I'm ready!"

The use of fixed-wing aircraft militarily first begins in this war. These are initially used for reconnaissance and ground attack. To shoot down enemy planes, anti-aircraft guns and fighter aircraft soon come on the scene. Principally the Germans and British create strategic bombers, though the Germans used Zeppelins as well. Towards the end of this conflict, aircraft carriers begin to appear on the scene.

Technological innovation is made at a rapid pace in the few years since the Wrights invention of the first flying machine. In 1914, only a few generals view aircraft as anything more than a tool for observation and reconnaissance. Toward the end of the war, both sides are integrating aircraft as a key part of their strategies.

With the growing importance and influence of aircraft, the need arises to control the air, and thus the fighter is born.

The Vickers Company is first to build airplanes armed with a machine gun. The airplane's crew consists of a pilot and a gunner. The gunner sits forward of the pilot with an uninterrupted field of fire ahead of the aircraft. This design proved unsuccessful in test flights. Many other designs are tried and discarded as being not practical.

A distant cousin to Jim and Charles, Troy Rainwater, grows up in Carrolton, Georgia, graduating from Georgia Tech. Troy learns to fly as a teen-ager at the Candler Field in Hapeville, Georgia. Flying is his first love.

His mother, Aunt Pet, tells him, "Son if God meant for us to fly, he would have given us wings."

"God gave us Wilbur and Orville and He allowed these brothers to design wings for us."

"I guess you got me, Troy, my boy."

"Mama I am joining the army to join Cousin Jim in France."

"Troy, that's no surprise to me."

Troy joins the army and ships out to Ohio for training in the small Air force, a wing of the U.S. Army. In his training, he flies the new Vicors FB5 all over the Midwest having the time of his life.

During Troy's training, a class discussion about fighter planes and there use in warfare is the subject.

Troy says, "I have the answer."

His surprised captain asks, "Really Troy! What's your solution?"

"As you know aiming a machine gun from one plane moving in three dimensions to an enemy plane moving in three dimensions is extremely difficult. I believe the perfect configuration is to place a fixed machine gun pointing forward to allow the pilot to aim the entire aircraft toward his target. This will eliminate the need for a gunner. The pilot becomes the pilot-gunner."

Captain Rogers is skeptical and says, "Troy, the propeller will be in the way with that configuration because the machine gun needs to be located close to the pilot to allow him to reload and service the gun should it jam. I'm not sure your idea will work."

"I know an engineer at Vickers who tells me he has a solution for the problem you have pointed out."

"What's his solution?"

"A timing mechanism that synchronizes the machine gun's burst of firing timing with the propeller rotation."

"I'll pass your idea on to the General."

The General request the idea be explored.

Troy, a Georgia Tech engineer works with his Georgia Tech engineering friend at Vickers. The idea works perfectly on the initial prototype model. The Army Air Force's top brass, pleased with the success, insist that this design be incorporated immediately. Planes with out a gunner in the rear are much lighter and therefore much faster and maneuverable. This is another plus for the design.

At the end of his training, the General promotes Troy to Wing Commander, to Troy's surprise. Troy is well qualified for this promotion.

> **"Granddaddy, did any of your ancestors fly**
> **an airplane in the war?"**
> **"Yes, my second cousin, Troy R. Rainwater,**
> **flew as a wing commander."**
> **"Tell me more about him, please."**

"All right."

Troy ships out from New York with his wing group, heading toward England. The troop ship includes his Army Air Force Wing and a battalion of infantry troops. Of course, the navy sailors that operate the ship are everywhere. After arriving in England, three weeks later, all the soldiers and sailors are relieved that no German U-boats attacked their ship.

In England, at a makeshift airport training station, Troy's wing meets the other American and British aviators. Several weeks of orientation and flying practices prepare Troy and his pilots for raids on the German military lines in France and Germany.

Troy loves the friendly English girls, although they have a funny accent, he thinks. At night, Troy visits the local pub to try to pick up the girls. He is all business at the base and all play at the pub. The English girls are fund of the American soldiers because of their sacrifice to help fight for their freedom. As Troy learns that the girls are friendly but have no part in any hanky-panky it suites him to just enjoy the times.

American General John J. Pershing, having pushed the French and English into use of more doughboy frontal attacks on the German entrenchments, asks for Troy's Air Force wing to go to Paris to offer air fire on the German trench lines. The French gave up on the frontal attack strategy as Pershing convinces them it is the best way to beat the Germans. The use of air power will enhance the strategy.

Paris

Troy arrives in Paris in the spring of 1917. His Wing flies in from England unscathed by the German fighter planes. As Troy, in the lead plane, observes the direction of the windsock, he leads his wing pilots into a landing pattern into the wind.

On ground, the pilots met by American doughboys in French trucks who take them to their temporary tent quarters. At the quarters, they receive their first orders for strafing the German lines 75 miles from Paris. Troy gives his pilots the rest of the day and night off to visit Paris before the flying mission the next day.

Troy heads to the nearest Paris bar. He has read that the French girls are out of this world. At the bar, he focuses his eyes on two Mademoiselles sitting at a small table in the corner. As he looks at them, they pay no attention to him.

Troy steps away from the bar and walks over to the girls and says to the blond one, "Hey, sweetie, let's go out."

She snaps back, "Je ne vais pas avec vous."

"Hey, we can have some fun."

"Sortez ici de l'yankee."

Troy, not understanding their French, feels that they do not like him. He thinks these French girls are not friendly like the English girls.

He walks back to the bar and knowing the bartender speaks English, he asks, "What did those dames say?"

The bartender laughs and says, "When you said, 'Hey sweetie, let's go out' she said, 'I'm not going with you', and when you said, 'Hey, we can have some fun' she said 'Get out of here Yankee.'"

Troy is disappointed that he does not score with these girls. He leaves the bar and walks down the street to get a taxi back to his quarters at the airport on the outskirts of the city. Suddenly he sees a familiar face about a block down the street. He thinks it might be his distant cousin Jim Rainwater.

As he gets closer, he sees Jim and says, "Well bless my soul, if it isn't my distant cousin."

Jim surprised to see Troy, smiles and greets him, "It's a small world isn't it. I never expected to see you Troy. What are you doing here in Paris?"

"We flew over from England to help you doughboys win the war. Say, I thought you were on the front fighting the Germans."

"Yes, I have been, but some of us have a rest period here in Paris."

"Didn't you just get out of the hospital? Someone told me you were gassed by the Germans."

"You heard right. I have now been out of the hospital for three months."

Troy is glad to hear that Jim is all right. As he looks at Jim he says, "Maybe you can change my luck with the girls. There are two good-looking girls over there in the bar. Let's go pester them."

"You know I'm married to Lamora and I don't cheat on her."

"Oh! Did you marry that good looking Hart girl?"

"I sure did."

"Come on Jim, I won't tell Lamora. Let's go have some fun with the girls."

"No, I told you I don't cheat on my wife."

The two walk for a spell and talk about the experiences of the war.

As they sit on a bench near a park, Troy asks, "Jim is your Grandmother and my Grandmother Cousins?"

"Yes I'm thinking; uh I believe you are right."

"Well what kin does that make us?"

"About fourth cousins I think."

It is getting late and Troy needs to get back to his quarters for the campaign tomorrow. He catches his taxi and Jim returns to his hotel as they bid each other good night. They plan to get together again soon.

Trench Warfare

Germany starts a huge advance after Russia surrenders, allowing them to move many troops to the Western Front. Using new storm trooper tactics, the Germans push forward some tens of miles and, by March 1918, the German advance comes to within seventy-five miles of Paris.

In the Battle, the American, Australian and Canadian infantry divisions spearhead a frontal attack successfully, with the help of Commander Troy Rainwater's Air Force Wing and his strafing of the German entrenchment. The Allies manage to advance 10 miles on the first day alone. These tactics end trench warfare and begin a return to mobile warfare.

Mobile Warfare

The machine-gun directly influences the organization of the infantry and air force and, by the middle of 1918, puts an end to the tactic of company-sized waves. Platoons and squads of men, with coverage from above by the air force become a winning strategy.

Jim Rainwater, with a division of American infantry troops, fights hand in hand with the use of light automatic machine guns. The Lewis Gun is the first true light machine gun capable of operation by one person, though in practice the bulky ammo pans requires an entire section of men to keep the gun operating. That is why it takes an entire division to advance swiftly while battling and chasing the retreating Germans.

Jim says to Oscar, a fellow infantryman, "See that airplane shooting a machine gun at the retreating Germans in front of us."

"Sure I see it. His actions are saving our lives."

"That's my cousin. He's the commander of the whole wing."

"Thank God for the air force!"

Troy, sitting in his fighter plane thinks, *I wonder if Jim is down there.*

Troy is having the time of his life, aiming his airplane toward the ground and pulling the trigger of his machine gun as Germans scatter about below him. It is a great thrill to then pull up his craft and fly toward the rear, loading his ammo belts for another round of attacks. He thinks *this is the most fun adventure since I first learned to fly at Chandler field in Hapeville, Georgia as a teenager.*

Unlike his cousin Troy, Jim is not having fun killing the Germans, even with the new more efficient weight weapons.

When he shoots and kills a young German, he is sad as he wonders if the soldier has a wife and children back in the fatherland. The fact that he is fighting for the freedom of all democratic countries of the world somewhat eases his conscience.

French Women

Jim and Oscar are hiding behind a French barn as they wait to advance further. A French girl looks around and smiles. Oscar says to the girl, "Embrassez-moi le chéri."

The girl runs quickly up to Oscar and kisses him on the lips.

After the girl runs back into the house, Jim asks, "Oscar what did you say to that girl?"

Oscar smiles as he replies, "I said 'kiss me sweetheart'."

"Where did you learn to speak French?"

"While we were stationed in Paris and you were busy writing to your wife, I was out talking to the girls and picked up a few handy phrases."

"My cousin, Troy, thinks the French girls are not so friendly."

"He's wrong. Most of the ones I have met are happy to see the Yankees who have come to liberate their country."

The French girl sticks her head out the door and says, "Battez lez allemands."

Oscar replies, "Oui jeune femme." The woman smiles and returns inside and closes the door.

Jim looking at Oscar questions, "What did you two say?"

"She said, 'Beat the Germans' and I said, 'Yes young woman.'"

"Oh! I understand now."

"Granddaddy, why is it called a World War, wasn't most of the battle in Europe?

"Much of the main fighting that affected America was in Europe, but there were war zones in Africa, India, the Pacific area, and Russia had it's own little revolution heating up between the Tsar and the Communist people. Some of the earliest fighting was in Africa, where French and British captured some of the German outposts. In India the people were fighting for their independence from Great Britain."

"Wow, it really was a World War!"

"Are you ready to hear some more?"

"Yes Sir, Granddaddy."

The Great World War Ends

Jim and Oscar march forward with their infantry company as the Germans retreat. Blessed with great tank and air protection, gives the men a relatively safe feeling. One of their last battles is at the Hindenburg Line.

Many German towns fall to the Allies and in Berlin, Kaiser Wilhelm is told that Germany has lost and must now surrender. There are no advances in the fall as details of the surrender are negotiated, leading to the Armistice on November 11, 1918.

Soldiers and civilians join to celebrate the end of a terrible war. Champagne and beer seems to flow everywhere. The streets of New York and London filled with celebrating crowds mark the order of the day.

Coming Back Home

"James Rainwater" the General's clerk hollers out at the ocean dock in England.

"Here" Jim answers, knowing that he may now pick up his duffel bag and walk up the gangplank to board the troop ship. Other soldiers stand silently, awaiting their name to be called to go aboard for the long voyage back to New York.

British men, women, and children are everywhere holding large signs that read 'Thanks Yankees!' The doughboys are thrilled to see such a turnout to offer thanks to the departing American troops.

Somehow, it makes it all worth it. Jim thinks about the thousands of men who will not be coming back—the ones that were killed in this war. He thinks to himself, *I guess God is not ready for me yet.*

Then his thoughts turn to Lamora, such a pleasant thought! He will be home for Christmas and away from all this foreign stuff will be behind him.

Suddenly as he stands on the troop ship deck, he hears the clerk call out the name 'Troy Rainwater.'

Then he hears his cousin answer, "Here." *Being with Troy will make the long voyage across the Atlantic less boring* he thinks.

As the steam engines churn away and the smoke stacks puff into the sky, the ship heads out to sea with New York City the destination. Several thousand troops are on board and all are tired and anxious to get home.

Thanksgiving dinner is served on the second day out at sea. Some are already seasick and do not enjoy the special dinner. Rations for the rest of the trip will not be as good as this day's food. Jim and Troy are two soldiers that dived into the dinner and ate with pleasure as they think of Grandma's cooking back in Fairburn, Georgia. Jim is the doughboy and Troy is the flyboy.

Troy says, "When I was strafing the Germans in their trenches, I wondered if you were down there doing some of the ground fighting."

"Yes I was Troy, in fact I saw your plane flying over and knew you were there helping us to win the war."

David lifts his hand and I ask, "Do you have a question son?"

"Yes Sir, Granddaddy."

"What's your question?"

"I am wondering if they used radios in World War I."

"That's a good question David, as a matter of fact radio was in it's infancy at that time."

"Do you mean it was just invented?"

"Well, the invention occurred several years before, but its practical use and commercialization of it was slow in starting.

"From 1896 through 1904, Guglielmo Marconi's groundbreaking demonstrations caught the attention of many in the military and especially in the Navy. Wireless telegraphy began to be used by ships for navigation and for distress signals. It still uses the Morse code as opposed to voice as we know radio today. In fact dot dot dot-dash dash dash-dot dot dot is the distress signal for *save our ship* (SOS)."

"That is interesting Granddaddy."

"Let me tell you some more about radio in the story"

Radio in the Great World War

The troop ship Commander, Alex Turner, walks over to Jim and Troy and asks, "You two are from the Rainwater family aren't you?"

Jim and Troy jump up, salute the ranking officer, and say in unison, "Yes Sir."

Turner says, "Gosh, I know about how the Rainwater men of the last century were quite innovative in the communications field as members of the U. S. Army Signal Corps. Are you part of that family?

Jim says, "Yes we sure are. My Uncle and my Grandfather were both actively involved in the early telegraphic communication technology."

"Troy, how about your family?"

"Well Jim and I are distant cousins, so I guess his ancestors are mine too."

"Men you might be interested in the new radio communications we now have on board. Hey, you may see our radio room now if you like." Turner suggest as he invites the two to go with him.

"Sure." Jim and Troy reply as they follow Turner up the steps to the ships bridge where the radio room is located.

"Rainwater your uncle and grandfather were primarily responsible for getting the military into more modern communications during the late 1800s.

"What you see here at this desk is the latest means of communications for the U.S. Navy and its ships everywhere. Since 1905, the U.S. Navy has equipped its entire fleet with transmitters, and set up an extensive chain of coastal stations. Radio is also employed as an aid to navigation.

"By 1913, numerous shore stations start to handle commercial traffic in areas where there are no private stations. "Finally, in April, 1917, with the entrance of the U.S. into this war, the government, led by the Navy, took over control of all radio communications for the duration of this conflict." Turner gives a little history to the boys.

Jim says, "Thank you, sir, this is very interesting."

Turner continues showing Jim and Troy the equipment as he says, "Let me introduce Seaman O'Henry, he is our operator for this shift. O'Henry this is Jim and Troy Rainwater.

"Nice to meet you gentlemen. Say the Rainwater soldiers are known throughout the military."

"Good to meet you too." Jim and Troy say.

"Well I know about the contributions of the Rainwaters to the communications in the Army Signal Corps. Are you any kin to those Rainwaters?"

"Yes we are." Jim and Troy answer simultaneously.

The ships commander asks, "O'Henry tell these soldiers about the latest technology in ship-to-ship and ship-to-shore communications."

"Yes Sir" as the commander leaves the room.

Then he turns to Jim and Troy and says, "With this key, I can send Morse code via radio to most anywhere in the world. The code goes through a modulator and then to the transmitter and on to the antenna where it radiates into the atmosphere. When these waves hit the stratosphere they reflect back to earth around the globe."

Jim interrupts to ask, "Can you send voice over the radio like we can do on the telephone?"

"Yes, I have a second modulator that I use for voice transmissions. You see this microphone here. I can speak into it and a voice signal transmits to those who are tuned to our frequency."

"Say that is very neat." Troy says.

O'Henry continues to explain the technology of radio. He explains that most of these new items are just now being used in a practical way.

He says, "Their use made a big difference in the war that has just ended."

Jim asks, "Can one pick up the worlds news via radio and type out a newspaper at sea?"

"Yes that's exactly right. Some of the passenger ships are now equipped to do just that. This keeps the traveling passengers updated to the latest news and financial developments, too."

The two cousins thank O'Henry, return to the ships deck, and enjoy each other's company during the trip as they play cards and read books to pass the time. After three weeks at sea, the ship pulls into the New York Harbor. The troops are to be disembarked according to their military units, the infantry first, and then the air force and so forth.

After standing on firm ground, in good old America, both Jim and Troy phone relatives in Atlanta to tell them they will be home soon. They spend the night in the Algonquin hotel in New York located on 44th Street in Manhattan.

Jim tells Troy, "This hotel seems like new even though it has been here since 1902."

"I like it, hey let's go get a drink in the Oak Room."

The two Southerners walk in to the bar and order bourbon and water.

The bartender recognizes the two as southerners as he says, "Youse guys must be from the South."

Troy asks, "How do you know?"

"I love your accent and most people around here drink Scotch whiskey."

"Well we drink bourbon and corn liquor in Georgia." Jim informs the bartender.

As the bartender goes to get the drinks, Jim says, "My mother and father don't believe in drinking alcohol, although I have seen them take a little wine for medicinal purposes."

"I have to slip around to do my drinking, too." Troy tells Jim.

After a couple of drinks, the two enjoy dinner, and then hit the sack, since they have to catch the early train for Atlanta the next morning.

Home Again

After a 13-hour train ride Troy and Jim arrive at the Union Terminal in Atlanta. Troy leaves for Carrolton and Jim catches a taxi to go home to Lamora and his four children in Flat Rock, just south of College Park, Georgia.

It is one sweet reunion as the doughboy embraces his wife and children. Lamora makes a pot of hot chocolate and the family sits

around the dining room table bringing Jim up to date about what
has taken place at home while the war was going on.

Lamora says, "Guess what! Your brother Charles and Bertie
have a new baby boy."

"When was he born?"

"He was born May the thirtieth about six months ago."

"What's his name?"

"Oliver."

Jim's eleven-year-old daughter Lillian looks at her daddy and
asks, "Did you get shot at during the fighting over there?"

"Yes, but I'd rather not talk about it."

> **David lifts his hand again. "Do you have
> a question son?"**
>
> **"Yes Sir, Granddaddy."**
>
> **"What's your question?"**
>
> **"Is Jim your uncle?"**
>
> **"Yes he is my father's brother, so that makes
> him my uncle."**
>
> **"Why did he not want to talk about the
> fighting in the war?"**
>
> **"I'm not sure about him, but most soldiers
> do not wish to talk about the memories of
> the horrifying times of their war experiences.
> Perhaps that's why Uncle Jim said that he'd
> rather not talk about it."**
>
> **"Thank you Granddaddy, you give good
> answers."**
>
> **"Thanks David. Now let's continue."**
>
> **"Okay"**

Lamora and her young children have a warm feeling now that
their man is home again. Before bedtime, they make plans to visit
Charles and Bertie, who live nearby, the next morning.

Little Ralph asks, "May we go see Grandma and Grandpa, too?

Jim quickly says, "Yes we will! I want to see Mama and Daddy too."

Aftermaths of the Great World War

While Jim is happy and feels good about being home, he still suffers from the nightmares of war. In the middle of the first night home, Lamora awakened by his wrestling with his pillow as she hears him yell out, "Shoot those Germans, now!" He is perspiring profusely at the same time.

"Wake up! Wake up Jim!" Lamora cries out.

When Jim awakes, he says, "I guess it is a nightmare."

He soon falls to sleep again.

Lamora lay beside her husband wondering how long he will suffer from this war stress problem.

The next morning after breakfast, Jim and Lamora load the four kids into the back seat of their Model T Ford and then go over to see Charlie and Bertie.

As they arrive at Charlie's house, Jim is greeted as a hero returning from war by his brother's family; but he does not wish to brag or talk about his service duties, however he is glad to see them. Jim's children Ralph, Lillian, Grace, and John love to play with their Uncle Charlie's children. Earl and Agnes are old enough to play with their cousins, so they all go out into the yard to do what kids like to do–play. Young Charles is only three and Oliver is not even a year old yet, so they stay in the house with the adults. Oliver is in his baby cradle and Evelyn is playing with paper dolls on the rug.

"Jim its sure good to have you back from the war!" Charlie says.

"I'm happier than any of you that I'm home. It seems like ya'll have all grown a lot since I left."

"I guess we have." Charlie pats his stomach, indicating that there is where he has grown.

Everyone laughs as Bertie says, "Oh! Charles you are not fat; you are just well rounded and that gives me more to love."

As truck farmers, Charles and Bertie have plenty of healthy food at their house and all of their children are extremely healthy. Bertie, having Saturday off, from her school teaching job, is in the process of canning some of the produce for later eating. She excuses herself to go to the kitchen to put the canning aside so she could enjoy visiting with her brother-in-law and sister-in-law. When she returns to the parlor, she asks, "Jim have you seen your mother yet?"

"We are going over there from here. Do ya'll want to go with us?"

"What do you think Charles?" Bertie asks.

"Sure, I always like going to see Mama and Papa. We'll need to take our truck to handle all the kids and adults." Charles states.

They all jump into the back of the truck with Charles, Bertie, and Lamora sitting up front. Jim sits in the back to watch the children as they drive to Fairburn to see Grandpa and Grandma.

Little Earl speaks up saying, "I love riding in this truck with the cool air blowing over my face."

It is always a merry time going to Grandma and Grandpa's house for all and especially for the children. Grandma Mary Ann has a way with the little ones and they love the attention she pays them. Her teacakes are always a delight.

On the way, Jim points out to the children the Bethlehem Baptist Church where Grandma and Grandpa attend. Devout Christians, his mother and father are very active in this church. Just a short distance away the truck pulls into the sandy yard of the home where he and his siblings grew up. To the right of the house there is a huge rock extending six to eight feet above ground. The kids love playing on this rock.

The smell of fried chicken sizzling in the pan on the wood burning stove is everywhere in the house. Just in time for dinner, Charles and Jim know that Mama will have hot biscuits and enough food to feed an army of Rainwaters and their children. Grandma greets everyone as she wipes her hands on her apron. She says, "Hey, I hope ya'll are hungry."

Around the dinner table all become very quite as they eat chicken and sop up their biscuits in the brown gravy.

Charlie brags on his Mama, "Mama this cooking is the best!"

Bertie says, "How about my cooking. I don't see you turning it down."

"That's because it is the best, too."

Bertie thinks *I should not have said what I said.* She places her arm around Charlie's shoulder and says, "Thank you honey."

After dinner, the Rainwater clan moves to the parlor to discuss the War with Jim.

Ephraim says, "Son, you are too young to remember the Spanish-American War; but it must have been some war over there in Germany and France; tell us about it."

"It was pure hell! I believed I was a goner when the Germans gassed us with that mustard gas. The medics saved me by taking me to the field hospital so quickly. Thank goodness, I didn't breathe in too much and that was a blessing from God."

Mary Ann asks, "Jim are the French girls as pretty as they claim?"

"Yes and no Mama. Some are very pretty and some are ordinary looking."

Lamora says, "Jim which one did you like?"

"Well some are friendly and some are not and I didn't have time to go with any of them. I was faithful to you sweetheart."

Mary Ann asks, "I hear that you ran into Troy. He's single and I'll bet he dated some of those French cuties."

"That's another story. You'll have to ask him about that."

Ephraim asks, "Jim is the telegraph still used like it was in my war?"

"Daddy it is used some; but we have telephones too. You will be interested in the wireless system that is just now being used on ships at sea. I think radio is the thing of the future."

Ephraim having an interest in communications from his Signal Corps days says, "I believe you are right Jim. I once gave a report about the new wireless when it was first being developed back in the late 1800s. I'm glad to see it being used as a communication tool for the Navy and the Army."

Jim is hesitant to talk too much about his times in France and Germany because it brings back too many bad memories, so he changes the subject.

He says, "Hey I notice that the old gas street lamps in Atlanta have been changed to electric lamps. When are you getting electricity out here in Fairburn?"

Ephraim answers, "That's a good question. They say it could be years before they stretch lines out here in the country; but you know we don't have electricity and it doesn't bother us even though it is the twentieth century and already 1918."

Ephraim realizing that Jim is uncomfortable talking about his war duties decides to ask one more question anyway. He asks, "Jim do you think that war was the war to end all wars?"

"Daddy I hope so. I understand that the President is working on a plan to prevent such wars in the future."

"That's right; I like President Wilson and hope he succeeds in his efforts."

Charles, looking at his watch, says, "Bertie we need to get the children home before dark. What about you Lamora?"

Bertie and Lamora agree it is time to take the children home.

They all kiss grandma and jump into the truck.

President Woodrow Wilson

On the way home Jim sits in the front with Charles, who is driving; the two women sit in the back of the truck with the children. Charles wants to know more about the President's peace plans because he is afraid some of his children might be in a war in the future.

To get the conversation started Charles says, "Jim I like President Wilson, but tell me about what news you have about his policy that will bring lasting peace."

"Well he is a devout Presbyterian and that should help, even though he is not Baptist."

"I'm not interested in his religion; I'm interested in his war policies."

"Okay, Jim as everyone knows, Wilson, a Democrat was elected President back in 1912. He proved highly successful in leading the Democratic Congress to pass major legislation including the Federal Trade Commission, the Federal Farm Loan Act and many other programs. As you may know, these legislative changes have been helpful in the growth of the South. That's why I like him.

"Wilson worked with others to negotiate peace in Europe.

"I hear that he plans to go to Paris next year and with his proposed *Fourteen Point* peace plan, try to create a League of Nations which will protect countries in the future from wars."

Charles says, "Thanks Jim, you have enlightened me and I do appreciate it. I guess since I wasn't in the war and since I spend most of my time down on the farm, I don't know about what's going on in Washington. I do know that Wilson is a smart man. You know, he graduated from Princeton and served as its President. Before becoming our President, he was Governor of New Jersey. I sure hope he succeeds in this League of Nations idea.

The Rainwater families arrive back at Charles and Bertie's place in the truck safely. Charles lay awake that night wondering about the League of Nations plan.

"Was the League of Nations like the United Nations?"

"Yes it was son."

"What happened to it?"

"Let me continue and I'll tell you."

"Okay."

The League of Nations

The League of Nations is an international organization founded as a result of the Peace Treaty. It encompasses Wilson's Fourteen Point Peace Plan recommendation.

The League's goals include disarmament, preventing war through collective security, settling disputes between countries through negotiation, diplomacy and improving global welfare. The League lacks an armed force of its own and must depend on the strong powers to enforce its resolutions.

The Republican majority in Congress, during Wilson's last years, is at odds with the president and the United States does not ratify the plan.

Charles and Bertie Rainwater

Living on the farm is hard work but rewarding for Charles and Bertie. Charles loves his time in the field planting and growing produce that people need and enjoy and most of all paying him good money for the upkeep of his family. Along with Bertie's salary at her teaching job at Flat Rock School, the happily married couple enjoys a prosperous living.

In 1920, Charles now 37 years old and Bertie 35 years old, enjoy their five young children. The oldest is Earl and at eleven years old, he is already a fine farm hand helper for his dad.

Agnes nine years old is always having fun, but stops to help mother wash the dishes and do other household duties. Evelyn is seven and learning how to primp in the mirror. Charles and Oliver, five and three enjoy playing together in the yard.

Bertie says to her husband, "We have three boys, but only two girls. I want another girl."

"You'll have to get pregnant first."

"I think you know how to get me pregnant Charles."

"I'm ready! How about you?"

"Not now Charles! It's the middle of the day."

"Yes mam! You know God has blessed us with five healthy children and I am so thankful for our life, aren't you Bertie?"

"We do have a lot to be thankful for. It seems only yesterday when my farm boy from Fairburn met his city girl from Hapeville."

"Time does fly! I am so happy with my city girl. I hope we have ten children together."

"Hey! Hold on. We don't need ten children.

"What ever happens is in God's hand."

Bertie returns to her housework and Charles returns to the farm with Earl and two other farm hands. Dinner has been good, but they need to get back to work.

During the rest of the 20s, the family prospers but with the struggles, that most Americans are going through during this post War depression time. The defense contracts and manufacturing of war materials has ceased causing some hard times for the working class people. Many people are still looking for jobs. The year 1921 starts great for Charles and Bertie as they have a bumper crop from the year before and have good winter crops, too.

Bertie announces, "Charlie guess what?" I have a surprise for you."

"Tell me about it.'

"We are going to have a baby. I'm pregnant!"

"When is the baby due?"

"Let's see, it is March now. So it will be sometime next fall."

In the fall of 1921 Bertie feeling her labor pains getting closer together rings the dinner bell outside to announce an emergency to her husband in the field. He drops his plow and runs to the house.

"What's the problem honey?" Charles says as he races into the house.

"I'm about to have the baby! Get Susie down the road. She helped me last time."

Charles rushes to Susie's house and the two run back to deliver the baby.

Susie says to Charles, "Get some towels and a pail of hot water."

Charles does as he is told.

Susie says, "Now you go in the living room and stay calm. I have everything under control here in the bedroom."

In a little while, Charles hearing the new babies' cries from the bedroom, jumps up, runs to the bedroom, and asks. "Is it a boy or girl?"

Bertie says, "My wish came true! It's a girl. Have you decided on a name?"

"No, I want to know what you think."

"How about Odell, what do you think, Charles?"

"That name has a nice ring to it. Let's do it."

Charles and Bertie now have six fine children with Odell born on November 18, 1921 as their last addition.

The small recession following the Great World War and the flu epidemic at the end of that war are hard times for all families and that includes the Rainwaters. "The 20s seem to be a different economic situation, don't you think Bertie?" Charles remarks.

"Well we are doing all right here on the farm and with my school teachers job, I feel good about the situation. Let's pray that it will always be good." Bertie said.

"Say Bertie, we haven't seen your mother and father in a while. Perhaps we can visit them after the baby is old enough to travel, if you like."

"Yes I do want to go down to Louisville in South Georgia if you think our truck will make it."

"Oh it's in great shape. Just let me know when we you are ready to go."

In January of 1922, Charles and Bertie bundle up all the children and take the truck down to Louisville to see Grandpa and Granma Henderson.

"It is good to see Mama and Papa." Bertie confides in Charles.

While in Louisville Bertie's brothers Clarence and Lunnie open a new car dealership.

"Chevrolet is giving Ford a lot of competition now." Clarence says.

Pointing to Charlie's Ford truck Clarence says, "You better get one while you are here."

"I have no problems with my Ford except the flat tires. Only two tires went flat driving down here and that's not bad."

Selma and Kitty are happy to see their sister.

Selma asks, "Bertie when are you going to stop having so many babies?"

"Bertie surprised at her sister's comments does not let it bother her because she knows that Selma has a sarcastic streak in her personality.

Bertie answers by saying, "When the good Lord thinks I have enough I guess." With that comment, the conversation ends between the two sisters.

After three days at the Henderson home, baby Odell's fretting and Charles' anxiety to get back home, they pack up and head north to their home in Flat Rock.

On March 19, 1925, Charles and Bertie are happy as their seventh child, a boy, is born.

Bertie says to Charles, "Look at all that red hair!"

"And you were worried that he would be bald like your brother John T. Henderson."

"Thank goodness he isn't bald like my kid brother."

The family receives God's blessings as the twenties experience an economical growth in America like none the country has ever seen before. Truck farming is prosperous as the city folk around Atlanta are happy to buy fresh produce from Charles' loaded new Ford truck. Earl, now 16, is plenty of help to his daddy and even Charles and Oliver do their part as younger children.

Bertie has plenty of help with her new baby. Agnes at 14 seems like a second Mama to her little brother Julius. She calms him down in her lap with rocking and a sweet singing voice.

Ephraim Dawson Rainwater is named after his Grandfather, because he is born on the same day and month as his Grandpa on March 14, 1927.

Bertie says, "He is the cutest baby of all."

Charles asks, "What shall we call him, Ephraim or Dawson?"

"How about Dawsie? I like that better than Dawson or Ephraim."

"My daddy will be proud to know that he has a grandchild who is named after him."

"I worry about raising a bunch of boys to fight in wars and I sure hope we are not." Bertie, looking at Charles, expresses her concerns.

"The Great World War was the one to end all wars. It was 10 years ago and I still have hope."

"Let's pray and hope it is the end of wars; but the Bible said there will be wars and rumors of wars as a sign of the end of time."

Charlie does not have a comment after that sermon from Bertie.

Earl lands a job at the new Chevrolet plant in Lakewood and Charles misses his help on the farm. Charles says to Bertie, "You know, I am feeling too tired to continue all this farming by my self. Little Charles and Oliver are of some help but not enough."

"Are you feeling all right Charles?"

"I guess I get tired easily now, but I'm okay."

"Why don't we move closer in to Atlanta and you can have just a small garden in the back yard to grow some vegetables to sell? Maybe that will be of help to you."

"Well, I will give the idea some thought. Hey, it does make sense to me. Let's do it."

College Park, Georgia

The family looks for a home to rent with a large back yard in Hapeville or College Park, just south of Atlanta. They find one on East John Wesley Avenue in College Park. The back yard is not as big as they desire, but it will have to do. Bertie can teach at the local grammar school and Charles can grow vegetables and have a cow and chickens in the back yard. Earl can ride the streetcar to work in Lakewood. This works out for the Rainwaters as Charles has less pressure to farm such a large one like the Flat rock farm. Julius is now three and Dawsie is one-year old. The good Lord is about to bless this family with their ninth child.

Bertie says, as she holds the newly born baby at Grady Hospital, "Finally, another girl, I am so happy!"

This is the first baby to be born in a hospital. All the other eight were born at home using a midwife.

Charles says, "Bertie I am so glad we didn't have to go through the berthing process at home like in the past. It is so much easier this way."

"You got that right, honey, and it's safer, too."

Charles' father and mother come up to the hospital to visit their new granddaughter.

Ephraim asks, "How do you know it's your baby, Bertie?"

"I just do! I trust the doctors and nurses to keep the babies identified."

When they bring the baby home, Agnes, now seventeen, is a godsend.

"She is so good at taking care of babies." Bertie says.

Bertie is pleased to have so many helpful children at home. She thinks, *'That's why God blessed me with so many children.'*

The Great Depression

The year Nineteen Hundred Twenty Nine is bad news for the stock market. Everything is bad and a depression seems inevitable for not only the country but also the world in general. Secretary of the Treasury Andrew Mellon advises President Hoover that shock treatment will be the best response.

Mellon says, "Liquidate labor, liquidate stocks, liquidate farmers, and liquidate real estate. That will purge the rottenness out of the system. High costs of living and high living will come down. People will work harder and live a more moral life. Values will adjust and enterprising people will pick up the wrecks from less competent people."

Hoover rejects this advice, not believing government should directly aid the people, but insists instead on 'voluntary cooperation' between business and government.

Charles worries about how is family will survive.

He says to Birdie and Earl, "The rent on this house is more than we can afford."

Earl says, "There is one for rent down the street that has more land for gardening and for our cows and I think it rents for less than this place."

"Well let's go look at it before we make a decision." Bertie suggests.

"Okay let's go." Charles agrees.

After looking it over, Bertie says, "It does have more yards for growing things and the pasture is very large for our two cows and the bull."

Charles asks Earl, "What do you think son?"

"It will be crowded in the house. It looks like the young ones will have to sleep in the hall and I'll have to sleep in the same room with Charles and Oliver. If I get married soon, that will free up some room." Earl tells his father.

They make the move down the street. Early Saturday morning, Earl, Charles and Oliver load up the Ford truck and after several short trips, move everything to the new rental house. Earl walks the cows down to their new home one by one. Charles places all the chickens in a cage and loads them on the truck for a final trip.

"I think we should go back to kerosene lamps and stop paying Georgia Power Company for our light bill. We cook and heat with a wood burning stove and fire places, so why not?" Bertie suggests.

No one objects to that decision. Most of the people in the neighborhood do have electricity and even a telephone, but the Rainwater family and its nine children can't afford those luxuries. Bertie continues to teach school as Charles seems to have health problems that just will not go away. Earl and Agnes help with their jobs, even though employment is hard to find in the 30s.

"President Hoover has not done much to improve the economical situation." Charles says to Bertie.

"We should not have elected a Republican."

"Well, why did you not vote last time Bertie?"

"You are the man of the house! I depend on you to vote for us."

"I hear that Franklin D. Roosevelt is running for president on the Democratic ticket this November. Most of the South will vote Democratic and that includes me."

"Let's pray that he can steer our country in the right direction."

The year, Nineteen Thirty Two, is a bad year for most of the population and it is no better for the Rainwaters. Bertie gives birth to her tenth child, a boy they name him Calyer Henderson using Bertie's maiden name as his middle name. Henderson is born on January 19 leaving Bertie without an income for several months. Charles develops rheumatic fever making him unable to garden, but he does get a few part-time jobs early in the year to help feed the family. Earl marries Kate the year before. Earl and Kate have a baby boy born in January. He is a junior. Earl Sr. is unable to help his mother at this time.

Many people in the world are starving, but Bertie and her children are able to grow enough food to keep the Rainwaters from starving. Son Charles has to quit high school to help his mother feed and clothe the family. Agnes marries Leonard Horton in May of 1932 and that took away her ability to help her Mama and Daddy at a time when the father is seemingly getting worse in his health.

Death

When things seem to be at their lowest level Bettie's husband Charles Edward Rainwater dies on a hot day in Georgia on August the Second of 1932.

Julius, the seven-year-old, knows something bad is about to happen, since Evelyn asked him to take Jean and Dawsie out to go play in the sand box. Baby Henderson is in his crib near Odell.

Dawsie 5 and Jean 4 play in the sand as Julius talks about Papa's death.

Dawsie says, "That part-time job roofing caused him to die."

Julius does not reply because he does not understand the cause of his Papa's death.

Julius walks over to the corner of the front of the house and watches two men with his daddy on a stretcher passing through the front door. One of his daddy's hands is sticking out of the edge of the sheet. The hand bounces against the door facing and throbs around like a drumstick. Julius goes back to the sandbox trying to hide his crying from his younger siblings.

The next day a kind neighbor takes Julius and Dawsie by the hand and walks with them to the barbershop on Main Street in College Park to get haircuts. That night Grandma and Grandpa Rainwater and Grandpa and Grandma Henderson and lots of uncles and aunts come to the house bringing food. It is a very sad time for all.

The funeral is at the Hemperley's Funeral Home in East Point, Georgia. The entombment is in the graveyard at Bethlehem Baptist Church in Fairburn.

President Franklin D. Roosevelt

The economy continues to slump further each month. Franklin D. Roosevelt is elected President in November of 1932 on his 'new deal' reforms. He promises to give the government more power to help ease the depression. Never in the history of the United States has unemployment been so high and business activity been so low. Banks, stores, and factories close, leaving millions of Americans jobless, homeless, and penniless. Many people come to depend on the government or charity to provide them with food. The new Democratic president takes office in 1933 after his landslide election in the fall.

Bertie, a strong industrious person, works at three jobs to provide for her family. She teaches school in the daytime, tends the Carnegie Library in Atlanta at night and sells corsets to women on the weekends.

Bettie's family is not hungry during these hard times as are many who line up at the soup lines to get food to keep from starving. Julius, Dawsie, Jean and Henderson do not know they are poor since they are so young. Earl and Agnes are starting their own families. Evelyn and Charles will marry soon, respectively to Nolan and Dorothy. Oliver is still in high school and Odell is just 12 years old but wiser than most girls her age.

These experiences make strong individuals of Bettie's children as she teaches them how to face life and work for a living. In addition to the cows and chickens, Bertie is able to hire a Negro and his mule to continue plowing the garden for planting of food for the family. She even plants a whole section in the field with rows of Jonquil flowers for selling in late January and February and early March.

When Dawsie and Julius reach the age of eight and ten, Mama wraps several dozens of bunches of Jonquil flowers, using damp newspaper around each bunch and places them in four market baskets. She sends her two young boys to Atlanta alone to sell the flowers. Every little bit of money comes in handy for clothing and feeding the family. Julius and Dawsie carry the four baskets to the streetcar line in College Park each Saturday morning during these cold months, heading to Broad Street and Whitehall Street in downtown Atlanta.

Julius says to Dawsie, "You know the Government is passing out hams to needy families but Mama wouldn't let then leave one for us."

"Why? I like ham."

"You know our Mama, she is so independent. She doesn't believe in accepting charity. She said we should work for what we get. She said some people are lazy and that's why they accept charity."

The two brothers return home Saturday night having sold all their flowers. They present their mother with seven to eight dollars to help feed and clothe the family.

Chapter 7

The Second World War

In the late 30's the depression worsens. By 1937, the American economy takes an unexpected nosedive, lasting through most of 1938. Production declines sharply, as do profits and employment. Unemployment jumps from 14.3% in 1937 to 19.0% in 1938.

Bertie Rainwater still working three jobs is barely making enough to keep her family going. Thanks to her older children who help make up the difference. Rent in College Park is more than she can afford, so with Earl's advice she finds a place to rent in Hapeville, an adjoining little town nearby. This new place saves some money; so, she stops teaching and works the day shift and evenings at the Atlanta Carnegie library.

Oliver marries Elizabeth and the two live with his Mama to help pay the rent. This helps him, his new bride, and his Mama too. Odell attends Russell High school in East Point nearby. Oliver graduates from Russell High. Julius, Dawsie, Jean and Henderson all attend College Street grammar school, just up the street from home. Bertie wants all of her children to get a good education.

WW II

With the grace of God, Bertie and her family survive the worst
of times. By 1939, the depression begins to ease up, as jobs are
now more plentiful. Odell graduates from Russell High School;
Julius enters the new high school in Hapeville; the three younger
children are still in grammar school. With the money from
Odell's job and Julius' paper route, their Mama works and is able
to provide for the family.

> **"You know you still have your World War
> II uniform Granddaddy."**
> **"Yes I do son. You still like to try it on
> don't you?"**
> **"The dress coat comes down below my
> knees, but it makes me feel like a soldier."**
> **"The moths have just about eaten it up."**
> **"That's okay Granddaddy. Tell me when
> did we get into World War Two?"**
> **"I'm getting to that. Just be patient."**
> **"Yes sir, I will. Did Hitler start it?"**
> **"Youngman, I'm proud of you! You know
> your history; don't you?"**
> **"I know a lot more now that you are telling
> me about the Rainwater family and how some
> of them fought in wars."**
> **"Thank you David. Yes, Hitler did start
> World War Two in my opinion. Let me tell you
> about it as we continue the story."**
> **"This is so interesting; please tell me some
> more."**

Adolph Hitler, who has risen to power as Chancellor of
Germany in the early 30s, makes a speech to the German people
on January 30, 1939 in which he predicts the annihilation of

the Jewish race in Europe. In September, just nine months later, Germany invades Poland without warning. By the evening three days later, Britain and France are at war with Germany and within a week, Australia, New Zealand, Canada and South Africa join the war. The world is now thrust into its second world war in 25 years.

Many Americans join the Canadian Royal Air Force to aid in the war effort. As more and more supplies are needed to aid the Europeans, rationing of gasoline, sugar, and meats becomes necessary at home. Ordinary families have a limit of three gallons of gas per week.

The rationing does not bother Bertie Rainwater, as she does not own an automobile. Her family is accustomed to doing without, so they are doing their part in saving things for the war effort; she reminds her young children.

Julius asks, "Mama, Do you think the United States will have to fight in this war?"

"I think Roosevelt is taking the stand that we'll help with supplies but so far we haven't declared war on Germany as our friends in Canada have done." Bertie says as she continues, "Lord, I hope not because I have six sons that are and soon will be old enough to serve in the armed services."

Many young men are joining the army, navy, and marines even though the United States is not at war. Signs everywhere in storefront windows show the red, white, and blue Uncle Sam pointing at the onlooker with the words, "*I want you.*"

Julius the oldest son still living at home is just 16 with only two more years before graduating from Hapeville High. Bertie isn't worried because a man has to be 18 before he can join the services. The Merchant Marines will allow a boy to join when he is 17.

At the new Hapeville High School, Julius becomes friends with several boys in his class. It seems as if this group of friends enjoys all the same things and hang out together doing what teenage boys do. Jim McLaughlin, Jerre Williams, Hansel Barnett,

Dillard Rosser, Lamar Foster, John Haralson and Bud Kincaid are all friends with Julius. The boys ride their bicycles to hangout and have fun. As the war in Europe progresses, these boys wonder if they will ever be involved in it. Their mothers hope not. Bertie, in particular, with six sons certainly hopes that Julius will not have to serve in the World War. The United States, so far has only participated by manufacturing war materials for the Allies.

Julius' friend Hansel is the first to buy a car. With help from his father, Hansel buys a 1934 Ford. Hansel with his *'pride and joy'* uses it to deliver papers for the evening paper *The Atlanta Journal*. Since Julius has the same territory in Hapeville for his delivery of the morning paper *The Atlanta Constitution*, they deliver their papers on Sunday mornings together; this utilizes Hansel's newly purchased used '34 Ford, to the delight of Julius.

It seems that all of Julius' friends work to help their families and to provide spending money for themselves. Jim McLaughlin and Jerre Williams run a small fruit and vegetable stand near the downtown area of Hapeville. This fruit stand, on busy Highway US41 running parallel to the railroad tracks, is a favorite hangout spot for Julius' friends. There they smoke cigarettes freely and drink their cokes with peanuts to satisfy their appetites, away from their meddling parents. All of the boys have parents at home except Jerre who has moved in with the McLaughlin family.

When Jerre was 16, he and his mother visits Shreveport where she becomes ill, under goes an operation and dies of pneumonia at the young age of 38. Jerre is an only child and his stepfather does not know what to do with the 16-year-old punk kid.

Jerre receives a letter from Jim McLaughlin inviting Jerre to live with his family until he finishes High School, with the approval of Jim's parents. He pays room and board.

His stepfather is glad to get rid of him. His alcoholic stepfather agrees to pay the room and board; but sent money only for two months, moves to New Orleans and Jerre never hears from him. Jerre goes to work at Chapman's drug store to earn his own money. That is how he came to live with the generous McLaughlin family.

A Date, Which Will Live In Infamy

The year 1941 is going smoothly since war defense jobs are plentiful and prices are still low because of Roosevelt's reconstruction policies placed into policy during the depression days.

Julius and his friends like to hangout together on Sunday afternoons. After attending church at either the First Baptist Church of Hapeville or the Methodist Church of Hapeville, the boys meet at Jim's house to play together. Jim's cousin, Gloria Welch and his sister, Betty, both now 13, like to hang around with these 16-year-old boys. Gloria, visiting with her mother from Sylvan Hills in Atlanta, seems to be more sophisticated than her country friends in Hapeville are. She does not know it, but Julius hopes someday he can date Gloria.

On this Sunday December 7, 1941, Julius, Hansel, Jerre, and Jim leave the young girls behind and ride in Red's (Hansel has red hair) '34 Ford coupe to his house to listen to some new records he purchased last week. At Red's house, as they listen to records, Mr. Barnett sticks his head into the room and yells, "Did you boys hear the news?"

"What news Daddy?" Red asks.

"The Japanese have just bombed Pearl Harbor in Hawaii." I'll bet this will mean war."

Red closed the record player's lid as he says, "Let's go tell the girls at your house, Jim."

Off they go, wondering if they will have to go into the service.

Jim says, "We are just 16-years-old. We don't have to register for the draft until we are 18."

"If this brings us into the war, I'll bet it will be over before we are 18." Julius says.

"I hope so." Jerre says.

"Were you afraid of going in Granddaddy?"

"No, I was too young to be scared. The whole story about war seemed adventurous to me and my friends, too."

"What did you do?'

"Being only 16 nothing much changed for me. I was finishing high school the next year and then another year after that before turning 18, so I just went on like nothing happened."

"That's cool Granddaddy. When did you learn about the details at Pearl Harbor in Hawaii?'

"Let me tell you."

"Okay."

When the boys arrive back at Jim's house, his daddy has the radio on and everyone sits in the living room around the family radio to listen to the latest news.

On the radio, everybody listens intently to this news report:

A Japanese carrier fleet has just launched a surprise air attack on Pearl Harbor. The raid has destroyed most of the American aircraft on the island and has knocked the main American battle fleet out of action. Three battleships have been sunk, and five more are heavily damaged. Four American aircraft carriers now at sea have escaped destruction.

Jim's father, whom Gloria calls Uncle Jim, says, "Kids I think this is going to bring on war involvement for our country. We'll have to wait until tomorrow to hear what the President has to say."

The boys leave to return to their respective homes not knowing what to expect next.

On December 8, 1941, President Roosevelt addresses Congress and the Nation on the Radio. All ears listen to his address as America, shaken by the news of yesterday, listens to what the President will tell Congress. The president addresses the nation:

"Yesterday, Dec. 7, 1941 - a date which will live in infamy - the United States of America was suddenly and deliberately attacked by naval and air forces of the Empire of Japan. ......

....

I ask that the Congress declare that since the unprovoked and dastardly attack by Japan on Sunday, Dec. 7, a state of war has existed between the United States and the Japanese empire."

You Are In The Army Now!

At Hapeville High School, everyone is talking about the President's address. The teachers, with permission from the Principle, allow the pupils to listen to the message on the radio. Many of the seniors are leaving to join the armed services.

"Jim, I wish we could join." Julius says.

Jim says, "We have to be 18 you know."

"Oh I know and my mother tells me to get joining the service out of my head until I graduate from high school."

In the next day's Atlanta Constitution morning paper, further news about the Japanese attack:

At Pearl Harbor, the main dock, supply, and repair facilities are repaired quickly. Furthermore, the base's fuel storage facilities, whose destruction could have crippled the Pacific fleet, are untouched. The attack united American public opinion to demand vengeance against Japan. The United Kingdom declared war on Japan the same day President Roosevelt asked Congress to declare war on Japan. Now the United States is part of the Allies fighting against the Axis of Germany, Italy and Japan.

"**What are Allies and Axis Granddaddy?**"
"**The Axis was the bad guys and the Allies were the good guys.**"
"**Which countries were the Allies?**'
"**Prior to December 7, Most of the European countries including the United Kingdom and its colonies and possessions around the world were part of the Allies.**"
"**What about after December 7?**'
"**Let me tell you in the story.**"
"**Okay.**"

After the attack on Pearl Harbor, Panama becomes an Ally on December 7.

Then, of course, the United States including American Samoa, Guam, Commonwealth of the Philippines, Puerto Rico, U.S. Virgin Islands, Costa Rica, Dominican Republic, El Salvador, Haiti, Honduras and Nicaragua all join the Allied forces on December 8.

On December 9, China, who has been at war with the Empire of Japan since 1937, Guatemala and Cuba become our Allies.

Later, on December 16 the Czechoslovakian government-in-exile joins the Allied group.

Graduation 1942

The first class that began as freshmen in the new Hapeville High is now ready to graduate in June of 1942. It is also the first wartime class to graduate, as many of the boys in the ROTC will go directly into the service when they reach 18 years of age. The rest of the 17 year old students leave graduation and seek full time jobs to support themselves and some, like Julius, will help support their mother and siblings.

Julius tries several jobs before he finds a good paying job as a carpenter's helper at the Fort Gilliam Quartermaster base being built in nearby Conley Georgia near Forrest Park. Not having a car, he bums a ride each day with one of the carpenters that live in Hapeville. *The work is hard* Julius thinks but he is used to that, having worked at some type of job since before he was 10.

The Hapeville friends begin to lose contact with each other during the weekdays but get together on weekends. Saturday night is especially fun when Gloria's mother invites the gang to come over and dance to records in her living room. She pulls the carpet away to make a space for dancing on the hardwood floor. Julius does not know how to dance but he tries to learn by dancing with Gloria, who can dance. Her beautiful blonde hair and soft feminine body is a thrill to touch. Julius does not know what love is all about but he has a desire to find out.

In the fall of 1942, several of Julius' friends join the service. The rest of the gang misses them but know that their time will come soon enough. Julius leaves his job as a carpenter's helper and works in a special radio class at Georgia Tech as a stock boy. Radio technology has always intrigued him. During January and February of 1943, Julius becomes a student of this class and learns from good teachers about radios. The WSB AM radio station was born in Atlanta the same year that Julius was born, 1925.

This form of bringing news and entertainment into the home has always been of interest to Julius.

Studying hard at the radio class does not stop Julius from having fun. A few dates with Gloria, going to a movie or eating somewhere in Atlanta brings the male hormones in the growing teenager, who has much to learn about true love. Having no car, he and Gloria take the trolley to downtown Atlanta for the few dates when time permits.

> **I am the one interrupting the story this time as I say, "David are you listening?"**
>
> **"Yes I am. Why did you stop?"**
>
> **"I stopped because I'm thinking about all the events in the war. If I try to cover all of these, it will be too much for both of us.**
>
> **"Which parts can you tell me Granddaddy?"**
>
> **"You know David, I am most familiar with my experiences in the War over in the Pacific and my friend Jerre has some interesting times in England during the War, so I am going to tell you about the two of us. Is that all right David?"**
>
> **"What ever you say Granddaddy, it is all right with me."**
>
> **"Good, this will let me tell you about the Japanese war zones and also the German war zones.**
>
> **With David's blessings, that is what I will do as I continue with Jerre first.**

Jerre 1942

Jerre Williams refuses to receive his Hapeville High School diploma unless he is credited him with the Scientific Course, which will allow him to enter any college of his choice. To achieve this Jerre takes the required Science courses during the summer of 1942. At the end of that summer, he receives his diploma. He is still living with the McLaughlins and working at Chapman Drug store as a *sweet water chemist.*

His real father, a master machinist with the Louisiana & Arkansas Railroad in Shreveport, invites Jerre to take a job with the Railroad, where he is employed. Unfortunately, his father does not send money for a bus ticket. Being a resourceful person, Jerre takes his valued portable dry-cell radio that he has bought with money he has earned earlier as an Atlanta Constitution carrier to Dr. Chapman and asks if he could swap it for a one-way train ticket.

With that even swap deal, he arrives in Shreveport, Louisiana twelve hours later. He checks into a three-story boarding house costing $5.00 for two weeks rent. His landlady provides him with a room, breakfast, sack lunch & supper. He shares the one bath with six others.

Having just turned 17, Jerre starts working at the railroad as a Machinist Apprentice. Jerre thinks *this $1 per hour is a good hourly rate for a punk kid.* Always up at 5AM having breakfast and with his sack lunch in hand, he rides the streetcar to the roundhouse where he works. Sadly, Jerre's father, second wife and stepson do not invite him to live with them and he seldom sees them.

War Time Service for Two GI's

(The experiences for Jerre and Julius are representative of many soldiers and will cover both theaters of the War.)

Jerre 1943

Jerre, now 18 is a young and healthy draft candidate. He ponders the decision about his future. He has always dreamed of being a pilot so, he takes the U.S. Army Air Corps exam and just barely

misses passing it. Rather than hang around Shreveport he decides
to volunteer, provided he can be placed in the Army Air Corps.

In December 1942, he is sworn into the service at Fort
Hamburg, Louisiana on the Red River. He remembers, when as
a child, visiting that city where he and his friends played in the
24-inch sewer line, which empties into this river.

Thirty new inductees, including Jerre, leave Fort Hamburg
on a Greyhound bus for the trip to Camp Polk, Louisiana where
initial training takes place. While waiting for basic training
assignment, Jerre works with the quartermaster issuing uniforms
to new arrivals. Jerre witnesses some of the red neck southerners
playing pranks on new Negro inductees and although born and
raised as a Southerner he is sensitive to the feelings of the Negros
and dislikes seeing them abused.

On a cold day in January 1943, Jerre and his fellow new
soldiers are to board a troop train for an unknown destination.

After loading his gear for an all-night trip, Jerre says to Jake,
one of his fellow soldiers, "I feel like I'm catching a cold. I'm
aching all over."

"You need to go to the sick bay and let the doctors treat
you."

"Oh, I'll just rub some Vicks salve on myself. I don't need a
doctor."

After loading on the troop train, Jerre feeling hot opens the
window in his train compartment to cool off as he tries to sleep
over the rickety rack rickety rack train sounds.

Arriving at Sheppard Field in Wichita Falls, Texas just south
of Oklahoma the next day and feeling sick, Jerre asks, "Sir, may
I see a doctor?"

The Sergeant in charge barks, "Okay soldier you came here
for basic training and not to be sick."

Jerre then asks the Lieutenant the same question.

The officer feels Jerre's forehead and says, "You have a fever.
Go to the Doctor now."

The Field Doctor examines Jerre and diagnoses the high fever; he sends Jerre immediately to the base hospital where he spends more than a month recuperating from double pneumonia. After discharge from the hospital, he is still weak but must still complete his basic training.

Basic training in the Army Air Force is just as tough as it is for regular ground troops. Jerre qualifies on the rifle range, learns to exist on plants and roots for food and water, is shown how to sneak behind an enemy and hold a knife blade over his throat to cut his vocal cords so he could not call for help. Such is the life in basic training.

Jerre learns that Jim McLaughlin is also at Sheppard field for his basic training where he is to be a Bomber Tail Gunner.

When Jerre finds Jim, he asks, "What's up buddy?"

This surprises Jim as he turns to see his friend Jerre.

"Jerre don't surprise me like that! Man its great to see you!"

The two high school friends talk about old times, wondering how Julius, Hansel and the other friends are doing.

Later, Jerre hears that Jim has a kidney infection and as a result, he receives a medical discharge.

Jerre classified as a 747 Aircraft & Power Plant Mechanic is assigned to the Dallas Aviation & Air College at Love Field in Dallas, Texas for the class of March 15, 1943.

Jerre says to Jake, "This place is great! The barracks are almost like home, they are wonderful."

"You got that right, kid. The food is great too! It's like eating in a nice cafeteria."

That is not all that is nice about Love Field. Jerre and Jake meet some lovely country girls who have an apartment in Dallas. Janice and Mary Kay are not only good-looking dames, but very friendly as well.

Janice says, "Jerre how about you and Jake coming up to our apartment and we'll give you something."

"What will you show us-uh-I mean what will you give us?"

"We will give you a home cooked dinner."

The dinner is wonderful for the two GIs and so is the company of two friendly working girls. Jake and Jerre have many other pleasant times with these nice girls.

Upon graduation, Jerre and his fellow soldiers receive promotions to Corporal.

Julius 1943

A few days after Jerre's Love Field training and Dallas fun, Julius' birthday March 19, 1943 now means he has reached the draft age of 18. The war is going strong in Europe and in the Pacific, meaning the armed forces need many additional new soldiers for the action. Julius does not volunteer but with in a week of turning 18, he receives notice to report for service at Fort McPherson. His brothers already serving, Oliver is a CB and Charles is in the Army Quartermaster. Agnes' husband Leonard is in the Navy. Earl and Evelyn's husband Nolan work in defense plants.

Bertie, hoping none of her children is wounded or killed, bids Julius goodbye as Gloria and her mother, Luna, take him to the base at Fort McPherson where he will be inducted. It is almost dark in the evening and Julius, being a bit bashful is hesitant to kiss Gloria goodbye.

Gloria says, "Kiss me soldier boy."

He bashfully kisses Gloria goodbye.

"Don't forget to write me Julius."

"I will send you my new address. Please write me too." Julius says as he holds her hand and bids goodbye once again before they turn to leave.

He reports in to the base induction center not knowing what lies ahead. He feels uneasy about having to go, but something inside him is exciting as he thinks about what adventures may be ahead.

The next morning Julius is sworn in along side of about 75 others. Next, he is outfitted with new olive drab clothing and other essentials to start his Army life. After that, he has an interview by one of the induction officers, who tells him, "Private Rainwater you are assigned to the U.S. Army Signal Corps and will be leaving for your training post by troop train tomorrow."

Julius asks, "Where am I going?"

"That is censored information Rainwater."

"Well what's my address? I need to tell someone where I will be located."

"When you arrive at your base for basic training you will know where you are, but your address will be an APO number which will follow you no matter where you serve."

"Thank you sir."

That night Julius calls his mother and Gloria to tell them he is in the Signal Corps and will be leaving the next day for where ever the basic training center is located. He has trouble sleeping during the night as he thinks; *I'll be in communication technical stuff with radio and all that good stuff.* Julius finally dozes off to sleep.

He awakes as the reveille sounds. *I guess I'll have to get used to that sound,* he thinks as he scrambles out of bed, washes up, dresses and heads to the formation outside his barrack.

The First Sergeant addresses the men as he barks, "Youse guys will have to get in line faster than you have this morning when youse get to your destinations. Please do not forget what I have just said! Discipline and promptness are primary in our army."

Julius' thinks, he *must be a Yankee. I wonder if he is trying to scare us.* Then he realizes that the Sergeant is correct in getting the civilians oriented properly the first day.

The Sergeant smiles and says, "At ease."

Julius knows that he does not have to stand rigidly at attention, so he relaxes to listen to the orders from the Sergeant.

The Sergeant bellows, "Youse guys will go to the mess hall for breakfast and then pack your stuff in your duffel bag and form a line at the troop train waiting across the field."

Then he says, "Dismissed."

Julius boards the troop train that morning in utter wonderment about what lies ahead. He has never been on a train before and this will be only his second trip out of Georgia.

The first time going out of Georgia, is when he was 15 and went on vacation with the McLaughlin's to Charleston's Folley Beach. Jim's family invites Julius to go to Jacksonville Florida with them; however, Julius' mother, fearful of the warnings of Polio outbreaks at beaches in Florida, did not let Julius go. The good people that the McLaughlin's are change the destination to Folley Beach to accommodate Julius. He has fond memories of that trip where he saw the ocean for the first time.

As the train leaves Fort McPherson, Julius' thoughts are on the journey to Fort Monmouth New Jersey where he has just learned it is to be his basic training station. *What's it going to be like?* Flutters through his mind.

"It will be tomorrow morning before we reach Ft. Monmouth." The conductor tells Julius.

"Why will it take so long?"

"This car will be switched in Washington, D.C. to another engine which travels via Ft. Monmouth on its way to New York City."

"Thank you, sir."

It is a long night and sleep is hard to get, as the train's rickety rack sound is disturbing as it speeds toward Yankee land. Julius looks out the window as the car disconnects and then switches to a long train headed to New York. He guesses it will probably be several hours before arriving in New Jersey. His guess is right as the train pulls into Red Bank, N.J. near the Fort Monmouth base at eleven o'clock on the morning of April 1, 1943. A large olive brown army bus with a sign up front: **'Ft. Monmouth – Home of the Signal Corps.'** is waiting to take the 25 to 30 new GIs from the train to the base.

The new GIs carrying their duffel bags file into the bus for the short journey to the base. Temporary quarters for the new soldiers are nearby. The sergeant in the barrack informs them that orientation will begin the next day and the group may go to the canteen or just relax the rest of the day. He points out the schedule for dinner and supper at the mess hall.

Julius becomes acquainted with Floyd Rogers from Macon Georgia and Chris McNair from Atlanta. The three southerners go to the canteen to get something to drink. Julius will think *Coca-Cola* but Floyd and Chris are used to drinking Beer.

When they arrive at the canteen Chris says, "I'll get us a pitcher of beer and you fellows grab a table."

Before Julius can say anything, he is setting at a table with a glass of 3.2 beer in front of him. Before that day, Julius has never drunk anything alcoholic. At first, Julius sips it and then acquires a taste for it. After several glasses of beer, they all relax and discuss their backgrounds.

Julius tells the two about his recent completion of the radio course at Georgia Tech.

Floyd says, "I'm a farm boy and not sure I'm going to like it up here with these Yankees."

Chris says, "I'm from Buckhead in Atlanta and I have been to New York many times with my mother and father, so I will be enjoying myself here."

Julius says, "I'm with you Chris. This is my second trip away from Georgia and I'm ready to explore the world and New Jersey and New York are two good places to start."

The canteen is full of soldiers making a lot of noise as they drink beer and talk with each other. Julius notices that most of the crowd is from the North.

Julius says to Chris and Floyd, "It looks like we are in the minority; most of these fellows are Yankees. I can tell by their accent."

"You are right Julius, they are." Chris observes.

"Yes they are." Floyd echoes.

Early the next morning after breakfast, about one hundred fifty soldiers assemble into a large auditorium for orientation. The officer at the front talks mainly about soldier discipline and customs of the military. Each soldier is given an information profile sheet to complete.

Julius fills in his name and then he has to look at his dog tag to write in his serial number. He has not memorized it yet. He knows that he needs to so, he says *34769949* repeatedly in his mind. After completing the sheets, the soldiers are dismissed for lunch. They are to re-assemble in the auditorium at 14:00 o'clock.

Back to the auditorium, assignments are ready for each soldier. Assignments are for the following categories: some to Signal Corps construction teams, some to technical repair teams, some to clerical teams, and some to radio operator teams. Julius, assigned to the radio operator team is happy. He figures that the profile sheet each has completed gives the officers an indication of how to make these assignments. His new acquaintances Chris and Floyd are assignments to different teams; Chris is to be in the technical repair team and Floyd is in the construction team. The technical repair team and radio operator team will be station at nearby Camp Elgin for their basic training and specific skills training. Chris, Julius, and about 75 others transport to Camp Elgin that afternoon.

Camp Elgin is near Red Bank and not very far from Ft. Monmouth. The camp is set up specifically for preparing troops for this war.

After six weeks of strenuous and hard training climbing tall walls, crawling under barbed wire as bullets zoom overhead, camping in the Jersey forest without food, and other rough task, the boys become men. A three-day furlough to rest up rewards the men. This is not enough time to ride the train back to Atlanta so Julius and Chris decide to go to New York. Chris calls Floyd over at the Fort and invites him to go too.

Chris' father made reservations for the three at the Waldorf-Astoria Hotel with all rooms paid for in advance, since the soldiers cannot afford to stay at this luxury hotel on Park Avenue in Manhattan. They enjoy the train ride to New York. When they check in at the hotel, the reservations are for two rooms. Floyd and Julius have one of the rooms and Chris shares the other room with his girl friend that happens to be in town.

The three days go by too fast for Julius and Floyd. They walk across the street to Central Park and at night see Broadway and all its lights, but they do not see Chris much during the stay in New York. He spends most of his time in the room with his girl friend.

When it is time to checkout, Chris shows up in the lobby of the hotel and introduces his girlfriend to Julius and Floyd. She is a beautiful girl. The three guys bid her goodbye and head for the train to report to their respective bases. It is a great three-day break but they must return.

The first night, Julius has Gloria on his mind so he writes a letter to tell her about seeing New York City. He also sent a letter to his mother in Hapeville.

The next day it is time to start classes to learn about radio communications as used by the U.S, Army Signal Corps. Julius is in a class with 33 other men all from New Jersey, Philadelphia, Brooklyn or the Bronx. He is the only Southerner. His friend Chris is assigned to another class where he will learn to make repairs on the modern radio equipment and other accessories used by the Corps. Floyd back at Fort Monmouth will learn about erecting antennas and Quonset Huts used for the fixed stations in the war zones.

Semaphore signaling is still taught as part of the bag of tricks available on the battlefield to the amazement of Julius. Signal lights with short and long burst of light used, especially from ship to ship in convoys at sea. Julius spent many weeks and months learning the Morse code. He listens to code with his earphones and types the messages on a typewriter, practicing repeatedly. The Sergeant pats Julius on the back and says, "Soldier you are learning fast. I think you are ahead of the class already."

"Thank you sir, I'm trying."

Julius receives his first promotion just a week later. He is now a corporal. In addition to his training, he is to assist other students in order to make sure the class will finish on schedule. Unfortunately, some soldiers do not pass the work. The ones, who do not pass, transfer to other branches of the Army. Some go to the infantry and some to office clerical jobs.

Julius, Chris and Floyd celebrate the Fourth of July Holiday at Asbury Park beach. This resort ocean town is only 45 minutes away. They notice a stream of girls getting off a bus from New York. The boys can't believe their eyes when each girl is selecting a soldier with whom to spend the evening. Julius, with his girl Dawn Nice sits on a park bench along side of Chris, Floyd and their girls. Julius wonders if this girl Dawn Nice really has that name. He has not been out much with girls and none at all with Yankee girls. The evening goes just fair for Julius and the girl since he does not try anything too aggressive. Later he wonders *was she disappointed.*

After three days at the beach, the three soldiers report in at the base. Julius has sunburns all over his legs requiring medical treatment. The medic at the base hospital reminds Julius that being sunburned is a dischargeable offense in the army; but he does not report Julius. The medic supplies Julius with a salve to heal and ease the burn.

At the end of the summer 1943, Julius and 29 other trained Signal Corps Men are given assignments to Camp Crowder near Joplin, Missouri. During the long train ride, Julius notices that he is the only one from the South. He makes friends with the others who are from New York, New Jersey, and Pennsylvania. The group plays polka and smoke cigarettes as the train moves through the countryside. Julius enjoys the company of two friends from New York and the three became friends during the trip. Emanuel Hernando Cortez from Flatbush and Sidney Silverstein from the Bronx are Julius' new friends. Cortez is of Spanish descent while Silverstein is Jewish. Coming from three different cultures the three young men enjoy comparing backgrounds during the journey to Missouri.

Cortez and Silverstein are amazed to see so many farmlands along the way. These two have lived 18 years in Flatbush and the Bronx seeing only pavement, and no farms.

Julius asks Cortez, "How many tits does a cow have?"

"I've never seen a cow. I don't know how many tits one has."

"Well, a cow has four tits."

On the way to Camp Crowder in Missouri, the scenery is beautiful with all the fall colors glistening in the forest as the train rolls past the countryside.

Jerre 1943 - 1944

Jerre and his soldier mates, having completed basic training in Dallas, are now ready for real 'on the job training' at the Ford Motor Company Rotunda plant in Detroit Michigan. Another long troop train across the country to Detroit brings Jerre above the Mason-Dixon Line for the first time in his life.

Jerre says, "Hey guys this is my first time in Yankee Land. I'm glad its summer time instead of winter."

The Ford plant converted for the manufacture of the Pratt & Whitney R-2800 engine used on heavy bombers, such as the B-17 & B-24 and other military aircraft. Jerre learns how to maintain the engine in all kinds of conditions even to being able to time the engine with a cigarette paper.

Detroit is a beautiful city and the people are very respectful of GI's. All entertainment and transportation is free. When a soldier enters a bar and orders, the civilian customers insist on paying the soldiers bar bill.

One night Jerre says, "Let's go down one side of this street and have a drink at each bar and then come back on the other side and do the same."

"Let's do it!" The other fellow soldiers cry out.

Half way around the street Jerre says, "I want a tattoo. How about you guys?"

Jackson says, "Great idea Jerre! Let's all get a tattoo."

The men walk into the tattoo store and tell the manager, "Hey we want a tattoo."

"Are you guys drunk?"

"Not me sir." Jerre says.

The others, in unison say, "No sir."

They all get their tattoos; Jerre's is his Army serial number on his left arm *18209806*. After the stop for tattoos the boys continue their bar hopping trip. They made it all the way without passing out.

Jerre and the other men are not all play. Much work is necessary to gain knowledge in aircraft power plant machinery. Jerre, who passed his basic at Love Field in good standing, gains the knowledge at Ford easily as he is a quick learner.

The real on the job training is next. This takes place in Alamogordo, New Mexico.

Jerre says, "I'm ready, bring it on!"

Ready or not, the troops are again on a troop train to travel across the country one more time. This time the trip is from Detroit to Alamogordo. Unfortunately, some of the soldiers who do not qualify in Detroit transfer to other outfits.

Alamogordo, New Mexico (White Sands National Park) is all white and glary and has cold desert nights. Jerre works the night shift on B-24 Heavy Bombers used during the day to train Air Force flight crews.

For recreation, Jerre and his friends take leave and hitchhike to El Paso to visit Juarez Mexico, just a hundred miles south.

Jerre says, "Juarez is a dirty wicked city."

He says this after Pedro, a little Mexican boy, says, "Soldier, have my sister she is a virgin."

Jerre says, "No thanks!"

Since counterfeiting is so prevalent, the silver dollar is the only American currency accepted.

Jerre says, "These coins are so heavy my pants are pulled down to my knees."

Joe, one of Jerre's friends, says, "We all have that problem."

Silver dollars used to buy Mexican bourbon that is very good and inexpensive. Jerre bought a couple of bottles, as do his GI friends also. To get through the MP security at the base, Jerre and his friends place the bottles in their socks under their pants in order to hide it.

After several weeks of training in the desert, Jerre's outfit is now ready for POM (Prior to Overseas Movement) training. This means another troop train ride. This time going northwest through the Rocky Mountains and the beautiful sights to Kearns, Utah some ten miles southwest of Salt Lake, City and ten miles southeast of the Great Salt Lake. As Jerre peers out the train window he thinks, *I am lucky to see so much of our country.*

Here Jerre receives his wartime clothing, arms, final instructions and training. The soldiers in preparation for overseas are restricted to the base.

Jerre says, "I wish we could have seen Salt Lake City."

His preparation training for overseas duty lasts only a few weeks before the Eighth Army Air Force unit with full battle equipment boards on to a troop train. This time the destination is Camp Shanks, New Jersey where they will prepare for the trip across the Atlantic.

As Jerre arrives, he does not know that Julius has just left New Jersey for Missouri; nor does Julius know that Jerre has just come to New Jersey from Utah.

Camp Shanks on the Atlantic Coast is the place where Jerre and the Eighth Army Air Force will load on the Queen Mary for its voyage to Scotland and the UK.

The soldiers have one day away before boarding the Queen Mary. Where will Jerre and his friends spend that day?

Jerre suggests to his friends, "I've never been to New York City. Do ya'll want to go?"

Joe replies, "I do!"

Michael and Jackson are ready to go, too.

The army provides a GI bus for those who wish to go to New York that night. Jerre and his three fellow soldiers are on that bus. When the bus arrives in New York, Joe says, "Let's hail a cab."

All four get into the cab and Joe says, "Take us to the Stork Club."

The driver says, "That place is an exclusive club and expensive."

Joe, who is from Oklahoma, tells the cabbie, "We still want to go to the Stork Club. My friend, Sherman Billingsly from Oklahoma is the owner.

The cabbie shuts his mouth and off they go to the Stork Club.

After the headwaiter seats the four, they order drinks and Joe asks the waiter, "Please advise Mr. Billingsly that we are here."

Billingsly arrives and sits with the GIs during introductions.

After introductions, he asks for a phone and calls a woman friend and asks, "Ethel will you be willing to entertain four GIs for the night."

Jerre, listening to the phone conversation, gets the message that the woman is either booked or not willing to take on four young and horny soldiers. Billingsly excuses himself.

The waiter says, "Drink up; the drinks are on the house."

A beautiful woman photographer in a short skirt takes their picture.

After several more drinks, it is time to report to the GI bus, for the return trip to Camp Shanks in New Jersey.

The next day, Jerre and lots of other GIs, Officers and equipment load onto the beautiful Queen Mary. It is late fall of 1943 and the weather is cloudy, cold and windy. The Queen Mary is a converted liner with soldiers housed down in the bottom in a stateroom designed for two third class passengers but now it has six GIs and is crowded, smelly, and loud at night with snoring.

Jerre expects the crew to be British, but he does not know about the food. The first meal served is kidney stew, to his disappointment. Jerre is seasick and the stew makes it worse.

Jerre says, "Please excuse me but I need to *hit the rail*"

He runs up the many wide stairs to the upper outside deck and runs into someone he recognizes from Hapeville. It is Forrest Gilbert an MP.

Before he can talk with him, Jerre says, "I have got to puke. I'll talk to you later."

Later, with Jerre feeling better, he meets with Forrest and they talk for several hours.

Jerre says, "It is good to see someone from my home town."

The fine Queen Mary is subject to being hit by German submarines and must zigzag with one minute to the right and one minute to the left and so on. With the bad weather the ship yaws left to right so when Jerre tries to walk down the hall to his bunk he finds himself walking on and above the handrails then back to the hall floor and then to the other side. If he is not sick, he soon will be. Jerre is seasick most all the way.

Before boarding, the men are warned that the ship will not stop for anything, even if someone falls overboard. Unfortunately, one GI does fall overboard. However, Jerre once heard that the Queen Mary did stop in the Atlantic for seventeen minutes so that an Army doctor could perform surgery on one of the GIs.

Julius 1943 - 1944

As the troop train arrives in Joplin Missouri in the fall of 1943, Julius thinks, *I have seen more of our country in the last six months than in my whole life.* Waiting nearby are a line of olive drab U.S. Army troop buses. The troops grab their duffel bags and line up to board a bus. Julius, Cortez and Silberstein sit near each other, wondering what's ahead at Camp Crowder.

Camp Crowder, established south of the city of Neosho, near Joplin in 1941 is the U.S. Army Signal Corps Training Center is on about 43,000 acres.

As the buses enter into this area, they pass hundreds of white barracks on each side of the street.

Julius remarks, "I'll bet there are fifty thousand soldiers here."

"You may be right." Cortez agrees.

Silberstein says, "I wonder which one of these barracks is ours."

Two of the buses stop and a U. S. Army Captain greet the soldiers as each one embarks the bus.

The Captain says, "Welcome to Camp Crowder. Please form two lines."

Then he points to the area where the soldiers are to assemble.

"Soldiers in Company 3922 will answer as I call your names." The Captain bellows out.

"Adams."

"Here!"

"Private Adams, you will be in Barrack 312."

"Atkins."

"Corporal Atkins, you will be in Barrack 312."

He continues alphabetically calling the names and assigning the barracks as he calls, "Cortez."

"Here!"

"Private Cortez, you will be in Barrack 313."

When the Captain reaches the Rs, he calls, "Rainwater."

"Here!"

"Corporal Rainwater, go to Barrack 313."

Julius, with his duffel bag, follows Cortez to Barrack 313. Later Silberstein joins them.

Cortez says, "I'm glad youse guys are in with me."

"So am I." Julius and Silberstein echo.

After reviewing the bulletin board just outside the Sergeant's private bunkroom, they notice that Sergeant Davis is in charge of their Barrack 313.

Julius grabs a top bunk just above Cortez and adjoining the Sergeants room. Silberstein takes the upper bunk next to Rainwater and Cortez. They unpack their belongings into the locker case at the end of the bunk and sit on their bunks awaiting orders from Davis.

After all the bunks are taken by the new arrivals, Davis walks out of his room and says, "Attention."

All men jump up and stand at attention in the aisle in front of their bunk.

Davis says, "At ease."

Everyone is at ease awaiting word from the Sergeant.

He speaks, "Men, I welcome you to Camp Crowder where you will receive training as professionals in the use of communication equipment under warfare conditions. In other words, this is a place for fine-tuning the Signal Corpse Company 3922 to be at its best under battlefield conditions. Some of you will qualify and some you will not, therefore work hard. It's going to be tough. Just remember guys, I will be pressing you guys every day, so hang in there.

"Your duty roster will be posted by 2100 to night. Please read it carefully for your name because it will be different for each specialty. In this barrack, we have radio code operators, radio technicians, fixed-station construction crews, and cryptographic personnel. I will be responsible for your discipline; other instructors will be responsible for your technical training.

"You are free for tonight but don't leave the camp and you must be in your bunks by 11:00PM. Does everyone understand?"

"Yes sir." The entire group yells back.

The three: Rainwater, Cortez and Silverstein head for the canteen along with half the barrack's soldiers. They order several pitchers of beer and enjoy a few hours of relaxation.

"Granddaddy is beer good for you?"
"If you are old enough, it is a good way to relax if you don't drink too much."
"Well Grandmother said it is not good for you."

"She is right; too much beer is not good for one."

"Did you drink too much Granddaddy?"

"No!" I said quickly, hoping we could go on with the story, although there were times when I did drink more than I care to share with my grandson.

"Do you drink beer now?"

"No I do not anymore, David."

"Okay, tell me some more of the war story."

The next day Julius and his friends follow their duty rosters as posted on the bulletin board. Julius, Cortez, Silverstein and 12 other radio operators go to their classes at the radio code room.

Julius says, "This is exciting! We are learning how to copy from real live signals sent out by other Signal Corps companies."

Cortez says, "Julius you are too much. Why get excited about this stuff. All I want to do is get this war over and go back home to Flatbush."

Silverstein says, "Cortez don't be so critical. We need to be conscientious about what we are doing. Julius is right; let's do our best and that will help to end the war."

With that discussion, Cortez goes back to his station desk. Julius and Silverstein return to what they are doing at their desks.

That night Julius picks up a copy of *Stars and Stripes*, the official military newspaper to catch up on the war news. The headlines:

October 1 1943 -	*After Mussolini Re-establishes Fascist Government Allies Enter Naples, Italy*
September 4, 1943 -	*Allies recapture Lae-Salamaua and New Guinea.*

October 7, 1943 -	*Japanese execute approximately 100 American POWs on Wake Island.*
October 26, 1943	*Emperor Hirohito: "My country's situation is grave."*

As Julius reads the articles, he wonders *where my Hapeville friends are now*. In the letters he receives from home, he understands that Jerre is in the Air Force and is in Europe. Some one wrote that Hansel is in the infantry and is stationed near Tulsa, Oklahoma. *Maybe I can go visit Hansel* he wonders.

He turns to Cortez and asks, "I wonder where we will be sent. Do you think it will be Europe or the Pacific?"

Cortez says, "I'm not sure but I hear rumors that we will be sent to the Pacific."

Julius says, "I like that. I hope we do go to the Pacific."

The extensive training at the Signal Corps training center familiarizes Julius and the rest of the group in the complete operations of a fixed radio communication station. Morse code is extensively used. Signals sent by the use of a key to send the dots and dashes through the transmitter to the antenna and out around the earth. The *'bug'* is a key that semi-automates the process. Julius is quite good at the use of the *'bug'*. His maximum speed is fifty words per minute. This speed he reaches after eight weeks of constant practice at the radio desk.

Early in December 1943, the company captain calls all the men of Company 3922 to a special meeting in the auditorium. Cortez asks, "Julius do you have any idea what this is about?"

Julius says, "I hear that some of us will receive promotions."

"Man I hope so." Cortez says.

"When the company assembles in the auditorium, Captain McMaster congratulates the men for doing well in the training at Camp Crowder. He then announces promotions. Julius promotes to sergeant while Cortez and Silverstein promote to corporal. Other soldiers receive promotions as well.

On the way back to the barrack, Cortez asks, "Julius why are you a sergeant and we are only corporals?"

"I'm just lucky I guess."

Silverstein says, "I know why he is a sergeant."

Cortez asks, "Why?"

"Because he has shown more leadership abilities than anyone else as he focuses on his program responsibilities."

That afternoon, Cortez suggests, "Let's go to Kansas City."

Everyone agrees and off we go, hitchhiking to K.C. During the war, it is easy to catch a ride for soldiers. Five hours later, the three arrive in K.C. and check into Hotel Phillips. It is Friday night and the men do not have to return until Sunday night. Everywhere they go during the evening the civilians pick up the tabs. At one bar, three girls invite themselves to have drinks with Julius, Cortez and Silverstein. This turns out to be a great party; the time is fun.

When the girls say, "We need to be going home."

They will not let the boys pay the bill.

Over the weekend, the city is kind to these lonely soldiers away from home. Hitchhiking back South to Camp Crowder is easy enough. They return just in time for taps and lights out.

At mail call, the next day Julius receives a letter from Hansel Barnett, his friend from high school. Hansel writes:

Dear Julius

"I am down in Tulsa and I heard that you are up in Missouri. Let's get together down here. If you can come this weekend, I'll be at this address: 226 River Road, Tulsa. I stay at this nice rooming house when I want to get away from the Army base on weekends. If you can't come write me, but if you can come don't write. Hope to see you this weekend.

Your friend, Hansel

Julius asks, "Cortez do you want to go to Tulsa with me this weekend."

"What's in Tulsa?"

"I have a high school friend stationed there."

"I don't think I want to go."

"Okay, perhaps Silverstein will go with me."

On Friday afternoon, Julius and Silverstein hitchhike on Route 66, the Will Rogers highway, to Tulsa. When the two arrive in Tulsa, they find 226 River Road. It is a run down old rooming house near downtown. The woman that runs the rooming house lets us know Hansel is out and will be back in about two hours.

Julius and Silverstein walk around looking for a bar. They soon learn that mixed drinks are outlawed in Oklahoma so they search for a liquor store. They find a liquor store on the corner and purchase two pints of Scotch whiskey. Back at the rooming house, they find Hansel is back. Julius and Red (That is what Hansel's friends call him.) are happy to see each other. Julius introduces his friend to Hansel. Hansel's hair is still as bright red as ever.

Julius asks, "Red where do we sleep here?"

As it turns out the room has only has only one regular bed. There are no other rooms available. Soldiers are used to making the best of any situation, so they agree that they will all sleep in the one bed.

Before bedtime, they get some ice and soda and drink some of the Scotch whiskey. At first Red does not want Julius to know that he takes a drink of alcohol. Before the evening is over Red consumes more of the Scotch whiskey than Julius or Silverstein. It is a good visit with Red and all three sleeps like babies during the night.

On Saturday and Sunday, Red invites the Signal Corpse boys to visit his Infantry training center. After a bus ride out to the base, Julius and Silverstein are impressed with the facilities. *Tulsa is a beautiful city* Julius thinks as Red shows them around the town.

Sunday evening Julius and Silverstein get back on Route 66 to hitchhike back to Camp Crowder. Around 10:30PM, their first rider drops them off at a small town just inside Missouri. Eighteen-year-old boys are always hungry so they go into a hamburger joint and fill up on hamburgers and cokes. When they get back on the Highway to finish their journey to their camp, they accidently start out on the wrong side of the highway. A beautiful girl in a convertible stops to give them a lift. Julius and Silverstein like having such a pretty woman to give them a ride toward their destination. (At least they think they are heading in the right direction.) She is a very nice person and so trusting of the sleepy GIs trying to get back to Camp before reveille.

After about a half-hour the girl asks, "I'm going to Los Angeles; where are you guys going?"

Julius says, "We are going to Joplin in Missouri to Camp Crowder where we are based."

"Well I'm going in the wrong direction for you fellows. I passed Joplin about two and a half hours ago."

"Well we better get out and head back east."

"I'll take you back to that little town where I first picked you up. I don't want to leave you out here in the boondocks."

Julius and Silverstein accept her kindness and say, "Thank you mam."

When they arrive back to the little town, Julius asks, "How much do we owe you?"

"Don't be silly; you don't owe me anything. You are fighting for my freedom and that's enough payment for me. Good luck on your trip back."

She turns her convertible around and heads west as the two lost GIs wave goodbye.

Julius says, "Let's make sure we are on the right side of the highway Silverstein."

Luckily, they have a ride within 15 minutes and arrive back at Camp Crowder just two hours before reveille. It is a short night before the bugle calls for the two sleepy GIs to wake up.

On December 20, 1943, the U.S. Army Signal Corpse Company 3922 finishes their extensive training at Camp Crowder.

The next chapter in the military career begins as they load onto a troop train heading west. *Julius thinks I'm really getting to see a lot of my country.* Across Oklahoma and Texas, oil wells are seen everywhere from the train's window. The train passes through dozens of little small towns. Many civilians wave at the train as it passes their towns. The GIs wave back.

The train arrives in El Paso Texas on their third day out. The train stops here and the troops are can walk around the little town for a couple of hours and have lunch before the train pulls out. Julius, Cortez, and Silverstein walk down near the river where they discover a little restaurant that serves chili.

Cortez asks, "What is chili?"

Julius says, "It's a beef concoction that we eat in the South and its good."

Silverstein says, "I've never heard of that."

"Let's eat some, okay." Julius suggests.

They do order a bowl of chili each; and to the surprise of Julius, the two Yankees enjoy it.

Silverstein says, "I wonder if it is kosher?"

"What do you mean kosher?" Julius asks.

"Jewish people are supposed to eat only kosher food. It's clean food for the Jewish body."

Cortez says, "Silverstein I saw you eat some ham this morning. Is ham kosher?

"I pretended it was corned beef."

The southern boy Julius has not been around many Jewish people so he is learning more about them from his friend Silverstein. Cortez is Catholic, but doesn't seem to practice his religion very much. Julius, being Protestant, is learning a lot about other people in America.

On the afternoon the train leaves El Paso, Silverstein comes to Julius and is crying as he says, "Julius have you noticed how the other guys make fun of me because I'm Jewish."

"I haven't paid any attention to that. Why do they make fun of you?"

"Well many people hate Jews and it makes me very uncomfortable; that's why I'm crying." Silverstein confides in his friend Julius.

"Do like I do; many people kid me about being a rebel, because I'm from the South. I just slough it off."

"That's different Julius; they are just kidding you but they really want to hurt me just because I'm a Jew." Silverstein says.

"If they continue it let me know and I'll tell them how wrong they are."

Silverstein put his arm around Julius and says, "Thank you pal!"

After a long train ride, the troop train arrives in San Francisco. The troops settle down in temporary quarters awaiting their departure date to board their troop ship for the Pacific Ocean. All destinations kept secret to avoid the Japanese learning about troop movements.

Christmas in San Francisco is not like back home in Hapeville Julius thinks as he and his friends explore the city. The cable car ride is fun and different from the Atlanta streetcars. China Town is interesting, too. Bar hoping is a treat as the civilian customers will not allow the soldiers to pay for their drinks.

January the second is the day the troops board the Liberty ship to head into the ocean away from San Francisco. The Liberty ships are cargo and troop ships built in the United States during the war. These are British in conception but adapted by the USA, cheap and quick to build, and come to symbolize U.S. wartime industrial output.

The troops sleep in the belly of the ship in five-high bunks with crowded, smelly and noisy conditions. The heads (latrines) and showers are small and do not allow privacy for the GIs. Julius *thinks it's a good thing we don't have women in the Army.* There are nurses on board but they live midship in upper deck officer's quarters.

Julius standing aft at the stern is wondering where his brothers are now. His mother's letters tell him that Charles is somewhere in the Pacific and Oliver is in the CBs, she thinks. Leonard is in the Navy. Odell has married Paul a soldier. Dawsie is thinking about joining the Merchant Marines. Looking back at the West Coast Julius views the city and mountains as they fade into the background of a mountain range along the seashore.

Five days later, the Liberty troop ship sails into Pearl Harbor. The troops are ready to disembark and get their land legs back.

Jerre 1944

The Queen Mary arrives in Glasgow, Scotland three weeks after leaving New Jersey. Before the ship docks, Jerre went to his commander prior to disembarking in Scotland and asks, "May I volunteer for TAT duty?"

Jerre hears that TAT, standing for *'To Accompany Troops',* will allow him to help supervise the loading and unloading of equipment once the ship arrives at doc side. He thinks *this will keep me from getting bored hanging around on this ship doing nothing.*

His Captain says, "Okay Sergeant Williams, you have my permission. Please report to the unloading supervisor at 1500 o'clock this afternoon."

"Yes sir."

Jerre salutes and departs the area smiling, knowing that he will be one of the first to embark and be doing something useful.

Jerre and several other TAT volunteers do go ashore first with some of the outfit's equipment, which is loaded on a troop train waiting nearby. It takes several days to unload and reload the equipment giving the TAT crew several days in town.

Jerre and his friends enjoy the time as they visit some of the pubs and find it interesting to watch the prudent Scotch men fill their pipes without dropping a grain of tobacco and drink their beer to the very last drop.

The British troop train transports the Army Air Force crews and equipment to Attlebridge near Norwich in Eastern England and only 200 miles north of London.

Jerre says, "Look the B-24s are already here."

His Captain says, "The 466 Bomb Group arrived several days ago. There are four Squadrons sharing eighty B-24 Heavy Bombers."

The little town of Attlebridge, named after a bridge built by Ættla a 7th century Catholic Bishop is only 30 miles from the North Sea. Its airstrip has been modified to accept the Air Force's B-24 Heavy Bomber airplanes. The air base, AAF Station #120, is used by the 466th Bomb Group. Prior to this, it was originally built for the RAF No. 2 group light bombers.

The Southern boy Jerre likes new experiences. He and several of his friends visit Norwich to eat at a local quaint restaurant. Jerre notices *Welch Rarebit* on the menu and says to his friends, "I'm going to have *Welch Rarebit* because I've never tried it."

He orders this when the waiter came over to take their order. When the waiter serves it, Jerre looks at the toasted sliced bread covered with a cheese sauce and says to the waiter, "Where's the rabbit?"

She said, "Oh, Yank you are so funny." Everyone laughs and that day Jerre learns about *Welch Rarebit*. He thinks, *Gosh I have a lot to learn in this world.*

A few days later, Jerre and the rest of his crew receive an alert that the first mission is one to bomb Berlin.

Jerre says, "I'm anxious to see the big bird B-24s takeoff."

The ground crew watches them take off like flying Eagles. When it comes time for these birds to return, to their utter dismay, 64 fail to return. Some destroyed, some crashed in enemy territory, and some land in neutral countries. The Army's Eighth Air Corps is almost destroyed. This causes a setback in the United States war efforts at the time.

Jerre says to the ground crew, "I am pleased since at least some of our brave flight crews have returned safely with little damage to the bombers."

Each B-24 has a three party ground crew, a chief, an assistant and a member. Jerre signs on as the member. Bombing has to stop until the manufacturers can make and deliver new aircraft. It takes several weeks before the new shiny planes arrive.

Jerre says, "The manufacturers have been pressured to deliver without taking time to paint the camouflage on each airplane. These shinning planes look odd among the few remaining old ones."

When the missions began again, the situation requires a complete schedule change in the war lives of all the fighting men. A typical schedule is up at 0400, eat, go to the planes, preflight them and thoroughly check them out and provide a reliable and safe bomber for the brave crews that have to spend two to eight hours flying in enemy skies. Fortunately, Jerre's plane makes sixty-three successful missions. On one occasion, the pilot, 2nd Lt. McAfee is killed by German flak. The crew calls in the sheet metal mechanics to repair many flak holes, however Jerre knows of no other brave men who have been killed or injured.

Jerre's ground crew likes to sit by the takeoff runway and watch the planes glide up into the sky. Sometimes these bombers are loaded with heavy 500-pound bombs. One morning while watching Shoo Shoo Baby take off the pilot accidently dips his right wing onto the runway and the entire plane explodes and burns. Jerre's ground crew has the assignment to search for body parts. Jerre finds a left hand with his wedding band still on the finger. One ground crew member is missing; they find his remains wrapped in one of the wings as the plane dived into the ground crew on the ground.

Jerre tells his Commander, "This is an assignment that makes me feel bad all over my body."

The Captain says, "That is understandable Sergeant. Take a few hours break and rest up."

The nickname *Shoo Shoo Baby*, named by the original crew chief T/Sgt. Hank Cordes after his favorite song sung by *The Andrews Sisters*. The name given to another aircraft and in May 1944, a third *Shoo* adds to the name. Most of the planes get their names from the pilots and crews. There isn't any normal procedure to cover this. A name picked by the crew and the crew chief sees to it that the nose art is completed.

Jerre tells Rick, one of his crewmembers, a story about Charles Seth.

He says, "Charles Seth is a navigator for two different Liberator bombers on which he navigated. Charles is the navigator on *Lovely Lady*. After 12 missions over Germany, it is too damaged to fly again. His crew names a later model B-24 *Lovely Lady's Avenger*. On its 23rd mission the ship damaged has to make a crash landing. The pilot has a choice of back to England 500 miles away or the neutral country Sweden 100 miles away. The Pilot chose the shorter distance and crash lands just before the beginning of the landing strip with none of his crew hurt."

Rick says, "Someone told me about that crash. The plane crash-landed near Malmo, Sweden didn't it?"

"That's right."

In-between missions Jerre and his crew friends visit the local pubs and on several furloughs, Jerre goes to London. On one of these furloughs, Jerre meets a lovely young Welsh girl by the name of Freda Williams. He visits her city on the Irish Sea. The two agree to keep in touch.

In that Welsh city, everyone who lives on one street have the name Williams, on the next street, everyone has the name Owen and so on. These people are very clannish.

On Jerre's second furlough to London, he dates a nurse. While the two are walking through Hyde Park at night, they hear a Buzz Bomb.

Jerre asks the nurse, "Shouldn't we go for cover?"

She says, "Love, don't worry as long as you can hear the buzzard. When you can't then hide and worry."

About that time, the buzzard ran out of fuel and they hear nothing. Jerre grabs her, as they both hit the ground. In a few seconds, it explodes some two miles away.

Still in London later in the week, Jerre is knocked out of bed by a German V2 Rocket. He concludes *those Germans are trying to kill me. I feel safer back in my Nissan hut at the airbase.*

On two occasions, his guardian angels save his life. One time is when a friend in the hut is cleaning his 45 automatic and it accidently fires, just missing Jerre by three inches. Another time he is flying with his crew over Germany when ground fire hits the plane and the bullet misses his leg by four inches.

In between missions, and when the bombers are on their long missions, Jerre helps in Special Services as a projectionist at the base theatre and when available he helps with the USO shows.

After the unit's one hundredth mission, as an award they are given a '100 Mission Party'. The unit's officers arrange for all available young girls from the villages to be there for the GIs dates. Glenn Miller and his band play for the dance.

Jerre says to Glenn, "Will you autograph these two English Pound notes at the watermark?"

Glenn Miller says, "Gladly soldier boy."

Jerre thinks as Glenn signs his signature to the pound notes *I'll save these pound notes and give them to a lovely young Hapeville girl when the war is over.*

Julius 1944

The troop ship, loaded with thousands of troops, arrives at Pearl Harbor in Honolulu where the troops will disembark. Honolulu on the beautiful island 0f Oahu, is surrounded by a gorgeous blue ocean. From the deck of the ship the soldiers have a great view to the right of the white sandy Waikiki beach and at the far end of the island, Diamond Head stands tall above the palm trees and white beaches,

As the GIs depart from the troop ship, Julius says to Cortez, "I have always wanted to go the Europe Zone, but this I believe is better, don't you think so Cortez?"

"I know I'm going to enjoy this place even better than England or Europe."

They notice the sunken remains of ships in the harbor and plan to visit the sight of the December 7, 1941 Japanese bombings later.

Olive drab army buses line up just outside the docks to transport the troops, fresh from the States, to their barracks on the Island. The buses arrive at Schofield Barracks in the middle of the island of Oahu, Hawaii in the City of Honolulu.

Julius says, "It looks to me like there are mostly Infantry troops here."

Silverstein says, "I understand the 25th Infantry Division is here on this base. Also, I saw signs that the 1st Marine Division is here."

The U. S. Army Signal Corps Company 3922 moves into a spacious barrack in one corner of the large military base of Schofield Barracks near Hickam Air Force Base. The first few days, mostly filled with orientation conferences are interesting. The communication arm of the army training facility in Honolulu, located in Diamond Head is where Julius and his friends in the Radio field will further train for whatever mission is in store for them in the future.

The three friends Julius, Cortez and Silverstein get into the fun of the beautiful island and its warm weather quickly.

Cortez suggests, "Let's go up in the mountain nearby and see what's there.

Julius says, "Hey look! Is that a water fall up there. Maybe we can go swimming. Are you fellows ready to explore it with me?"

Cortez says, "Julius you are always looking for fun things to do. That's why I like you, even though you are a rebel from the South."

"Okay you Flatbush Yankee, I like you too."

"Silverstein are you with us?" Cortez questions.

"What are we waiting for? Let's go!" Silverstein answers.

After a two-hour hike, the three are at the waterfall near the top of the island mountain. They all agree such a beautiful sight is right in their view.

Julius suggests, "Let's go skinny dipping in the cool water below the fall."

Off come, their clothes, into the water, they jump.

"Wading up under the fall feels like a masseur working on my shoulders and neck." Julius remarks.

"Swimming naked feels gooooood!" Cortez yells.

"I wish some young girls would come by right now." Silverstein says.

Julius says, "No such luck; there is no one within a mile of us right now."

After swimming in the small pool beneath the waterfall, the boys climb out and onto the large flat rocks. They sun dry themselves before dressing themselves for the hike back down the mountain to their barrack.

Before returning to their barrack, they drop by the canteen for a cold beer. Several of their fellow soldiers at the canteen wonder where the three have been.

Josh Wikens asks, "Julius how did your hair get so messed up?"

"We've been skinny dipping."

"Did you have girls with you?"

"Yes we had three of the cutest girls"

"You are kidding me."

Julius never tells Josh the truth.

Across the room at another table, Julius sees a marine he thinks he knows. Julius excuses himself and walks over there. The marine is James Clay from Hapeville Georgia; Julius surprises James as he taps him on the shoulder and says, "Hi James. What are you doing here?"

"Well bless my soul if it is Julius Rainwater. I am her e in the 1st Marine Division. We are shipping out tomorrow, heading to the South Pacific."

The two talk for a while. Catching up on what is happening.

On a sunny Saturday afternoon, Julius takes a trip down to the main street in Honolulu, which runs parallel to Waikiki Beach. As he walks alone down the sidewalk another soldier stops him and asks, "Julius what are you doing here?"

Julius looks up to see who is speaking to him and he cannot believe his eyes. Standing before him is his older brother.

` "Why Charles, I didn't know you were here in Hawaii.'

"I've been here since last November. Hey, I am surprised to see my kid brother here too."

"I've been here since January."

The two brothers warmly hug each other, sit down on a nearby park bench under a palm tree and discuss family and military information for a long time. They exchange APO addresses and agree to keep in touch.

After a great time together, Charles says, "I must go because we are shipping out tomorrow."

"Where are you going?"

"I don't know. I won't know until I'm there, I guess."

The two Rainwater brothers bid each other good-bye, promising to write each other often.

Training in the bowels of Diamondhead where Julius learns much about the Signal Corps' most modern radio communication equipment, proves very successful for him. Julius placed in charge of a complete shift of radio messaging operations where he experiences real live wartime coded communications. Because of his good performances, his Captain promotes Julius is to Technical Sergeant. This means: more responsibilities, more money to send back to his mother in Hapeville and more to spend on extras himself.

The other men, not receiving promotions, question Julius' promotion. These questions get no response from Julius as he continues to take his responsibilities very seriously.

During the spring of '44, Julius enrolls himself in the United States Armed Forces Institute, a college level free study, provided for soldiers in the service on a voluntary basis. His subjects are Algebra, Geometry, Trigonometry, and Physics. In his high school studies, he has covered some of these subjects very lightly and to get in Georgia Tech he will need more knowledge in these subjects. When not on duty, he spends time at his bunk studying these courses.

Julius says to his friends, "I hear that today we will receive orders to pack up and get ready for our next destination."

Cortez asks, "Where is the next destination?"

"I'm not sure, but I'll bet it will be to the South Pacific."

The First Sergeant officially announces the new orders: The troops will leave the next morning for the troop ship now docked at Pearl Harbor.

The next morning the soldiers have packed, ready to board onto the busses, which will take them to Pearl Harbor. Julius remembers when his brother, Charles, left several months before.

On the Liberty ship, there is equipment and troops crowded into every nook and corner. Julius is on the top bunk of a five-tier bunk in the bowels of the ship.

One day out at sea, the personnel, both Navy and Army aboard, are excited to hear the news over the PA system of the D-day in the European war zone. June 6, 1944 is the day on which the Battle of Normandy begins—commencing the Western Allied effort to liberate mainland Europe from Nazi occupation.

"Maybe this is the beginning of the end to this war." Julius is surmising.

Silverstein says, "Julius, I hope you are right."

"But how about the Japanese battle, when will the beginning of the end come for us?" Cortez asks.

No one knows the answer to this question.

The U. S. Army Signal Corps troops bunk together in the aft belly of the ship. They soon get used to sleeping with the noisy propellers roaring night and day. Julius, Silverstein and Cortez take their sheets and pillows up onto the deck to cool off and sleep during many nights. The decks are crowded with other GIs doing the same thing.

Most all troops go up on deck during daytime to play cards, read and sleep. The deck is wall-to-wall men lying everywhere. To walk across the deck requires skill to step over the bodies lying about. Julius enjoys beating his Yankee friends at polka, but even that soon bores him. He does spend sometime browsing his Armed Forces Institute studies.

Not much news is available to the troops on board as the Stars and Stripes newspaper is not available to ships at sea. Julius wonders what is happening to Jerre and Hansel. *Hansel must have been on the invasion at Normandy* he thinks. He has not heard from Jerre; but understands he is in the Army Air Force.

Julius meets with Josh Wilkens, another member of his Signal Corps Company who is a fast typist and is noted for excellent newsworthy writings.

Julius says, "Josh, I have an idea. I need your opinion."

"What's your idea Julius?"

"We can't receive much news here on the ship. If the ship's commander will let me copy the news off the radio, the two of us can produce a newspaper for the troops."

"That is a lot of work; don't you think Julius?"

"Not at all; it will be a weekly newspaper and consist of only one page. I have checked and the ships bridge adjoining office has a typewriter, a mimeographing machine and plenty of paper.

I'll copy the news items from the Morse code addition on the ships radio from the news agencies if you'll type the newspaper format. We'll both run the sheets on the mimeograph machine and distribute the paper. What do you think, Josh?"

"Julius it sure looks like you have done your homework! Okay I'll help."

The two walk up to the Commander's office and make their idea known to him.

Commander Jacobs says, "I like your idea! When do you want to start?"

"Right now." Julius and Josh agree and say to the Commander.

"Here is a typewriter and Rainwater you may use this radio desk to copy the news." Jacobs instructs the two volunteers.

Josh asks Julius, "What do you think we should name the newspaper?"

"How about *The Poop Deck?*"

"Sounds good to me."

Josh and Julius get busy.

The Poop Deck has its first issue on July 9, 1944 with the following headlines:

The Poop Deck
July 9, 1944

June 19, 1944 -	*The "Marianas Turkey Shoot occurs as U.S. Carrier-based fighters shoot down 220 Japanese planes, while only 20 American planes are lost.*
June 27, 1944 -	*U.S. troops liberate Cherbourg.*
July 3, 1944 -	*'Battle of the Hedgerows' in Normandy. Soviets capture Minsk.*

July 8, 1944 -   *Japanese withdraw from Impala. British and Canadian troops capture Caen.*

Commander Jacobs is well pleased with Rainwater and Wilkins' results. Everyone on the ship likes what he sees and looks forward to the next week's edition. Jacobs is so pleased that he moves Julius and Josh to two spare bedrooms in the Naval Officer's quarters near the bridge office. In addition to having more room to sleep and study, Julius and Josh are eating with the officers meals that are more delicious.

Josh says, "Rainwater your idea has turned out to be better than I thought it would."

"Thanks Josh, I love it too. To show our appreciation to Commander Jacobs, let's publish it twice a week."

"Good idea, let's go for it."

In August when the convoy of ships arrives near their destination toward the Palauan Islands, the sailors in the radio room tell Julius and Josh, "We are mad at you two because you have started something that the Commander says we must continue."

Jerre 1944 -1945

Jerre and the ground crew men prepare the Bombers during the daylight hours because every night is a lights-out situation to avoid enemy planes from homing in on their base. Luckily, their base in the northern part of U.K. does not have darkness until 10:30 or 11:00 PM. The crews take advantage of the light. The chow hall remains open until midnight providing chow for the hardworking crews at those late hours.

Jerre says, "Thank the Lord that provides us with cooks at night when we are tired and hungry."

All of the crew agree with Jerre's comment.

One night, told about an important coming invasion, the men work all night that evening preparing the Bombers for the largest invasion ever. The bombers take of one by one with *Dirty Girty* the one Jerre's crew prepares for its take off sequence time. The news, June 6, 1944, on which the Battle of Normandy begins, for the liberation of France and the European countries, spreads throughout the base.

As the planes return from this mission, the *Dirty Girty* ground crew is too excited to sleep as they keep looking at the sky expecting their plane to return and return it does to make many more missions.

When General Patton and his tanks are driving through France in the fall of 1944, he ran out of fuel. Jerre's Air group has orders to stop bombing missions and to install bladder tanks in the Bombay area of the aircraft. The ground crews work hard night and day to complete this job as rapidly as possible. These tanks are filled with gasoline and other equipment Patton needs. In the plane that Jerre modifies the flight crew invites him to fly with them. The plane lands on a grassy landing strip outside one of the French villages and they unload the fuel tanks and a kitchen sink Patton ordered. Jerre asks, "Why does Patton need a sink?"

No one could answer that question except one soldier who says, "I guess when he orders everything but the kitchen sink; you must have missed the last part of that order."

Jerre laughs as he says, "That's funny."

Near the end of December 1944, the allies have made gains into Germany and the Russians have pierced Germany's Eastern front. Unknown to Jerre and Julius, their friend Hansel, captured by the Germans, is now a prisoner-of- war. During the Battle of the Bulge, many GIs, killed or captured, is very disheartening.

Jerre hears about the Germans'Ardennes Offensive through regular Army Air force news sources. On Christmas day 1944, he wonders to himself, *Hansel is in the Third Army and I hope he's all right,* not knowing that Hansel that day is sitting in a German prison camp.

This German offensive, known to most as *The Battle of the Bulge,* begins on December 16 and continues to Christmas day. Germany's plans for these operations to split the British and American Allied zone in half, capturing Antwerp, Belgium and then proceeding to encircle and destroy four Allied armies, forcing the Western allies to negotiate a peace treaty in the Axis Powers favor. The German military has been in almost total radio silence leading to a surprise for the allies. The weather, cold and a heavy overcast, compounds the situation causing a lack of Air Force Bomber support from weather grounded aircraft.

Most of the American casualties occur within the first three days of battle, when two of the U.S. 106th Infantry Division's three regiments surrender. Hansel is in that Division.

"The Battle of the Bulge is the bloodiest of the battles that U.S. forces have experienced so far in World War II." Jerre's Captain says.

Jerre, hearing this, worries about his friend Hansel Barnett.

The German objectives do not materialize. In the wake of defeat, as German survivors retreat, many experienced German units become depleted of men and equipment.

The Army Stars and Stripes newspaper list several headlines in its February 15 1945 issue. These are:

Jan 17, 1945 -	*Soviet troops capture Warsaw.*
Jan 26, 1945 -	*Soviet troops liberate Auschwitz.*
Feb 04, 1945	*Roosevelt, Churchill, Stalin meet at Yalta*
Feb 14, 1945	*Dresden destroyed by a firestorm after Allied bombing raids.*

"This is good news." Jerre says as he reads the newspaper.

"It looks like we are winning the War." A friend in his crew says as he also reads the news.

Indeed these two crewmembers are right as the bombers they cared for continue to hit their targets and destroy entire German towns, such as Dresden. Jerre is happy as he sees the direction the war is taking.

Each day as the planes take off and as they return, fewer and fewer bombers are lost. To the delight of the ground crews, most all of the bombers return safely after each mission.

Jerre spends time at the USO with his friends in between missions.

He says, "You know this gives me rest, but I'll not feel fully rested until I am home in Hapeville, Georgia."

Julius 1944-1945

The convoy of six ships, three Liberty Troop Carriers, two support Destroyers fitted with anti-aircraft guns, radar and forward-launched ASW weapons, in addition to their light guns, depth charges, and torpedoes and one submarine battle ship are plowing through the blue Pacific Ocean heading south toward the Islands.

Julius is in the Radio Room listening to a Tokyo Rose propaganda broadcast with Commander Jacobs looking over his shoulder. Suddenly Jacobs reaches over and switches the broadcast to the PA system so the entire ships population can hear Tokyo Rose and her American popular music. Over the loud speakers, the GIs hear several popular songs making them homesick. The songs: *Sentimental Journey* by Les Brown; *Bless 'Em All* by Bing Crosby; As *Time Goes By* By by Rudy Vallée; *Moonlight Serenade* by Glenn Miller Orchestra; *Hot Time in the Town of Berlin* by Woody Herman & His Orchestra; *Bell Bottom Trousers* by Art Kassel are among other titles.

Julius asks Jacobs, "Where does she get all that music?"

"I'm sure she copies them from American broadcast. You know Tokyo hopes to persuade the GIs to become so homesick that we give up."

"She doesn't persuade any of us. It seems to me we have the Japs on the run and are nearing their defeat."

"I agree with you Julius….." About that time, Tokyo Rose announces the Imperial Navy sinks three Liberty ships, the USS Silversides Destroyer, the USS Brom Destroyer and the USS Cobia submarine. Jacobs continues, "Hey, those ships are ours in this convoy. Thank goodness its propaganda and not a fact." He reaches over and switches off the PA system.

"How do they know the names of our ships?"

"Your guess is as good as mine."

The GIs on the ship hear all of this and laugh knowing that it is just propaganda crap. Julius walks down to the deck and looks for Cortez and Silverstein. He finds them in a polka game and asks, "Hey fellows can I join in your game and win your money before Tokyo Rose sinks us."

They laugh and say, "Come on join us."

Two days later, Commander Jacobs asks all men to listen up as he speaks on the PA system to all aboard.

"Our convoy has been ordered to pass below the Equator and remain at sea until the Palauan Islands are secured by our brave Marines and Infantry. In the meantime *The Poop Deck* will keep us abreast of significant news about the war."

With that announcement Josh and Julius, get busy publishing their next *Poop Deck* issue.

While Josh and Julius are working, the ship passes over the equator, which brings on an initiation rite commemorating a sailor's first crossing of the equator. The older and more seasoned sailors on board named as 'Sons of Neptune' pour sour liquids over the un-imitated first timers. None of the Army GIs on board have ever crossed the equator so they, known as 'Pollywogs' are at the mercy of the Sons of Neptune. Other scary acts keep the Pollywogs scattering, as King Neptune seems to rule. When the controlled chaos returns to established order and the ceremony is complete, each Pollywog receives a certificate declaring his new status as a Son of Neptune.

Julius says, "Whee, I'm glad this is over."

Josh says, "Now that we have passed over the equator we'll never have to be initiated again."

"That's right; now let's publish *The Poop Deck*."

———————————————————————

The Poop Deck
September 21, 1944

Sept. 13, 1944 -   *U.S. troops reach the Siegfried Line*

Sept. 15, 1944 -   *U.S. troops invade Morotai and the Paulaus.*

Sept. 17, 1944 -   *Angaur and Peliliu taken from the Japanese by a force comprising the first Maine Division and the US Army's 81st 321st and 322nd regimental Combat Teams.*

Sept. 20, 1944 -   *Commander Maj. Gen. Paul J. Mueller announces that the Islands are secure.*

———————————————————————

Commander Jacobs calls in Julius and Josh into his quarters and says to the two GIs, "Thank you for keeping our crews and troops abreast of the news these past two months. We are deeply grateful for your hard work. I have a letter of commendation for each of you. This will go into your military records."

"Thank you, Sir." Julius says.

Josh adds, "Yes Sir, Thank you. It has been our pleasure."

The ships are now one day away from the Islands of Anguar and Pelilu where the Signal Corps will set up the Fixed Radio Station for the South Pacific in preparation for the invasion of the Philippines. An airstrip is to be build for Air Force Bombers to use for the invasion.

The convoy arrives the next day near the shores of Anguar and Pelilu. Several Navy LKT amphibious cargo ships transport the troops, supplies and equipment to shore. The Signal Corps troops find that temporary use of pup tents is required for sleeping. Each soldier carries a backpack loaded with one-half of a pup tent, K-Rations, and other personal items. Julius has his study course books in his pack. These supplies will tide the men over for several weeks as construction crews build barracks, mess halls and other more permanent structures. Julius and Cortez share a pup tent.

Radio communications begins in two days, when the mobile radio room that has been unloaded from the ship. Placed on a temporary slab near the men's pup tents, it is accessible. This mobile radio room has its own gasoline generator attached for powering the transmitters and receivers. Julius as the T/Sergeant in charge of the radio operators posts a schedule of shift assignments for his men. Josh Wikens the T/Sergeant in charge of the cryptographic team posts his schedule along side Julius' list.

From a distance Julius sees a group of marines walking nearby. As they grow closer he notices one of the men is James Clay, his High School friend from Georgia. Julius waves to the group as he says, "Hey James, I didn't expect to see you down here."

"Neither did I expect to see you Julius. Our outfit is leaving tomorrow for the invasion of the Philippines." James says to Julius.

"Man I heard you fellows had a rough time taking these Islands from the Japanese."

"Yes it was rough; but some of us survived, thank the Lord."

"James take care in the Philippines."

As the marines march away, James says, "I'll see you in Hapeville Rainwater."

Although the Island has been secured, there may be a few Japanese soldiers hidden in the hills. Night guards, scheduled to watch for any Japs that may wonder down from the hills at night provide protection. Each Signal Corpse soldier carries a carbine rifle for which he has been well trained in its usage. One soldier stands guard duty from 1800 to 2400 and another from midnight to 0600 as assigned by Julius and Josh.

The radio room is busy with hundreds of messages each day. This keeps Julius and his men from getting bored as they operate the radios and typewriters. All messages are in code, so the operators do not know what they are typing as they copy the Morse code, further coded from English. For example, a coded message has groups of five letter words and may appear like this:

```
jklmt rspmo vwplt arqtoc umted npock lovkj jokme suptx teape negem marsh varie lttpp acekt
zocet l adim notme qrted npock lovkj jokme suptx jklmt rspmo vwplt arqtoc jadim kotme
fryhe teqpe nellm mddea carsh pptwo maybx npock lovkj jokme suptx teape negem marsh varie
```

The above message could be from the USAAF Pacific Headquarters in Honolulu ordering a bombing mission on the Philippines for a certain time and date to coordinate with the Navy ships at sea.

Some times when Julius is copying code, the Japanese harmonize in on his frequency to try to disrupt him by suddenly substituting letters into the five letter coded words. One example: kotme nellm if_ _ _ (the "f" word) us_ _ _ (the "s" word). When that happens, the cryptographic team questions Julius, but is able to work around the miss-typed words anyway.

In between shifts, Julius and his friends swim at the beach in the beautiful blue Pacific Ocean.

Julius says, "I wish we there were some girls on this Island."

Josh reminds Julius, "There were only 200 civilians on this Island and the Marines moved them over to Pelilu before we arrived."

"Oh, I remember that. I still wish we could have some girls here."

"Yes we all do!" Cortez chimes in.

"We do have movies that have girls in them over in the auditorium tent some afternoons. I wish we didn't have night blackouts so we could see movies at night." Josh says.

Julius asks, "Have you noticed that all the cigarette buts are gone from the theater area every morning?"

'I know why." Cortez answers.

"Why?"

"The Japs slip down at night and pick them up."

"I hadn't thought of that. You know you're right Mr. Cortez."

"Have you seen any Japs near the Radio Room on your guard shift?"

"No, I haven't, but did you hear about one of the Air Force guys standing guard heard something and shot at it? The next morning they find a dead cow."

"Do you really mean that?"

"That's what the Captain tells me."

"He should know."

"Have you noticed that we haven't received mail this week?"

"Maybe the mail will be here tomorrow."

Now that the new barracks are completed, Julius enjoys studying more at his bunk. It is too crowded in that little pup tent to study. Tomorrow the crew will move into the new large white framed Radio/Cryptographic Room. Julius is looking forward to more space for his radio operator crew.

Josh says, "Hey Julius, we have plenty of room in my area now, too."

Julius asks, "How do you keep unauthorized people out of the Cryptographic Room?"

"We have a combination locked door and once in the person must give the pass word for the day. Only our people know the lock combination and the daily password."

"Who assigns the password?"

"My Lieutenant gives it to us in secret each morning."

"Josh, how about the cryptographic codes you use for the messages we copy? How do you get those?"

"Each morning we receive a new code for the day from Honolulu headquarters in Diamond Head. The code is changed every single day."

"Wow! Has it ever been broken by the Japanese?"

"Not to my knowledge."

News copied by Julius and his men avoids waiting for the *Stars and Stripes*. Recent headlines and the articles behind them keep the troops at Anguar up-to-date with war victories in Europe and the Pacific.

Some recent ones for the Pacific are:

October 11, 1944 -	*U.S. Air raids against Okinawa.*
October 18, 1944 -	*Fourteen B-29s based on the Marianas attack the Japanese base at Truk.*
October 20, 1944 -	*U.S. Sixth Army invades Leyte in the Philippines.*
October 23-26 '44	*Battle of Leyte Gulf results in a decisive U.S. Naval victory.*
October 25, 1944 -	*The first suicide air (Kamikaze) attacks occur against U.S. warships in Leyte Gulf.*
November 11, 1944 -	*Iwo Jima bombarded by the U.S. Navy.*
November 24, 1944 -	*Twenty-four B-29s bomb the Nakajima aircraft factory near Tokyo.*
December 15, 1944 -	*U.S. Troops invade Mindoro in the Philippines.*

Some recent ones for Europe are:

Oct 2, 1944 -	*Warsaw Uprising ends as the Polish Home Army surrenders to the Germans.*
Oct 10-29 -	*Soviet troops capture Riga.*

Oct 14, 1944 -	*Allies liberate Athens; Rommel commits suicide.*
Oct 21, 1944 –	*Massive German surrender at Aachen.*
Nov 20, 1944 -	*French troops drive through the 'Beffort Gap' to reach the Rhine.*
Nov 24, 1944 -	*French capture Strasbourg.*
Dec 4, 1944 -	*Civil War in Greece; Athens placed under martial law.*
Dec 16, 1944 –	*Battle of the Bulge in the Ardennes.*
Dec 17, 1944 –	*Waffen SS murder 81 U.S. POWs at Malmedy*

Julius writes his mother on Christmas day 1944 as follows.

Dear Mama,   Dec. 25, 1944
This Christmas day, I miss being home with family. I wish for you and the family a Merry Christmas.

Here at the end of 1944, it appears that the Allies are winning on most fronts. In the Pacific Theater, the Philippines fall before the Military Strategist had forecast; as a result, the need for Anguar as an Air Force bomber base is gone.

The Signal Corps center is still staffed as it has been from the beginning. Most of the Air Force troops have moved on to closer Islands near the Philippines that have been secured by the Marines and Infantry. Other Signal Corps Companies have been assigned to those Islands.

Maybe I'll be home next year. I hope so!
Love, Julius
P.S. Call Gloria and tell her I'm okay.

Julius, realizing that not every radio operator is required on each shift, says to his crew, "Since we are receiving only two or three messages each day, I will let you fellows have off every other day. In other words, one-half of our crew works one day and the other half will work the next day. We will begin this slimmer shift on January 1, 1945."

There is a loud yell of approval from Julius' crew!

For several weeks, the slimmer crew works fine, however, Julius works every day and does not alternate days. However, on 1 February, Major Doug Ragsdale calls Julius to his office. Julius walks in and salutes the Officer. Ragsdale returns the salute and says, "Rainwater I hear that your crew is only working every other day. Is this correct?"

"Yes sir, that is correct." Julius answers.

"Who gave you permission to do that Sergeant?"

"No one sir, I as the crew chief made the decision because our work load has dropped to a point that everyone is not needed every day. Besides, I have noticed that the Lieutenants have started doing the same thing. Instead of two Officers on duty each shift, there is only one."

"Rainwater, start back to full shifts and I will not punish you this time. Do you hear me Sergeant?"

"Yes sir, loud and clear. Your command will be followed, sir." Julius says as he salutes and then leaves Ragsdale's office.

His men do not like hearing this, but understand why Julius must change back to full shifts.

Two weeks later Julius learns that the GI Officer (Government Inspector Officer) is investigating the affairs of Major Ragsdale. Julius thinks *I hope Ragsdale doesn't squeal on me.*

After the GI Officer leaves the Island, an announcement is posted that Major Ragsdale is relieved of his duties and will be shipped back to the States. The scuttlebutt is that he has been drinking to excess and has lost the respect of the Officers beneath him.

Julius is glad to hear this bit of news.

Julius' men ask, "Where did the Major get his liquor? We non-commissioned soldiers don't even have beer at our canteen."

Julius says, "The Officers Club is well equipped with wine, Scotch whiskey, bourbon and beer. But the club is off limits to us."

Captain Jody Marcus, the officer just beneath Ragsdale promotes to Major in charge of Julius' outfit. Marcus calls Julius into his office and congratulates Julius on a job well done.

Julius says, "Thank you sir, I try to get the job done to the best of my ability."

Marcus says, "I have always noticed that Rainwater. By the way, I think your idea about alternating your crews to an every other day shift is a good one. Why don't you reinstate your schedule since our work load is so small now?"

"You have made my day Captain, I mean Major Marcus. I'll do it right away, sir. May I ask you what has happened to Major Ragsdale?"

"Rainwater you hear the scuttlebutt going around. It is all true I am sorry to say. The drinking has been clouding his brain for sometime now. He will return to his home in New Orleans. He needs treatment for his alcoholism soon and perhaps will be able to return to active duty. You know he has 20 years in the service and I do wish the best for him."

"Thank you, sir."

Back at the barrack, Julius lays aside his study books and writes a letter to Gloria. He has always liked Gloria Welch since he first met her when she was 13 years old. He thinks *I hope Gloria and I can be close friends when I return home.*

Dear Gloria,   *Feb. 14, 1945*

313

This Valentines day, I miss being home and seeing you. Maybe next year I can see you, I hope.

I have been studying my Algebra, Trigonometry, Geometry and Physics lately. I would be bored if I didn't have my studies to do. I do swim at the beach most days and we do watch movies sometimes.

Since there are no girls on this Island, I can't get in trouble. Pleas think about me and I'll do the same for you

Maybe I'll be home next year. I hope so!

Love, Julius   *OXOX*

Although there are probably no Japs left in the hills, a night guard schedule is still in affect outside the Radio Shack just in case. Tonight is Julius' time to guard the Midnight to 0600 o'clock shift. He sits on the ground facing the hills with his carbine rifle in his lap. It is dark as midnight so he can't smoke due to the blackout restrictions. Julius pinches himself every once and a while to keep from going to sleep. He thinks *this is the most boring thing I have to do in this man's army.*

About three in the morning, Julius sees something crawling toward him. The object is about 300 feet away so he dare not shoot at it at that distance. As the hours go by the object creeps closer and closer. Julius remembers the time recently when a soldier shot a cow one night. Julius doesn't want to be blamed for something like that. He has his carbine cocked and ready to fire as soon as he can figure out what this dang object is.

As the darkness slowly begins to turn to morning light, he sees the object still moving toward him. He still can't figure out what it is. At about 6:00AM, just before his shift ends he looks closely at the object and figures out what it is.

It is a crumpled piece of newspaper moving ever so slowly as the wind blows it toward the Radio Shack. Julius lays down his carbine and thinks, *I'm glad I didn't fire at it!* He walks to his barrack and gets in his bunk to catch up with his sleep.

"Now that General MacArthur is in command of all U.S. ground forces and Adm. Nimitz in command of all naval forces, I feel that it will not be long before all of the Philippines, Iwo Jima, Okinawa and Japan itself will be under American control." Major Marcus announces to the Signal Corps troops on the Island of Anguar.

The word from Marcus is welcome news for the men who are anxious to move on from the dull duty on this small Island with no civilians and especially with no girls. Marcus then makes an announcement that thrills the troops.

"We have good news to day for you. On March 20, we are giving everyone a little R&R. We will shut down operations here for three days and all of us will board an Australian Luxury Cruise Liner for a cruise down below the Equator to Papua New Guinea. You guys deserve it and so do I."

Julius looks at Cortez and says, "Man that should be fun."

Everyone is happy and can hardly wait for March 20 to arrive.

On February 28, Julius wakes up with a toothache. He reports in to sickbay where the Doctor sends him to the Dentist tent down by the beach. He sits in a high dental chair overlooking the beautiful Pacific Ocean with white choppy waves lapping at the beach. He thinks *this is not bad at all especially if my toothache goes away.* As the Army Dentist pumps the foot pedal, he feels the grinding on his tooth, the sight of the beach goes away and each time it hurts. The wartime military dentist in remote places like Anguar do not have electricity so they use foot power to the dismay of Julius.

When it is all over the military dentist asks, "Do you feel better Sergeant Rainwater?"

"Yes thank goodness!"

Back at the Radio Shack, Julius and Cortez copy the latest war news for the troops. Some of the headlines behind the news are:

315

March 2, 1945 -	*U.S. airborne troops recapture Corregidor in the Philippines.*
March 3, 1945 -	*U.S. and Filipino troops take Manila.*
March 10, 1945 -	*Fifteen square miles of Tokyo erupts in flames after it is fire bombed by 279 B-29s.*
March 10, 1945 -	*U.S. Eighth Army invades Zamboanga Peninsula on Mindanao in the Philippines.*

The big day, March 20 arrives! This is the day all of the Signal Corps troops board the Australian cruse ship *Captain Cook I*. It is also the day that British troops liberate Mandalay, Burma.

Just after sun up, Julius and the other men line up to take a small craft out into the deep water to board the cruise liner. Julius has never been on such a ship. As he climbs out of the small craft and onto the cruise ship, an Australian sailor greets him, "Welcome aboard mate."

Julius finds the ship has luxurious bedrooms and spacious decks. The ship reaches the port at Papua New Guinea in mid-afternoon. The ship is their quarters for the three days.

On land, there are civilian men, women, and loads of sailors and soldiers from many areas of the south Pacific. Some of the women look strange to Cortez and Rainwater. They have no covering over their breast, which, for some, hang down to their waist.

Julius says, "That's not a pretty sight."

"You got that right! Hey guys let's go into the canteen, okay?" Cortez says.

"Suits me." Julius replies as they walk toward the canteen, which is next to a jewelry store.

In side the canteen '*Guinea Pub*' operated by the American Quarter Master Corps, they find hundreds of tables with sailors and soldiers enjoying their drinks.

Julius says, "I have never seen such a large crowd."

Cortez replies, "Me neither. Say look at that pretty WAC over there."

Julius turns his head and says, "Wow!"

The beautiful blonde WAC is surrounded by several high-ranking Naval Officers, so Julius and Cortez feel they do not have a chance. They find a table, order a pitcher of beer, and enjoy themselves.

The next few days they continue relaxing by looking into some of the shops and talking to GIs from around the South Pacific. Nights on the *Captain Cook I* are restful as they sleep like babies while the ship rocks with the waves at night. The food on the liner is Australian and very good. Julius has lamb chops for supper. This is his first time having lamb and he likes it. Cortez does not care for his lamb. He prefers the roast beef.

March 23, the unit boards the liner and heads back to Anguar and to the same old grind ahead for the troops.

The war news is good. On April 1, the U.S. Tenth Army invades Okinawa. In addition, a few days later, U. S. Carrier-based fighters sink the super battleship *Yamato* and several escort vessels which had planned to attack U.S. Forces at Okinawa.

April 12, 1945 is a sad day, president Roosevelt dies and Truman becomes President. Hitler thinks that the death of Roosevelt will help the Nazi efforts to regain the offensive. He is wrong.

Six days later, all of the German forces in the Ruhr surrender. Three days later, the Soviets reach Berlin.

On April 28, 1945, Italian partisans capture and hang Mussolini. Two days later, Adolph Hitler commits suicide.

VE DAY

"The most special day so far in this war is today." Julius yells as he runs out of the Radio Shack and continues, "The Germans surrender. We have won!"

May 8 is *Victory in Europe Day*. The day, which will forever be known as VE Day, is now!

The Officers close down operations and open up the Officers Club to all GIs. What a day it is as Scotch whiskey, bourbon, and gin and vodka flow like a river. Julius, not having been used to drinking, gets a little too much as he celebrates the victory in Europe with his fellow soldiers. He is not the only one as soldiers are staggering everywhere.

The next morning Julius wakes up lying in a field about a hundred yards from the barracks, not knowing how he got there. He will never forget this experience. He staggers to his barrack and climbs into his bunk to sleep over the hangover.

He privately tells Cortez, "That's the first hangover I have ever experienced. I guess it is worth it to be able to celebrate the defeat of the Germans. I can't wait until we defeat the Japanese."

"I hear we will be leaving here soon. Do you know anything about this?"

"No, but the way things have been going I'm sure we will leave this Island and go to where there is action."

Jerre 1945
VE DAY

News of Hitler committing suicide and the German Armies surrendering is wonderful news for the pilots and crews at AAF Station #120 in Attlebridge, England.

Jerre and his friends celebrate the victory in Europe with the English civilians praising the Yanks for their part in the War. There is dancing in the streets, as jugs of beer are free to all the GIs. The girls are kissing the Americans as if they do not want to see them leave. Jerre is eating all this up as a cute blond haired girl yells, "Comere and kiss me soldier boy."

Jerre says, "Winning from the Germans brings on many benefits. I'll take a lot of this."

When celebrations end, Jerre and his fellow crewmembers are awaiting reassignment, thinking they might have to go into the Pacific War to help finish off the Japanese. In the meantime, they must modify all the aircraft for the flight back to the good ole USA.

Jerre asks the flight pilot, "How about letting me fly with you to the States."

The Captain says, "Sorry Jerre but only flight personnel are allowed to return with the aircraft."

"Dang it!' Jerre says with a smile.

As Jerre and the ground crews prepare the Bombers for the flight back to America, they have no concerns about night blackouts.

Jerre says, "It's strange that we can have all of these lights on and can light our cigarettes at night. There is no fear of German airplanes being in the air looking for us. I hope the Germans never again try to start another war."

The outfit packs everything for the trip back to Scotland to board the beautiful Queen Mary for the trip back across the Atlantic. Before leaving Attlebridge, they say their goodbyes to the English friends. Jerre sheds a few tears as he sees his English friends crying.

It is a warm July day as they board the Queen Mary for the trip back.

Jerre says, "Look at this good old American food. He remembered the English food on the original trip over.

The ship sails straight with no zigzagging as before. There is no fear of enemy submarines or aircraft. The passenger soldiers enjoy the warm July sun and relax on the deck with shirts off to soak it in.

The news over the PA system:

1,000 B-29 bomber raids against Japan begin.
Liberation of Philippines declared.

> *U.S., British, and French troops move into Berlin.*
>
> *Atlee succeeds Churchill as British Prime Minister.*
>
> *The first U.S. Naval bombardment of Japanese home islands begins.*

Jerre listens to the stories behind these headlines and thinks *I'll probably not have to go to the Pacific because things are looking good over there now.* He watches from the deck of the Queen Mary as the ship floats into the dock in New Jersey.

After disembarking, the Georgia boys are sent to Fort Jackson South Carolina where they await reassignment.

Jerre asks his superior officer, "May I have a few days leave."

"Sure Williams, you deserve it."

It is a hot August day as Jerre catches the Greyhound bus for Atlanta. From the Atlanta Bus terminal, he catches the Trolley to go to Hapeville. He goes to his home away from home—the McLaughlins.

Jerre enjoys the family that took him in during the 30's. He and Jim, Jr. are like brothers. Myrtle and Jim McLaughlin are fun to be with especially when celebrating. The news from the Japanese front is a great reason to celebrate.

Jerre and Jim are listening to the radio in the McLaughlin living room on August 6 when they here that a new kind of bomb has been dropped on Hiroshima, Japan.

As they listen, Jerre says, "Wow this must be some whopper to do the damage the announcer is talking about."

The radio announcer says, "This huge bomb dropped from a B-29 Bomber flown by Col. Paul Tibbets has destroyed an entire city."

Jim says, "He calls it an atomic bomb. I've never heard of that kind of bomb."

Two days later, they hear that Russia declares war on Japan.

Jerre says, "You know I don't trust those Russians. They have grabbed most of Eastern Europe after Germany was defeated. I know they were our ally but I still don't trust them."

The news on August 9 tells about a second Atomic Bomb. This time, dropped on Nagasaki from a B-29 flown by Maj. Charles Sweeney.

The radio announces, "These two bombs may help to end the war. The rumor is that Emperor Hirohito and Japanese Prime Minister Suzuki may decide to seek immediate peace with the Allies."

Jerre says, "I hate that it came to this considering the civilian casualties, but I sure am glad the war may be over soon."

Jim says, "You know Gloria told me that Julius is in the South Pacific. I bet he is jumping up with joy right now."

Jerre says, "Man it'll be good to see old Julius again."

VJ DAY

President Truman declares Victory in Japan Day on September 2, 1945 as the formal Japanese surrender ceremony takes place on board the Missouri in Tokyo Bay.

The McLaughlin's, along with Jerre, celebrate until the wee hours of the next day. It is a joyous time; but Jerre has to return to Fort Jackson the next day to learn where the Air Force will send him next. He thinks *since the war is over now maybe I'll get my discharge; I hope.*

On the bus to Fort Jackson, he recalls that GIs receive points for their service longevity and a person with the most points is first to receive a discharge. At the base, told he does not have enough points yet he wonders what's up.

"Sergeant where will I spend time waiting until my points are enough to be discharged in Georgia?" he asks his Sergeant.

"Williams, you have a 30 day furlough which will allow you enough time to report in at Sioux Falls Air Force Base."

"Okay, I'm outahere."

Jerre learns he will begin training as a mechanic on B-29s. On his way to Sioux Falls in his 30-day furlough, he goes to Hapeville and has a great time with Jim and the McLaughlin family.

It is a sad day when he has to leave to catch the train in Atlanta but it is something he must do. Jim's grandmother, whose grandchildren call *Other Mama,* asks her husband Ron Carter, "Ron, why don't you take Jerre to the train station?"

Carter says, "I only get 3 gallons a week ration cards for gasoline, but I'll spare some for this good soldier."

Jerre, Jim and the McLaughlins jump into Carter's '38 Chevrolet and head to Terminal Station in Atlanta.

Jerre loves milk so much that when his train stops in Chicago, he buys and drinks a quart at the station right out of the bottle. *That milk is a mistake* he thinks as he arrives at Sioux Falls feeling very sick. He reports in at the base, but within four days, his gums are swollen and sensitive, so he goes on sick call.

The doctors diagnose his problem as trench mouth. He remains in the base hospital for two weeks, receiving shots to cure the ailment. While there, he almost bleeds to death one night. When he feels better, he thinks to himself, *the Lord took care of the matter.*

At the Sioux Falls USAAF base, waiting for discharge or reassignment, Jerre volunteers to serve as a flight training dispatcher. During that time, pilots could retain their 20% flight pay if they fly a number of hours each month. Dispatching these pilots is Jerre's job. To show their appreciation some of the pilots often ask Jerre to fly with them.

These men fly the single engine AT-6 (Advanced Trainer) which is fun to fly and to ride in as a passenger. These young pilots often fly very close to the ground, hedgehopping and blowing the shingles off the local farmhouses. Jerre enjoys these rides, but prays that God will take care of him.

Since Jerre, at one time, lived in Shreveport and is familiar with the area, two of the pilots who are from the Shreveport area have a weekend pass.

They ask Jerre, "Why don't you come along with us to Shreveport. You can be our flight engineer."

Jerre says, "Okay, let me ask my Sergeant if I may have a pass."

"Sergeant Kincaid, may I have a three day pass to go with the two pilots going to Shreveport?"

"No you cannot, Williams. You may be scheduled for an assignment this week-end."

"Well I'm going anyway!"

Jerre knows that his time is short for staying in the Air force, so what difference does it make.

They take off Friday afternoon in an AT-10, a twin-engine trainer.

After several hours in flight, it is getting dark and the pilot asks, "Jerre, how are we doing on gas?"

"Its getting low, I think we should go down to refuel within the next 30 minutes. I suggest you pick a place to land for refueling."

"Okay, let's land and refuel in St. Joseph, Missouri."

Some twenty minutes later, the pilot lowers down and sees a field next to a river. He lowers the landing gear, sets the flaps at 10 degrees and then the switches on the landing lights, but discovers that only one light is operative.

The co-pilot says, "My maps do not show a river at the St. Joe airport."

The pilot says, "We are committed and must land."

Skillfully the pilot lands without incident. A group of Navy vehicles drives up and tells the Air Force men that they have landed at an U.S. Navy field. The Navy comes to the Air Force's rescue with fuel while Jerre tries to repair the inoperative landing light.

Seaman First Class Hindman says, "You guys look hungry, come and have supper with us."

Jerre and his pilots eat up, thank the Navy, and go on their way.

The plane lands at the City field in Monroe, Louisiana. After parking and mooring the airplane, Jerre hitchhikes on down to Shreveport where he visits with his aunt and uncle. He also visits with his Dad on Sunday and then takes a bus to Monroe. He meets up with his pilots and they take off for Sioux Falls.

Jerre returns to his barrack to find all sixty-nine bunks gone. His bunk is the only one remaining.

"Where is everybody?" Jerre screams as he begins a search for his fellow soldiers.

Tom Killpatric, one of Jerre's acquaintances drops by and says, "Man where have you been? The Sergeant called your name and when you didn't answer, he tells everybody to forget Williams. I suggest you run as fast as you can to Building 500 and ask them where you are to go."

Jerre rushes to Building 500 as fast as he can. He sees a line of men in front of a clerk's desk. He gets in the line and when his time comes to speak to the clerk, he asks, "My name is Jerre Williams, where am I being sent?"

The clerk looks in his file cabinet and turns to Jerre, saying, "Williams, we wondered where you were. I have processed your discharge. You are out of the Army. Here is your honorable discharge certificate."

"Thank you very much!"

Jerre hails a taxi and says to the driver, "Take me to the busiest highway heading south."

With duffel bag in hand, he hitchhikes south toward home. The cars always stop for GIs making his trip successful.

As nightfall comes, Jerre finds a hotel, no matter how small the city. Early each morning he is back on the highway hitchhiking again. He has no difficulty having people pick him up. One man picks him up and Jerre notices his eyes are glassy and his speech is slurred and he thinks *this man has been drinking.*

Jerre says, "Stop the car and let me off here."

Jerre, glad to get out, continues his hitchhiking journey south. When he reaches Dallas, Texas, he contacts his stepfather and his wife, Jo Kellogg. They enjoy a short but nice visit before Jerre has to leave to hitchhike to Houston, Texas. There he visits his mother's sister before leaving for Shreveport and another visit with kinfolk.

Jerre finally arrives in Hapeville, Georgia, where he settles back into civilian life. He enters the University of Georgia in Athens, Georgia using his GI Bill privileges.

Jerre falls in love with a lovely girl, Sara Weinberg. It is now 1946.

Julius 1945-1946

Cortez says, "Julius, you are right! Did you see the notice this morning?"

"No, what notice?"

"We are scheduled to board a troop ship tomorrow. They are closing down this Island base and moving us up to Saipan."

"Where is Saipan?"

"I don't know."

Julius finds a map and learns that Saipan is in the Northern Mariana Islands just north of Guam. He shows Cortes and Silverstein the map. Everyone begins to scurry around, packing for the next chapter in their lives to begin as GIs in the Signal Corps.

Travel on the troop ship is just like the one that they came down from Hawaii on last year, only shorter. It is a hot July day when the ship arrives in Saipan.

Julius and his crew, housed in a very comfortable barrack at a large military camp at the Southern tip of the island, like the location. Company 3922 is mixed with Company 3689. The soldiers from Company 3689 have been on the Island for eight months so they show Julius and the others the ropes to the camp.

Julius writes this letter to his brother Charles:

> *Dear Charles,*   *July 16, 1945*
> *I am now in Saipan and have been in Anguar for almost a year before being shipped here. Things are going great. It looks like the war is going our way.*
>   *Maybe the invasion of Japan is next, but we don't really know.*
>   *Where are you now?*
>   *Love, Your brother Julius*

Julius spends most days at the Signal Corps communication building. The 3689 men actually are staffing the operations; however, they do ask Julius to help occasionally.

One of their men, Fred Langley, tells Julius, "You know there are still Japs up in these hills."

"How do you know?"

"The cigarette butts are all gone in the theater area every morning and it's the Japs that slip down at night to pick them up."

"Has anyone ever seen them?"

"No, but our helicopter crews have seen them sneaking around by the river in the hills. Sometimes they steal food from the mess hall at night. They take cans of beans and other stuff."

"That's interesting."

Another chapter is about to begin Julius thinks as he reads the notice that his Company is to leave on a troop ship Sunday August 3, 1945.

He tells Cortez and Silverstein, "There are rumors that the Marines and Infantry left two weeks ago for the invasion of Japan. I guess we will follow up after they secure the country to set up a Fixed Radio Station like we did in Anguar."

Cortez says, "I'll bet it will be tougher for us this time."

Silverstein says, "I'm scared, we may get killed."

Early Sunday morning, Julius and several hundreds of other soldiers, holding their duffel bag, are standing on the dock anxiously awaiting the time to board the troop ship.

Julius says, "Well Cortez, it's another chapter for us."

"What Chapter are we on now Julius?"

"Let's see, there was New Jersey, Missouri, Honolulu, Anguar and here in Saipan and now it'll be chapter six."

"I hope we are as safe in this new chapter, as you call it, as we were in the first five,"

"Let's pray that we are." Julius continues as Major Marcus interrupts the crowd.

Everything goes quite as Marcus speaks through a portable PA system to the congregation of soldiers, "Listen up men. We have orders to return to your barracks. Don't unpack, but remain there until you receive orders to board the ship."

"What's up, Julius?" Cortez asks.

"Your guess is as good as mine." Julius says.

At the barracks, Julius and Cortez go over to the canteen and enjoy some beer.

Several Infantry soldiers sitting nearby are talking to each other; one says, "I hear that the Infantry and Marines at sea have been asked to turn around. This means that the invasion of Japan is off, at least for now."

When Julius hears this, he asks, "Do you really think so soldier?"

"Yes sir Sergeant, my officer says it is true."

The next few days are lazy times since the men have no duties. Instead of twiddling their thumbs, the men play polka and shoot craps. Julius does not want to unpack his study books, so he plays and wins some money. He does unpack his toiletries so he could brush his teeth. His beard is now long so he doesn't have to shave.

The news three days later on August 6 is that some sort of huge bomb drops on the city of Hiroshima in Japan literally destroying it. Julius runs to the Signal Corps Communication Center to learn more. What he learns is unbelievable.

The Department of War in Washington has a news release coming over the radio news channel stating, "President Truman has authorized the use of a nuclear bomb on the Empire of Japan to make them surrender." It further reads, "After six months of intense firebombing of 67 other Japanese cities, the nuclear weapon '*Little Boy*' was dropped from a B-29 on the city of Hiroshima on this day August 6, 1945."

Julius tells his crew, "I'll bet hundreds of thousands of civilians were killed. If Japan surrenders, it will save millions of lives in our military and in Japan's military. Look at what happened in France and Germany at the invasion on D-Day."

"What is a nuclear bomb?" Silverstein asks.

"I have no idea." Julius answers.

The troops are waiting for news that they are to board the ship for Japan. Several days pass and they hear that a second nuclear bomb, dropped on August 9 on the city of Nagasaki has destroyed the city. A B-29 flown by Maj. Charles Sweeney drops the bomb.

For several days, rumors are floating around that Emperor Hirohito and Japanese Prime Minister Suzuki are seeking peace with the Allies.

VJ DAY

Six days after the detonation over Nagasaki, on August 15, Japan announces its surrender to the Allied Powers. The signing the Instrument of Surrender on September 2, officially ends the Pacific War and therefore ending World War II.

The Island of Saipan rocks that night. Julius is careful not to imbibe too much as he did on VE Day. He remembers the hangover headache, which reminds him to watch his booze. He enjoys VJ Day much more than VE Day. *No more war for Julius* he thinks.

The next day Julius, reports to the Signal Corpse Radio building.

As he walks in, Major Marcus greets him and says, "Sergeant I want you to work with this Japanese radio operator to send messages to all the Japanese soldiers on the Islands that we have bypassed to let them know the war is over. Now we also have helicopters dropping leaflets notifying them that Japan has surrendered and that the war is over."

"Yes sir, I'll do my best."

Through an interpreter, Julius is able to aid the former Japanese prisoner of war send messages in Japanese to the surrounding Islands. Julius notices that the former prisoner is very polite and willing to cooperate, but it is an uneasy feeling to be so close to a former enemy.

The dropped leaflets, in the mountains of Saipan, do the trick. Three days later, eighteen Japanese soldier holdouts come walking, in military formation, from the mountains to surrender to our American forces. The holdouts who survived several years in the mountains now look very clean in their worn-out ragged uniforms. The mountain river has been their source for drinking water and bodily cleansing needs during that time. Julius is impressed with their dignity in surrendering themselves.

The news that General MacArthur will head the occupation forces in Japan is good news. In addition, Julius learns that General Wainwright, a POW since May 6, 1942, released from a POW camp in Manchuria is now free. Instead of bombs, the USAAF B-29s are now dropping supplies to POWs in China and Korea.

"All troops formally scheduled to ship out must form in the assembly area immediately." Blast out from the PA speakers in all of the barracks.

All of the troops including Julius and his fellow Signal Corps men grab their belongings and head to the assembly area. After the roll call, the soldiers hear from Major Marcus, "Gentlemen, we are to board the troop ship today. Our first stop will be Yokohama Japan. Please file on to the trucks now."

"Finally, we are going this day of September 16, near my mother's birthday. We don't have to worry about fighting the Japs anymore, thanks to the nuclear bombs." Julius says.

Silverstein says, "I've always wanted to see Japan. I wonder if the Japanese will be glad to see me."

Cortez says, "Who cares."

"That's not nice Cortez." Julius tells Cortez.

Aboard ship, Julius thinks *we have been at sea many months during this war, but now we don't have to worry about war.* He sits down on a cool spot on the deck and writes letters to his mother and to Gloria. Then he thinks about his brothers and wonders where they are now. Oliver is in the Navy CBs somewhere. Dawsie is in the Merchant Marines. Charles is in the Army Quarter Master in the Pacific. Julius thinks *I guess we are all in the Pacific somewhere right now.*

After two days at sea, Julius goes up to the bridge and asks, "Sir is it possible for me to get a message to my brother?"

The First Class Seaman says, "Sure soldier, I can do that for you. What is his name and APO address?"

"Charles Rainwater, APO 3122890."

"Hey, are you a Rainwater boy?"

"Why yes, I'm Julius Rainwater."

"Do you know Oliver Rainwater?"

"That's my brother also; he's in the Navy CBs."

"His Naval Construction Battalion outfit built the airport landing strips for the B-29s back in Saipan."

"Gosh I wish I knew that back then; we could have contacted each other, while I was there."

"His outfit left for the States last week. I guess with the war over they do not need to construct air strips and bridges anymore."

"He has been in the service about two years more than I. He must have enough service points to be discharged when he gets back."

"Well Rainwater we have the information about your brother, Charles, is now in Korea at the Quarter Master post in Seoul."

"Great! I understand we will be dropping supplies off in Yokohama Japan and then sail around to Incheon the port city to Seoul. Am I right?"

"Sergeant Rainwater, you got it right. In fact, we will be arriving there in Incheon just before Thanksgiving Day."

"That's a month and a half from now. Why does it take so long to get there?"

"Sergeant, we are going to Yokohama which is the port city for Tokyo on the Pacific Ocean. We will be there about three days to unload supplies. From there the ship sails down the Eastern coast of Japan around Okinawa through the Sea of Japan and then down South around Korea on the Yellow Sea and way up North to Incheon. It'll take every bit of that time."

"Could you relay a message to my brother that I'll be arriving in Incheon and want to see him?"

"Promise you want tell the other soldiers about this, because I can't be swamped with message sending chores. However, for you I'll do it. It's easier now since we don't have to code everything."

"Thanks, uh uh what's your name?

"I am First Class Seaman Jack Tripper."

"Thanks so much Jack. I'll check back with you later."

"Jack asks, "Say aren't you the Signal Corps radio operator who started a newspaper on a sister troop ship in 1944."

"That is me!"

"Well you are known all over the Navy. You might have noticed that I have that duty in our ship's newspaper."

"Yes I have noticed and the name *Poop Deck News III* is similarly to the one we started. You do a nice job Jack."

"Thank you Julius. If you want to help me I'll let you."

"I am still trying to complete some courses I am taking with the Armed Forces Institute. I plan to study on this trip; in fact, I need to go do it now." Julius says as he walks out backwards through the door.

It is a dark cool fall day as the troop ship approaches Japan's coastline. Just as the ship reaches the dock at Yokohama, the ships Commander on the PA system announces, "Please listen up! We are no longer enemies of Japan and the Japanese, having surrendered, are now not our enemy. The Commander of all U.S. Navy Forces and General MacArthur request that all of you behave like gentlemen and treat the Japanese as you like to be treated. Do not do anything that will reflect on the conduct of American Military. This is an order."

Julius and Cortez are on the ship's deck as they hear this announcement. The deck is about 30 feet above the dock below. The Japanese are busy down below handling the tie-down ropes and look like small ants below.

Cortez says, "I still don't like those dirty Japs. I think I'll pour a bucket of cold water on them."

"You shouldn't do that Cortez. Did you not here the Commanders order?"

"Oh, okay, I'll be careful Julius."

Since nighttime has begun, the ship's GI passengers, not allowed to debark, must stay aboard until the next morning. All during the night, the noise of cargo lifting from the ship's hole keeps the GIs from some of their sleep.

As Julius awakes, he is anxious to go on land to see a little bit of Japan. The troops, advised to change their American Dollars into Japanese Yen at a bank near the dock to be legal. Julius walks down the ships long stairway to the dock below and finds the Japanese people to have a downcast appearance. Few of them speak to him perhaps because they don't understand English. Julius certainly doesn't understand Japanese.

As Julius approaches the bank, a US Army Air Force Major stops him on the street and offers Yen for his Dollars. Julius takes this opportunity to save a trip to the bank. He exchanges 60 Dollars into 900 Yen.

At the markets down in Yokohama he has fun bargaining with the merchants with his Southern English and the Japanese language it is impossible, except for the fact that money talks. A colorful silk kimono caught Julius' eye. He offers 20 Yen and receives a signal "no no" from the merchant. Finally, he agrees to 45 Yen ($3.00) as the purchase price. *This will be a good gift for Gloria* he thinks as he pays for it.

At other shops, Julius purchases Japanese jewelry and other items typical of the Oriental customs to be souvenirs to take home.

That night, back on the ship, he shares with Cortez and Silverstein about the day's activities. His two friends just wonder around looking in the shops but do not buy anything.

Julius says, "I didn't have to go to the banks to change my money."

"Where did you get your Yen?" Cortez asks.

"A Major on the street swapped Yens for my dollars." Julius answers.

"Julius, did you know you did him a favor instead of him giving you a favor."

"What do you mean?"

"Soldiers in the Occupational Army are not allowed to send Japanese money home for their wives to exchange for Dollars and place in the bank. This eliminates the black market trade. In addition, the American Occupational Dollars can only be spent in the occupied country. The Major needed your real American Dollars."

"I didn't know that! Anyway, it did save me a trip to the bank. He gave me the bank exchange rate of 15 Yen for each Dollar."

"Did you do something wrong Granddaddy?"

"No I didn't son. Maybe the Major did something wrong?"

"Well, I am just wondering."

"You do have good questions David."

"Thanks Granddaddy, but when did you come home?"
"I'm getting to that. Just be patient."
"Yes sir, I will."
The story continues.

On the third day at the dock in Yokohama, the ship prepares to depart Japan for the long voyage to Korea. Julius takes advantage of the long trip to continue his studies. He figures he is about halfway to the finish.

Recreation consists of card playing on the deck. None of the men wants to stay down in the ship's belly with the five tier bunks. It is dark down there and the diesel fueled engine smell covers the ships lower decks. The engine's roar is constantly interrupting one's sleep and thinking process. That is why everybody congregates to the top deck during times awake. That's where Julius does his studying, even with hundreds of GIs around him.

Julius likes to play polka and blackjack and usually wins. When he enters a card playing game, the others say, "Oh no, Julius is going to take our money again!" In one game, as the ship soars through the rippling waters and the salty air splashes across the faces of the players, Julius' luck goes down hill. Down to no dollars, he sells the kimono to another GI for $20.00, which allows him to get back in the game. He thinks, *sorry Gloria I'll get you something else.*

On November 22, the ship's cooks serve Thanksgiving dinner to the soldiers on board. All the GIs, longing for home, enjoy turkey, dressing, sweet potato casserole, cranberry sauce and other goodies.

Julius visits the ship's radio room to talk to Tripper. "Jack I thought you said we will arrive in Incheon before Thanksgiving Day."

"For some reason, this year Thanksgiving is on November 22 for some and for others it's on the last Thursday November 29. You know it has always been on the last Thursday of November, but this year it has been confusing to have two Thursdays for Thanksgiving Day."

"When will we arrive in Incheon?"

"Let me check the log. It looks like we will be there on November 28."

"Please send a message to my brother Charles to meet me at the dock."

"Sure thing Rainwater."

The next week passes very quickly; soon the troop ship sails into the Incheon dock. Julius comes to the stairway entrance to the ship waiting for Charles. Most of the sailors and GI passengers left to visit the Korean town, but there is no Charles.

Suddenly Julius hears a soldier say, "Hey soldier do you know where I can find Julius Rainwater?"

Julius recognizes his brother and says, "Don't you recognize your kid brother?"

"Julius, is that you behind that beard and mustache?"

"It's me Charles."

"When I last saw you in Honolulu your face was clean. You look like a wolf man Julius."

The two brothers embrace and walk down the ship's stairs to the deck together.

Charles has driven over from Seoul in a Quartermaster Jeep. During the twenty mile drive from Incheon, he and Julius talk about family and there military careers.

Julius asks, "When do you think you'll be going home?"

"I'll be leaving in three weeks. How about you?"

"I don't have enough points yet. Our ship leaves for Okinawa in two days, that's where I'll wait out the rest of my time until my point priority allows me go home."

"I guess I'll be home before you Julius."

"It looks that way Charles."

"I have a surprise for you."

"What's the surprise?"

"Thanksgiving dinner is being served at my base tomorrow and you're invited."

"Great, that makes two Thanksgiving dinners for me. Last Thursday we celebrated Thanksgiving Day on my ship."

Charles drives into the Quartermaster base in Seoul and shows Julius around the camp.

"What's that awful smell?" Julius asks.

"The sewer system here in Seoul consists of open sewer trenches running down the streets. There are no main sewer pipes. That's what you smell. I have gotten used to it and it doesn't bother me."

"I wonder why they don't have underground sewer pipes like we do in Atlanta."

"The Koreans are far behind the rest of the Western world in many of the modern facilities we take for granite in America. You'll see as I show you around the city tomorrow."

"I'm looking forward to tomorrow."

It is Thanksgiving Day at Charles' base and after a good nights sleep in Charles' barrack; Julius and Charles have a light breakfast before visiting the area.

Julius says, "I hope these people are thankful for the Americans liberating them from the Japanese."

"You know, I think they are. It's difficult to communicate with them since they don't understand English and I certainly don't speak Korean."

"I see these people smoking cigarettes quite a bit."

"We pay fifty cents for a carton of cigarettes at the base Post Exchange and these gooks will pay us $20 for a carton. It's against the military rules to sell cigarettes on the black market to these people."

"Wow! Have you tried selling on the black market?"

"No, I don't want to do something to mar my record." Charles reminds his kid brother.

"Come on Julius, it's almost time for Thanksgiving dinner. We need to get back to the base." Charles reminds Julius.

There are about 100 soldiers in the dinning room, where Julius is the guest of his brother Charles. The feast before them is delicious looking and smells good too.

"What's that in the tall brown bottles?" Julius asks.

"That's Japanese Saki Beer. Do you want some?" Charles asks.

"Sure, I'll try anything."

After tasting the rice beer called Saki, Julius says, "It's warm but taste good."

After three full glasses, Julius begins to feel good, but decides not to drink anymore for fear of getting drunk.

"The turkey and dressing is wonderful." Julius says.

"Our chef is from Georgia."

"I think it tastes like some of Mama's Southern cooking."

"He does a fine job."

Later that day, Charles takes Julius back to the ship, which leaves early the next morning.

Julius says, "Good bye, I'll see you back at home."

The ship heads for Okinawa, arriving there on December 3, 1945.

Okinawa has plenty of civilians; however, the GIs never encounter them because the Army base is a huge land area with signs in Japanese telling civilians: **DO NOT ENTER**.

Julius takes his duffel bag and other belongings and stores them on a shelf near his bunk. He reports to First Sergeant Doug Simpson as instructed.

Simpson says, "Sergeant there is nothing for the Signal Corps men to do but hang around and wait for their point priority to allow them to go home. Since you as a T/Sergeant are the ranking non-commissioned officer, what can I do for you?"

"I will be studying my Armed Forces Institute courses, but other than that I don't want to just hang around. Do you have something I can help you with?"

"How about helping us dispense the beverages supplies to the soldiers? We do that twice every week as the supplies arrives."

"Sure, I'll do that Doug."

As it turns out it is a lucky break for Julius. Carbonated beverages and 3.2 beer are available to the troops free. Each GI can have 12 cans of one or the other twice a week. Any beverages left, Doug and Julius agree to split. The carbonated drinks go fast with none left over. The beer has plenty left for Julius and Doug to divide.

Rather than wasting time sitting around sleeping and getting bored, as Cortez and Silverstein are doing, for the next few weeks, Julius spreads his Geometry, Trigonometry, Algebra and Physics books out on his bunk and studies all the time except when he and Doug dispense the beverages.

Under his bunk, he accumulates twelve cases of 3.2 Beer. He studies, has a beer, and studies, has a beer, and studies, has a beer, then goes to the split trench to relieve him of the beer. He comes back, studies, has a beer, and studies, has a beer, and studies, has a beer, then goes to the split trench again. So goes Julius' military days while he awaits his time to return home.

Cortez asks, "Julius why do you study all the time?"

"I plan to go to Georgia Tech and I am just preparing myself."

He finishes his courses and feels relieved having done so.

On January 8, 1946, Julius' time has come. He has enough points to return to the states for discharge. Another long troop ship voyage is in store for Julius. This time he will be returning to civilian life soon.

He knows what to expect on the cramped Liberty Troop ship since he has been on so many of them during the past several years. He makes friends with the Naval Radio operator, since this is something he likes. He meets First Class Seaman Clark McElroy and the two discuss their experiences as radiomen. He seeks and receives permission to send a message to his mother and to Gloria to notify them of his approximate time of arrival.

Most days Julius sits on the deck either shooting craps or playing polka with fellow soldiers. He wins some and loses some coming out even in the end.

He looks up and with the salty sea breeze flowing into his face; he sees the United States main land mountains in the distance. His heart seems to beat faster as he thinks *I'm going to kiss the ground when we land.* The ship is approaching Portland, Oregon.

After docking in Portland, the troops transport by military buses to a large staging camp full of barracks where discharge preparations happen. The soldiers separate to sleeping quarters according to their geographical destinations in the country. Julius bids his two Yankee friends, Cortez and Silverstein, goodbye.

"Hey guys lets keep in touch, okay?"

Cortez says, "We will."

Silverstein says, "Me too."

The three friends exchange home addresses and depart to their assigned sleeping barracks.

Julius meets Sgt. James Thomas, an MP from Macon, Georgia and Corporal George Phillips, an armored vehicle mechanic from Lilburn, Georgia. They decide to leave the camp and go into Portland for a few hours.

Julius, James and George meet three girls on the street who treat them like war heroes. The girls are so friendly that Julius thinks *I am already in the South.* This is the first time any of the men are around American girls or any girls in several years.

The girls take their soldiers to the USO where they dance until the wee hours of the next day.

About 2:00 AM Julius says, "We need to get back to camp because we head South tomorrow."

Julius' date says, "I love your Southern accent and then she reaches over and smacks him in the lips with her lips."

Julius thinks he is in heaven for a moment. His face turns red, but he kisses her on the lips too. He thinks *I left as an 18-year-old boy and am retuning as a 21-year-old man.*

The three Southerners bid the girls goodbye; grab a taxi and head back to camp. They get a few hours sleep before breakfast and then board the troop train to go south.

The long journey across the country from Portland to Atlanta is intriguing for Julius as he enjoys seeing several states and cities for the first time. The train passes through Boise Idaho, Salt Lake City Utah, and then Denver Colorado before Julius falls asleep.

He dreams of seeing Gloria and his family again after three years away in the Army.

In the afternoon of January 26, 1946, the train pulls into Fort McPherson. Julius learns that his discharge papers will be available the following day and that he must stay on the base until then. He rings his Mama, "Hello." His mother Bertie answers the telephone.

"Hello Mama, this is Julius. I've just arrived at Fort McPherson."

"I recognized your voice Julius. When will you be here?"

"It will be tomorrow before I can leave the base. I will be there some time in the afternoon. I'll call you when I know before I leave."

"Great! Everybody in our family will be here tomorrow night. We are having a welcome home party for you. You are the last one to come back from the war."

"Wonderful, I am sure looking forward to seeing everyone."

"We want to see you too. Call ahead of time tomorrow because Earl wants to pick you up at the base.

"Okay Mama. I love you. Goodbye."

"Goodbye."

Julius calls Gloria. He remembers her number as Raymond 3331. She answers, "Hello."

"Gloria, I'm back!"

"Really, Julius? When can I see you?"

"I'm at Fort McPherson. Can you come over?" Julius remembers that the Welch family live near the Fort.

Gloria says, "I'll ask my mother to bring me over. Where shall we meet you?"

"I'll be at the front gate."

"We'll be over in less than 30 minutes and I can't wait to see you."

"Thanks, Gloria. I can't wait to see you either. Hurry!"

"Okay."

Julius stands at the front gate of the Post, anxiously waiting and wondering what Gloria will think about him. After all, when Julius left, he was 18 and Gloria was 15. Now he is 21 and and she is 18. He sees a car approaching. It pulls up beside him and out jumps a beautiful blond haired young woman. She runs over to Julius and gives him a big hug and the two embrace in a long kiss.

Gloria pauses to say, "You really kiss me soldier boy!"

"I love it Gloria." Julius says.

Julius has learned a lot about kissing girls during the past three years, so this time his kiss is very smooth.

Gloria asks, "have you had supper yet?'

Julius is not ready to stop the kissing but says, "Not yet. But I have to be back by 11:00 tonight."

"Jump in the car. We've got supper ready for you at home."

Gloria jumps in and sits in the center beside her mother.

Julius gets in and says, "Hi! Mrs. Welch."

Luna Welch says, "My how you have grown since we dropped you off here in 1943."

"I guess I have Mrs. Welch."

As Gloria and Julius snuggle next to each other, Gloria thinks *he sure did get handsome too.*

Just a few minutes away, the three arrive at 1657 Sylvan Road, a place that brings back pleasant memories to Julius. He remembers the Saturday Night dances at this house when he was just a high school student.

After supper, Julius and Gloria excitedly talk as they sit close together on the living room sofa while Luna and Athas Welch let them have their privacy. Julius feels very comfortable with Gloria and feels that she is the woman I love. He does not tell her how he feels since he knows the two of them will require time to be sure.

Gloria enjoys being with Julius and wonders *is this the man I have been looking for?*

Gloria has not yet learned to drive so she and her mother drive back with Julius to the Fort to assure that he is there before 11:00 PM.

Finally, the next day Julius has in his hand what he has been looking for some time—discharge papers. He receives an honorable discharge with several metals to wear on his military coat.

Earl, his oldest brother, picks him up for the trip to Hapeville. When they arrive at Mama's house, what a welcome party he sees as the whole family is present to greet him.

The Rainwater Family - January 27, 1946
Back Row L-R: Julius*, Nolan & Evelyn Dobbins, Odell & Paul*
Minton, Dorothy & Charles*, Elizabeth with Baby Margaret &
Oliver*, Earl, Jr.
Second Rowe L-R: Dawsie*, Bertie, Henderson, Agnes & Lenard*
Horton, Charles & Jean Adams, Earl & Kate
Bottom Rowe L-R: Charles & Betty Horton, Douglas Minton,
Yvonne & L.R. Horton
*WWII Veterans

Mama Rainwater, overcome with joy, dines with the six boys who served in the war and who are fortunate to come home now. Several of her neighbors have a **Gold Star** card in the front window representing a son killed in action. Julius is the last to come home and Mama asks him to give a prayer of thanks before eating supper.

Bertie says, "I wish your dad could be here to see what you boys have done."

Julius says, "Mama I'll bet Grandma and Grandpa are proud of us too."

Julius you haven't heard that Grandpa Rainwater died while you were overseas, have you?"

"No! I'm so sorry. When did he pass away?"

"It was back in July of 1944."

"Well, I want to go see Grandma when I can. Does she still live in Fairburn?"

"She does. Uncle Homer Cochran and Aunt Ida have moved in with her to take care of her."

"Is she doing all right?"

"She is an amazing woman. She'll be 89 in April, but she seems as active and strong as she was twenty years ago."

"Maybe she will bake some of her famous tea cakes for me."

Julius, Charles, Oliver and Dawsie are the four Rainwater brothers who served in the war; Paul Minton and Lenard Horton are the in-laws who served. All answer questions from their mother and sisters and the young ones. Like most veterans, the men really do not care to bring up war subjects; however, out of politeness they do tell some experiences when questioned to do so.

Charles mentions, "I guess Julius and I are the only ones who saw each other over seas. Julius and I ran into each other in Honolulu and then we met for Thanksgiving dinner in Korea last fall.

Julius says, "Charles and I enjoyed a great Thanksgiving together.

"I did see Hansel Barnett in Oklahoma, but haven't heard from him since then. I met up with James Clay in Honolulu and also at Anguar Island in the South Pacific."

Dawsie says, "Hansel is home; I saw him the other day and he tells me he has been in a German prison as the war ended in Europe. I saw James Clay the other day. He is now discharged from the Marines and is going to work for the Hapeville police department."

Bertie says, "You know, Uncle Felton's son George was injured by the Germans."

Julius asks, "Is he alright?"

"He limps when he walks, but otherwise he is okay."

Bertie asks, "Julius how is Gloria?"

"She's doing okay. As you know, she and her mother picked me up last night."

"Julius, when you were in the Pacific, Gloria and I compared notes as we received your letters. That one picture you sent to us looked like you were one of the Island natives."

"I had a long beard in that picture and wore a fake grass skirt, that's why."

"When did you shave it off?"

"When I was in Okinawa waiting to come home."

Dawsie and Julius compare their travels with each other. Dawsie served in the Pacific with the Merchant Marines and later in the Army. Julius served in the Signal Corpse like his granddaddy, Ephraim Dawson Rainwater.

Julius asks Dawsie, "Are you going to go back in the service?"

"No, I'm not. What do you plan to do Julius?"

"I'm going to use my GI Bill to go to Georgia Tech."

"What are you going to study?"

"I plan to study Electrical Engineering with the Communication Option."

"That ties into your Signal Corps experience, doesn't it?"

"Yes, it sort of does, but much more."

"Good luck Julius."

"Thanks Dawsie."

Sleeping in the bed at his Mama's house feels strange to Julius that first night. He dreams about his Army days and about Gloria and about Georgia Tech. These dreams seem like wondering thoughts while awake lying in bed, trying to go to sleep.

> **David looks up into his Granddaddy's eyes and asks, "Did you think about going back in the Army?"**
>
> **"I did think about it son; but it's like this. I would not take a million dollars for the experience, but I would not give a million dollars to go through it again. Do you understand?"**
>
> **"I think so."**
>
> **"Are you ready to hear more of the war stories?"**
>
> **"What about your brothers; what did they do in the war."**
>
> **"Let me tell you about Dawsie. Listen up."**
>
> **"But Granddaddy there was six brothers in your family in the service. What about them?"**
>
> **"Remember I told you about meeting with my brother Charles. Now listen up."**
>
> **"Okay I'll listen up."**

Dawsie Rainwater
Merchant Marines and U.S. Army
WWII

The next day, Julius wanting to know more about his brother Dawsie's activities in the war sits on the front porch with Dawsie.

Julius says, "I read what President Roosevelt said about the Merchant Marines when he was still alive. Did you ever read that dawsie?"

"No I didn't; what did he say?"

"Well he praised the Merchant Marines for the great service they rendered in the war effort.

"Dawsie, I'm proud of what you did during the war. Many people do not understand the fact that the men who served as Mariners are heroes and many of them gave their lives for America. We hear a lot about the Marines, the Air Force, the Navy, the Infantry and many other Army units; but we don't hear much about the Merchant Marines."

"I guess you are right Julius; but, I never thought about it. I just did my job when I served."

"Dawsie, I was already in the Signal Corps and didn't follow much about your service in the Mariners. Tell me about how you served."

"It's a long story. I was in high school enjoying playing football at Hapeville High, but didn't like studying that much. When you left for the service, I turned 16 and wanted to do what my older brothers were doing—serve in the war effort. I didn't want to wait 'till I was 18, so I, went with several of my friends to join the Navy. I was broken hearted when all of my friends got in but I was rejected."

"Why did they reject you?"

"I was color blind."

"What happened when you couldn't get into the Navy?"

"The Navy officer-in-charge says, 'Rainwater if you really want to sail the seas, go across the street to the Merchant Marines recruiting office; they will let you join.'

"So I went across the street, signed up, and was accepted on the spot. They must have needed me really bad, because they told me to go home, pack your clothes and report back the next morning."

"Is that what you did?"

"Yes I did. Mama didn't want me to join; but, I was hard headed and did anyway."

"Well what happened?"

"The very next morning at 8:00 AM., the recruiting officer put me on a train for St. Petersburg, Florida. I spent two months of rugged training to be a Merchant Mariner in warm Florida.

"In July of 1944, I was placed on a train for San Francisco. While there, several of us young boys enjoyed walking down Market Street and riding the cable cars up and down the hills of that beautiful city. We played fun games along the way at the penny arcades. We remained in San Francisco for about a month preparing the Liberty ship for departure.

"I began to grow up very fast as I was around a bunch of *'old salties'*. Those *'old salties'* taught me about everything: card playing, drinking and some things I'll not mention.

We find ourselves heading out to sea when the big ship turns around and heads back to port because Japanese submarines are spotted ahead. When we did leave port, there was a fleet of nearly one-hundred ships in our convoy. There were battleships, destroyers and many Liberty cargo-troop ships, including ours, the SS William H. Stewart. We were well protected by the U.S. Naval Armed guards as we traveled to the South Pacific."

"Where did you go in the South Pacific?"

"In November of 1944, our ship was one of many that went into the Battle of the Philippines at Leyte. I was lucky because the Japanese Zero planes didn't bomb our ship. Many Kamikaze pilots dived into other ships during this battle. At night, we were forced into total blackout so the Zeros couldn't see us. Of course our aircraft carriers have fighter planes that have dog fights with the Zeros and did shoot hundreds of them down."

"Were you scared Dawsie?"

"I guess I was too young and adventuresome to be scared. You know I never thought about death. However, many merchant mariners died during this battle. Someone told me that there were more Mariners killed in that battle than all the other services combined."

"That sounds scary Dawsie; I'm glad you made it back brother. By the way, what did your ships transport?"

"Mostly food supplies and some troops were transported by us. We carried lots of K-rations and other food products. We even transported Australian troops in the South Pacific."

"Did you go to Australia?"

"Yes and I also went to Borneo and quite a few of the Islands in the South Pacific."

"Did you ever go to the Southern Palau Islands?"

"We went by those Islands on the way to the Philippines. There were a lot of Merchant Marine ships lost there in early 1944 in the battles for Anguar and Pelilu."

"Did you know that I was on Anguar Island?"

"That's what you said last night when we were talking about our experiences with Mama."

"What did you do to pass the time on the ship when you were traveling through the ocean?"

"We played polka, blackjack and shot craps with the dice. The *'old salties'* have something to drink for us, even though they were not supposed to bring it aboard. The ships commander closed his eyes to what they were doing. Maybe they supplied him with his scotch whiskey."

"When did you come home?"

"Our ship arrived back in San Francisco in February of 1945."

"What did you do when you came home?"

"Well I was discharged from the Merchant Marines and then I went back to Hapeville High so I could play football. You know that was my first love!"

"I hear that you then went into the Army. Is that correct?"

"Yes, when I turned 18 in March of 1945, I was eligible for the draft. In June, the draft called me up. I first went to Fort McPherson. Guess who was drafted at the same time with me?"

"Who?"

"I'm sure you remember Ray Nash and Bob Camp and our cousin Allen Rainwater .They were at Fort McPherson with me."

"Well that was just last year. What happened?"

"I eventually wound up in Saipan just before the war ended. When the war ended, we were just making time. You know Saipan is an interesting place. Just 22 miles long and 3 miles wide, it must have been about a mile high. Our station was at the radar station on top of the mountain."

"Wow Dawsie, I was there and didn't know you were there, too."

"Where were you stationed Julius?"

"I was down near the southern coast. We were preparing for the invasion of Japan when the war ended. After the war's end, we left Saipan and delivered supplies to Japan and Korea before I was discharged from Okinawa. Dawsie what did you do there?"

"I volunteered to be a cook. I made out, as I pretended to know all about cooking; I did know how to fry eggs and make S.O.S. toast and a few other things. I could open canned food. I really fooled them. What helped is that I remembered how Mama used to cook turkey, dressing, corn bread and mashed potatoes, so I started cooking like Mama cooked and the men loved it."

"Dawsie tell me some of the interesting things you saw in Saipan?"

"Julius did you hear about '*suicide leap*'?"

"Yes, but I never saw it."

"It was near our camp at the top of the mountain. When the American Marines were advancing up the mountainside, hundreds of Japanese soldiers retreated to the *'suicide leap'* and jumped off the deep cliff to their deaths."

"That's interesting Dawsie. Do you have any more interesting stuff?"

"As the cook, I surprised the men one time with bunches of bananas I picked off the trees down below the mountain. I hung them all around the mess hall and they went fast. Those were a big hit."

"You were a Sergeant; isn't that right?"

"Yes I received a field promotion to Staff Sergeant to replace the mess hall sergeant who was eligible to leave Saipan and return to the states."

"Did you play polka?"

"I did and I usually lost when I played. I sent most of my money home to Mama."

"Say when did you come home?"

"I was discharged just last month, just before Christmas."

"That is about a month before I was discharged two days ago at Fort McPherson."

"That's right Julius."

"Thanks a lot Dawsie for bringing me up to date. We were in the South Pacific at the same time and did not know it. You have two service involvements; that is more than most of us. Aren't you glad it's all over?"

"I sure am!"

Chapter 8

After the War

Julius (1946)

Julius rides the trolley to Gloria's house everyday for the next few weeks. They enjoy being with each other and find that the movies shared at the movie house are more fun together than as individuals.

The most special day in Julius' life happens on February 14, 1946. He and Gloria express to each other that they are so in love with each other that they agree to announce their engagement to be married. They decide to marry only after Julius completes his degree at Georgia Tech. That means waiting four years.

Julius enters Georgia Tech in September that fall, after working part time selling shoes at the Butler Shoe store in Atlanta during the summer to support him before entering Tech. Between dating Gloria and the many telephone calls with Gloria, his grades the first quarter suffers, although he passes every subject. Julius and Gloria change their minds and move the wedding date to December 22, 1946.

Julius' mother asks, "Julius what happened to the four year wait?"

"We both can't wait that long Mama. My study needs will be better served when Gloria and I don't have to just date with my spending so much time at her house. When we get married, I can study during the day while Gloria works. The GI bill pays more for married students too." Julius explains to his mother.

"Where will you live?"

"Gloria's mother and daddy have two rooms in the back of their house, a kitchen and bedroom where we will live."

"Julius you know you have my blessing."

"Thank you Mom."

With that blessing and Mr. Welch's permission, Julius and Gloria, marry on December 22. The two will spend their early marriage days with Gloria working and Julius studying at Georgia Tech.

Dawsie (1947)

After Julius and Gloria marry in 1946, Dawsie meets Mary Gilmer, a beautiful Hapeville girl and the two fall in love.

Julius is busy studying at Georgia Tech but still has time to visit his brother Dawsie who is still at home with their Mama.

When Dawsie and Mary's marriage is approaching, Dawsie asks, "Julius old buddy will you help me get ready for my marriage?"

"You know I will."

On Friday night before the wedding, the two brothers are sitting on the front parch at their Mama's house when she walks out the front door.

"Dawsie do you mind going into the house. I need to ask Julius something." Bertie asks.

"Okay Mama?" Dawsie says as he leaves, puzzled at why his mother ask him to leave.

Julius asks, "Mama what do you need from me?"

"Son, please talk to Dawsie about marriage and you know *'the birds and the bees'*. He is young and you, as a man, can tell him better than I can."

"Okay, I will Mama." However, in his mind he knows that Dawsie, now 20-years-old, knows about as much as he did when he married Gloria the year before. After all Dawsie has spent two times in the service during the past war and a fellow learns a lot about girls and sex during those years.

Dawsie and Julius later laugh about what Mama wanted Julius to tell his younger brother.

Dawsie says, "Julius tomorrow is the big day. I need you to go with me to get the license and the ring."

"You know I don't own a car so you'll have to pick me up. Oh, and I am going to the Duke Football game tomorrow. It's home coming at Tech."

"That's okay, I'll pick you up first thing tomorrow and we will go to the marriage license bureau and to the jewelry store before your game. Then I'll pick you up after the game to go to the wedding at the Justice of the Peace. You are my best man."

"It's a deal."

The next day, November 1, 1947, it rains so hard that Julius remarks as Dawsie picks him up outside Grant Field, "It rained *cats and dogs* all through the game, but Tech won because Bobby Dodd is such a great coach."

"Thanks for helping me today. I'm as nervous as a *cat on a tin roof.* I bet you were too when you married last year in a church wedding."

"You'll get over it tonight when you and Mary check into the motel for your honeymoon."

The marriage is a good one; their adjustment as newlyweds goes smoothly.

He and Mary move into a nice little apartment where Julius and Gloria visit several times when Julius could pull himself away from his studies.

Dawsie finds work at the new Ford Plant in Hapeville.

Julius' Army Friend Cortez

At Julius' house, he is the main cook for supper since he comes home from school early and Gloria works at the Southern Bell office in downtown Atlanta. His choice of menus may not be the best but it is the best for a young man studying all afternoon and then preparing supper for him and his wife. This night's menu is creamed corn, butter beans, cabbage and iced tea. He prepares just enough for himself and Gloria. It is simmering on the stove to keep it warm as Gloria walks in and gives Julius a big hug, as she smells the food. They sit and talk in the living room before supper.

"Julius, I hear some one at the door." Gloria says as she motions for Julius to answer the door.

Julius says as he walks to the front door, "It's probably someone for your parents."

When he opens the door, he sees a friend from the Signal Corps. It's Cortez and a woman. Julius greets his WW II friend and invites them into the living room.

"Gloria, do you remember me telling you about Cortez. This is him!"

Cortez says, "Glad to meet you Gloria, so youse guys got married I see. Let me introduce my wife Florentine."

"I'm so happy to meet you folks. Julius has told me a lot about you Cortez. Glad to meet you both. Julius never told me your first name Cortez." Gloria says.

"I have six names altogether, so most people just call me Cortez. You might know that Spanish people sometimes have five or six names. Mine are: Emanuel Hernando Horacio Benito Antonio Cortez."

Gloria says, "I'll just call you Cortez."

Florentine speaks, "I call him Honey but sometimes Cortez, too."

They all sit down and talk about what's happening with each other and begin reminiscing about Julius and Cortez's wartime experiences.

To the surprise of Julius, Cortez asks, "Why not quit Tech and get a job like I have. There is a lot of money to be made out there."

"If I get a degree from GA Tech I believe my chances are much better for getting a job that I like. Where are you working Cortez?"

"I am a radio operator for RCA."

Julius thinks *that is not much of a future* but says, "I hope you like what you are doing."

Soon Cortez remarks, "We are on our way to Florida. I guess we must bid youse guys goodbye. Are you ready Florentine?"

After goodbyes, Julius rushes back to the kitchen to be sure the food has not simmered away.

Friends, Inc.

Julius and his high school friends: Jerre Williams, Jim McLaughlin, Dillard Rosser, Hansel Barnett, Lamar Foster, John Harrelson and Bud Kincaid decide to meet every month at alternating homes to keep their post-war friendship alive. They play penny-ante polka as they reminisce about the past. This becomes a lasting friendship group.

Jerre says, "Say why don't we call ourselves *Friends, Inc.*"

"Hey I like that idea." Julius says.

So the group, meeting each month, is forever known as *Friends, Inc.* This arrangement goes on for a couple of years when the wives say, "Hey! How about letting us be a part of Friends, Inc?"

All the men agree to include the wives. Gloria Rainwater, Sarah Williams, Velma McLaughlin, Melba Rosser, Betty Barnett, Sybil Foster, Pearl Harrelson, Betty Stancill (Jim's sister and her husband Weldon Stancill are now included.) and Ophelia Kincaid join the group of men each month, not to play polka, but to socialize in a more civilized manner. The men having gotten tired of just playing polka each month welcome this change. Besides, the feminine side is more enjoyable to look at each month.

Julius graduates from Georgia Tech in the fall of 1949 just a month before his pregnant wife, Gloria is to give birth to their first child.

Gloria's mother says, "Julius your timing is perfect, you finished Tech before having to provide for a baby."

Gloria says, "I have something to do with that timing too Mama."

Dawsie and Mary give birth to their first born-Lonnie Rainwater. On October 11, 1949, Lonnie is born and named after his grandfather, Mary's father.

Julius and Gloria give birth to Hank Rainwater the next day. On October 12, 1949, Julius Henry Rainwater, Jr. is born. They call him Hank to distinguish him from his daddy Julius.

Luna Mae, Gloria's mother says, "You can't call that little sweet baby, Hank! That sounds more like a cowboy's name."

Nevertheless, the name Hank it is and it sticks.

At Crawford Long Hospital in Atlanta, there are now two Rainwater babies. The nursery ward Nurse-In-Charge, Estelle Hilton, places Hank on the third floor and Lonnie on the fourth floor to keep them from getting mixed up. Estelle Hilton, the sister of Bertie, is the aunt of Julius and Dawsie. You can bet that Lonnie and Hank receive excellent care.

> **David looks up and says, "I didn't realize my daddy has a cousin born about the same time as his birth."**
>
> **"Yes it really happened and did you know that my mother was born on October 10, 1865. We celebrate three birthdays, on October 10, 11, and 12."**

**"Really? Did the hospital keep the two
babies separated alright?"**
"Yes they did David."
"Tell me some more Granddaddy."
"Okay."

Dawsie works at the Ford Plant and Julius works at The Warren Company, a commercial refrigerator manufacturing company.

Julius' friends group, *Friends Inc.,* all begin to grow their families, too. The monthly meetings sometimes change to allow the wives to give birth to new offspring.

At one of their meetings, Julius says, "I hope our children will never have to fight in an American war."

Hansel says, "The United Nations is supposed to prevent future wars, I thought."

"The Russians seem to be our biggest threat now." Jerre says.

Jim says, "Since Russia was awarded East Germany and North Korea, these countries have become Communist nations siding with Russia. I'm not sure what the U.N. can do."

"Communism, I believe will be our future enemy." Julius says.

Sarah asks, "Why can't the world live in peace?"

Gloria says, "It's because of greed and power hungry men."

"I hear my baby crying, please excuse me." Velma says as she checks on her baby daughter Vicky.

The discussions that these friends are having are typical of the discussions on the minds of most Americans who have just recovered from the most devastative war ever, only a few short years earlier.

**"I know a little bit about the Korean War,
Granddaddy; did any of the Rainwater family
get involved in that war?"** David asks.
"What do you know about it David?"
"Not much I guess."

"Well to answer your question; we did have Rainwater's in the Korean War."

"Who was it?"

"It's time for your nap son. When you rest awhile I'll tell you."

"What are you going to do Granddaddy?

"I'm going to the bathroom and then grab a nap myself."

"Okay Granddaddy, but don't forget to tell me when you wake up."

As David walks toward the bedroom, I think to myself, *I need to collect my thoughts about the Korean War while he's napping.*

Chapter 9

The Korean War

On June 25, 1950 at approximately 4 a.m. (Korean Standard Time) on a rainy Sunday morning, Democratic People's Republic of Korea Army (North Korea) artillery and mortars open fire on Republic of Korea (South Korea) Army positions south of the 38th Parallel, the line then serving as the border between the two countries. North Korea claims South Korea's forces attacked North Korea in the west area and their declaration of war is in response to this attack.

This claim is bogus. President Harry S. Truman returns from his home in Independence, Missouri, to Washington, D.C., arriving in early afternoon. Meanwhile the U.N. Security Council passes a resolution calling for the immediate cessation of hostilities and the withdrawal of North Korean forces to north of the 38th Parallel.

As all hell breaks out in Korea, Dawsie calls his brother Julius on the telephone, "Julius I have been called back into service."

Julius questions, "But you have already served in the last war, why are they calling you back?"

"I guess they can because I am a member of the reserves."

"When did you join the reserves?"

"It was just after Mary and I married. Some of my friends were joining the Army Reserves, so I joined too. I was able to keep my Staff Sergeant rank and the extra reserve pay helps. I only have to meet twice a month. There is nothing for me to do but answer the call and go.

Julius says, "Let me know if I can help in any way."

. As an Army reservist, Dawsie reports to Fort McPherson in August of 1950. Sent by train to Fort Eustis in Newport News, Virginia where men train for upcoming military service. Dawsie is surprised at the size of this base. The United States Transportation Center serves all vehicle training for all branches of the army.

Dawsie asks his Sergeant, "Man this is a big place. What all do they do here?"

"Rainwater, this is an education and on-the-job training center for all modes of transportation maintenance." Sergeant Jackson answers.

With Dawsie's experience, they ask him to serve as the Mess Sergeant for his outfit. This is to his enjoyment because he loves being around the food in the mess hall. All the other men have to take basic training. He enjoys drinking his coffee in the mornings waving bye to the men as they march out for training. Some of the men laugh at Dawsie because he has to work in the mess hall; but he loves it.

After about three weeks, Dawsie has a chance to relax and make friends with some of the fellow soldiers. He and Mike Jordan decide to visit the city outside the Fort.

Mike says, "Did you know that this was a great battle site during the Civil War?"

"No I didn't know that." Dawsie answers.

"As we walk along the Great Warwick Road, I think about the battles that took place here during the Civil War. This is where the American navy was born."

"Where did you learn that stuff Mike?"

"My father is a history teacher back home in Alabama and he told to me about this place many times."

The two soldiers walk out to the docs and watch the great ships floating gently along the bay.

They walk into a museum and learn a little more about the history of Newport News.

Dawsie says, "We see where Civil War soldiers are being honored. I wonder if the World War Two soldiers will ever be honored like we see here."

"That's right; you were in that war too. I'm sure that your war hero efforts will be honored one day. I was too young for world War Two. Say, why are you in this war?"

"Because I joined the reserves and here I am." Dawsie explains as he thinks, *I wish I could be home with Mary and Lonnie."*

"Hey Dawsie, let's go pick up some girls tonight. Do you want to?"

"Look man, I'm an old 23-year-old married man. I can't do that."

"Oh! I forgot about that."

"Why don't you ask Joe Mitchell? He's a young single buck and may be anxious to find a girl."

"That's a good suggestion Dawsie. I'll do that."

That night Mike and Joe go looking for girls.

Dawsie stays at the base and calls Mary. "Mary this is your handsome husband."

"Hi! Handsome what are you up to?"

"I'm just sitting here thinking about you and Lonnie."

"Do you really miss me Dawsie?"

"I miss you so much I could kiss you over this telephone. Smack Smack."

"Smack Smack." Mary responds as she misses Dawsie very much.

"Say Honey how's Lonnie?"

"He's doing just fine, Dawsie."

"Mary give Mama a call and tell her that I'm okay, please. And call Julius and Gloria too."

"I will sweetheart."

"I guess I better go because this long distance telephone call is costing us a fortune. Bye Bye."

"Bye bye sweetheart."

The next morning at breakfast, Dawsie leaves the kitchen and sits with Mike and Joe in the Mess Hall.

Dawsie asks, "Did you guys get a date last night?"

Joe speaks first, "We did. We found some hot blonde-haired girls. Man you should have been with us."

Mike says, "He's teasing you Dawsie. Don't believe a word he says."

"Tell me what really happened."

Mike says, "We did find two nice girls and they invited us to a prayer meeting at their church."

"Did you go?"

"Yes we did; but I think Joe was bored."

"Is that right Joe?"

"I was looking for a little more action."

Vigorous training for the troops, except in Dawsie's case, continues as the men await assignment to Korea. The *Stars and Stripes* news keeps them abreast of happenings in Korea:

Stars and Stripes
October 1, 1950

Gen. MacArthur receives permission from President Truman to employ U.S. ground support forces and to carry the war into North Korea and the waters offshore but to stay well clear of the Manchurian and Soviet borders. Later, he receives permission to deploy one Regimental Combat Team to Korea to establish a defense line in Pusan area to assure retention of the port. The order is expands to

*two combat divisions and with permission to employ
these forces against North Korean forces in the Suwon
area. The United States is now fully involved in the
Korean War.*

*The Thirty-Fourth Infantry Regiment and
Twenty-Fourth Infantry Division are maintaining
the port at Pusan on the southern tip of Korea and
are advancing northward toward the North Korean
strong holds.*

Dawsie, Joe, and Mike ponder their destinies as they hear the news. They know that the United Nations is backing this war and also other countries such as Britain, Australia, Canada and many freedom-loving countries are in support positions; but it is still a dangerous venture for American young men to face.

The general public opinion of this war for Americans is a mixed one. Since WW II was over just five years before, many question our motives in Korea. ***Who are we to police the World*** is the headlines of some of the liberal newspapers.

It doesn't take long for Dawsie to become very homesick. After two months, Mary and Lonnie move to Newport News. Dawsie, Mary and Lonnie share a two-bedroom apartment with an army friend, Jason White, his wife and little girl, Betty Joe, about Lonnie's age.

Four months later, the army outfit must go to Korea. Mary, Lonnie, and all the other army wives return to their respective homes. Mary moves in with her mother and dad while Dawsie is away.

The outfit leaves Fort Eustis by train for San Francisco California. A month later, the troops board a plane for Hawaii their first stop to re-fuel. Hawaii, a beautiful and warm place where Dawsie wishes he could stay. The troops will now board planes for their trip to Japan.

With the flight attendants on the plane, looking after the troops as if they are vacationers it takes away from the fact that they are going to war. The plane lands in Japan where they remain about a month awaiting shipment to Korea.

Finally, on a troop ship heading to Korea, Dawsie thinks, *this is nothing but a smelly old cattle boat.* The sack lunches three times a day do not make the two-day trip any more enjoyable. On board Dawsie meets several soldiers, wounded, sent to a hospital in Japan and now returning to the fight on the front lines in Korea. The sight of the wounded begins to worry Dawsie as he thinks *what if I am hurt or killed. What will Mary and Lonnie do?*

These thoughts bring Dawsie to the side of the ship alone where he looks up and prays to God.

> *"Dear God, keep me safe, bring me back home to my family. If you will do this, for me now I'll always put You first in my life. Please do this for me God."*

Dawsie knows he should not make deals with God but he does anyway. God made sure he never forgets his promise because anytime he steps out of line, God reminds him of this promise.

God is watching over Dawsie as the ship arrives in the port city of Puson in the South Eastern tip of Korea. The 425th Transportation Division transports to Taegu up in the mountainous farmlands of ROK. The region, known for its apple trees has beautiful farms everywhere.

As mess Sergeant, Dawsie has two teams of cooks, one baker, five Korean mess boys, and one stove man. Dawsie knows a lot more about cooking now than he did in his WWII days. He enjoys what he is doing. He has some great cooks and begins to gain wait. His team feeds 100 men and 25 officers 3 meals a day. He has a jeep and a truck at his disposal. Dawsie plans all the daily menus for two shifts, orders the rations and picks up the rations.

The 425th Transportation Division has men in many areas of Korea but mostly behind the fighting lines. The headquarters at Taegu is relatively safe for Dawsie. God is living up to Dawsie's prayer request and Dawsie is living up to his promise to God.

General MacArthur wants to drop the atomic bomb on North Korea; President Truman relieves him of his command because of these views.

Dawsie says, "I think MacArthur is right. We should use the bomb to end this killing."

Dawsie's Captain says, "I think the United Nations and the other countries will look down on us if we do that."

"I guess you are right sir."

It is April 1951 when Truman removes MacArthur from command for publicly disagreeing with his Korean War Policy.

Many people do agree with MacArthur especially because of his military dictum, "In war, there is no substitute for victory." However, MacArthur warns, "The soldier, above all people, prays for peace, for he must suffer and bear the deepest wounds and scars of war."

Dawsie thinks *MacArthur is a great General he has fought in WW1, WW2, and this war. He has risen to the rank of General of the Army.* Public opinion back in America is two fold: those who think we shouldn't be in Korea and those who feel we must protect our freedom from the Communist.

Dawsie goes about serving faithfully disregarding the public opinion. As a volunteer in the reserves, he lives up to his duties. He is thankful for not having to be in harm's way on the front lines.

One day, several of the cooks along with Dawsie go fishing at a nearby lake. Dawsie fell into the lake, nearly drowning before artificial respiration, by one of the cooks, restores his breathing. He never fishes again in Korea.

One of Dawsie's special good deeds that he enjoys is the feeding of the Korean children. Left over's at each meal, he hands through the fence behind the mess hall to a group of happy hungry children. He pads his food orders to have plenty for left overs.

On a night a month before Dawsie leaves Korea, he is going over to the mess hall when one of his men stops him and says, "You can't go over there now."

It is Dawsie's 25th birthday. The baker, cooking Dawsie a birthday cake, asked the man to keep Dawsie away until the cake is ready.

The man continues as he says, "You better act surprised."

Dawsie does act surprised and enjoys every bit of the birthday celebration on that March 14, 1952.

The Korean War truce talks began last year but the only agreement between the two sides is on the 38th Parallel as the line of demarcation. Gen. Mark Clark assumes command of U.N. forces in Korea, in May of 1952. He is confronted with a military deadlock on the front lines; he steps up military pressure believing that the Communists only understand force.

It is Dawsie's time to return home. Other fresh troops will replace men in his outfit. Dawsie has many Korean friends, especially the young children. It is a tearful time as he bids these people goodbye. The little children are sad to know he is leaving them. However, Dawsie is happy to be returning to the good old U.S.A.

His troop ship arrives in Seattle in May 1952. All the soldiers from Georgia take a train to Augusta, Georgia for discharge from the army. Mary and Lonnie meet him in Augusta with open arms.

As the three arrive home in Jonesboro, Dawsie says, "Honey it is so good to be home with you and Lonnie."

That night Dawsie and Mary make up on a lot of missed loving.

The war in Korea continues into the summer of 1953. An armistice, signed in Paris by the United States, North Korea and China on July 27 ends the war but fails to bring about a permanent peace, as South and North Korea do not sign a peace treaty.

War is horrible! During the war, nearly thirty thousand service members die in battle, or from battle-related injuries.

Dawsie is happy as he ponders his promise, *God I haven't forgotten my promise to You.*

Back at work at the Ford assembly plant in Hapeville, Dawsie settles down and enjoys family life again.

Epilogue

Wars after WW II

The Author's Perception of these Wars

After WWII, there continued to be a period of tension and competition between the United States and the Soviet Union including their respective allies. This period, known as the 'Cold War' began in the mid 1940s. These two superpowers tried to outdo each other, not only militarily, but in ideology and in technological developments. As a result, massive defense budgets occurred. Espionage was rampant on both sides. The race to nuclear arms, while very scary, eventually led to an agreement to limit the nuclear arsenals in both nations. Even now in April of 2010, Barack Obama and Russian President Dmitry Medvedev agreed to sharp cuts in the nuclear arsenals of both nations.

Toward the end of WWII, meetings held between Roosevelt, Churchill, Stalin and later Truman to agree upon who would occupy or control the destinies of the defeated German Nazi country. Russia occupied East Germany, the Eastern countries surrounding Russia (Russia forms the '**Union of Soviet Socialist Republics**'.), and North Korea (after the Korean War). North Korea and China became Communist allies of the Soviet Union.

The United States, United Kingdom and France jointly controlled West Germany. Later the United States occupied the defeated Japanese country.

The largest city in East Germany, Berlin, was divided into four sectors controlled by U.S., U.K., USSR and France. The West, surrounded by the Soviet occupation zone, supplied their troops and the population using truck convoys and rail cars traveling from West Germany through East German rail lines and an Autobahn to reach Berlin.

Early in 1948, the Soviets flexed their muscles by blocking the west from having access through the eastern zone for trains bringing in supplies to the Berlin west zones. The Berlin blockade was the beginning of the Cold War era, with many more Soviet threats to follow. Later in the same year, the Soviets announce that the Autobahn leading into Berlin from West Germany is closed. Air lane lanes had been agreed upon so the West began the greatest Airlift in history to force the Soviet Union into backing away from their bluff. It worked and Stalin lifts the blockade in May of 1949.

The most serious event of the Cold turned into a *'Hot War'* when the Korean War began in June of 1950 as communist North Korea invaded South Korea below the agreed upon 38° Parallel border between the North and South. I wrote about this War in Chapter 9 since my brother, Dawsie Rainwater a member of the National Reserve, was called back into service for this war. The war continued into the summer of 1953 when an armistice, signed in Paris by the United States, North Korea and China in July ended the war. Friction between these two countries is precarious even today in 2010. Neither side officially signed a peace treaty.

The most horrible *'Hot War'* occurring in the Cold War era was the Vietnam War. We in America, at first, viewed this crisis as Indochina fighting in a colonization feud with the French; but it turned into the worst and only war that the U.S. ever fought and lost. China and USSR backed Ho Chi Minh's regime in the North. Like Korea, Vietnam was divided at the 17° Parallel.

Under the terms of a Geneva Convention agreement civilians could move freely between the two states. Communism ruled in the north, under Ho Chi Minh, while democracy ruled in the South, under Ngo Dinh Diem. The U.S. involvement began as an aspect of its advisory role to France in 1950, when Truman was President. Presidents Eisenhower, Kennedy, Johnson, Nixon and Ford all inherited this war. As the U.S. increased its position from advisor to fighting ally and finally all out war, there were ever increasing casualties. Public protest against our involvement took to the streets. Finally, after a ceasefire and evacuation agreement was reached in Paris in 1975, the war ended! I remember seeing on television the helicopters evacuating the last of our embassy representatives. It was very hectic with Vietnamese civilians begging to be evacuated. The South Vietnamese did not sign the Paris agreement and people were left to fend for themselves within Ho Chi Minh's dictatorship. Some people say today that Iraqi was President George W. Bush's Vietnam.

President John F. Kennedy had his hands full during the beginning of the Cold War era. The Vietnam War was not his only concern. Closer to our own shores, Castro's Cuba adopted communism, with the backing of USSR. In an attempt to overthrow Castro's regime, the U.S. used Cuban exiles to launch an operation in Cuba, named after the Cuban bay called the '*Bay of Pigs*'. The Cuban army defeated these exiles in about three days during the spring of 1961.

A year later our country was at the brink of a nuclear war with the Soviets as Kennedy sent war ships to block a fleet of Soviet ships in the Atlantic loaded with nuclear missiles headed for Cuba. This major confrontation with the Soviets had our people scared and afraid that a nuclear war was eminent. I'm not exactly sure how the threats and negotiations went; but several weeks later, the Soviets backed away and promised not to deliver nuclear missiles to Cuba. I think the deal breaker was that NATO agreed to remove missiles from Turkey. My wife Gloria and I were relieved when this threat was over. Our daughter, Jan, remembers "nuclear war drills" in grammar school because the children had to hide under their desks, or were timed on how quickly they could run home if this became necessary. Some Americans even built 'bomb shelters" in their homes.

While this book is about wars, I will divert to a day I remember it as if it were today, when President **John** F. Kennedy was assassinated. I was at the Atlanta airport that Friday November 22, 1963 when the news first broke. *'Did the Russians do this?'* flashes in my mind. Many women (and some men) were crying that day in the airport terminal. *Now we know that the Soviets were not involved,* I think. It was a sobering weekend as all television programs ceased and changed to religious themes. People all over America mourn the loss of its leader for many days. My family was driving home from church that weekend, when it was announced on radio that Kennedy's assassin, Lee Harvey Oswald has been shot by Jack Ruby.

Johnson, the Vice-President, is installed as president. Nixon is the next president followed by Ford. In November of 1976, Gloria and I stood in line for three hours to vote for the next president of the United States. We canceled out each other's vote. Gloria voted for Jimmy Carter and I voted for Gerald Ford. Gloria won! Jimmy Carter became the president in January of 1977. I believe Carter won because the nation was tired of wars and the new president advocated peace around the world, especially in the poor undeveloped countries. Carter sought to have more dialogue with Moscow. One of Carters greatest achievements was his efforts in negotiating a peace agreement between Egypt and Israel.

Now back to America's wars and the Soviet Union's war with Afghanistan. Americans call this the Soviets *Vietnam War* because it lasted a long time and the Russian population became impatient. Of course, unlike the USA, open protests against government policies were not allowed. The soviets fought the rebels from 1979 to 1989 when Gorbachev ordered an exit of all troops. This war was an embarrassment for the Soviets. The U.S. helped the Afghanistan rebels win by supplying arms from Pakistan.

Carter faced a crisis in the fall of 1979 when the entire U.S. embassy in Iran was taken hostage during a revolution involving Islamic students and militants. This seems to be a common occurrence in 2010 Iran; but thank goodness, we do not have an embassy there now. Carter tried rescue operations but did not succeed. He lost the election in 1980 to Ronald Reagan. The hostages were released on January 20, 1981, the day that Reagan was inaugurated as the new president. How and why this happened I do not know. The Americans were held hostage for 444 days.

As president, Reagan advocated a limited government, substantial tax cuts, and a massive military build up in an arms race with the Soviet Union. In an address to the British Parliament in 1982, Reagan predicts the fall of communism when he said, "Communism is another sad, bizarre chapter in human history whose last pages even now are being written." History has proven his predictions true for the former Soviet Union.

A few days later while standing at the Berlin Wall's Brandenberg Gate Reagan made his famous request, "Mr. Gorbachev, tear down this wall!" This was the beginning of the end of the Cold War. We know now that Gorbachev was listening to Reagan because things changed over the years. In 1989, the Berlin Wall was torn down. The Soviet Union collapsed in 1991. There is no Soviet Union; there is Russia surrounded by countries such as Georgia, which were formerly part of the Union. East and West Germany are reunified. Countries like Hungary and Poland are not aligned with Russia anymore. While all of this is true, we sill have times of friction with Russia.

The stream of wars continued when George H. W. Bush became president in 1989 and studied the Panama situation where the military leader tried to keep control against the will of the people. As the situation grew brutal, Bush orders an invasion of Panama to capture Noriega and return the country to its properly elected president. U.S. operations continue for several weeks, as Noriega remained at large. Fierce action by the U. S. Army routs Noriega and he surrendered on January 3, 1990. Noriega is placed on a military plane and sent to Miami for detainment and trial in the United States. Most Americans and I are proud of Bush's actions. Noriega was convicted of racketeering and drug trafficking charges in April 1992. To my knowledge, he is still in a Miami prison.

George H. W. Bush faced another challenge in the summer of 1990. Saddam Hussein led his country Iraq in the invasion of its neighbor to the south, Kuwait. Bush condemned this action and sought support from allies in Asia, Europe and Middle East. I remember Saudi Arabia being very helpful in allowing our aircraft and troops to use their land. I'm sure King Fahd of Saudi Arabia was anxious to help for fear that Iraq would invade his country. Gloria and I were at prayer meeting on January 16, 1991 and there was much talk about our air force getting ready to drop bombs all over Iraq that Wednesday night. With Congress approval and a UN resolution mandate, the Persian Gulf War began that night. All eyes were on CNN that scary night, including my eyes. We prayed that night for those who might loose their life. The *'Desert Storm Campaign'*, as it was called, ended on February 27, 1991 when Bush announced the complete liberation of Kuwait and a withdrawal of the few remaining Iraqi troops. Many Americans wished we had continued the fighting to eliminate Saddam Hussein. Sometimes I wonder if that was why the first President Bush's son later wanted to finish what his father did not. Hindsight tells me that if the first president had taken all of Iraq we would not have had the Iraq War that started in 2002 and ended in 2012. Wouldn't that have been a blessing? I also wonder if it would have staved off the 911 terrorist attacks.

President Bill Clinton had his war situations, too. Problems in Bosnia and Herzegovina began after Yugoslavia was broken up when communism dissipated at the end of the Cold War. This was such a convoluted problem that I'm not sure I can explain it. I do know that Slobodan Milosevic, President of Serbia (one of the breakaway states) was accused of genocide in Bosnia because it was in the news a lot back in 1989. When Clinton became President in 1993, an all out international war in Bosnia and Herzegovina caught his attention because it progressed all the way to the International Court of Justice. In 1994, Clinton sent delegates to try to reach an accord to cool off the situation and stop the massacre of innocent women and children. In 1995, NATO with U. S. aircraft bombed Milosevic's territory and sent troops to capture him. That brought about peace and Slobodan Milosevic faced a trial in the International Criminal Tribunal in The Hague. He was sentenced to life imprisonment. I remember the trial so well because it was shown on the news many times during the nineties.

President George W. Bush became president in 2001 and we all know that there have been two wars during his presidency. If the terrorists did not attacked us on September 11, 2001, perhaps this decade would have been one of peace in this new century. All of us know where we were on that day, just as I remember where I was on December 7, 1941 when the Japanese attacked America. These terrorist acts were planned in Afghanistan by Osama bin Laden with Al-Qaeda as the enemy. They **commandeered four of our passenger aircraft, on this day and flew** them into the two World Trade Center Towers in New York City, the Pentagon, and a field in Pennsylvania.

The War in Afghanistan began in 2001 with the full backing of Congress, our allies, the UN and NATO with the sole purpose of routing out the Al-Qaeda and finding Osama bin Laden dead or alive. That war continues today during President Barack Obama's regime. Obama has authorized a surge of additional troops with the plan to end the war. I hope he succeeds, but I personally believe that we should leave Afghanistan as soon as it has a stable government and use our military resources to protect our homeland. The terrorists are everywhere and not just in Afghanistan.

The Iraq war started in 2003 as a result of intelligence claim that Saddam Hussein posses weapons of mass destructions, or did it start so that Bush could finish the job that his father did not complete? Over time, the intelligence data has been proven wrong; but in the meantime, we have spent billions upon billions of dollars fighting this war. Bush did plan a surge there to bring the war to and end. Obama made sure the plan to leave Iraq is implemented. At the time of this writing, it looks as if the end will occur in 2011. We may have a skeleton advisory force there for sometime. It is my humble opinion that, at least, we have established another ally in that region. This is more than the Russians can claim.

However, the enemy is a different one than ever before. We are not at war with the Afghan Political structure; rather we are at war with extremists, bound together with the aim of the destruction of Israel and the United States, especially. They know no 'rules of engagement' and have nothing to lose, as they eagerly give their lives for the cause. This may truly be a non-winnable war.

The Question

Why does America fight? I believe everyone will agree that it is to defend and protect the freedom we enjoy in America. God bless, thanks to all the soldiers who have served, and to those who have given the ultimate sacrifice to preserve the freedom we enjoy, going back to George Washington's time.

As this story ends, some readers may wonder why David, my grandson, has not asked questions in the last several pages.

Sadly, David was killed in an automobile accident at age 18 in 1997.

I have dedicated this book in memory of my grandson who dearly loved history so much that he inspired me to tell my story.

The End

The Rainwater Tree
1469 to the Present Time

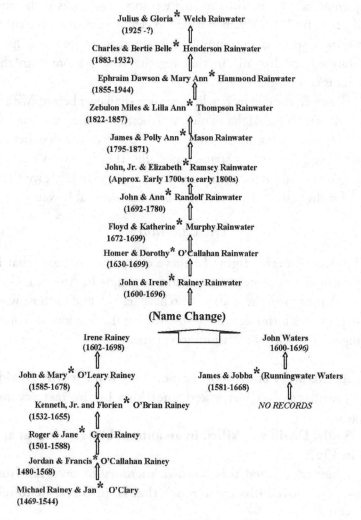

Julius & Gloria * Welch Rainwater
(1925 -?)

Charles & Bertie Belle * Henderson Rainwater
(1883-1932)

Ephraim Dawson & Mary Ann * Hammond Rainwater
(1855-1944)

Zebulon Miles & Lilla Ann * Thompson Rainwater
(1822-1857)

James & Polly Ann * Mason Rainwater
(1795-1871)

John, Jr. & Elizabeth * Ramsey Rainwater
(Approx. Early 1700s to early 1800s)

John & Ann * Randolf Rainwater
(1692-1780)

Floyd & Katherine * Murphy Rainwater
1672-1699)

Homer & Dorothy * O'Callahan Rainwater
(1630-1699)

John & Irene * Rainey Rainwater
(1600-1696)

(Name Change)

Irene Rainey
(1602-1698)

John Waters
1600-1696)

John & Mary * O'Leary Rainey
(1585-1678)

James & Jobba * (Runningwater Waters
(1581-1668)

Kenneth, Jr. and Florien * O'Brian Rainey
(1532-1655)

NO RECORDS

Roger & Jane * Green Rainey
(1501-1588)

Jordan & Francis * O'Callahan Rainey
1480-1568)

Michael Rainey & Jan * O'Clary
(1469-1544)

*The Grandmothers

About the Author

Julius Rainwater is from a large southern family; he was born in 1925. He spent his childhood days during the great depression years.

Julius' service to our country in the 3922nd Company of the U.S. Army Signal Corps during World War II qualifies him to tell this war story. Julius received his discharge from the Army in January 1946.

He now resides in Conyers, Georgia with his lovely wife, Gloria Welch Rainwater.

The author completed his studies at Georgia Tech in three years, receiving a BSEE degree in Electrical Engineering.

Most of Julius' career has been in the engineering fields. Several technical papers, he authored, have been published in leading technical journals.